WOMEN OF IRON

Catherine King

sphere

SPHERE

First published in Great Britain in 2006 by Sphere
This paperback edition published in 2007 by Sphere
Reprinted 2007 (twice), 2008, 2010

A CIP catalogue record for this book
is available from the British Library.

Typeset in Bembo by Palimpsest Book Production Limited,
Grangemouth, Stirlingshire
Printed and bound by CPI Group (UK) Ltd, Croydon, CR0 4YY

Papers used by Sphere are natural, renewable and
recyclable products sourced from well-managed forests and certified
in accordance with the rules of the Forest Stewardship Council.

Mixed Sources
Product group from well-managed
forests and other controlled sources
www.fsc.org Cert no. SGS-COC-004081
© 1996 Forest Stewardship Council

Sphere
An imprint of
Little, Brown Book Group
100 Victoria Embankment
London EC4Y 0DY

An Hachette UK Company
www.hachette.co.uk

www.littlebrown.co.uk

Catherine King was born in Rotherham, South Yorkshire. Her father, grandfather and great-grandfather worked with coal, iron and steel. A search for her roots and an interest in local industrial history provide the inspiration for her stories.

She is the author of four saga novels, all published by Sphere. Visit her website at www.catherineking.info

To the memory of Edmund Humphrey King

Acknowledgements

I should like to thank the staff of Rotherham Archives for enabling me to find the inspiration for this story, and my friend the novelist Elizabeth Gill for her encouragement and support in the writing. Thanks, also, to my agent Judith Murdoch and editor Rosie de Courcy for their advice and direction in its completion.

Chapter 1

1830

'My God, this child will be born with or without its mother's help! I swear it will! Push, I said!' the doctor urged her. 'You must push when I say so. You must.' He turned his tired, lined face to Grace. 'Help her, woman! Tell her what she must do. She will listen to you!'

The girl let out an anguished protracted scream as another wave of grinding torture seared through her body. She clutched at Grace's hand and begged her to stop the pain, to stop the infant, to stop her life. The bed, once smooth and white, was now tumbled, stained and rank with the smell of childbirth. Grace supported the young mother's shoulders and mopped her flushed, damp face with a torn piece of linen. The coals, banked as high as possible in the grate, gave out a fierce heat and a flickering light that danced shadows across the girl's frightened eyes.

'Keep breathing like I told you, miss,' Grace murmured

soothingly, 'and do as the doctor says. It will all be over soon. First timers always take longer.'

'Not this long,' the doctor commented grimly. 'Both of them are growing weak.'

Grace looked up sharply at the concern in his voice. She had seen difficult births like this before, both mother and baby worn out by the ordeal. If they were lucky and the doctor was good, he might save one of them. Best tend to the mother, she thought. She can always have another child, next time inside wedlock.

The girl screamed again, an agonising wail that tore at Grace's heart. The girl did not deserve this. She had brought shame on her family, but, Lord in Heaven, the poor girl did not deserve this.

'Let the baby go,' she muttered quietly to the doctor. 'Save the mother.'

The doctor, if he heard her, did not respond except to say hurriedly, 'Fetch a parson. As quick as you can, woman.'

Grace picked up a storm lantern and scurried away, snatching her heavy winter cloak from its hook by the back kitchen door and stopping only to bark at the timid maidservant, 'Keep this fire banked up and fill another scuttle for upstairs. I shall take it up when I return. You stay down here, do you hear me? You stay down here tonight and make hot toddies for the men.'

She would go herself for a parson. Young servants were unreliable. Also, servants gossiped. Grace knew that because she was one herself. The less the other servants knew the better. She pulled up her hood and bent her head against icy driving rain.

The parsonage was set near to the church, a little way up the hill in this tiny coastal village, far away from London Town. An onshore gale helped her with the climb, but coming back, accompanied by a sleepy dishevelled clergyman, it took her breath clean away. She paused only once, before they entered the bedchamber, to hand the parson a coin and plea for his discretion.

The doctor had removed his waistcoat and rolled up his shirtsleeves. His hands and forearms were smeared and bloody, and, miraculously, the mother's screams had quietened. Had the doctor eventually given her some laudanum?

'Ah, you're back at last,' he said. 'Get over here, woman. I need your assistance.'

The baby was finally coming, its head was through and the mother had fallen back on the pillows in a faint, tired out by her ordeal. The infant, too, was exhausted when, eventually, she slid into this world, a lifeless skinny thing with long limbs and black hair.

Grace held out her arms for the baby. 'Shall I take her, sir?'

The doctor shook his head. 'Do what you can for her mother.'

She pulled a sheet over the bloodied bed and offered some brandy to the girl's lips, already drained of any colour. Leaning very close she whispered urgently in her ear. 'Come on, miss. It's all over now and you have a baby girl. What will you call her? You must give her a name.' Grace thought that even if the infant died, at least she would get a Christian burial if the parson baptised her now. 'What will you call her, miss?' she repeated.

'Mama, Mama,' the girl breathed. She did not, or could not, open her eyes.

'A name, you must give her a name,' Grace insisted.

''Liss. 'Liss.' The first syllable was lost as the name came out in a fading sigh and her head fell sideways.

Grace smoothed her sticky, tangled hair. Now she could sleep. Maybe by morning she would be stronger. But the infant . . . ? Through the lamp's yellow glow she watched the doctor tending the babe. There was no sound from her yet. Perhaps she had already gone. Hopefully not stillborn, but the parson wouldn't know that unless the doctor told him. He would need a name for the infant. Liss? Aliss, was it? No, it couldn't be Aliss. That was her mama's name, a name for one of the gentry and not for one born out of wedlock and shunned by her family.

A thin wail emerged from the babe. She was alive! Not for long, no doubt, if a baptism was nigh. But, if she did survive, she was likely to end up as a servant. Best not call her Aliss and cause raised eyebrows. Aliss – 'Liss – Lissie – yes, Lissie would be better. Yes, Lissie would do. Grace glanced at the infant's mother. There was not a movement from her as the child's wail developed into a cry. The doctor had given her too much laudanum to quieten her screams. He had been tending her for eight hours now. Poor man, he looked all in, as if he were ready to sleep on his feet.

She took the crying baby from him and wrapped her up for the parson. He baptised her quickly, by the flickering embers of the fire, using a chipped kitchen bowl as the font. The child was skinny all right, but long

limbed, like her mama and her mama's father. Maybe
she was a fighter like him. Maybe she stood a chance.

A male voice interrupted Grace's thoughts. 'Parson!
Over here. Quickly! You are not here for the child. The
mother's need is greater. You should have tended to the
mother first. I believe you will be too late.'

The exhausting, painful struggle had been too great
for the girl. Her brief life ended during that stormy
winter night in a soiled and bloodied bedchamber, far
away from her family home. Grace held the young life
that she had helped bring into the world and contem-
plated this unexpected turn of events. If anyone had to
die this night, why should it be the mother? The mother
was young and pretty and could have married and had
more children. Why had the babe not died instead?

What hope was there for a babe-in-arms with no
father to speak of, and now no mother to look after her?
Her ladyship's orders had been clear. The girl's family
wanted nothing to do with a bastard child. The infant
must be farmed out to some worthy farmer who would
pocket a purse of gold and not ask any questions in
return for an extra pair of working hands when the child
grew older.

The doctor interrupted her thoughts. 'You will be in
need of a wet nurse. I attended a young woman two
days ago who can provide. She's healthy enough. You
have money?'

Grace nodded. Oh, yes, she thought. For the first time
in my life I have money. She had been well paid to hide
and care for her pregnant charge in this isolated fishing
village on the windswept Yorkshire coast.

'I'll see to it then. Give the babe to me,' the doctor went on briskly as he dried his hands on a square of linen and rolled down his shirtsleeves. 'You know what to do with the body.' It was a statement rather than a question.

Grace nodded again. 'There's meat and drink in the kitchen and a maidservant to wait on you. I'll be with you when I have – when I have finished here.'

As soon as the room was empty but for her and her charge's lifeless form, Grace carefully removed the locket and chain that also carried the casket keys from around her neck, then began the process of laying her out. The girl had kept her jewels in the casket. And money. Grace needed money.

Less than one week later, Lissie whimpered and grizzled in the biting east wind as her mother was laid to rest in a bleak and barren churchyard. It was a discreet occasion. Grace had seen to that. Only the two of them and the parson stood by to watch a plain wooden coffin being lowered into the ground. Nearby, a worn and mossy stone covered a vault that guarded the decaying remains of distant cousins on her mother's side of the family. The parson had no objections to another departed soul joining those already laid to rest in this neglected corner of his graveyard. Grace had paid him well, with enough for a local mason to add another name on the ancient stone slab.

She stamped her feet to warm them as the wind whipped round her ears. The baby in her arms began to wail. No doubt hungry again, poor mite. No one from the girl's family came to the funeral just as no one had visited her while the child grew in her belly. Why should they? She was a family disgrace. They had done their duty. They had leased an empty house for her, far away on the Yorkshire coast. She had an elderly distant cousin, a childless bachelor, living on the other side of the moor who might have attended. But the weather was evil for travelling at this time of year.

It was God's will, and for the best, thought Grace, shrugging her new wool shawl closely around herself and the little one. By gum, she thought, these local fishermen's wives knew how to fashion a warm shawl. The rain began to fall in icy drops that stung her eyes and spiked her cheeks. It would turn to snow on the moors. She should get the infant home quickly now the deed was done.

Grace would have to send a letter to the girl's family in London, telling of recent events. She sighed. Poor, wretched girl. Not fifteen years on this earth. The scandal of it all had brought her low and a putrid fever did the rest. But the infant, well, the infant was a bonny, healthy lass with a fine appetite and a strong pair of lungs. Did the family want to know about the infant? Did they *need* to know? Lissie grew heavy in her arms as Grace walked away from the churchyard.

Any barren farmer's wife would pay well for such a child and be thankful, even if she was a girl. Girls made good dairymaids and, if they were handsome, made good marriages too. Grace had no need for a purse of sovereigns to farm out this little mite and she wondered if she might keep her to herself. She wrote to the family that the child was a puny boy who might not thrive and would be hard to place unless he grew stronger. She reasoned to herself that a bastard boy with a claim to the family name would be better dead as far as the family were concerned. They would want no scandal attached to them. She finished the letter by saying that she would stay in Yorkshire and do her best by him. Grace needed time to think about how she could get far away from the family.

The doctor had been as good as his word and a wet nurse had arrived promptly. She was a ruddy-faced, hungry fisherman's wife whose latest baby had sickened and died within the first few days of life. Little Lissie, having survived her fight for life at birth, carried on her demanding ways, took to a stranger's breast well and thrived.

Grace, for her part, had weathered the northern winter in a pleasant haze of warm fires and French brandy, courtesy of the grateful suppliers of her household needs. She had kept a good table for Lissie's mother, and continued to patronise the local tradesmen for herself and the baby and her wet nurse.

She needed to consider her future. If she kept the baby and the gold in the dead mother's casket, where would she go and what would she do? She could travel a long way with all that gold, but not so far at her age with an infant in tow. There was no hurry; this coastal house was comfortable and it would be madness to travel anywhere before the spring. Grace bided her time while Lissie ate, slept and grew.

It was Ruth, the wet nurse, who gave her the idea. Lissie was suckling contentedly at Ruth's breast and, already, her skinny limbs were filling out. She had lost the shock of black hair she was born with soon after birth. Now it was growing back, just as black, but her skin was not olive as Grace had expected. It was pale, almost translucent, lightly tinged with a baby pink, and her eyes were turning a smoky shade of green.

Ruth heaved Lissie over to her other breast. 'Blooming 'eck, she's getting heavy. I think she puts on weight every day. And eat! Look at her, still going at it! Shall we try her wi' some bread and milk tomorrer? 'Ave you thought what you're going to do with 'er, Grace?'

Grace was mulling a tankard of ale for each of them by a good fire in the upstairs drawing room. She had cut two thick slices of bread and speared one to the end of a long-handled brass fork. 'I don't know yet. I can't keep her with me, whatever I do.'

'Do you want to go back down south?'

'No, I don't.' Grace shrugged, and then thought for a moment. 'Well, it doesn't matter where I am really, only I don't want to go back into service with the gentry. I've had enough of running round after them and I've done a good job here without having to take orders from any gentry.'

'Oh aye, you 'ave that. Everybody says so. You've had this place all cleaned up and cosy for the winter. Where did you learn how to do it all?'

'In the poor house when I was a nipper. Over in the South Riding. I was born there, you see. The Admiral's family used to come up to Yorkshire every year for the shooting and I was sent from the poor house to help out at the lodge.' Grace became thoughtful for a moment, shaking her head gently. 'I wouldn't wish the poor house on this little mite.' Then she brightened. 'I was good with the children and in the sickroom too, and, one year, they took me back to London Town with them. The master was a captain in the navy then and lived in a mansion near the Thames.'

'You were lucky to get out o' the poor house like that.'

'Not so lucky with my husband though. I married a sailor and he was always at sea. I had to get used to being on my own.'

'Didn't he come home ever?'

'Oh, aye! But when he did, he spent all his money, an' most of his time, in alehouses!' Grace became thoughtful again and sighed. 'He didn't come back from Trafalgar though. That was twenty-five years ago. I went to work for the Admiral again. He was a hero by then, and he knew the Regent and the old King and everybody.'

'Will you go back there?'

Grace curled her lip and shook her head. 'They don't want anything to do with the little 'un. They're too grand now, with all their fancy ways. No, after a lifetime of that I've had my bellyful o' the gentry. I'll move out of here in springtime. I shall find somewhere for the babe to keep her out of the poor house and will look for a little lodging house of my own.'

'A lodging house? There i'n't much call for them around here, or up on the moors. You will 'ave to go to t' big towns for that.'

'A town would suit me. I'm used to London Town.'

Lissie was slowing down now, snuffling at Ruth's breast and becoming sleepy. 'Best put her down,' Grace suggested, 'and come and get yourself something to eat.'

Ruth laid Lissie on the sofa, sat by the fire with Grace, and continued, 'There are ports down the coast, all around the river Humber. Always money from sea-going ships and canal barges down there, my Joseph says.' She took some toasted bread and butter and sank her teeth into it with relish. The butter ran down her chin and she wiped it away with the back of her hand. 'My Joseph says you can make a good living from the Humber. It's rough though, wi' all the sailors and gangs o' thugs about.'

Grace knew from her days on the Thames what it was like to live near docks. She was familiar with the comings and goings on wharfs, and the ways of sailors, whether they sailed with merchant ships or the King's navy, and she wanted none of it. No longer young, she wanted something easier for herself. 'Aye,' she replied, 'I know about living in ports well enough. And I know I've had enough of sea-going men.'

'Well,' Ruth added, 'they have plenty o' trade in the South Riding. There's coal and iron and they say they'll soon have railways as well. They'll be all over the Riding one day, my Joseph says. Three of the fishermen have already left their boats to work down the pits or on the furnaces.'

Grace's memories of the South Riding were grim. Brought up on the parish, her young life had been one of humility and hardship, constantly scrubbing away the ashes and soot belched out by the ironworks chimneys. Men and women worked hard, they sweated hard and drank hard. Her escape to London Town had been a welcome release from this at first. But she quickly realised that emptying slops and cleaning grates for the gentry was no different from the poor house, except that she wore cotton aprons instead of sacking.

The Admiral did not travel to Yorkshire for the shooting any more. Since Trafalgar he had suffered from an injured leg that pained him constantly and tried his patience. But the wealthy Riding ironmasters he knew from previous journeys often visited him in his elegant London house. And they brought their sons with them.

Lissie's father was one of those sons. A young gentleman he was, full of his own importance, based on his father's money and his university education. Lissie's mother was the Admiral's youngest child, fourteen at the time and a wild, wilful girl who was taken in by the young gentleman's charm. Some gentleman! Grace had heard them at it regularly, like a pair of rabbits, in the old attic nursery and was not surprised a few months later when she was asked to take the girl away somewhere and farm out the child. The young gentleman did not even know and nobody considered telling him.

The towns of the South Riding were grimy, and the gentry lived on the surrounding hills away from the smoke and dirt of the manufactories in the river valleys. But Grace remembered the soft wind and rain, sheltered as it was from driving westerly gales by the Pennine chain. Years ago the woollen trade had thrived there, but now the hills were scattered with ironstone pits and coal mines to feed the greedy furnaces of ironworks by the river.

The South Riding was prosperous, Grace considered. It had plenty of trade and men with money to spend on good lodgings. A woman could make herself a living there, she decided. She took another piece of toasted bread and spread it generously with fresh butter.

'Well, you were born in Yorkshire, so why not come back for good?' Ruth suggested. 'As you're on your own, like. Unless you think you'll wed again, o' course? You'd have no trouble wi' that, you being such a good cook an' all.'

As Ruth chattered on, between mouthfuls of toasted bread and warm, spiced ale, Grace's thoughts wandered. What about the babe though? She would not be able to run a lodging house with a babe in arms, and it would be years before the infant would be old enough to work. Grace went to sit by her on the sofa. She did not want the child to end up in the poor house. What would the poor house do for her? Work her hard and then place her as a servant when she was ten years old? The poor house did not look after its destitute folk for no reward. They expected, and they got, payment for the years their inmates had lived on the parish. Most of the payment never went back to the parish either, but into the pocket of the poor house master and his wife, if he had one.

Little Lissie already showed promise of becoming a real beauty with her large eyes and pretty mouth. She was too lovely for the poor house and a life as a drudge or a farm servant. Grace could do better than that for her. She owed it to her and her poor ma, if nothing else. There must be many a body who would pay well for such a beautiful, healthy infant. Then, Grace calculated, she would have her ladyship's purse from the casket, and more besides for her trouble. With all that gold and silver she could make a nice life for herself somewhere else, and she wouldn't have to go back to the beck and call of the gentry ever again.

Grace gave a rare smile and swallowed another mouthful of mulled ale. 'What did you say, Ruth? You think she is ready to take some bread and milk? Well, I'm sure you're right. We'll start her on that tomorrow. Your time with her is nearly done.'

As soon as the days began to lengthen and the weather turned warmer, Grace planned her departure from the Yorkshire coast. She told all those who asked that she was going back down south, from where she came with the infant. She would take the same route out that had brought her and the girl here at the beginning of winter, by turnpike south to the Humber and then she would take a coastal vessel to London. The first part was true. She would take little Lissie with her to the estuary. And then, who knows where she might go.

Travelling with a babe in arms in a coach and four was hard work for Grace now that she was no longer agile. Her joints were stiffened by sitting and ached when she moved. But her fellow passengers were entranced by Lissie's infant beauty and ready smile, and they were more than willing to hold her while Grace took a nap or ate her bread and cheese. And while she travelled, she thought about her plan and her future.

A babe like this might grow into a fine young woman, maybe catch the eye of a rich husband. She had breeding too. The blood in her veins was gentry. If Grace had been a younger woman she would have considered keeping her. But the exhausting carriage journey made her realise that she no longer had the energy to look after a little one as well as herself. And a child would cost her a good deal of money until she was old enough to work.

No, she would have to move her on and a healthy little beauty, as Lissie was, would fetch a good price from the right buyer. Besides, with all that gold she could take a house in a nice part of town, and provide lodgings for gentlemen to earn her daily bread. Once the babe was off her hands, she decided, she would transfer to the cheaper canal barges to reach her destination. Until then, she would stay in a respectable inn and she asked her fellow travellers to recommend one.

The North Star, near to the coaching inn where the horses were changed, was suitable. It was away from the squalor and noise of the docks, yet within easy reach of the waterways for those travelling on. Night had fallen when Grace arrived, followed by a boy and handcart with her luggage. The saloon was alive with drinkers and the landlord carried her boxes upstairs while an exhausted Grace wrestled with a tired and fractious Lissie.

Grace surveyed her room. 'I'll have my dinner in here, as soon as you can. Bring me some warm milk and toasted bread for the babe. You got a crib somewhere for her?' The landlord nodded and muttered something about his wife finding one. 'Good,' she continued, now well used to dealing with tradesmen and the like. 'Have you got a girl who can give me a helping hand with her? I think the poor mite's got her first tooth coming through.'

The landlord disappeared quickly, anxious to get back to the familiar territory of his saloon. Babbies, he thought, were women's work. However, a short while later a young woman knocked on Grace's door and offered her services as nursemaid. By the time Grace had eaten her dinner and Lissie had been quietened with a teaspoon of French brandy in some milk and honey, Grace had learned from her gossiping helper all she needed to know about the inn's regular visitors.

She waited until late, when most of the inn's drinkers had gone to their homes and wives, before going down for a tankard of porter. It was dark outside and the nights were cold, so the only people remaining were, like her, staying at the North Star. She took her drink to a seat by the fire, next to a genial-looking fellow in a respectable tweed jacket, with a round face and a belly to match. The nursemaid had described him well.

He looked up and gave a nod. 'Evening.'

Grace nodded in return.

'Saw you arrive earlier,' he said. 'With a babe in arms. Have you come far?'

'North Riding,' Grace answered, swallowing the greater part of her drink with relish.

She didn't want him knowing too much of her business, even if she was going to move on. The gentry all knew each other round these parts and it would never do for any word to get back to the Admiral's family about the child. Her mind began to race as she made up a story of the child's origins.

Her new companion leaned forward, threw a couple of logs on to the dying embers of the fire and shouted over his shoulder, 'Landlord! More whisky for me – and another of whatever the lady is drinking.' He raised his eyebrows in Grace's direction.

'Ta very much,' she replied, emptying her tankard. 'The name's Grace, Grace Beighton.'

'Luther Dearne. Pleased to meet you.'

They carried on exchanging pleasantries until Grace was satisfied she could talk business with Luther. He was a rogue and a crook, she didn't doubt, but he sported a fine wool waistcoat with a gold watch and chain across his ample belly. The nursemaid told her that he was known for being a soft touch with the landlord's children, having none of his own. For her part, Grace concentrated on covering her tracks regarding Lissie's story. She needed to have the story straight in her own head before she told anybody else.

The child, she decided, was a foundling and would have died of exposure if Grace hadn't rescued her, and she was such a beautiful child she deserved better than the poor house and a menial life as a laundry girl or scullery maid. But Grace herself was a widow, which was true, and no longer young, which was also true, and she needed help to look after a baby as she had very little money of her own. What she was seeking was someone with a need for a lovely, healthy child for their own. They had to have means to compensate Grace for the trouble and expense of rescuing the infant. And she was such a pretty lass, you only had to set eyes on her to take to her . . .

Luther interrupted her thoughts. 'How long are you staying here?'

'Just till I've completed my little bit of business,' Grace replied.

Luther stared at her. She was nothing special to look at, he thought, but she seemed respectable enough. Plain dress though, the sort of thing a housekeeper to the gentry might wear. 'And what line of business is that then?'

Grace lowered her voice and leaned forward. 'I've got something to place that needs a special kind of buyer.'

Luther drew his chair closer to Grace's. 'Tell me more. I do a bit of dealing myself.'

Grace told him her brief story about the 'foundling' child and before long she could see that he was interested.

'That was the child?' he asked. 'The one you brought with you? Can I 'ave a look?'

She faked a yawn to stall him. 'I've been travelling all day, my friend, and I need to rest. Tomorrow is time enough for that. I'll bid you goodnight for now.' She took a candle and retreated upstairs to where Lissie, soothed by her teaspoonful of brandy, slept soundly in an old and battered wooden crib. Lowering the light to see her better, Grace was pleased with the way the nursemaid had washed and changed her before tucking a clean blanket around her. In the yellow glow, her skin looked as soft as down and her tiny lips like rose petals. Her silky black hair poked out of the pretty white night bonnet her mother had lovingly sewn for her.

Grace stroked Lissie's cheek with the back of her

knuckle. 'Little beauty, aren't you? And eyes so green, a smoky green like I've never seen before. You'll fetch me a good price, I'll wager. Enough for old Grace to set up her own little place and see out her days in a bit o' comfort. And well away from your poor ma's family and their prying eyes. Sleep tight, my little one. Your old Grace has a nice big fat fish on a hook for you.'

Chapter 2

Luther Dearne loitered on the dockside, thinking about the woman at the inn last night who called herself Grace. He wondered if she was wed and what kind of deal she would strike with him.

Pity she was so plain though, for he did like a pretty face to look at over a tankard of ale. Not that he had a particularly roving eye for the women.

Not like his mate Mickey from the Navigator Inn back home. Mickey just could not keep his hands off anything in a skirt when he was a young man. He had mellowed a bit of late, but even nowadays nobody's daughter was safe when Mickey was around!

No, it wasn't the woman herself who had caught Luther's attention. Truth to tell she was a bit of an old trout. It was seeing her when she arrived, carrying that babby up the stairs, that had pulled at his heart.

It was the way of things, he knew. Mickey and his missus had three lads and a lass now, while he and Edie had none. He stood watching that Svenson fellow who had come in on the clipper with iron to sell. There he was with his woman and their little lad, arm in arm and happy, talking together with the kid playing round his mam's skirts, and Luther knew he was missing out on something.

He should have realised on his wedding night that Edie was going to be no good to him in the bedchamber. He thought, then, that she was young and not experienced in these things and that excited him because he looked forward to teaching her a few tricks to help things along.

'Give us a kiss, lass,' he had said as he got into bed. Luther was proud of his manhood and it had not let him down that night, so he had left off his nightshirt to show off his strength. Edie did not seem impressed and was clothed up to her ears. He put his hand up her nightgown and played around between her legs with his fingers, but she was as dry as old sticks.

'You're not frightened o' me, are you, lass?' he asked.

'No. Me mam said to keep still and let yer get on wi' it. She said it do'n't last long.'

'Your mam 'a'n't seen my cock. Put yer hand on it, lass. You want to know what you're getting, don't you?'

'What do you mean, Luther?'

He pushed her nightgown further up and rolled towards her so that she could feel his hardness on her thigh. 'What do yo' think o' that, then?'

Edie did not know what to think and stayed silent. Her mam had said if she did not like what he did it was best just to lie there quiet until he'd finished.

Luther continued to probe around between her legs, but his heart was sinking fast. 'Bloody 'ell, Edie, the tarts on the cut would be begging me by now.'

'Well go an' find one o' them, then,' she retaliated, fed up with all this playing around.

Luther gave up his attempted foreplay and snapped, 'Oh shurrup then and oppen yer legs.'

She always let him do it, whenever he wanted. But she didn't rave on like the other women he'd been with. Maybe she'd be better when she had a babby, he thought. And they did it that often, he'd been sure he'd get her with child soon. But he had been wrong.

If only his Edie would give him a son, or even a daughter, their life would be better. But, no matter how much he tried, he couldn't get Edie with child. Now, even the sweat of all that trying was beginning to pall and this vexed him even more. Edie had lost her youthful bloom and he, too, was well past his prime, so it was hard work these days.

He'd really loved Edie when they were first wed, but she still never did anything for him in the marriage bed to help things along. Not that Edie ever complained about her duties in bed. She was a good wife to him in that respect. But he'd known from that first night, and her weary sighs when she rolled over for him, that he wasn't really welcome. Still, she always did her duty. Though it was nigh on ten years since they had wed and no sign of any babbies at all.

Oh my, he thought, Edie had been such a pretty little thing when he married her, like a china doll with brown ringlets and pink cheeks that dimpled when she smiled.

Now she seemed just like dried-out skin and bone. She could do with fattening up a bit, he reckoned, if she was ever to bear him a healthy babby. Yes, that's what she wanted! A fine ham or a joint of salt beef might set Edie to rights.

He stroked his ample chins and wandered over to where the barges and Yorkshire keels were unloading their cargo of fire grates and ranges for that foreigner Svenson to ship down the coast to London. He knew the bargeman well.

'Leave those till last,' he muttered to him under his breath as he was about to move the first of the ornate fire surrounds and mantelshelves. He slipped a half sovereign into the bargeman's palm and added, 'Wait until the foreigner has gone and then hire a wagon and a couple of hefty lads. Keep what's left o' this for yourself and there'll be the other half and a good dinner wi' a flagon of ale for you if you get a couple of those fireplaces safely to the stable yard behind the North Star after nightfall.'

Luther reckoned that Svenson wouldn't miss a few pieces from his payload, and a stylish fire grate and surround for the best room at the North Star should easily take care of what he owed the landlord at the inn. The other would take care of his winter larder at home with no questions asked and a bottle or two of gin for Edie to keep her sweet.

That Svenson fellow, the foreigner, had driven a hard bargain for his cargo. But Luther knew ironmasters who would take all he could get of Swedish bar iron for their furnaces and forges in the South Riding, and he had finally secured some at a fair price. It was not cheap by any means. This Swedish iron was the best there was, and Svenson knew it, by God. Luther also knew that a barge-load of new cast-iron cooking ranges to ship down the coast to London would be good business for Svenson too. He could strike a deal with any man, dealing was in his blood, and the foreigner had seemed satisfied.

The bargemen were under pressure to keep their transporting prices down, now that they had a bit of competition from railways. Their Yorkshire keels, when they were empty of fire grates and ranges, would be loaded with bar iron to carry back through the canals and cuts to the South Riding to be forged into wheels, axles and beams for steam engines and railways. The new cut went right up to Tinsley now, making it easy to get the heavy stuff right into the heart of the South Riding.

Even so, the bargemen were uneasy about their future. There was a lot of talk of the success of the railways in the North Riding, and of how the waterways had had their day. They feared for their livelihoods on the barges, and that of their families. Luther knew this and used it to get the lowest prices he could for transporting the iron. With his contacts on the wharfs and in the coal-field manufactories, he could guarantee barges had full payloads both ways. This kind of dealing meant that there was always a bargeman who owed Luther a favour, and who would give him free passage back home when his business was done.

Luther spent the next couple of hours bartering the remaining cast-iron fireplace with its fashionable brass trimmings. He had trading cronies near the docks who knew a bargain when they saw one and asked no questions. His blood was up when he got back to the North Star at the end of the day. Doing deals always fired him up in this way, it was what he lived for. Some good ale and a hot dinner was what he wanted now. If only he could sort Edie out with a babby, his life would be perfect.

It was late when he finally sat down to some hot food, but the old trout was still there at the inn. She was in the same place by the fire with her tankard of dark stout, which she raised to salute him as he strolled into the saloon. Luther tried to keep calm but he was bubbling underneath. His day had gone well and it wasn't over yet. He hoped the old woman was not spinning him a line about the babby.

He played for time by eating his dinner first. But he wolfed down the roast mutton and greens and gulped his ale. Finally, he wandered over to the fire. 'Evening, ma'am,' he began. 'Had a good day?'

'Fair.' Grace was in fine fettle, having spent her day recovering from yesterday's journey and arranging her onward passage. 'You?'

'Usual.' Through a haze of wood smoke, he thought she didn't look too bad in the flickering light of the fire. He drew up a chair and stretched out his legs. 'You still got your bit o' business to finish?'

'If you mean the business we talked of last night — aye, I have.'

Luther's spirits soared. 'You still got hold o' the goods then?'

Grace raised her eyes to the ceiling. 'Still up there. I

want a good price, mind. You'll see for yourself that she's a little beauty and I know she's from good stock.'

'It's a girl then.'

'Didn't I say? Are you looking for a boy?'

'Might be.' A girl, Luther thought. A girl would do. A little beauty, the woman said. When she grew up, she'd be like Edie was as a young girl. A little beauty! Edie would be bound to love her, like Mickey's wife loved their little Miriam. He tried to calm himself. 'Good stock, you say? I thought you said she was a foundling.'

'Take my word for it, she's gentry.'

'How do you know?'

'I know because I brought her into this world. I looked after her ma and her ma was a lady.'

Luther persisted. 'Last night you said she was a foundling.'

'Aye, well, she is. Her ma died and there was no other family to take her in. She was destined for the poor house.'

'What about her pa?'

'Nobody knows who he was,' she lied. 'Born the wrong side of the blanket, y' see.'

Luther believed the woman. 'Let's have a look then.'

Grace rose to her feet. 'Bring a lamp and follow me.'

Luther knocked back his drink and went upstairs to the bedchamber. As he approached the battered crib in the darkest corner of Grace's room he felt the excitement rising in his chest until it nearly choked him. This little babby was everything the old woman had said. Here was his future with Edie! A child. A beautiful child. Their very own child. He couldn't believe his luck! He almost forgot he was a dealer in his haste to talk terms. Almost.

'Well, well, yes, she is a little beauty, just like you say. Does she 'ave a name?'

Grace shrugged. 'When she's yours you can call her what you want.'

'Nay, I know nowt about girls' names.' And Edie knows even less, he thought.

'What did her ma call her?'

'Lissie.'

'Lissie? Not heard o' that one afore. Pretty, though. I like it.'

'It's short for Aliss. Her ma called her that afore she went. But we baptised her Lissie.'

'She's baptised then?'

'The . . . I . . . I thought she was going to die as well as her ma, so I fetched a parson.'

'Parsons cost money.'

'There was a bit of money from her ma. It's all gone now and I can't afford to keep her.'

The air was silent while Luther absorbed this information, then he asked, 'Are there any papers or letters?'

'Nothing, I swear it,' Grace lied. 'If you buy her, she'll be yours, don't you fret.'

Grace reckoned that even if the girl's family knew about her they wouldn't want her. No, she was best dead as far as they were concerned. She had found some trinkets and papers in the locked casket with the gold. These keepsakes were too good to throw away but she'd probably burn the papers when the babe had gone. Grace began to get restless. She wanted this business over and done with and demanded impatiently, 'Do you want her or not?'

Luther thought he had better cover his tracks, just in case somebody came after her. 'Oh aye, I want her all right. Not for me, you understand. It just so happens that I know of a couple looking for a babby to bring up as their own. They're not gentry but they have means and good connections.'

'What sort o' connections?' Grace demanded. The last thing she wanted was any gentry poking their noses into this deal.

'They're in trade,' he answered, 'and they live a long way from here.'

'Whereabouts and how far?' Grace wanted to know. It wouldn't do for the babe to go back to the North Riding, even if her cousins there were distant ones.

'Nigh on middle o' the country if you're going coast to coast. They are good folk though, and they live away from the 'factories. Cordwainers they are. Folks allus want boots so the little 'un will never want for owt.'

Luther never had any trouble in enlarging on the truth. He was well-practised in the art, and he continued, 'Of course, there'd be my expenses in getting her there, but I'll take full responsibility for that. If they don't like the look of her I wouldn't bring her back to you. I'd find somebody else for her. Mind you, a girl is harder to place than a boy. But, no matter, I can take her off your hands for good if you want – at the right price, o' course. What do you say to a deal?'

He was good, Grace thought, at pretending the babe was for someone else. But she knew that he had fallen

for her, and the gleam in his eye told Grace he wanted
this baby, and he wanted her badly. Maybe he was telling
the truth and maybe he wanted to sell her on when she
was a bit more grown. But she could see that he'd set
his heart on her, and Grace was not going to let this
one off the hook. She named her price, adding, 'In gold,
if you please.'

Luther eyes rolled. 'That's a bit steep.' He offered a
smaller sum, like he did with his dealing, expecting to
agree a lower price.

Grace walked over to the door and opened it pointedly. 'No deal. That's her price. It's what she's worth. Take
it or leave it. I've got another body interested if you've
changed your mind.'

He thought for a minute. He could not let this chance
slip through his fingers. If he walked out now and offered
a higher price in the morning, he might be too late; she
might be gone. Oh what a pretty little babby she was,
wrapped up in shawls and slumbering in her battered
old crib.

As far as Luther was concerned she was his already.
He said, 'For that money, I'll want all her clothes and
everything – and your silence.'

'That goes without saying. Her things are in the crib
for you.'

'And I want to take her with me now. Tonight.'

'You got the gold here?'

'I 'ave that.'

'All of it?'

'Aye.'

'Done, then.' Grace spat on her hand and held it out.

Luther did the same and he grasped hers briefly as he did with the canal traders. Then he began to pat his tweed coat and breeches to locate the small leather pouches of gold and silver he kept secreted about his person. He counted out the coins on to the marble slab of Grace's washstand and put the remaining loose coins in his waistcoat pockets.

Grace watched him closely then picked up the money. She turned her back on him and hoisted up her skirts to reach the leather belt and purse around the waist of her under-drawers. When she had hidden the money from his view she turned back and asked, 'Have you looked after a babe before?'

'The landlord's girl has been helping you, hasn't she? Send her along to me.' With that closing remark, Luther picked up the crib with the babe asleep in it, and left. Lissie was his, all his. He had a daughter, a little beauty of a daughter and he couldn't wait to get her home to Edie.

'Edie! Edie, lass, look what I've got 'ere for yer!'

Edie Dearne jumped when she heard Luther's voice outside. She did not particularly like being married to Luther, but she reckoned it was better than being a pithead lass or a farm girl. Or a mill girl. Edie had heard terrible tales of working in the big mills hereabouts. She had never gone after the boys much, not like the other village lasses, so when Luther took a shine to her her mam had made sure he took her to the altar. But Edie never thought that being married was up to much and it suited her for Luther to go off for weeks at a time doing his deals. He was generous with the money he made and she could do exactly as she pleased all day and every day when he was away.

She was in the front room trying to get a fire going so that Luther could sit in there with a jar of ale after his dinner. He was fussy about that when he came home, and had sent word ahead with one of the bargemen that he was on his way. He liked things to be ready for him, a good dinner, some strong ale and a comfy chair by a roaring fire. And Edie looking pretty.

She patted her ringlets and took off her pinny. It was hard to keep looking nice all the time. Her mam used to help her afore she was married, and afterwards until she died. But Edie found it tiresome to curl her hair on her own. Luther was strict with her as well, about her not going over to the Navigator when he was off down the canal doing his dealing. He said she had enough to do keeping up with the house and garden when he was away.

She stared out of the front-room window. Luther was striding across the clearing in the trees with a sack over his shoulder. And behind him was a woman carrying a bundle. No, not a bundle, a babby. The woman had a babby in her arms. What was going on?

Fear clutched at Edie's stomach. Luther was *her* husband! What was he doing with another woman and a babby? She hurried through to the back kitchen and opened the scullery door to let him in.

'Ee, lass,' Luther said, 'you'll be right pleased about this.' He turned to the woman behind him. 'Ta, love. Step inside a minute.'

The woman nodded at Edie and laid her bundle on the kitchen table, then loosened a pack strapped to her back, dropped it to the floor and held out her hand. Luther counted out a few coins, murmured, 'Much obliged,' and the woman left as silently as she had arrived.

'Who was that?' Edie demanded, looking aghast at her departing back.

But Luther, excited to have Lissie home at last, was focused on the sleeping child. 'Isn't she a beauty?' He smiled.

'She looks like any other barge gypsy to me,' Edie responded sourly.

'Not 'er. The babby. I've fetched us a babby, Edie.'

Edie felt herself go rigid all over. 'I can see that. Whose is it and what do we want wi' it?'

'It's ours. O' course we want it. It's a little lass, just like Annie Jackson's Miriam. All 'er things are 'ere an' all. She's ours, Edie, love. All ours.'

Edie thought Luther had lost his wits and said, 'Well she's not mine and I don't want owt to do wi' 'er.'

'Course you do, Edie. We've been wed ten year now. That's a long time to wait for a babby and you're not a young lass any more.'

'You don't have to tell me that, Luther Dearne,' Edie scowled. ''Ave you been carrying on wi' that barge whore who brought 'er? Is she 'ers?'

Luther didn't like the way Edie was talking. He thought she'd be as pleased as he was to have a babby at last. But she was not taking to the little 'un at all. 'I told you,' he said firmly. 'She's ours.'

'Oh aye? Are you 'er dad, then?'

Now he was getting impatient with Edie. She had no right to question him like this. She was his wife and she'd damn well do as he told her. 'What if I am?' he answered angrily. 'You 'a'n't given me any, 'ave yer?'

'Well, it i'n't fo' want o' trying,' Edie snapped sullenly.

She di'n't want any babbies anyway, spoiling it between her and Luther. If she allus did as Luther said she never went short o' coal or food on t' table. An' he brought her snuff and gin when he was flushed wi' money. An' she could do what she pleased when he was away, as long as she stayed this side o' the canal.

'I don't want 'er round 'ere, Luther,' Edie continued. 'Why can't her own mam look after 'er?'

'You're her mam now, Edie. Look at 'er, she's lovely.'

But Edie was stubborn. 'I don't know how to look after a babby.'

'Yes you do. You're a woman, aren't you? Empty one o' them cupboard drawers to put 'er in for now. I've got some more of her things waiting on the wharf.'

Edie began to whine. 'Tek 'er back where she came from while you're down there. And bring me me snuff. You 'ave got some snuff for me, Luther, 'a'n't you? You allus brings me some snuff.'

But Edie's pleading fell on deaf ears. Luther walloped 'er one if she didn't get on wi' things. 'E spent all 'is money on things for the babby and left Edie on 'er own to do the extra washing and feeding. She got fed up wi' 'im allus cooing an' gurgling at the little 'un so as 'e 'ad no time for 'er any more. She 'ad no snuff neither. And when Luther said 'e'd on'y fetch her some from the Navvy if she looked after the babby right, Edie realised

that she had moved to second place in Luther's affec-
tions.

In contrast, Grace was satisfied with her deal. Luther
Dearne was soft about the babby and the landlord's girl
had said he had a wife and a house and money in his
pocket. She was sad to part with the infant, but she had
already booked a passage on a Yorkshire keel heading for
the South Riding. She planned to find a position to keep
her while she looked for a house of her own.

She obtained a place as a housekeeper and nurse to
a merchant and his dying wife. Mr Sowden, a successful
grain dealer, had acquired two stepdaughters when he
had married their widowed mother. The elder girl had
packed her box and gone before Grace moved in. But
the younger daughter, Clara, would not leave her dying
mother.

They were reasonably well-to-do, though the house
was small and inconvenient and they did not keep a pony
and trap. Only Mr Sowden went out, alone and on horseback. Grace did not like him, but she reckoned that his
wife would not live much longer and then her position
would come to an end. She spent three months of her
life trying to organise his dilapidated household while
cleaning up the soiled bed and washing the decaying
body of his dying wife.

On the day Mrs Sowden died, Grace stood in the
open door of his study and informed him. 'Your wife
has passed on, sir,' she said.

He was unemotional. 'Do what you have to,' he said
dismissively.

'Shall I arrange the funeral as well, sir?'

'Yes, yes!' he replied irritably. 'And do not bother me with this matter again.'

'As you wish, sir.' Grace bobbed a curtsey. 'I'll lay out her body in the sickroom.'

Mr Sowden, she thought, was a harsh, mean-spirited man. His cold grey eyes became flinty in their bony sockets. Grace left the study quickly.

He called after her. 'Wait,' he barked. 'Come back here.'

'Sir?'

'Send my daughter to me.'

'Yes, sir.'

Miss Clara was a grown woman, but her stepfather treated her like a servant. Paid servants, Grace realised, did not stay long and now she understood why. But the position, located as it was on the edge of the South Riding, had suited her until she got to know the Riding better. Although the house was cold and dank and dirty, she had done her best for mother and daughter in the time she had been there. She hurried to the kitchen where Clara was helping with supper.

Clara had been crying and Grace's hardened heart melted a little. 'I am so sorry, Miss Clara. I did all I could for your mother.'

Clara wiped her eyes with a soggy handkerchief. 'I know you did, Mrs Beighton. You have been a great support for me too. You are a good woman. Do you think Father will keep you on?'

Grace had no intention of staying. But she frowned at the idea of leaving Miss Clara with her stepfather. He was a nasty man.

'I cannot say. He wants to see you in his study.'

Grace noticed the alarm in her eyes. Such a pity her life was so miserable for she was quite lovely to look at, Grace thought. Just as she imagined her little Lissie would be when she grew up, with fair skin and grey-green eyes, and glossy black hair dressed in coils at the back of her head. Lissie's eyes had been green, whereas Clara's were blue. She hoped that Luther was being kind to Lissie.

Grace Beighton did not shed tears easily. She had lost a few when she heard of her husband's death at sea, and when Luther Dearne left the North Star with Lissie. And now, as she saw the grief and fear in Clara's eyes, she allowed herself a few more. Since Clara's sister had left the household, all Mr Sowden's bidding fell to her.

'It's going to be awful here without you,' Clara said. 'Just me and him, and no one else to turn his anger on.'

Her sorrow was heart-breaking for Grace to see. Despite her position as servant, she walked around the kitchen table and took Clara's hand in hers.

Clara did not snatch it away. She held on to it, took a deep breath and said, 'You are such a help for me.'

Grace nodded slightly. Life was hard for women when the master was cruel, she thought, even in a well-to-do merchant's house like this one. And this master was cruel. Grace was uncomfortable in his presence, recognising, as she did, a man of dubious appetites. He had married an older woman for her property, yet preferred the pleasures of younger flesh, which he sometimes brought back to the house. Clara's mother's second marriage had been ill-judged and poor Clara was now alone with this brute of a stepfather.

'Best not keep him waiting,' Grace advised.

Clara dried her eyes and remembered just in time to take off her apron and smooth down her hair before she entered her stepfather's dusty study. He was a thin, bony man with greying hair and copious whiskers around thin lips and a receding chin. Her mother had told her he had been a charming young gentleman fifteen years ago when they had married. And a successful shopkeeper.

Clara stood in the middle of a worn square of carpet, gritty with spilled ashes from his warm study fire. Her stepfather stood up and examined her appearance in detail before he spoke.

'You are the lady of this house now. If you attempt to run off like your sister I shall find you and flog you. Do you understand?'

'Yes, Father.'

'And be sure that you do not fall ill and die on me as your mother has done.'

'She only became ill because you treated her so badly,' Clara muttered.

'What did you say?' he breathed angrily.

'It's true!' she cried. 'You treated my mother like a servant and insulted her by bringing your . . . your women into her house!'

'How dare you speak to me like that!' he shouted.

'This was my mother's house, *her* house, left to her by my own dear father, and you defiled it with your . . . your whores!'

The back of his hand across her face sent her reeling to the floor. 'This is *my* house. *Mine.* Your mother was *my* wife. Everything here belongs to *me*.' His flinty glare swept over her again and he added, 'Including you.'

'Well, I shall be twenty-one soon,' Clara replied, 'and then you cannot own me.'

He grabbed her by her hair and hauled her to her feet. 'We shall see about that. Go to your chamber. Now.'

Grace had heard the argument from the kitchen and hurried to the study, opening the door without knocking.

The master was furious. 'Leave this instant, Beighton. I did not call for you.'

'But, your daughter, sir, she has a cut on her face.'

'I ordered you to leave!'

'Yes, sir.' Grace retreated to the kitchen. She glanced at Clara as she left and saw the fear in her eyes.

Clara's fear was justified. Her stepfather was unpredictable and he was a frightening sight when he was angry. He had taken out his temper first on her mother and then on her elder sister. Now they were both gone and Clara remembered the last rational words her mother had spoken before she died. She had pleaded with her to leave this house.

'Do not let him break you as he has me,' she had begged. 'Follow your sister. I am finished now. He can hurt me no more.'

'Daughter.' Her stepfather never used her name. 'You will go to your chamber. I shall deal with you presently.'

Clara hurried away. Her face was stinging where he had struck her. She sat on the edge of her feather bed and nursed her swollen cheek. He would beat her for this outburst. The long wait for her punishment made her nervous. She wondered how many lashes from his strap she would have to endure this time, and whether they would be across her hands or her back.

Eventually the stairs creaked and she stood up, swallowing anxiously. He came into her bedchamber and closed the door behind him, turning the key in the lock.

'You are not in your nightgown,' he observed.

She remained silent, not wishing to annoy him further.

'Why are you not in your nightgown?' he demanded

'It is early in the day, Father, and we have not yet eaten our supper.'

'But I sent you to your chamber, Daughter.'

'I . . . er . . . I thought, that is, I . . . I am twenty years of age, Father.'

He stepped close to her and glowered. 'Then it is high time you learned how to behave in my house. When I send you to your chamber you put on your nightgown.'

'Yes, Father.'

'Do it then.'

Clara frowned and looked about her. 'I do not have a screen. If you would leave my bedchamber . . .'

He sat down on the only chair in the room and stated baldly, 'I am your father.'

Clara's fingers shook as she fumbled with the buttons of her bodice. He was going to thrash her back without the protection of her chemise and corset to dull the pain. He watched her impassively as she took her long white nightgown from the chest in the corner and draped it over her body while she removed her corset and stepped out of her drawers. Then he got up and walked slowly around her as she stood silently with bare feet in the middle of the room.

He had his cane with him, the one he used to beat off street urchins and dogs. Would he use the cane instead of the strap today? She could not see his strap anywhere.

'Are you sorry for what you said?' he demanded suddenly.

Clara stared at the bare wooden floor in silence.

His voice lowered threateningly and he poked the cane painfully into her stomach. 'I asked you if you were sorry . . .'

'Yes, Father. I am sorry,' she answered quickly.

'Will you speak to me like that again?'

'No, Father, I shall not.'

'No, Father, I shall not,' he repeated softly. 'That is good. You wish to please me, do you not, Daughter?'

'I . . . er . . . I—'

'Do you wish to please me?' he demanded loudly, pushing the cane harder into her flesh.

'Of course I do, Father.'

He looked satisfied. 'Very good. Now you may kneel by your bed and say your prayers.'

Shakily, she lowered herself to her knees. He was going to beat her back with his cane as she knelt, she thought. The worn floorboards were hard and cold but the soft edge of her familiar satin quilt provided comfort. She clasped her hands together, squeezed her eyes tight shut and waited for the pain to start.

She heard him moving about and imagined him taking off his jacket, flexing his arms and testing his cane for strength. He would be smiling, she thought. Her stepfather enjoyed beating people.

'I cannot hear your prayers,' he snapped. 'Speak up.'

'Please God, forgive me for the sins I have committed. I have been disrespectful to my dear father who has looked after me and my mama. Take care of my dear mama and receive her into the Kingdom of Heaven. Bless my father and his house for my father is a good man . . .'

She choked on the words and her voice dwindled to a whisper. The bedstead creaked as he sat down beside her. She kept her eyes tight shut and tensed her body, waiting for the blows. If she held her breath she might faint and not feel the pain. A draught came in under the door, making her legs and feet feel icy cold. How long would it take to faint? She could smell him close to her. He smelled of strong drink and stale tobacco, with an underlying sourness of wet dogs and his chamber pot.

She let out a small, surprised squeal as he grasped her clasped hands in his. Her eyes opened smartly. He was sitting on the bed in his shirt and with his breeches opened and pushed down around his ankles. He yanked her hands across to his lap and shoved them down towards his private parts.

'No!' Horrified, she tried to pull her hands away, but his hold on them was firm.

'Yes,' he growled. 'This is your punishment. Look.'

A vile sight confronted her as his shirt parted to reveal a brown quivering arch of flesh struggling to raise its head.

'Look!' he ordered harshly. 'You see this. This is your punishment. Kiss it.'

'I . . . I c-cannot,' she whispered hoarsely.

'Kiss it!' he demanded. 'And hold it. Like this.' He

pulled her clasped hands apart and folded them around his trembling flesh.

It felt hot to her chilled hands and as he pushed her face towards it it seemed to shrink beneath them. But when her lips collided with its smelly brown skin it grew again and raised itself strongly in her hands.

'Aaaaah.' A low growl came from her stepfather's throat. 'Yessss. Move your hands. Like this.' He covered her hands with his and moved them up and down his hot, rigid flesh.

'You do it,' he snapped.

'I . . . I cannot. Please don't—'

'Do it! *Do as I say, you whore!*'

Sick with loathing and fear of this vindictive man, she obeyed as best she could until her wrists were tired and her body ached with tension. The gruesome sight before her sickened her further and she shut her eyes to blank out her ordeal. But it did not take away the disgusting smell and feel of him. Or the bark of his voice when she slowed.

'Faster, whore, faster!' At some moment during her nightmare he took his own hands away. The growl in his throat became a louder and more frequent pulsating groan as he threw back his head and cried out, a strangled animal-like snarl that made her open her eyes in fright.

His flesh pulsed and throbbed in her fingers, and quite suddenly her face and hands were covered in a sticky white mess that shot out of him, first as a dribble and then as a prolonged spurt that clung to her skin and tasted salty on her lips. His snarling quickened and then faded as he fell backwards on her quilt. The pulses slowed and his flesh went limp in her hands. Numb with shock and hatred, she stared at it, a soft crumpled heap of wrinkled brown skin and sticky, greying hair.

The vomit rose in her throat and she choked it back, overwhelmed by disgust. He revolted her, lying there helpless and groaning, with his eyes closed and a lick of spittle leaking from the corner of his mouth. She did not think that she could hate her stepfather any more than she already did. But now she knew she could. She despised him for living.

Was this the reason her elder sister had left? She had thought it was the beatings, just the beatings, and they were used to those. Beatings tore at your body but your body healed. This – this assault on her sensibilities had poisoned her mind. She wanted to kill him. A knife – a kitchen knife – would suffice. If she had one with her she would do it now. She knew that if she stayed with him she would surely kill him. She knew that this was why her sister had left and she must do the same.

Calmly, she wiped her face and hands on the bedcover, staining the beautiful satin sheen with his poison. She kept her eyes on the damp smears as her stepfather recovered, sat up and said, 'Your duty, Daughter, is to please me. If you please me I shall not beat you. When you are finished in your duty you must ask if you have pleased me. Do you understand?'

'Yes, Father,' she answered meekly.

'Ask me, then!'

She swallowed wearily. 'Did I please you, Father?'

'For the present, Daughter. For the present.' He grasped

a handful of her skirts and wiped away the stickiness from his own flesh, then pulled up his breeches and left her bedchamber, taking the key and locking the door behind him.

Grace had eavesdropped outside the door without shame. She had heard Mr Sowden's groans inside Clara's bedchamber and knew them for what they were. Now she darted along the landing to hide in the sickroom where her mistress's dead body rested. As soon as the master was downstairs she returned to Clara's door.

'Clara,' Grace whispered. 'Are you all right?'

'No I am not!'

Grace thought she sounded angry rather than weepy. 'Come to the door so we can talk,' she urged.

'What is it?' Clara demanded.

'I heard what he did to you. You don't have to stay here. You can leave with me.'

'Where would we go?'

'Anywhere. Away from him.'

There was a short silence, then Clara asked through the door, 'When are you leaving?'

'Tonight. I'll add some spirits to his ale at supper. When he's sound asleep, I'll take his keys and let you out. Do you have a travelling box?'

'Yes.'

'Put some clothes in it. Not too many because you must carry it yourself.'

The two women, shadowy figures wrapped and hooded in long dark cloaks, set off after midnight. They trudged steadily along the road, hardly uttering a word to each other until Grace, worried by the younger woman's silence, asked if she was all right.

'Yes, thank you,' Clara responded firmly. 'I was just thinking that I had learned something today.'

'What do you mean?' Grace asked.

'I learned that men have a weakness – even the strongest of tormenters.' She turned to Grace and added, 'That's useful for a gentlewoman to know, isn't it?'

They reached the turnpike as the first streaks of dawn appeared in the eastern sky.

'Let's rest a while and wait for an early-morning carrier,' Grace suggested. 'It'll take us to the far side of the Riding and away from your stepfather.'

Clara remained subdued as they sat on a mounting stone by the horse trough. 'I wanted to kill him, you know,' she muttered. 'I would have done so if I had stayed with him.'

'And ended up on the gallows for your trouble? No, Miss Clara. It is best you leave him to his dubious pleasures. You can make your own way in life now.'

'How? I have no money and only a little education.'

'Do you have nothing left of your mother's?'

'Some jewellery and a few silver coins that Mama kept back for us. She gave half to my sister and half to me.'

'Does he know about that?'

'I do not think so. Why?'

'Well, he may come after you for it, as you are not yet twenty-one.'

'Oh, Grace, I shall kill myself before I go back to him.'

'Then we must plan for your future. Or our future, if you wish it.'

Clara looked surprised and Grace continued. 'I have enough gold to take a house with bedchambers for lodgings. Times are changing in the South Riding. When I was your age there were only the gentry and their servants. Now, with all these manufactories there are more men like – well, in trade like your stepfather. They do not have land but they have money, money from ironworks and mills, from haulage and other callings. They travel and they buy from each other. They come from all over, from Manchester, even from London Town. So they need lodgings. Good ones, like their own homes. And wholesome food to eat at the end of their working day.' Grace paused for breath. 'I . . . I can't do it on my own, Miss Clara. But, if you wish, together we can make a decent living providing for them.'

'What if Father finds out and comes looking for me?'

'You have to take that risk. But I shall say that you are my niece. With any luck you'll be turned twenty-one before he catches up with us.'

Clara thought for a moment. 'I haven't run a household before, only helped Mama, then my sister, and now you.'

'I know what to do in the kitchen and laundry. Your manners and charm are all we need to impress our guests and gain a reputation.'

Clara was doubtful. 'I don't know whether I can do it.'

'I shall do all the housekeeping and as soon as we can afford it, we'll get a girl to help with the work. You are beautiful, Clara. You will make a fine mistress of the house, welcoming the guests, seeing that the rooms are as comfortable as their own homes, and that they have good fires and hot water for their shaves.'

'Yes, I could do that.'

'Then we could be equals in this venture?' Grace asked hopefully.

Clara nodded, warming to the idea and feeling an inner excitement welling. She would be independent, with money of her own, free of her stepfather and his evil ways. 'Equals,' she repeated. 'I like the sound of that.'

Grace smiled. 'We shall look for a house together and you can choose the furnishings.'

The sun's rays streaked across the early-morning sky, and in the distance a carrier cart plodded slowly towards them and their new life in the South Riding.

Chapter 3

One year later Grace and Clara had furnished three bedchambers for guests in a sturdy, stone-built house on the road to the moor just outside a busy Riding town. They had heard from the butcher's boy that Clara's stepfather had come looking for her, but no one in this part of the Riding knew Clara's real identity and he soon moved on to Sheffield in his search. And now she was twenty-one and free of him for ever.

It was almost the end of their working day. Grace had cooked a roast beef dinner that Clara had served to their three guests in their elegant dining room. Clara carried a tray of dirty china back to their spacious kitchen.

'Mr Hardcastle said the roast beef was especially good tonight, Grace.'

Grace was helping their scullery maid, Mary, to wash the pots. She called from the sink, 'This is his third visit to us. We shall soon be able to afford to mend the roof.'

'But what we really need is enough money to furnish another bedchamber so that we can take on extra help,' Clara stated wearily.

Grace wiped her hands and came through to the kitchen. 'I am sorry, Clara. I should have realised you would not be as used to hard work as I am. Sit down and I'll make you some tea.'

'Heavens no, Grace! I am thinking of you. I can keep going. But you are more than twice my age and I know how your bones pain you, especially in the mornings. You must let me do more in the kitchen and laundry. It is too much for you with only a girl to help.'

'No, Clara. You are the lady of the house. You need to look elegant for our guests, and to call on tradesmen in town. It is important for our reputation and our credit with the bank.'

'I suppose you are right. But the work is too much for you! I know it is!'

Grace sighed and sank on to a rickety kitchen chair. 'I manage. But you are right. We need another pair of hands.'

Clara picked up the heavy blackened kettle from the hob. 'A girl to do the laundry, as soon as we can afford it,' she said firmly. 'Do you want a hot toddy? Mr Hardcastle has asked for Scotch whisky for his nightcap.'

'Don't mind if I do,' Grace replied. 'Shall I take his drink upstairs for you?'

'No you shall not. You have done far too much today.' Clara mixed their best Scotch whisky with hot water, honey and spices in a jug, then poured it into a small pewter tankard. She pushed it across the table to Grace.

'Take this to bed and rest. Mary will turn down the lamps. I'll see you in the morning.'

'Good night, then.'

'Good night, Grace.'

Grace and Clara had small bedchambers on the second floor that was reached by the back stairs. There were attics further up where servants had slept in the past when the house was built. But the attics were damp and Mary slept downstairs in an anteroom that had once been the butler's pantry and now housed cupboards of china and plate for the dining room.

Clara placed Mr Hardcastle's nightcap together with a lighted candle on a silver tray. She flexed her aching shoulders and massaged the back of her neck before calling good night to Mary and going through a heavy, brass-studded door to the spacious square hall at the front of the house.

Clara was tired and her back hurt, but she thought that her life here with Grace was perfect. She was mistress of a fine house, finer than her own dear father's house, and without her cruel and vicious stepfather to dominate her. She was weary but she was content. Well, almost content. As she climbed the front stairs she thought how much pleasanter life would be with a little more income from the lodgings.

'Your nightcap, sir.' She tapped on Mr Hardcastle's door. He had asked for this chamber. It was one of their best, with a large bay window that looked out on to a village in the distance and the moor beyond. She had furnished it well, with a comfortable bed and a carpet on the waxed floorboards.

'Come in, Clara, my dear.' He was in his shirtsleeves, sitting at the side table reading documents by the light of an oil lamp.

'Over here.' His voice sounded heavy as he moved his papers aside to make room for the salver.

But as she put down the tray, his left arm snaked around her back to encircle her waist.

'Stay a while,' he said.

She was startled, but not frightened. 'I beg your pardon, sir?' she responded.

'Sit down and talk to me. Your work is finished and I am in need of company tonight.' He put down his writing pen and turned to face her.

Clara thought that he looked as exhausted as she felt. His days were taken up visiting ironworks and forges on behalf of the railway company that employed him.

'I . . . I don't know that I should, sir.'

'Oh, Clara, some distraction from this boring task of mine is long overdue. And the South Riding has very little to offer a weary traveller.'

'There are inns and taverns in town, sir,' she suggested.

'They are hardly to my taste,' he muttered. 'Not like you.' He raised his bushy, greying eyebrows and she did not mistake his meaning.

She took his arm from around her waist and said clearly, 'I think not, sir.'

'Why not? A man has needs when he is away from his wife. A woman can help him with his needs. Especially a beautiful woman like you.'

She stepped away from him and said, 'Drink your whisky, Mr Hardcastle.'

'Oh please, Clara. I need you to be a woman for me, not just a servant.'

'No, sir, I shall not oblige you.'

'Come along, my dear. You must crave a little distraction yourself at the end of your working day,' he persisted.

'No, sir, it is not distraction I crave,' she pronounced briskly. 'Rather, some well-earned rest.'

'Are we gentlemen too much work for you?' he asked lightly.

'Of course not! No, Mr Hardcastle. It is my Aunt Grace who causes me concern.'

'She is quite well, I trust?'

'She . . . she is getting old, I think.'

'Then she needs another servant,' he explained patiently. 'In the kitchen perhaps?'

'The laundry, actually . . .' she began. She stopped as she realised that he was simply humouring her.

He gave her a gentle smile. 'I believe we can help each other, Clara.' He reached under the table for a small leather travelling box that he opened with a key on his timepiece chain. He took out a small stack of gold sovereigns and placed them on the salver.

'How much extra help do you need?' he asked.

Clara stared at the coins. She was speechless and her heart began to thump in her throat. She knew what he meant. She knew the kind of proposition he was suggesting. Her mouth opened but no sound came out. But neither did she flounce from his chamber as she had imagined she might.

'I can see that you are tempted,' he persisted calmly. 'You need have no fear of me. I shall not harm you.'

Clara thought of her stepfather and shuddered. But Mr Hardcastle was not like her stepfather. Mr Hardcastle was a cultured man, kind, well-educated and from a good family in Manchester. Clara thought also of Grace, who had rescued her from an intolerable future and provided everything to set them up here. She would always be in Grace's debt for that. Perhaps it was now her turn to provide for Grace? Her heart continued to thump.

'What . . . what do you want of me?' she asked nervously.

'I want nothing that you are not prepared to give,' he said, then added, 'I promise you that. But I would like to see you without your gown – if you are willing?' Again he used his small, gentle smile to entice her.

She should have talked to Grace first. But Grace would have said no. Definitely no. And Clara felt a frisson of excitement run through her. She was frightened, but she felt a strange thrill at the same time. She had never lain with a man, but she knew of their weakness, even though her only knowledge was that of her stepfather's needs.

She wondered again what she would have to do, and in the next moment she realised that she did not care. Men may be powerful and dominant in life, but they all had this weakness in the bedchamber. Mr Hardcastle was being honest with her about his. He was a businessman and, to him, this was a business deal.

She took a deep breath and nodded. 'All right,' she said.

She began to remove her bodice, skirts and boots until she was down to her corsets, drawers and stockings. He watched her silently, then asked her to help him take off

his own clothes. He stood there impassively as she undid
buttons and peeled away the layers. He was so passive
she had to ask him to assist her, murmuring, 'Lift your
arms, sir. Step out of your breeches, sir.'

'Call me Master Henry,' he asked.

She did not question him. 'Of course, Master Henry.'

'Now my under-drawers.'

She swallowed and knelt on the floor, rolling them
down to his feet, not having the courage to raise her
eyes.

'Is it time for bed now?' he asked quietly.

'Yes, Master Henry.'

He walked over to the bed and she dared to look at
him. He was a pale, skinny man, but unclothed she could
see that he was capable of physical work. His arms and
legs were sinewy and his shoulders and chest, though
narrow, were muscled. His greying hair had once been
black and he had a small amount on his chest, and more
between his legs where a fleshy projection hung, limp
and forlorn. It flopped to one side as he lay on the bed,
resting his head on his hand.

'Walk around the chamber for me,' he asked.

She obeyed tentatively, her nervousness showing at
first, and then as her confidence grew she straightened
her back and held her head high. He seemed to approve
of this because he began to smile at her. But she noticed
that he did not stir with any desire for her.

'I do not please you, do I?' she uttered at last.

'On the contrary,' he sighed, 'you please me greatly.
You remind me of my first boyhood passion. She was a
handsome woman who valued her freedom.'

Clara thought that he was shrewder than he looked. His unassuming manner concealed a wealth of knowledge about the world and its people. She stood before him, her legs slightly apart and her hands resting lightly on her hips where her corsets met her calico drawers. She had no idea what to do next.

'You have not done this before, have you?' he smiled. 'Or you would know that an older man such as myself needs a little more persuasion.'

Her smile faltered a little as her mind raced. Her stepfather had been an older man. Should she touch him? Of course, yes, that's what he wanted. Nervously she knelt by the bed, pushing all memories of her stepfather aside. Mr Hardcastle was different. He was kind and cultured and he smelled clean and wholesome, of real soap and the cologne he used when he dressed. Tentatively, she began to stroke his thighs and his stomach.

He closed his eyes as she progressed towards his private parts, but still there was no reaction from him and she began to despair. Would she have to kiss it to make it stir? She glanced at his face and saw a tiny glitter of eye through his lashes.

'Do not look so worried,' he murmured. 'This is only a game.'

For you, maybe, she thought irritably. If she could not succeed at this, what was she doing even trying? Game, was it, Master Henry? She rose to her feet and gave him a sharp slap with the flat of her hand on his naked rump. 'Well, wake up and start playing!' she muttered desperately.

'Yesss,' he said softly and she heard him sigh. 'Again.'

Again, he'd said. So this was part of Master Henry's boyhood passion? She hit him again on his behind, hard, leaving red marks where her fingers had struck. He gave a little whimper in his throat and she could not tell whether it was from pain or pleasure. But he did not protest or ask her to stop and she hit him again, this time saying, 'Wake up, you naughty boy!'

Clara did not know why she said that, except that she was growing impatient with him and he had told her it was a game. But it was then that she noticed the first stirrings of his male desire. Her eyes widened and she swallowed. Her thoughts tumbled around her head as he continued the whimpering in his throat.

'Naughty, *naughty* boy,' she repeated. 'What are you?'

'Naughty boy, Nurse,' he whined.

Good heavens! she thought. His nurse was his boyhood passion! And this is what he *wants*!

'And what does Nurse do to naughty Master Henry?' she asked imperiously.

His voice had raised an octave to that of his childhood. 'Nurse beats him with the rule,' he replied.

Clara's mind raced. Beats him. Beats him with the rule? Ah yes, there was a wooden rule on his writing table that he used for making drawings. Quick as a flash, she crossed the room to collect the rule and a folded linen towel from the washstand.

'And where does Nurse beat him?' she asked, placing the linen carefully beneath him.

She did not need an answer as she saw the bead of moisture pushing out of his enlarged arousal. It was bigger than she'd realised, she thought absently as she rapped the wooden rule across his buttocks and heard him groan.

To her surprise it was all over quite quickly. The folded linen served its purpose and he was flaccid again. Gently, she cleaned him up with the towel and dropped it by the door. She stood watching him in the lamplight for a moment. He had rolled on to his back and his eyes were closed. Well, almost closed. She detected that tiny glitter between his lashes again.

'Can I put on my nightshirt now, Nurse?' he asked in a small voice.

Clara thought quickly and wondered what she should do next. Perhaps he expected more of her? She stood in front of him, still holding the rule in her hand.

'Is Master Henry going to be naughty again?'

'No, Nurse. Not tonight.'

'Then you may.'

She handed him the nightshirt that was folded on the wooden blanket chest at the foot of the bed. As he pulled it over his head he seemed to become his normal adult self again.

Was that it? she thought, and asked, 'M-may I get dressed now, sir?'

He nodded, giving her that small, secretive smile of his. 'Do you want help with your gown?'

Clara shook her head. The buttons were at the front and she fumbled with them, wondering if that was all she would have to do for a guinea.

He gave her two and said, 'You are good. I know other men who would pay you just as well. As much for your discretion as your services. It's a lucrative business, Clara. Think about it.'

Her hand was shaking as she took the money, knowing what she had become. But this was not how she had imagined it when she saw women loitering in the streets at night. She picked up the soiled linen and the candle and left. Once on the landing, she leaned against the waxed, wooden-panelled walls until she regained her composure.

What had she done? She felt a kind of fluttering excitement in her breast. She had been so nervous with him, but that had added a frisson of danger to her encounter. She realised that she had enjoyed the experience. And it had been easy! She did not deceive herself that it would always be this easy. But for the first time in her life she felt powerful.

The coins chinked in her hand and she thought about a laundry maid for Grace. Clara went to her bed wondering how she would approach talking to Grace about a new direction for their business. She fell asleep rehearsing the words.

The next morning, Grace and Clara were sitting at the dining-room table finishing their coffee while Mary stacked the breakfast dishes on a wooden tray.

'Oooh, they've left some kidneys this morning,' Mary squealed.

'Would you like them for your breakfast?' Clara asked, ignoring Grace's raised eyebrows.

'Ooh, yes please, Miss Clara.'

'Take them through to the kitchen then, and eat them while they're hot.'

When Mary had left, Grace chided Clara lightly. 'I could have put them in a pie for dinner,' she pointed out.

'I know, I know.' Clara took a deep breath. 'I need to talk to you.' She retrieved the gold coins from a small pocket in her overskirt and placed them on the polished tabletop.

'Where did they come from?' Grace asked.

'Mr Hardcastle. Last night.'

Grace raised her eyebrows again. 'Clara?'

'I didn't have to do much. Truly, Grace. Just hit him, really.'

Grace's eyes rounded. 'I warned you they might ask. Oh Clara, I told you not to get involved with any of the guests—'

Clara interrupted. 'But look how much he gave me for – for just beating him on his behind. That's all it took.'

Grace gave a short dry laugh. 'Well, well. That's what the Admiral used to like too.'

Now it was Clara's turn to be surprised. 'Did you do that for him?'

'And more. It started when he got the gout and I had to help him in and out of bed. He said it took his mind off his bad foot.'

'Mr Hardcastle wanted me to be his nurse.'

The two women stared at each other across the table.

'We can mend the roof,' Clara began, 'and get a laundry maid and—'

'No, stop. You're not doing this. You don't know what it can lead to.'

'Oh, Grace. Mr Hardcastle is a respectable man. He knows others like him. I can be very discreet. Anyway, I shan't need many if they pay this well.'

'I said no.'

'Why not?' Clara demanded. 'It will be on my terms, at my price. My choice, Grace. My choice.'

Grace laughed harshly again. 'When you're a servant you don't have any choice. I got myself out of service so I could have choice. But not this, Clara. Not this.'

'You said yourself that times are changing. There's a different way of life emerging in the Riding. I can provide a different kind of service here.'

Grace stared at her. 'You are determined, aren't you?'

Clara nodded.

'Carriage trade only?' Grace queried.

'Of course.'

Still Grace hesitated. 'No, Clara. You don't know anything about this kind of business.'

'But you do, don't you?' Clara suddenly knew that she was right. 'And I can learn.'

Grace stared out of the large dining-room window. It was raining again. She loved to watch the soft gentle rain washing the heather on the moor. But today it meant more damp in the attic and more coal for the fire to dry the laundry. The gold coins glinted among the break-fast-table debris.

'Are you really sure about this, Clara?'

Clara smiled. 'Then you agree. You will not regret it, I promise.'

Chapter 4

1833

Down at Mexton Lock one year later, Edie Dearne was becoming thoroughly fed up with her lively inquisitive toddler. When Luther came home, it was all 'Lissie wants this' and 'Lissie wants that' with no thought for Edie who was doing all the work. He just plays wi' 'er, she moaned to herself, talking at 'er like 'e were slow in the 'ead. And Edie didn't get 'er snuff if the house wasn't clean or there was no dinner on the table. Now he'd told her he was going on another trip down the canal.

'Don't go and leave me wi' 'er again, Luther!' she pleaded.

'And what are we going to live off, if I don't? Where am I going to get t' money for your snuff, tell me that?'

'Can't yer tek 'er wi' yer?'

'Don't be daft, Edie.'

'I thought you'd want 'er along, you're that soft wi' 'er all the time.'

'You know I can't take 'er on the canals wi' me. She's a good little lass fo' you now, i'n't she?'

'No! She's into everything now she's toddling!'

'She sits on t' po' for yer, do'n't she?'

Edie looked down at Lissie sitting on Luther's lap and playing with the chain on his timepiece. Luther was the one that was daft. He was that daft with the little 'un, it made Edie want to spit. A grown man gurgling and cooing at her, and bouncing her on his knees. Then he'd pick 'er up so that she could dance her feet on his legs and he'd go on and on about how big she was growing. But it was Edie who had to wash her mucky clothes and curl her hair and all sorts when he was home.

Edie put on her wheedling, whining tone and said, 'I don't know what to do wi' 'er on me own.'

'Not that again! It's time you grew up a bit, Edie lass. You just 'ave to get on wi' it, like all mams do for their little 'uns.'

'But I'm not 'er mam.'

'Don't start all that either!' Luther gave Lissie a last big hug and said, 'Now you be a good little lass fo' yer mam, and yer dad'll bring you summat back wi' 'im. Some spice or summat.' He gave her big sloppy kisses all over her face and added, 'Ee, lass, I could eat you.' He put her down on the rag rug in front of the hearth and turned on Edie. 'Now, you do as you're told when I'm away, else you'll get what for when I get back. I'll find out, y' know, if you go over ter Navigator or owt.'

'Well, bring me back some more snuff this time,' Edie cried as the back door slammed shut. 'It's allus summat for 'er these days.'

But Luther was already on his way, striding across the clearing towards the lock and thinking about a bargeman he'd heard was on his uppers. Might get some cargo at a good price to sell on, he thought, whistling cheerily to himself.

Edie turned her petulance on the child. 'It's all your fault! I didn't get owt from him this time, it were all stuff fer you that he brought! I may as well not be 'ere when 'e comes home now!'

Lissie grasped a piece of coal that had fallen out the bucket and lifted it up to show her mam, making a gurgling noise in her throat. But her pretty smile was wasted on Edie, who continued to scowl and mutter to herself.

'Well, I don't care what Luther says about me not going down to the canal wi' yer. I gotta 'ave summat ter keep me going. Put that coal down and get on yer feet.' She yanked at Lissie's arm and dragged her across the kitchen. 'Now sit there on yer po' while I get me shawl.'

Edie waited until she was sure Luther would be gone from the lock before she yanked again on Lissie's little arm. She let out a noisy sigh through her lips as a smell rose to meet her nostrils. 'Pooh, you mucky little gypsy. Stand still while I wrap this shawl round yer. We're off to see Rosa.'

Leaving the smelly po' in the kitchen, she went out of the back door dragging a whimpering Lissie behind her, following in Luther's footsteps across the clearing and down the track through the trees.

The main work on this side of the canal was timber

from the woodland. There was a big warehouse in which to store it and a permanent crane on the wharf for loading it into barges. The familiar smell of sawn wood mixed with an oily metallic stink from pulleys and chains that screeched and rattled endlessly.

Luther had said that trade had got steadily worse since he brought Lissie home, but folk always needed timber. And coal. There was plenty of coal heaped up that year as the ironworks were not taking much for the furnaces now some of the melting shops had closed.

Edie slowed as she reached the canal, not wanting anyone to see her, then hurried to the end cottage in Woodmill Row and rapped on Rosa's door.

'It's me, Rosa. 'Ave yer got any o' that snuff mixture? Luther's gone, but he's left me a few coins.'

The door opened. 'Aye, I saw 'im go. Come in outta t' cold. What's she crying fer?'

'I don't know, do I?'

'Is she wet?'

'Don't think so, she's been on the po' half the morning.'

Rosa bent down and lifted the hem of Lissie's skirt. 'Edie, she 'a'n't got any drawers or owt on. And she smells a bit.'

'I told you. She's been on the po'.'

'You 'aven't washed her though. You should gi' 'er a wash, Edie.'

'Oh, I don't know, Rosa, she's nowt but trouble. I wish 'e'd never brought 'er home. I liked it better wi'out 'er. Just Luther and me. He a'n't got any time fer me any more. It's all Lissie this and Lissie that, I could crack 'er one just thinking about it, I really could.'

'Here, try this, love.'

Rosa tipped a small amount of brown powder on to the back of Edie's hand. Edie sniffed it hard up her nostrils and held out her hand for more.

Rosa obliged then said, 'Come and sit down while I clean up the little 'un for you.'

'Oh ta, Rosa. I can't stand to touch her sometimes when I think where she's come from. I swear he's been wi' some tinker's whore. And I get lumbered wi' looking after her! It's not fair!'

'Di'n't Luther tell you her ma died?'

'Aye, but yer never know wi' Luther whether to believe all he says.'

'Well, you sit there while I gi' 'er a wash.' Rosa lifted the snivelling Lissie into the stone scullery sink and cleaned between her legs with a cold wet cloth wrung out from a tin bowl on the wooden draining board. She called through the open door. 'Fetch me that pot of salve from the table, Edie, she's a bit sore. 'A'n't yer got any drawers fer 'er?'

'There might be some in that pile of stuff that Luther brought on his last trip.'

Rosa placed Lissie on her horsehair couch by the kitchen fire and lifted down a stone bottle from her cupboard in the alcove. 'Try some o' this, Edie. It'll make you feel better.'

'What is it?'

'A drop o' gin.'

'Ooh lovely, I don't mind that.'

The two women sipped contentedly out of tin mugs.

'Don't you miss Luther when he's away?' Rosa asked.

'Not now. When he's home 'e 'as me running around all the time, dolling her up, I'm glad when 'e's gone these days.'

'You must be lonely at night though?'

'Not as long as I got me snuff.'

'Not even in the bedchamber?'

'Especially not there! I'm glad of a break from all that. Always at it, 'e is. I'm that fed up wi' 'im heaving and sweating like a pig all o'er me. I put up wi' it when we were first wed, and now I 'as ter do it when he asks, 'cos if I say no he wallops me one.'

'Don't you like it, then?'

'I've never liked it wi' 'im! It's the worst bit of 'im coming home. I allus gives 'im plenty of ale wi' 'is dinner now and then 'e goes straight off to sleep after 'e's done it ter me once.'

Rosa was looking at her with a little smile on her face. 'I never liked it wi' mine either. He cleared off and left me years ago.'

'D'you miss 'im?'

'On'y the money, when me rent is due.'

Edie took another sip of gin and thought how much nicer it would be if she lived here with Rosa, instead of up in the woods with Luther. She gave Rosa a shy smile in return. 'Well then,' she said, 'my Luther's generous to a fault when 'e's got summat in his purse, so we can share it when 'e's gone away.'

Rosa poured more gin into Edie's tin mug. 'Well, you can come down 'ere any time you like, Edie, m' love. D'you think the little 'un'll 'ave a sleep now?'

Edie shrugged. 'Don't know.'

'I'll put 'er over 'ere on the rocker then we can both sit on the couch, together like.'

'Go on, then.' Edie helped herself to another pinch of Rosa's snuff mixture and sat back with her gin. She thought how nice it was here with Rosa. She'd come down here more often when Luther was away. She liked Rosa much more than she liked Luther.

Chapter 5

1839

'Lissie Dearne, you get back here this minute, do y' hear me.'

Lissie heard all right and put her hands to her ears to shut out the screech of her mother's high-pitched voice. Her head ached from the rags that her mam had tied into her hair the night before, and her toes hurt as her feet squeezed into boots that were too small. She swung her legs, banging the heels against the boarded front of the privy seat. If she pointed her toes, they touched the ground now. The wooden seat felt safe and comforting against her bottom and, compared with the harsh icy weather outside, was smooth and warm.

'Lissie, I won't tell you again! If I have to come down there for you, I'll clip your ear 'ole!'

She would too, Lissie thought, rubbing her ears to warm them up. Her mother's hands were claw-like and bony and the back of her hand could easily knock Lissie sideways, and frequently did. She shuffled to the edge of the privy seat and slid off the end, pulling up long calico drawers under her woollen smocked dress as she scampered up the frozen mud path to the house. She was nearly nine and growing fast.

'My boots are too tight, Mam,' she complained, 'and my feet hurt.'

Edie pushed a dusty and battered tin bucket at her. 'Shut up and rake the ashes from the kitchen and the front room grates, then get on with cleaning 'em. And don't forget to put on your old pinny.'

'Can I have a drink of tea, Mam?'

The older woman bent down to Lissie and glared at her. 'We 'a'n't got any tea till yer dad gets 'ome, and anyroad, nobody can have a drink of owt until the fire's going, halfwit.' She gave the child a sharp clip on the back of her head. 'Now shut up, I said, and get on with what you're told.'

Lissie hated the scratchy rasp of dry cinders in her fingers, and the dust made her nose all itchy and twitchy when she heaped them into the bucket. Although it was heavy for her little arms, she managed to lug it down the garden to the dump behind the apple trees, and found a small juicy eater hidden under the criss-crossed branches as her reward.

Blackleading the grates was harder on her small hands as the blacking got into her sore skin and hurt even more, but at least she warmed up a bit while rubbing at the ironwork. The kitchen grate was worst because it was so fiddly with its bars and swing hob that held the sooty kettle. Then there was the bit o' brass on the oven door at the side to shine up.

Her dad was proud o' the new grate he had fitted in the kitchen chimney place. 'You look after it, Edie,' he had said. 'It were made for t' gentry.' Lissie thought it would have been best rubbed up last night while it was still warm from the fire; it was so much harder to get a shine on it now it was cold. She tried to say this to her mam but she only shouted back at her, yelling, 'Well, you were asleep in bed when the fire died down last night. Did you want me to wake you and make you clean it in your night-gown? No, I thought not. Get on with it now and make sure you rub it until you can see your face in it.'

Lissie finished the grates and laid both fires, then went outside again, this time to the woodshed for kindling wood to replace the sticks that had been drying in the bottom oven next to the grate. She was shivering with cold and very hungry by this time. Her mam had left a bucket of coals in front of the kitchen grate, as well as a flint and some old rags smeared in musty cooking grease to make sure the fire caught first time. Lissie could hear her next door in the scullery, pumping water to fill the kettle. The greasy rags crackled and spat at her but soon the flames were licking round the coals and giving out some heat.

'I've done it, Mam. Fire's going,' Lissie said proudly. 'Shall I do the one in the front room next?'

Her mother dumped a kettle full of water on the hearth and picked up an empty one. 'No, leave the front 'un till later. Just look at the mess you've made of the rug. Get out of it, you little toerag. You'll have to give it a shake now.' She landed another clip on the side of Lissie's head. 'Go on, roll it up and take it outside.'

'Ow!' Lissie held her ear where her mother's hand had caught her and looked at the rug. She had been extra careful not to spill any ash or coal dust on the rug and couldn't see anything that wasn't there before she started. Lissie tried ever so hard to please her mam, but she was so difficult, especially when Dad was due back from one of his trips.

It didn't matter what Lissie did, or how much she tried, it was always wrong and more often than not she'd get a clip round the ear for her trouble. Her lower lip trembled and she frowned as she gathered up the rug and went out once more into the cold. She hoped the first kettle to boil would be to pour on some oats for breakfast, and not for the pots. The dirty stone sink was piled high with greasy pots and she hated the cold draughty scullery in winter.

But Lissie was out of luck that morning and all she got to eat was some bread and dripping, and a mug of chilly dusty water that had been standing out all night, before she had to climb up on the old milking stool to wash the pots.

'Now get on with those and mind you don't break anything. Your dad will be coming home soon and you don't want me telling 'im you're a slovenly little brat, do you? When I get back I want all them pots washed and drying on the draining board.'

Dad! Her dad was coming home soon? Lissie drew in her breath sharply and asked, 'When will he be here, Mam?'

'When 'e's made enough money, that's when!'

What on God's earth possessed Luther to bring home

a *babby* all those years ago, she would never know. It must be eight or nine summers now that they'd had that little toerag causing rows and too much extra work for Edie's liking. Still, she had grown up fast and was becoming a good little help to Edie round the house. Edie thought that that was the only good part about keeping her instead of sending her out into service.

Well, she had heard that the ice on the canal was cracked and the barges were moving again, so she had better get in some bread and taters. She took a thick wool shawl from a hook behind the scullery door and slung it round her skinny shoulders.

'Where are you going, Mam?' Lissie ventured.

'Never you mind, nosy little madam.'

Edie slammed the door behind her. Lissie jumped and the old milking stool wobbled on the uneven bricks of the scullery floor. She grasped the rough rim of the stone sink to steady herself. Her hands were still filthy from blackleading the grates even though she had tried washing them under the pump. The water was icy cold this morning and didn't make any difference on its own. But Lissie knew from doing this in the past that scrubbing a sink full of pots and cooking pans would do the trick.

The soda in the water hurt her hands and made the skin red raw, but at least the blacklead had gone by the time she had finished. Then she took off her coarse jute apron and scrubbed some more to get the soot and blacking out of it. She looked forward to rubbing some salve on her hands and sitting by the fire while it soaked in.

Spreading the cold wet apron over a hedge to dry, Lissie lingered in the morning rays of an early winter sunrise. Night frosts had blackened the last of the flower heads and the beanpoles were falling over. When her dad came home he would straighten everything out, and Lissie would help him. She prayed for her dad to come home ever so soon. Her mam never made her do all the dirty jobs in the house when her dad was here.

As long as Dad made no complaints about the mess, they left all the worst chores until he went away again, when her mam asked him for extra money to get a girl in to clean up. Lissie was excited by this the first time she understood what her mam was asking for, as she thought it would be like having company and Mam might buy a cake from the inn by the lock. But when she asked her mam about 'the girl to clean up' all she got was another clip round the ear, told not to be so cheeky, and the scullery floor to scrub.

The frost had melted under the sun's rays and Lissie looked for some dock leaves to wrap round her chapped hands. Her mam was gone a long time so she went inside and wandered round the house for something to do. Better not light the front-room fire. She lifted the empty kettle from the brick floor and heaved it up into the scullery sink. She could pump the water to fill it but then it was too heavy for her to lift it down again. She climbed on to the old milking stool and played with the pots and pans on the wooden draining board for a while. Bored with that, Lissie remembered where her mam kept the old papers that dad brought in with him and sat turning the yellowing pages, looking at the patterns the words made and wondering what they meant. Hurriedly, she put them away when she heard her mam coming round the side of the house.

'Get the door open, Lissie. Look sharp, will you, these are heavy.'

Edie deposited a tin can of milk and an old sack filled with bread and vegetables on the scullery floor. The wholesome smell of fresh-baked bread filled her nostrils. Mam never went to so much trouble for just the two of them and Lissie's eyes lit up.

'Ooh, Mam! Is Dad coming home today?'

'Aye, lass, he is that. There's been some ice downstream but the ice-breakers 'ave got through it and the barges'll be here later on.' Edie spotted the kettle in the sink and immediately lugged it through to the hob that swung over the kitchen fire. 'I'm parched after all that carrying. The sooner you're big enough to do this for me the better.'

'I can go to the lock for you if you want, Mam. I can.'

'And there'd be hell to pay from your dad if you did. You know he says you haven't to go down there on your own. One o' the Jacksons 'd see you and tell him. Then there'd be no nothing for either of us, so shut your trap.'

'But I'm big enough, aren't I?' Lissie stood on tiptoe, squashing her cramped toes, and stretched as tall as she could.

'Aye, you are that. And you cost me a fortune to feed when your dad's away.'

I didn't believe him when he said she was six months old when he found her, Edie mused, and I still don't believe it. She looks more than eight to me. Anyway, if she was a foundling, how did he know how old she was?

'Will Dad be home soon, Mam?'

'Oh, give over, will yer!' A bastard, that's what she is, a filthy little bastard that he's lumbered me with! Probably his own, an' all, Edie thought, with that cheap floozy from the docks. My God, I hate the sight of 'er.

As Edie lifted her hand to give her a crack on the head, Lissie ducked and disappeared fast into the pantry, dragging the damp sack of potatoes and carrots and saying, 'I'll put these away for you, Mam.' She closed the door behind her and sat on a piece of old wood on the floor until the clattering in the scullery had died down and her little bottom was frozen stiff.

When everything went quiet Lissie knew it would be safe to go back with the empty sack. The door to the kitchen was open and her mam was sitting dozing by the fire with a mug of tea. Her nose was brown where she had been taking her snuff, and there was a bottle of spirits falling from her hand into her lap.

Lissie climbed on to a wooden chair and carefully poured herself some lukewarm tea from the big brown pot on the table. There was still only bread and dripping to eat, but when Dad got home there would be a feast! Dad always brought good things to eat when he came home. She wished she could go down to the lock to meet him, instead of having to wait here. P'raps he'd bring her some new boots this time, and a thick wool shawl like her mam's.

She scrambled down from the table and sat on the hearth rug by the fire to warm her chilled feet and legs.

She wondered why her mam was always so cross. She often grumbled that she didn't know what Luther was thinking of when he'd brought home a little gypsy. And when Lissie had been running around the garden in bare feet in the summer, with her long black hair flowing behind her, her mam had often called her 'a dirty little gypsy', and threatened to 'take her back to them and swap her for a pony and trap'.

Lissie leaned against the brass-buttoned leather of her dad's favourite chair by the fire. She hoped her mam would wake up soon and take the rags out of her hair as her head was hurting something cruel. Mam always twisted her hair really tight and when Lissie had asked her not to, she'd pulled it more and made it worse, snapping, 'Yer dad likes you wi' ringlets. I don't care if you look as if you've been pulled through a hedge back'ards! If it were left to me I'd cut the whole lot off.'

The glowing pile of coals in the grate fell, causing a few sparks to dance in front of the sooty fireback. Mam had put the new bread on top of the oven to keep warm and the blackened kettle was just beginning to grumble on its hob. Suddenly, Mam woke up and wiped her nose with the back of her hand. She put the empty mug and her spirit bottle down and roughly pulled Lissie towards her.

'Come here, thee. Let's get these rags out.' She tugged at the fraying strips of linen, catching and pulling strands of Lissie's long black hair.

'Ow, ouch, ooh stop, Mam, it hurts!'

'Oh, shut up whining. Your dad'll be here soon and you'd better look your best.' She grabbed the freed ringlets with her bony hand and tied them back with a piece of faded ribbon saved from an old petticoat. Then she opened a drawer under the alcove cupboard next to the fire. 'Here. Put this clean pinny on and no going into t' garden, d'you hear?'

'Ah, Mam,' Lissie pleaded, 'can't I go out and watch for Dad coming up the path?'

'No you can't. Go an' put a light to the front-room fire. You can watch from there. And as soon as you see him, you come straight in here and tell me. Straight away, d'you hear?'

'Yes, Mam.'

Lissie stood on the horsehair cushion of one of the high-backed front-room chairs and pressed her nose against the window. The house stood on the site of an old charcoal burner's cottage in a wooded area that stretched for about half a mile to the canal. It had been rebuilt in brick with a slate roof years ago by a young engineer working on the cuts and locks in the area. However, it was out of the way and not a handy place to live as there was no proper village nearby.

When the waterway was finished, the engineer and his new wife had gone overseas and the house had lain empty for several years. It was too dear for a farmer to buy to house one of his workers, having a front door and staircase leading up to the bedchambers. Workers' cottages had stairs in the kitchen and no front doors. Not that there were many farm workers around any more. Most had gone to work in the manufactories or collieries in the heart of the South Riding. Furnaces and forges that belched out smoke and grime crowded into

the Riding towns. They were some way upstream from
Mexton Lock where Lissie lived. But few folk from
Mexton ventured that far even though they were easier
to get to now, with the canal completed to Tinsley.

Luther Dearne had heard about the empty house as
a young barge hand grafting a living on the waterways
that linked the rivers Humber and Trent with the South
Riding, and he knew a bargain when he saw one. It was
perfect for him, far enough away from the merchants
near the coast and the factory owners in the Riding for
him to disappear quickly when his shady dealings went
sour.

The barge owner that Luther worked for as a young
man was a cussed old bugger who lived alone on his
barge. When he took sick one winter and died, Luther
tipped him overboard into the Humber and sold the
barge as his own. This was all he needed to be able to
set up home in the engineer's house with his new bride
Edie. He was able to stop working on the barges after
that, and rely solely on the gains from his dealings to
keep body and soul together.

That was nearly twenty years ago and trading had
been good at first. The ironworks and foundries had their
ups and their downs but there were always deals to be
made in coals and bar iron. He bought and sold materials on the coast and manufactured goods from the
town and arranged the transport of them in and out.

Nowadays, with regular business so unreliable, he tried
to deal for other people as much as he could because
there was less risk to his own money that way. Being a
broker meant that he had plenty of opportunity to cream

off more than his dues and that was something Luther could not resist. The traders never found out and, as they were all better off than he was, he reckoned that there was enough to go round.

Manufacturing in the South Riding expanded, water traffic increased and bargemen demanded a source of refreshment for themselves while they waited their turn to go through Mexton Lock. There had always been an inn at the lock, since the days when numerous thirsty labourers had cut the canal through farmland near the river Don.

The Navigator did a good trade and Mickey Jackson, with his wife Annie, worked hard. Annie kept clean rooms and cooked good food for travellers. Mickey, a burly, rough-and-ready man who spoke with his fists, preferred to keep the company of his regular ale drinkers in his saloon, one of whom was Luther. Mickey could always rely on Luther for extra muscle when he needed it.

Over the years, Mickey had added stables and livery to the inn for the workhorses that drew the heavy vessels through the oily black water. The youngest of Mickey's lads had recently set up as a horse marine for this stretch of the canal and the eldest was nearing the end of his apprentice bond with the blacksmith. The middle brother had taken over ale brewing from his father, who was now more interested in drinking it. A thriving community was developing on the bankside and there was a regular trade at Mexton wharf in timber and coal from a local land owner.

While Mickey's business grew, Luther was beginning to find work hard to come by. His reputation was not

good with respectable traders and big transport companies took the best trade. Luther had to confine his dealings to newcomers who had no knowledge of his past.
As his trade dwindled, he relied more and more on what
he could purloin from his deals. When challenged he
always blamed the other party's short supply, and if things
got really hot he simply disappeared until they had cooled
down.

Edie had turned out to be a disappointment to Luther,
but he easily found solace on his travels. There was many
a young widow or neglected wife in town or port with
a warm bed to offer in exchange for a piece of good
linen, a cooking pot or a brace of rabbits. And the child
was a joy to behold. Meeting that old trout in the North
Star all those years ago and buying little Lissie when she
was but a few months old had been the best deal he had
ever made.

As Luther lumbered through the woodland track, a
bulky sack bouncing over his shoulder, his heart lifted
at the thought of seeing his lovely little Lissie. She was
all that kept him with Edie now. He beamed at the sight
of her little white face and bouncy black ringlets peering
out of the front-room window. He saw her disappear
from view, guessing she was dashing through to the
kitchen.

Lissie squealed when she saw her dad striding up the
mud and cinder path that emerged from the wood into
the clearing that formed their front yard. Dressed in his
usual brown moleskin trousers and thick tweed jacket
that refused to stay buttoned, he sported a fancy new
waistcoat straining across his ample belly. She jumped

down from the chair and hurried through to the back kitchen.

'He's here, Mam! Dad's home!'

Edie leaped to her feet and smoothed down her apron, hissing at Lissie to behave herself and only speak when she was spoken to. Luther burst in through the scullery door shouting, 'Get the fire banked up, woman, I've got yer favourite leg o' mutton in here for you to bake wi' some 'taters!' He threw the heavy sack on to the wooden table in the kitchen, picked Lissie up by her elbows and balanced her against his corpulent belly. 'How's my little trooper today? My God, I believe you've grown some in only a month. You're so heavy now. Wait till you see what I've got for you.'

She was as pretty as a picture with her hair as black and shiny as wet coal. It was done up with a ribbon that bounced with her curls as she moved. She wore a white pinafore over her dark winter dress and black lace-up boots on her feet. Luther wondered again, as he had done many times before, what he had done to deserve a little lass that was such a vision of loveliness. He was never a church-going man but he reckoned he must have done something right in his dubious life for Him up in Heaven to bless him with Lissie.

Lissie jumped up and down on the spot. 'Where is it, Dad? What you brought me?'

'Wait on, lass. The barge is unloading as I speak. I've borrered Mickey's cart this time. Do you want to come down to the lock with your dad, and ride back with me? Do you?'

'Oh yes, Dad. I do, I do,' Lissie squeaked in excitement.

Her smoky green eyes shone and she forgot how much her boots pinched her toes, or how her hands felt sore and stinging. The recognisable warm smell of old tweed and tobacco filled her nostrils and comforted her.

Dad took her small hand in his large first. 'Off we go then.' He led her through the scullery, shouting at Edie over his shoulder, 'And cut one o' them cabbages from the garden, Edie. We can have a right good dinner tonight.' He turned to Lissie. ''Ave you missed me, lass? 'Ave you missed your old dad, then?'

'Oh yes, Dad. I have.' Lissie turned to say 'ta-ra' to her mam, who met her with such a scowl of spite and hatred that she recoiled in silence. What had she done now to upset her mam? Why did she hate her so and what, oh what, could she do to put things right? Her dad tugged at her arm, jolting her out of her stillness. But the edge was taken off her happiness as she wondered what her mam would do to her when her dad was gone again.

Chapter 6

Erik Svenson had struggled for eight years to establish his reputation in England. Dealers like Luther Dearne, who had no time for foreigners, didn't help him. But with the assistance of his wife, Ingrid, he had survived and prospered enough to employ a clerk to run his warehouse on the Humber. His son, Blake, now thirteen, was growing fast and Ingrid had found them a decent house in Goole, well away from the rats and diseases of the coastal ports. One of his buyers had recommended a good school in the South Riding to complete his boy's education, and Erik thought that he now had a future in England.

Blake jumped out of the family horse and trap leaving his neatly stacked boxes behind him and ran the last few yards to the red-brick villa that was his home. He scrambled through the damp, dripping shrubbery surrounding the building to reach the kitchen at the back of the house and darted inside, picking up a slice of fruit bun on the way.

'Papa! Mama! I'm home again!' Bursting into the drawing room he collided straight into the tall, upright figure of Mr Ephraim, his papa's clerk. 'S–So sorry, sir, I didn't see you there.'

'Evidently not.' Mr Ephraim was a serious man with curly dark hair and a greying straggly beard. He was dressed as always in dark sober clothes and carried a black felt hat with a low crown and wide brim. Blake's mama said that he kept Papa's manifests in good order and could remember the smallest detail when asked. Blake never saw him laugh, but his mama said he was a good man who was steadfast and loyal and they were lucky to have him in the business.

His papa was on his feet and walking across the thick Persian carpet that furnished their drawing-room floor. 'No need to call the maid, Ingrid, I'll see Ephraim out.' He turned to address his clerk. 'Thank you. I'll be at the warehouse first thing tomorrow to go through those documents.'

As Papa followed his trusted employee into the spacious hall they continued their conversation in hushed voices. Blake's mama remained seated as she gently chastised her son. 'Blake, you will behave more quietly in the house, please? Now come here and give your mama a kiss, then sit down. Your papa wishes to talk to you about your new school and Lucy will bring tea in a few minutes.'

Blake quickly swallowed the last of his bun and wrapped his arms around his mama. He kissed her on both cheeks. 'Mama, you look beautiful in that dress. The blue is the colour of your eyes.'

'Thank you, my dear. How was school?'

'Dull, I'm sorry to tell you, Mama. When can I leave?'

'Blake! How can you say such a thing?'

School had bored him a lot lately and it was good to be home. He was restless to be outdoors, to find his young friends in the town, or perhaps go with his papa on one of the keels down the Humber to their warehouse. But he settled reluctantly in one of the damask upholstered chairs that furnished their drawing room.

He answered dutifully while his mama quizzed him about his stagecoach journey to the post in town where their own horse and trap had collected him and his luggage. He had had a seat inside the coach but it was still freezing cold all the way and he hated sitting still. Maybe his papa would let him work in the warehouse after Christmas so he would not have to go back to school. He had had too much of school already!

'My boy! At last! Stand up and let me see how you have grown!' His papa strode back into the drawing room, filling it with his presence. He was a big man, broad-shouldered and strong. He was Blake's hero, and his mama's too. In Sweden he had sawn timber, mined coal and forged iron, before buying a share in a sailing ship to cross the North Sea and set up a trade with England.

Erik had heard that Swedish iron was always in demand with the ironmasters of the South Riding. There they had good coal and good men who knew how to forge iron. Yes, he conceded, they really knew how to forge iron in the South Riding! Trade had been steady, even in the bad times when some of the factories had closed.

Blake listened to his father telling his mother that closures were often due to poor handling of business and profits, for there was always a need for good iron in peace as well as wartime.

Erik Svenson was an outgoing, sociable man who drove a hard bargain but always dealt fair. In contrast, Blake's mother was quieter. But she was strong in her own way, listening and commenting in her unassuming manner. Often when his father discussed business with his mother over a glass of schnapps, she would simply listen as he talked and talked until he had decided what he would do next. Sometimes, his mother made a suggestion, but always, they talked it over together.

Mama had worked as hard as Papa in their early days of trading. She still kept her interest in the warehouse even now that they had Ephraim to help with the work. She liked England and the English way of life and they stayed, at first renting a small house in Goole, a pleasant town, well upstream of the brackish, estuarine waters and away from the lawlessness and smells of the Humberside docks. After a few years, with his wholesale trade established, Papa sold his share of the ship that had brought them over and bought this villa with its own carriage house and stabling, spacious cellars and attics for the servants.

Blake saw the pride in his father's eyes as he spoke. 'You are taller for sure, but you're pale and too thin. It is time you filled out a bit, I think. School is all book learning and not good for a growing boy.'

'He's only thirteen, Erik, and book learning is so good for his future,' his mama argued. 'You have the letter from his headmaster? He says Blake will go to the university if he wishes.'

Papa ruffled Blake's bright golden hair. 'You have your mama's wits, my boy,' he said, adding with a touch of regret, 'which is just as well, for I have no brain to speak of.'

Mama protested. 'Now that is nonsense, Erik, and you know it.'

'Oh, Ingrid, Ingrid. I should have known there were thieves about. You only need to look at the manifests to see—'

'Well, Ephraim has been right through the papers. We shall know the worst tomorrow.'

Blake's curiosity got the better of him. 'What is it, Papa? Have we been robbed?' One of his best friends had had to leave school because his father had been robbed of all their money. 'Papa, Papa, are we going to lose everything?'

'No, my son, we are not. But, but . . . well . . . we have been cheated and . . . and . . . robbed by an unscrupulous dealer.'

'Is it very serious, Papa?'

'Yes, it is. We have lost some of our goods and the profits from them.'

'If you want, Papa, I could give up school and work for you. Please let me give up school. I'll work with Mr Ephraim in the warehouse.'

His father gave him a benign smile. 'You are a good son and you can work in the warehouse when you're older. Your mama is right about school. This is a foreign land for us and you need to learn its ways as much as you can. We have found a better school for you, now you are a grown boy. It is further to travel – inland in the South Riding – but there will be other boys like you there, sons of professional men and factory owners. It will be better for you, I am sure. And if you want you can go to university.'

'But school is so dull, Papa! I want to be with you and Mr Ephraim at the warehouse—'

'You will be. You will. When you have finished your schooling. How about you come with me and Ephraim to get our stolen money back?'

'Erik, no! I do not think that is wise. He's just a boy.'

'And he'll soon be a man, Ingrid. He needs to know of the world outside school. Then he will be ready to handle himself with the bigger boys at school.'

'Yes, yes, Papa!' Blake jumped up and down with excitement. 'Can I come with you? Can I?'

'I have business in Doncaster to attend to first, but then we can travel on the waterways into the Riding towns.'

Mama continued her protest. 'But those towns are so smoky and dirty now. It will not be good for him.'

'Ingrid, I shall look after Blake. He is my son and I love him. We shall lodge outside of the towns and I shall not let anything happen to him.' Papa walked over to where Mama was sitting primly in a blue full-skirted gown, with her hands folded in her lap, and kissed the top of her head. 'Do not worry, my dear wife. He will be safe with me, I promise. I shall find an inn away from the manufactories. Ephraim has done all the work and we have letters from merchants in the Riding.'

He paused, stroking her hair gently. 'You know I have to do this, my love. Luther Dearne has cheated both me and the merchants who supply me and I must challenge him about his thieving ways.'

'Won't you go to the constables first?'

'I am a fair man. I shall give him a chance to own up. And pay up, of course. As soon as he sees the papers that Ephraim has prepared, he will know that his crooked little game is over. He will have to repay us, all of us, or his fraud will be exposed and he will most likely end up in the debtors' prison. I am sure he will not wish for that.'

Blake watched this exchange of views between his parents, his bright blue eyes dancing with excitement. Papa always listened to Mama where Blake was concerned, and he so wanted to go with Papa on this trip. His father had frequently taken him on to the estuary waters of the Humber where the sea was choppy and the keels had sails that agile sailors hauled up and down to catch the keen coastal breezes.

He pleaded with his mother. 'Let me go, Mama! Please let me go. Mr Ephraim will be with us too,' he cried.

'Mr Ephraim is older than your papa. He cannot help if ruffians and the like set upon you and rob you!'

'And why should that happen?' Papa argued.

'You know that bargemen can be very rough. They drink so much and they fight – and Blake is so young,' Mama complained.

'Ingrid! Do not judge too quickly. *Ja*, some of them are bad but I have my friends also among the bargemen. They are good men and they work hard. Besides, we shall travel by stagecoach as far as Doncaster and from there with a carrier that I know and trust.'

There was a silence before Mama said, 'Then if it is so safe, I shall come with you too.'

'No. This is men's work.' Papa's voice was firm.

Blake stared at his mother with wide pleading eyes. 'Mama?'

Ingrid sighed heavily. 'Bah! Blake, you are your father's son. What can I, a mere woman, say? Go! Go! Leave your mama to look after the warehouse. But you must take care. We – you – are foreigners in this land and so you will count for nothing if it all goes wrong. Promise me, Erik, that you will take very great care.'

Papa kissed her again. 'I promise. What do you say, my son, will you come along with your papa?'

'Yes, yes, yes! Oh yes, Papa, yes!' Blake jumped around the drawing room almost knocking over Lucy as she came in with the tea tray. He took some bread and butter in his hand and ran outside to help unload his boxes from the carriage.

Blake, his papa and Mr Ephraim took the stagecoach as planned from Goole to Doncaster. The weather was miserable, so cold and wet that the coach felt as damp inside as it did for those riding on top. At least the rutted turnpike was not frozen solid and they reached their destination mud-spattered, but without any mishap.

From there they were to travel on a feed barge taking oats and bran, and bales of hay for the horse marines along the navigation. Most of the barges carried heavy forged iron for recasting, or coal for the furnaces. They were long and wide, carrying a hundred tons or more and needing two horses to tow them. In winter, this meant a lot of feed for the animals and frequent changes at the horse marines to keep the cargo moving.

There was some delay in Doncaster as a biting and persistent east wind had brought a keen and lingering frost that had frozen the canals. Barges were backed up at the lock basins until teams of heavy horses hauled the icebreakers through. The local inns were doing a good trade in spiced, mulled ale for the stranded bargemen.

For Blake, the experience of travelling on the feed barge filled him with excitement. The bargeman allowed him to drive the fine Cleveland Bay along on the towpath. He showed him how to walk behind the horse, holding the long reins loosely, and he learned how to crack the whip to warn other canal users of their approach at bridge holes and tunnels. His special task was to re-fill the horse's nose can when it was empty, and to make sure he had fresh water at the stopping places.

The feed barge had a warm cabin below deck at the stern, with a stove where they could mull ale to keep out the cold and dry their muddy boots and breeches. The bargeman told Blake stories of how he and his wife used to live on board before he had made enough money to buy a cottage near the wharf in Doncaster. Now he could take paying passengers and was glad of the extra for his growing family.

While his papa and Mr Ephraim talked of business and the fraud, Blake darted about at locks and basins, heaving sacks of oats, holding mooring ropes and winding sluices up and down at lock gates. During quieter moments, he thought to himself that travelling on a canal barge was the best thing he had ever done and much more fun than going to school. Oh, why did it take so long to grow up? This adventure was over much too soon for him as the feed barge reached Mexton Lock, just outside the iron towns, where it changed horses and they reached their destination.

A weak winter sun was already low in the sky ahead of them. The barge emerged from under a stone bridge into a wider basin where the bargeman waited for his turn to go through the lock ahead of them upstream. On the north side of the canal lay a timber yard with a few cottages nearby. Stark bare branches of woodland trees in winter gave a bleak backdrop to the cottages. In the yard, piles of lumber and coal waited to be loaded into barges for hauling away to the towns.

In contrast, the south side of the canal was alive with activity, for there was an inn and other buildings serving the canal trade. A horse marine with barns and stables stood next to the inn, and beyond that was a blacksmith and forge. Further upstream a small, whitewashed house stood nearer the water than the other buildings, where the lock keeper stood guard to make sure all dues were paid.

Blake heaved their boxes on to the towpath and held out a helping hand for Mr Ephraim to climb ashore. Although Mr Ephraim lived by the tidal waters of the Humber he never sailed on them if he could avoid it. This was the first time he had climbed off the barge during the whole of their journey, being afraid of the water and the moving gap between the barge and bank.

They had been travelling since dawn and Blake was hungry and tired. His papa climbed ashore last and surveyed the scene around him. Soon the light would be fading and he was anxious to find where Dearne lived so that he could talk to him before nightfall. He buttoned up his warm overcoat and caught up with the others.

'Ephraim, you're looking pale! You need a brandy, man!'

'Yes, I do believe that would help. I hope the land-lord keeps a good fire.'

The small party hurried inside and arranged for their boxes to be brought in. Ephraim headed straight for the fireside and took off his thick winter gloves to warm his hands. Blake stayed near to his father and sat on a narrow bench next to the counter.

'Landlord, two glasses of brandy and a hot toddy for the boy, if you please,' Blake's papa called. 'We also need a good dinner and rooms – two rooms – and my companion needs a lively fire in his. See to it.'

Mickey Jackson, the landlord of the Navigator, reluc-tantly turned his florid face away from his regular customers. His expression was surly, but he recognised good custom when he saw it. He shouted over his shoulder to an unseen person through a door into the back, 'Miriam, get your ma!' then turned back to the travellers. 'Right away, sir. Come far have you?'

'Doncaster.'

Mickey Jackson also recognised foreigners when he heard them. 'Donnie, eh? And afore then?'

'What do you mean?' Papa sounded stern.

'On'y that I meant you're from foreign parts like, from over the sea.'

Papa nodded silently then added pleasantly, 'The brandy, landlord?'

'Aye, sir. Coming up. I were on'y thinking there's bin a bit o' ice Donnie way.'

'Yes, indeed. It has caused us some delay.'

'Aye. How long will you be wanting the rooms, then?'

'One or two nights. Perhaps more, for it depends on how long my business takes.'

'What kind of business might that be, sir?' He put the drinks on the worn wooden counter and nodded to a young girl who had appeared in the bar. 'Hot water and honey for the lad,' he barked and she disappeared as fast as she had arrived. When Blake's papa stayed silent, the landlord persisted. 'It's on'y that I know the folk round these parts if it's directions you need.'

Papa must have decided that a little information would keep the landlord quiet. 'Iron,' he volunteered. 'Bar iron, ready for the forge.'

Mickey Jackson was satisfied and noticeably impressed.

The girl brought Blake's toddy to the bench where he was sitting. He took it gratefully, savouring the warmth as it seeped down his throat and through his veins. She lingered, batting a wooden tray against her long skirts and blinking at him. He smiled at her and she stared back, pushing her lower lip forward. With her free hand, she twisted loose curls of hair round her fingers and swayed a little. Surprised, Blake stopped drinking.

She was just a young girl, he noticed, but she was

enticing him, making him look at her in a different way. She pulled a curl down on to her chest so that it trailed away to the lace that covered the tiny swell of her budding breasts. Blake felt a stirring inside him, and he began to look at her more closely. She was pretty, in a little girl way, with her honey-coloured hair and hazel eyes. He guessed that she was a few years younger than he was and wondered, briefly, if she behaved like this with the local boys.

He liked the feeling she aroused in him, the adolescent thrill that bubbled through his veins. It was a new kind of excitement and he relished it. He wanted more. He smiled at her, gulped down the rest of his toddy and shuffled along the bench to make room for her to sit with him. She sat very close and placed the tray across her lap. It jutted over his thigh and she moved it very slightly, backwards and forwards. He looked at her again and saw that she was smiling at him.

'Miriam!' The landlord's bark shattered their brief contact. 'Get in the back kitchen! Now! Go and help your ma with the dinners!'

Miriam rounded her eyes and looked towards the ceiling, then scuttled off leaving Blake wondering what she would have done next. He stood up and joined his papa at the wooden counter.

'Well, landlord,' his papa was saying, 'you may be able to help me. I am looking for a dealer called Dearne. I'm told he lives at Mexton Lock.'

'Dearne, eh? You got business with him, then?'

Papa ignored the question. 'This is Mexton Lock, isn't it? He lives around here, in the woodland I believe. Where might that be?'

'You done business with Dearne in the past, 'ave you?'

Papa leaned forward and breathed, 'If I had, my good man, it would be my business and not yours.'

Mickey Jackson scowled. He liked to know everything that went on around Mexton Lock. It was his patch, his manor. Luther was his crony. But he knew better than to upset a good spending customer. 'Pardon me, sir. The woodland is on t' other side o' the canal. You go over t' stone bridge downstream o' the lock, or you can walk across t' lock gates if you've a head for the deep water. Follow the track up through the wood and you'll come to Dearne's house. Only house there, in a clearing where the old charcoal burner's hut used to be.'

'Thank you, landlord. Do you know if he is home? I plan to visit him tonight.'

'Tonight?' He turned and yelled, 'Miriam! Miriam, answer me when I'm talking to you! Is Mr Dearne back yet?'

'Yes, Father. He came through on the icebreaker. He's just been over to borrow the horse and cart for his supplies.'

Mickey Jackson turned his attention back to his customers. 'There's your answer, sir. Will you take a lantern with you? It will be a cold 'un tonight for sure. You'll get a bit o' moonlight later on if you're lucky.'

'Good. We'll have dinner now. Over by the fire if you please.' His papa crossed the inn saloon to join Ephraim by the fire and Blake followed him. 'Are you warmed through yet, Ephraim?'

'Much better now, thank you, Erik. Wouldn't you rather wait until morning to confront Dearne?'

'I want to get this over with and also give the man time to think overnight. If he cannot see sense now, he might by the morning. I'll take the papers with me.'

'I've written out copies to show him. You can leave them with him so he knows how much you have on him.'

'You're a good man, Ephraim. You always think of everything.'

'Do you want me to come with you?'

'No, you need to rest after dinner. The journey has been long and cold and you need to keep yourself warm. If Dearne proves to be stubborn and difficult we'll move on to the magistrate in town tomorrow.'

'They are sure to send a constable for him with all this evidence.'

'I am a fair man. I shall give him a chance to pay back what he owes me first.'

'Be careful, Erik. You do not know this man.'

Blake, who had been listening closely to the conversation, echoed Ephraim's concern and urged, 'Don't go alone, Papa. I'll come with you.'

'There is no danger. I am going to talk business with this man, and that is all. But, my son, you can come along too if you wish. It is good for you to learn that business is not all profit and plenty. We shall have our dinner first, yes? I hope they will not be much longer with our food.'

Blake wandered outside to look at the lock, glad of his thick coat and good boots. There were a few children working on the other side of the canal, picking over a coal heap for slack and carrying it in buckets to a separate pile. They looked thin and chilled to him, and filthy with coal dust, but called cheerfully to each other and chased around, throwing about the slack they were supposed to be sorting.

A pair of heavy draught horses being led to the stables for the night got wind of the feed barge and whinnied and snorted, ignoring the stable lad's entreaties to move on. As daylight faded, Blake watched the huge animals with their fluffy white fetlocks eventually clomp slowly towards their own feed cans and a good rub down. The stable lad was not much older than he was, but he had a kind and calming manner as he coaxed them inside to the shelter of their warm, straw-filled stalls.

Then Blake noticed more activity on the other side of the oily dark water and shrank back into the shadow of the buildings. Keeping close to the rough stone wall of the inn, he watched quietly and covertly. There was a timber-built sawmill on the other side, as well as a row of stone cottages. The nearest cottage had its front window open and a plank set up outside it displaying small wares for sale. Daylight was fading fast and the progress of laden barges through the lock was slow. Someone lit a couple of flaring torches and Blake moved from the inn's protective shadow to the water's edge to get a closer look.

There was a man over the other side, a man he had seen before, just last summer when he had been helping Ephraim at Papa's warehouse on the Humber. The man had talked business with Papa and now Blake recognised him. He was striding around holding a lighted flare that caused flickering shadows on the muddy ground.

This must be Dearne! The man his papa said was a crooked dealer and a thief. He was a short, stocky man with a big round belly and a loud voice as he shouted at a couple of lads who were loading an untidy heap of sacks and boxes on to a cart.

When he had finished loading his cart and hitching up the horse, Dearne walked towards a row of cottages where a group of small children were playing around a stray log from the wood yard. The raucous squeals of their game of tag were savage, and by the light of the flare the laden barges transformed into monstrous shapes patrolling a deep dark crevice. He took one of the children back to the cart and prepared to leave.

Shadowy figures moving between piles of coals and timber seemed ghoulish and unreal. Lock gates creaked, and the winding machinery screeched. The sound of water rushing through open sluices caused an involuntary shiver to snake its way down Blake's back. In the darkness there was a malevolence about this place that scared him.

Undeterred, Blake walked right up to the water's edge and strained his neck for a closer look. But it was no good, the light had faded and the flare was almost spent. The horse and cart became a shadowy spectre as it trundled its way along a rutted track towards the woodland. As it passed the wood mill, where more flares were burning, the driver looked back at his load.

Blake could not see his face, only a fleeting picture of the man who had brought them on this cold dark journey to Mexton Lock. Already the injustice Dearne had caused his papa had insinuated itself into his head and etched itself in his mind. Papa was right. This man must pay for his double dealing! He watched until the cart disappeared through the trees and he heard his papa calling him back to the inn for dinner.

'He's here, Papa!' Blake exclaimed. 'I've seen him – the thief we have come to find!'

'Hush, boy, the landlord will hear you and he is a friend of Dearne. We do not wish to make the landlord our enemy as well. Now be quiet and eat your dinner.'

The food was good and wholesome, prepared that day by the landlord's wife. Erik and Ephraim dallied by the fire afterwards, and for the price of a few jugs of ale were able to question a few regulars about the Navigator Inn and its inhabitants.

They heard that Mickey Jackson was as tough as he looked and that he knew how to fight for what he wanted. Anyone who drank regularly in the Navigator learned very quickly to stay on the right side of the landlord and his two eldest sons, who were both from the same mould. The three of them were nothing but thugs, they were told, who would knock you down as soon as speak to you. Between them they saw to it that there was never any trouble at the inn save for the disturbances caused by the landlord himself.

Mickey Jackson finished most working days with a skinful of strong ale downed in the company of his sons and their cronies. More often than not, he slept it off by the fire in the saloon when all those with lesser constitutions had gone to their beds. All too frequently though, he caught the eye of one of the women who came in for the company of working men, women who knew by the end of the night which of the menfolk would have money left in their pockets to pay for a little more pleasure.

Mickey had a liking for women and his position and means in the thriving lockside community gave him his pick of them. A knowing look and a brief word would secure him some late-night company from any one of them who would be happy to indulge him in return for a coin. If she was especially pleasing to him she might acquire a length of dress cloth purloined from a passing barge, or a pair of fancy shoes bound for some merchant's wife in the Riding, before being sent off home in the middle of the night.

Mickey's wife Ann knew of his dalliances, of course, and had little choice but to ignore them. She gave her attention to the travellers staying at the inn, and spent her time in the kitchen rather than the saloon. Her daughter Miriam was her main consolation from being married to a bully and a thug. Miriam was her youngest child and her only girl. She had indulged her since birth, which made the boys jealous. If Ann wanted anything for Miriam, she could usually persuade Mickey to provide it.

Only their youngest lad, Peter, showed any kind of sensitivity or feelings. His two older brothers tormented him routinely, so from a very young age he had found solace in caring for animals. Horses were his passion, and already he was earning himself a good reputation with the horse marine next door to the inn.

Mickey's eldest lad would soon be a blacksmith and there was talk of him taking over the Mexton forge. He shared with his father the same controlling manner and liking for women and drink. The middle brother was fast learning these ways too, but for now had turned his strength to the brewing and heavy cellar work at the inn.

Blake watched and listened as he ate his dinner with his papa and Mr Ephraim by the fire in the Navigator saloon. He quickly realised that Mexton Lock, or at least much of the business on the Navigator side of the canal, had a Jackson's hand in it one way or another. The Jacksons were friends of Dearne. Papa was right. It was wise to keep your own counsel in these parts.

Chapter 7

During the years since Luther Dearne had first set eyes on Erik Svenson, Lissie had thrived. But she knew little of the world beyond Mexton Lock. Her young life had been spent mostly doing what her mam said and waiting for her dad to come home. Her only journeys were down the woodland trail to the canal to help with fetching and carrying.

For her those walks were exciting adventures and the constant activities on the wharf fascinated her. She loved to watch the heavy docile horses, heads down, straining their ropes, or waiting patiently on the towpath for the lock to fill or empty. When they stopped to feed, she stroked their huge noses and admired their chestnut leather collars and harnesses, decorated with polished brasses.

There was always plenty to see at the lock, and usually a convenient log to sit on while Dad went over to the Navigator or picked up a sack from one of the barges.

Her dad did not allow her to go over the canal, especially by the lock gates, for although they were wide enough to walk on, there was no rail to stop you falling in.

'When you're a bit older, lass,' her dad said, 'you can walk downstream an' go over t' bridge.'

The stone bridge was a hundred yards away and had been built to take timber and coal wagons out to local farms. Once over the bridge, the track went past the 'Navvy' and on through farmland, coalfields and pit villages before it reached the outskirts of town.

Dad always ordered her to stay on the woodland side of the canal until he came back from the Navigator. Sometimes, when he did return, he staggered over the lock gates carrying a can of ale to take home for dinner and Lissie was scared he would fall in the canal, but he never did.

There were times when he stayed a long time in the Navigator and Lissie went to see Rosa. Rosa's house was on the same side of the canal as the woodland. It was the end one of a row, built for labourers at the wood mill. The stone cottages faced the canal and they all had long gardens that backed on to the trees.

Rosa's husband had worked at the mill for years until one day he had suddenly cleared off and left her. Since then, Rosa had scratched a living from her garden and her kitchen. She kept a beehive and grew strong-smelling plants that she used to cook up all kinds of healing cures and salves to sell from the front door of her cottage.

Once, a bargeman's wife had taken most of her stock and paid her well in flour and lard, and a whole skirt of beef. So Rosa made meat pies and when they were done, she opened her kitchen window to sell them hot from the oven.

On rare occasions, when she got hold of a cone of sugar, Rosa boiled it up with liquorice to make a spice that she called pomfret cakes, which she kept for her favourite customers. Lissie was always sure of some spice from Rosa, if she could remember a bit of gossip to repeat. So she learned to become a good listener when her dad stopped to talk to the woodcutters or lock keeper.

'Mr Jackson's bought the stables, me dad says,' she related to Rosa, 'and he's going to set up his youngest lad, Peter, as the horse marine. Just as soon as he has rid of the one already there. He's going to put the rent up to make him go.'

'Ee, lass,' Rosa sighed, handing her a nib of pomfret. 'There'll soon be no room for nob'dy else but the Jacksons over there. Tell yer mam to come down to see me as soon as yer dad's gone off again.'

Dad didn't much like Rosa, but Lissie's mam was very friendly with her and when her dad was away they often visited her small, weird house full of dried herbs and stale air that made Lissie's head spin. Her mam liked Rosa and was always in a hurry when they went there.

'Pick yer feet up, girl,' she snapped, as her bony hand gripped Lissie's tightly and pulled at her tiny arm, dragging her down the woodland track. 'We're going to Rosa's,' her mam told her firmly, 'to buy a pie for dinner because we haven't got no coal to keep the fire going.'

This puzzled Lissie because when they eventually got

back home with the pie, the fire was still in and Mam would put the pie in the oven at the side to heat through. She remembered the visits well as she was usually left on her own in Rosa's kitchen to play. At first, the ugly bunches of drying plants and the odd smells frightened her. But eventually Lissie became fascinated by the tiny pots and corked bottles that Rosa kept on her kitchen shelves.

When they reached the cottage Rosa poured spirits from a bottle into two tankards and her mam sat with Rosa on her horsehair sofa, their heads close together, whispering and laughing.

Lissie knew that if she behaved herself and was quiet she would be given a drink of new milk, bought from the Navvy in a tin can, and a pomfret cake out of the locked cupboard by the fireplace. She sat on the carpet and played with some old pots and pans as her toys. Then her mam gave her another cake and told her to be a good little girl while she helped Rosa turn the mattresses. Rosa and her mam were giggly when they went upstairs, leaving her alone on a rag rug covering the stone flagged floor of the empty kitchen.

There was one visit when Rosa and her mam were upstairs for ages. Lissie climbed on to the window ledge to catch a glimpse of the barges with their cargoes of coal or iron queuing up to go through the lock, or watch timber or coal being loaded to take onwards to the towns in the Riding. But the canal was frozen, and she got bored as the floor was too cold to play on.

She listened at the door to the stairs and heard the creaking bedsprings and the groans and squeals of Rosa and her mam as they turned the beds. Lissie knew her mam did not like doing this at home, but with Rosa she never got bad-tempered like she did at home and she was always cheerful on days spent at Rosa's.

When they came downstairs she got another spice because she hadn't wet her drawers and cried. This was easier for Lissie now she had grown up, now she was tall enough to reach the back-door latch and go out to the privy down the garden.

Rosa mashed some tea and put in 'something to keep the cold out'. Lissie had a drink of it out of a saucer and fell asleep by the fire.

'Quiet kid, i'n't she?' Rosa commented.

'Good job too,' her mam replied. 'I never wanted her in the first place, you know. It was Luther's idea to have 'er. "To keep me company," he said, when he was away down the canals doing his deals and such like. That was afore he knew about you, like. Still, he doesn't mind me coming here when 'e's away, as long as I bring the lass wi' me.'

'She's a little beauty though. That black hair looks a bit foreign-like, to me.'

'Gypsy blood, I've allus thought.'

'Is she his?' Rosa asked.

''E says not, but I don't believe him. 'E's had some floozy down the Humber, I'm sure of it.'

Rosa gave her a sly smile. 'We-ell, you don't mind that, do you, Edie?'

Edie shook her head and giggled. 'Suits me and you, do'n't it?'

'Where's she from, the mother, like?'

'Down south, I think. Luther's got some trinkets and stuff from her, locked away in the old casement clock. 'E says she died and she was away from her own folk. There was a nurse wi' her, but she couldn't take her back to her family, the little 'un being a bastard, like.'

'Nurse, eh? They were well-to-do, then?'

'Oh, aye. Just born the wrong side o' the blanket.'

'Aye, well, there's plenty o' them about. We 'ad some Londoners through the lock two summers ago and they said t' old king had bastards all o'er t' place but he still couldn't manage to produce one for t' throne. And now we have a woman on t' throne. Whatever next?'

'Just a slip of a girl, I heard. Fancy that, Rosa. I don't s'pose it'll make any difference to us, anyroad.'

'She'll still 'ave a 'usband who'll tell her what to do, an' gi' 'er a tribe o' kids like this 'un. You're lucky Luther on'y brought home the one.'

'Oh aye, and she 'as her uses,' her mam declared. 'Luther, well, he fair dotes on her, and it keeps him off my back. She's right quick on the uptake and she's making a good little housekeeper now she's growing up.'

The two women exchanged smiles and finished their mugs of tea and gin.

At the other side of town, Grace's new business was thriving, and Clara was choosing fabrics and trimmings for new dresses. The dressmaker came to visit their home now, with her samples and drawings, and they all took tea in the small study before she left. And cakes. They ate cake every day now. They could afford it.

'Such a lovely house you have here, Mrs Beighton,'

the dressmaker sighed. 'Just the right distance from town, I've always thought.'

Grace smiled benignly at her visitor. 'It suits us to be away from the smoke and grime of the furnaces.' She stretched her hand, covered in a long, black lace mitten, to pat Clara's knee. 'My niece must have clean air to breathe.'

'But you are also away from the businesses, for your gentlemen – er – lodgers.'

'Guests,' Grace corrected her. 'As gentlemen, you understand, they have their own horses.'

'Or they hire carriages,' Clara added. 'Our guests are always gentlemen of means.'

The dressmaker, mindful of the cost of her own hired trap for the journey, took her leave. Clara showed her to the front door and wished her a safe journey home. She was a good needlewoman and, as such, important to Grace's household. After saying goodbye, Clara returned to the study. The furnishings were fashionably heavy and dark and it was a million miles away from the dirty smelly study she had left behind eight years ago.

'More tea?' Grace topped up the silver teapot from an ornate matching kettle keeping warm over an oil flame.

'Thanks. Do you think she knows?'

'Oh yes. I'm sure she does. She has the same customers as we do. Well, their wives and daughters anyway.'

'I suppose the wives know about us too,' Clara shrugged.

'And some of them are grateful to us. So don't you go fretting about that.'

'Do you mind all the changes we have made here, Grace? I mean, not taking lodgers any more?'

'Never! This is a far better use for the place. Well away from prying eyes and town gossips. Do you have regrets? It was your idea.'

'Yes it was, wasn't it? Well, Mr Hardcastle's actually,' Clara conceded. 'The lodging house was fine to begin with, but there was a lot more money to be made from my special services to the gentlemen. I had no idea there would be so much demand though. Or that we would need one or two other girls to help.'

'Me neither. But we must continue to be discreet. I am past fifty now, and I don't want to be run out of town before I'm ready to go.'

'You have no fears there, Grace. Not with Sir William as my personal client. And his private physician advising us.'

'And one of our new regulars is an alderman, I hear.'

'There you are, then. As long as we only take recommended clients.'

They sipped their tea and finished the cake. The coals fell in the fireplace, sending a few sparks on to the brass hearth rail.

Grace thought for a minute. 'You know, Clara, you are a very pretty girl, and not yet thirty. You don't have to do this. You could marry and get out of here if you want – I shan't mind if you do.'

'I don't,' Clara replied flatly. 'Any more than you wanted to wed that innkeeper who took a fancy to you when we first arrived here.'

'But I'm just a plain old widow—'

'A wealthy one though,' Clara reminded her.

'You could be proper rich,' Grace persisted. 'Sir William worships you—'

'Sir William has a wife.'

'You could be his mistress, set up in a house of your own, with servants.'

'That's just the same as being married. No, I vowed when I left my stepfather that no man would ever own me and I meant it.'

'You were distraught then. You—'

'Besides, I'd never leave you, Grace,' Clara interrupted. She got up and kissed Grace's brow. 'I owe everything to you.'

Grace squeezed Clara's hand. They were two of a kind, she thought.

That day, the day the foreigners came to Mexton Lock, Lissie was excited. Her dad was home again. With Christmas not far off, trade had picked up a bit and there was a lot of talk of a new era with the new Queen. Dad had brought clothes as well as extra food to see them through the worst of the winter. He was loading coal on to a borrowed cart to keep the kitchen fire going. He liked it kept in all day when he was home. When he was away, Mam was always letting it go out because she would forget to bring in the coals from the coal house next to the scullery. And then Lissie would get the blame and a clip round the ear.

Now she sat outside Rosa's cottage on one of the hewn logs that lay around, and watched, fascinated, as a long barge heaped with coals disappeared from view when the lock emptied as water drained away. Then, ages later, another rose from the depths as the lock filled again. She couldn't see what was in this one as it was covered in oily wet canvas. She would have liked a closer look but Dad had forbidden her to move from her seat until he returned.

The evening air was damp, and filled with a smell of horse droppings and the thick grease that kept the lock machinery moving. Huge, heavy wooden lock gates creaked and groaned as they were moved by strong young lads who leaned backwards against the wide levers to walk the gates open and closed. They shouted to each other across the canal, and to the bargemen who stayed aboard while their valuable craft went through.

Then she saw him. On the other side of the canal. A new face. As tall as Mickey's boys but not as thickset. Not quite as old as them, she thought, but better dressed in a neat dark overcoat with a thick shoulder cape. His boots were polished and clean, not even dusty from the towpath. He was wearing a proper cap made out of tweed, which he took off briefly, and when he did his bright fair hair glinted in the light from a window. He ran his fingers through that hair, combing it straight back from his brow in a quick fluid movement, then replaced his cap firmly on top of his head.

Lissie's attention was riveted by him. His clothes alone set him apart from the other boys playing around the lock. He didn't join in their games either, or help with the lock gates and winding the sluices. He just stood there, watching, as the canal folk went about their work.

Lissie stared, straining her eyes to see as much as she

could in the fading daylight, wondering who he was, where he came from and most of all, where he was going. With his cap pulled down to cover up that striking fair hair, he looked the same as any of the other better-off boys that sometimes came with their fathers to do business at the lock. But he wasn't from round here, she was sure.

Suddenly, and annoyingly, she was distracted.

'How's my little Lissie, then? Are you being a good girl?' Her dad stood with his sturdy legs wide apart and his arms behind his back, blocking her view.

She leaned to one side to peer round and catch another glimpse of the stranger on the further side of the canal. The boy was still there, he had not moved. He watched silently as a bargeman finished loading the cart.

'No peeking,' her dad chided, 'or it won't be a surprise, will it? Guess what I've got for you?'

Lissie's concentration was diverted as she jumped down from the log and squealed, 'Spice! Ooh, is it toffee, Dad? Oh, can I have it now, Dad? Please can I have it now?'

'Aye, lass, you can that. It'll be a while before tea's ready with the size o' the joint your mam's roasting for tonight. Don't tell her what you've been eating, mind. Y'know what she's like.'

Lissie unscrewed the top of the paper cone and placed one of the lumps of toffee in her mouth. Ann Jackson at the Navigator bought it in slabs from a traveller every Christmas, and sold it on to passing barges and keels. Sometimes Dad bought a small slab to take home. Then he would make a great ceremony of breaking it up in a cloth with his hammer and sharing it out. Lissie sucked and chewed with relish, thinking that it was the nicest thing that she had ever tasted in her life.

As soon as the wagon was loaded, her dad paid off the bargeman, who took one of the flares over the lock gates and went straight into the inn to spend his windfall. As the light flickered by him, Lissie noticed the boy was still there, keeping to the shady side of the inn and watching everything that was going on.

He was definitely one of the bigger boys, and one that Lissie would normally avoid – especially if he was in a gang. Big boys threw stones at the girls and pulled your hair if they got a chance. Her dad got really mad if big boys came anywhere near her when he was around. But she was safe from them this side of the lock. And anyway, this boy wasn't in a gang.

Dad lifted Lissie up and swung her round into the cart. 'You sit on the boxes there, lass, and don't go near the coal. Hold on to the side when it gets bumpy.'

'Yes, Dad.' Lissie pushed the last piece of toffee into her mouth. Dad led the horse and wagon up the dirt track through the trees, keeping to the well-worn ruts. She took one last look back but she could not see the boy. Where had he gone? she wondered. And why?

Chapter 8

Tea was very late that day, partly because it took Dad so long to get the coal loaded at the wharf and then to shovel it from the cart into the coalhouse next to the scullery. Then he had to take the horse and cart back to Mickey's and fetch a quart of ale for dinner. Mam had taken ages to cook the meat and Lissie was starving by the time it was ready.

It smelled so good she could hardly wait, and Dad kept calling from wherever he was in the house or garden to ask if it was ready yet. Only her mam seemed unimpressed and bored by all the fuss. But then, Lissie knew, she didn't like cooking and never ate that much anyway, preferring her bottle of spirits and pinch o' snuff to keep her going.

Dad often laughed at Mam saying, 'No wonder you're as skinny as a bird, you eat like one.' And then he'd tweak Lissie's nose and add, 'Not like my little Lissie, who knows how to enjoy a decent dinner.'

A clear sky promised another frost that night, but it was warm and cosy inside the house. Dad had dug some parsnips to roast with the potatoes and Mam had made a Yorkshire pudding with flour and eggs, baked in some of the drippings from the meat. They ate the pudding first, with lots of rich gravy, and after that Lissie had so much meat and vegetables that she could hardly get down from the table, she was so full.

Dad beamed at her as he helped himself to more slices of the roast mutton. 'I don't think you've eaten at all while I've been away. Either that or you've got hollow legs!' He looked under the table to where she had kicked off her boots. 'What do you say, Mam? Has she got hollow legs?'

Her mam picked at what she had left on her plate. 'She eats enough for two, that's for sure.'

'She's a growing lass, Edie. Why has she got her boots off?'

Lissie piped up straight away, 'They hurt me toes, Dad.'

Mam snapped at her just as fast, 'Speak when you're spoken to!'

Lissie shut her mouth and concentrated on her plate, but her dad continued, 'Edie, why didn't you say she needed some new boots? I could have brought some in with me.'

'There's plenty of wear left in them yet,' Edie muttered sullenly.

'Take 'em down to the wharf and swap 'em for some that fit tomorrow.'

'If you say so, Luther.'

'Yes, I bloody do. Are you sure she's getting enough t' eat?'

'She eats all right. You saw the way she scoffed her way through that little lot. God bless her belly, that's all I can say.'

Lissie's ears stayed alert as her dad persisted, 'But there's no spare flesh on her anywhere. What does she do all day when I'm away?'

'Not much, I can tell you! Always getting under my feet, so I can't get on with my work. And if I give her owt to do, I have to watch her like a hawk! She 'as to be shown everything.'

'She's not full grown yet, Edie.'

'Aye, Luther, don't I know it. The sooner she learns 'ow to 'elp in t' house proper, the better.'

Lissie kept her eyes focused on her plate and wondered if her mam was going to tell her dad how useless she had been, and if Dad would get cross with her and not give her the nice woolly shawl waiting in the front room. But Mam didn't, and Dad took another gulp from his tankard and settled back in his chair.

He said, 'Well, Edie, you might have a bit o' luck there.'

'Oh, aye? How come?'

'Mickey Jackson was telling me about a dame school up at Fordham.'

Lissie looked up quickly. 'What's a school, Dad?'

'I told you to speak when you're spoken to,' Mam snapped.

Dad ignored her and continued, 'Fordham is not too far upstream and Ann is sending their lass there after Christmas.'

'What? Their Miriam? I'n't she working wi' 'er ma at the Navvy?'

'Mickey says her ma wants her to do some learning.'

'What sort o' idea is that? A school is no place for a lass. School is for lads. I'd 'ave thought Miriam would be more use to her ma in t' kitchen.'

'Mickey thought it'd be a good idea for the two of 'em to go together.'

'What? Their Miriam and our Lissie? What for?' Mam argued. 'Waste o' good money if you ask me.'

'I've got a few pennies put by.'

'Aye and we'll need them if t' winter goes on like this.'

'It'll be good for her to learn to read and write, Edie.'

'Why? I never did. What use is reading to a girl? She has to learn how to clean and cook. And do sewing. Will they teach her that?'

''Course they will. They do all kinds of things. And there'll be other girls for her to learn with.'

Lissie saw that her mam was getting really het up about this and thought that whatever school was, she didn't want it if it made her mam any more cross with her than she was already.

'I need her here with me,' Mam said bluntly.

Dad persisted. 'She'll still be here with you, Edie. She won't have to live there. Mickey's lass is just going for the day.'

'What? There and back every day?'

'Aye.'

'Well, how far is it? Think of all the boot leather she'll need!'

'Edie.' Dad sounded stern. 'It'll be good for her.'

'Well, it won't be good for me. I don't want her to go. I want 'er 'ere wi' me.'

'I thought you said she was a nuisance to you?'

Lissie watched the talking between her mam and dad nervously. Her mam was always upset when Dad changed things at home, but Dad usually kept calm enough when he'd made up his mind. Though now she could see he was getting angry with Mam. She began to think about where she would hide if they started shouting at each other.

Mam must have also realised that Dad was angry, because she went quiet, got up from the table and said, 'I've done an apple pudding if you've still got some room left.'

Dad ate a plateful, and as Lissie's dinner had gone down a bit she managed to squeeze a bit more steaming food into her little tummy. Mam liked apple puddings sweetened with some of Rosa's honey more than anything, and did justice to her plateful as well. But neither of them had finished with the talk of school.

'I don't know, Luther. Going there and back every day? What about the big lads on the way? You know what they can be like with the little 'uns.'

'They'll be all right wi' two of 'em together. Anyroad, most o' the big lads know me and they'll have to answer to me if there's any trouble. Mickey says the same. And his eldest lad's got a fine pair o' fists on him nowadays.'

'She'll have to have a new dress and some more pinnies.'

'Yes, yes.' Dad sounded irritable now. 'They'll make the pinnies there. But she will need boots that fit her for walking. Ee, woman, why didn't you realise she'd grown out of her boots?'

Mam was getting mad now and she spat, 'I can't do everything when you're away! I never wanted a babby in the first place. Bringing her 'ere was all your idea.'

Dad retaliated sharply. 'We're not going through all that again!'

Lissie looked from her mam to her dad with some alarm. She did not want to be around if they started fighting.

Her mam was really cross and whined, 'Well, you spend more on her than you do on me! And now a fancy school, if you please! You 'ave better things to do wi' your money, Luther.'

Dad got to his feet and raised his voice. 'That's more than enough lip from you. I don't keep you short, do I? The lass is going to school wi' Miriam after Christmastide and that's it. Now mull some more o' that ale and bring it through to t' front room wi' another bucket of coal.'

Mam did as Dad had asked without further comment and Lissie, feeling sleepy after so much food, wandered after her mam and dad into the front room. A whole load of questions about school were beginning to crowd her mind. What was a school? Where was it and what would she be doing there? It was definitely something her dad wanted for her and Mam didn't, but she knew better than to keep on asking about it if Dad's temper was up.

Things calmed down once he had settled himself by the front-room fire with his ale and a pipe of tobacco. Mam cheered up a treat when Dad gave her a bottle of spirits and Lissie was more than pleased with her snug wool shawl. It was just like her mam's and she wrapped it round herself and waltzed about the front room.

'I've got summat else fo' thee, lass. Nip upstairs and fetch it down. It's on t' top o' me box in t' bedroom.'

Lissie looked quickly at her mam who scowled but said nothing, so Lissie scampered upstairs. On top of Dad's box, neatly folded, Lissie found a heavy wool cloak, a proper cloak with a hood! She ran downstairs, squealing with joy.

'Look, Mam, look what Dad's bought me!'

'Filched, more like,' Mam muttered through her gin.

Dad swallowed more ale and grinned. 'It's not new, lass, and it'll be too big fo' you now. But the rate you grow, you'll soon fill it up.'

Lissie flung it on and put up the hood. Her small shape was totally swamped and the hem trailed on the floor as she paraded across it, feeling like the new queen.

She saw Dad glance sternly at Mam as he added, 'It's just what she wants for walking to school in t' winter.'

Lissie had learned in the past not to start chattering on about something when Mam and Dad had a row, otherwise they would send her upstairs to bed. Wrapped in her woolly shawl, she took off her boots and curled up quiet as a mouse in the horsehair chair. She was as warm as could be with her new cloak draped over her as well and soon fell fast asleep. Tonight was no different from usual when Dad got home from his travels. Except that usually, while she was asleep, Mam and Dad put Dad's old shooting coat over her and left her there all night by the warmth of the fire.

But tonight *was* different. Something was going on. Roused from a deep slumber by all the noise, Lissie sat bolt upright clutching her cloak. The fire in the front room was low and the candles had burned out. Although Mam had closed the door to the hallway, the sound of raised voices came through it clearly. Dad was shouting and somebody else was shouting back at him. But it wasn't Mam. It was another man, and they were really mad at each other.

She heard her dad yell, 'Who d'you think you are? Coming round to my house like this? We finished our business weeks ago and I owe you nowt! Nowt, I say! Do y'hear me?'

A voice replied angrily in strange clipped tones, 'You are nothing but a common thief, Dearne. You have been stealing from me and others like me for years, and now it is time to pay!'

'Just you clear off out o' here,' Dad answered. 'I don't know what you're talking about. You're all the same you foreigners. I tell you, I don't owe nobody nothing!'

'You will pay me what you owe me! I swear I'll make you pay for your crooked deals!'

'You want to watch your tongue, saying things like that round 'ere! I got friends, y'know.'

Lissie scrambled to her feet on the high-backed chair to look out of the front-room window. The moon had risen high and it bathed the yard and clearing in a bluish hue. That boy was there! He was standing near to the house but he wasn't the one doing the shouting. He was watching, just watching everything that was going on. Lissie recognised his coat and cap straight away, and, closer to, she thought he was the most handsome lad she had ever seen. As she pressed her nose against the glass, he looked in her direction.

Lissie ducked down quickly, out of sight. She could not see the man he was with; he must have been right up close to the front door. Who were they and what did he want? She heard her mam's high-pitched whine join the row.

'Leave it be, Luther, it's freezing out there tonight. Come in and shut the door. He won't hang around long in this weather.'

'You are wrong, madam,' she heard the stranger say. 'I shall not go away. I have travelled a great distance to catch up with this man and I shall have the money he owes me.'

Lissie slid off the chair and leaned against the door to listen. The stranger talked in an odd way without the soft burrs of Yorkshire that Lissie knew. She was desperate to open the door and look at him, but knew it was more than her life was worth with Dad in such a mood. He shouted, 'Stay outa' here, Edie. This is men's business.'

But her mam was having none of that, having spent most of her day cooking, which, Lissie knew, always put her in a bad mood. 'I will not. I want ter know what's been going on.' An evening with the gin bottle had heightened her courage and she raised her voice even more. 'I want ter know what you been up to on the canal!'

Lissie's eyes rounded at her dad's angry response. 'Shut your mouth, you daft old witch! Get back upstairs and close t' door behind you!'

'Don't you speak to me like that, Luther Dearne. I told you, I want to know what all this is about.'

Lissie, by now riveted to the spot, concentrated hard to hear the stranger's response. Her smoky green eyes darkened with a mixture of fear and excitement as his strong voice came through the door. 'You will not like what you find out, madam. This man is a liar and a cheat and I can prove it!'

'Like 'ell you can! You're bluffing,' Dad argued.

'I have papers, sir. I have ship's manifests, invoices and loading notes. What do you say to that?'

'I say you're the liar and the cheat, trying to get more than your dues for that creaking tub you call a ship. Why don't you clear off back to wherever you come from!'

The stranger lowered his tone and paused before he replied in a slow deliberate manner. 'Because, as you well know, the manufactories in the South Riding need my best Swedish iron so that they can keep their furnaces and forges working. I am sure the magistrates will want to know that you are cheating your own countrymen as well as me.'

'Why you . . . you . . . bloody . . .' Dad sounded as though he was going to blow up. 'You . . . you wouldn't have the front.' He stopped for a second then added in a quieter tone, 'They won't believe you anyway, you're just a foreigner round here.'

The foreign voice responded, 'They don't have to believe me. I shall show them the papers.'

Dad yelled, 'Why you—'

'Luther! No!' Mam squealed.

They were fighting! Lissie heard the thuds and strangled cries as the two men struggled with each other on
the front door step.

'Papa! Papa! Stop it!'

That must be the boy! Was he joining in too? Lissie
scuttled across to the high-backed chair by the window
and peered through the glass. She could now see her
dad and the other man wrestling in the front yard, trying
to thump each other as they staggered around. Then the
foreigner broke free and hit her dad so hard in the
stomach that he was winded and went down. The ground
was solid with frost. Patches of ice crunched and cracked
as he fell heavily and rolled in the rutted track.

The foreigner stood with hunched shoulders and
clenched fists, ready for her dad to get up and fight back.
He did, picking up an old piece of timber that he waved
backwards and forwards in the air as he staggered to his
feet.

The boy moved quickly, retrieving a similar weapon
from the woodland floor and handing it to his father,
who had not taken his eyes off her dad as he ducked
and weaved to avoid the weapon. Lissie knew her dad
would win though. He was big and strong and always
said nobody had ever knocked him down in a fight.

But the boy's dad was big in a different way. He was
taller, and not as round as her dad. The two men clashed
and recoiled, holding the heavy timbers with both hands
as swords and cudgels. As her dad drew back his weapon,
the stranger swung in from his right and caught him a
slamming body blow that knocked him down again.

This time he couldn't pick himself up off the ground

quite so fast and the stranger moved in and stood over him, brandishing the timber. Mam was out there now, carrying the oil lamp, getting all excited and shouting at Dad to get up and thump him one and show him what for. Lissie had to press her knuckles into her mouth to stop herself crying out as well. If Mam knew she was watching she'd soon get a thump herself and be sent straight upstairs to bed.

'Come on, Luther,' Mam cried. 'Get up on your feet, man!'

But Dad didn't. He raised himself on one elbow and wiped a trickle of blood from his face with the back of his hand. He was breathing heavily and had split open the armhole of his tweed jacket.

The foreigner towered over him. He kicked the wood out of her dad's hands and then threw his own aside. Stepping back, he dusted his clothes down and reached inside his jacket to take out a sheaf of papers that he threw down, scattering them over her dad's heaving body.

'Read these, Dearne. Read them carefully. You have until midnight tonight to bring the money you owe me to the Navigator Inn. Otherwise, you'll be finished,' he said. 'Tomorrow I go to the magistrate with these papers.' He nodded, as though confirming the decision with himself. 'This is your last chance.' He turned to the boy, who had stayed close to his father throughout the fight. 'Come along, Blake. Our business here is done.'

Blake. Lissie held her breath and kept as still as she could. Blake? She didn't know any local lads called that, but she liked it. Even if his dad was a foreigner, he had a nice name. Blake. In the lamplight she saw him remove his cap and comb his floppy fair hair back with his fingers. He replaced the cap firmly, pulling it down over his brow. She noticed he had done that before when he was outside the inn. She wondered where he came from and whether she'd dare to ask her dad in the morning. Better not, she decided. She didn't want Dad to find out she'd been watching him fight.

Mam was all over Dad now. 'Luther, Luther, are you all right, husband? Get on your feet and come in the house. Your face is bleeding, let me wash it for you.'

But Dad was angry with her and he pushed Mam off, shouting, 'Get away from me.' He was shuffling through the scattered papers, cursing and crumpling them but not tossing them away. 'Go inside yourself, woman,' he growled. 'Get back in there and see if the lass's all right. Ask her if she heard owt.'

Lissie's eyes stretched wide open with alarm and she shot off the chair and under her new cloak on the horse-hair chair in a trice. The coarse tapestry of its uphol-stery was rough against her face and she pulled the cloak right up over her head. Her feet were sticking out from under the hem and they were icy cold, but she dared not move them. It seemed as if she held her breath for ages, and she only remembered to let it out and breathe normally when her mam opened the front-room door.

Mam walked a couple of steps into the room and her dad must have been right behind because Lissie heard him say, 'She's fast on. Slept through it all, thank God. Leave her be, Edie, and gerroff to bed.'

'Aren't you coming up, Luther?'

Lissie heard the rustling of the papers. 'No. I have to

do some thinking. I'll go through to t' back kitchen and smoke another pipe.'

'Shall I mull you some more ale?'

'I said clear off, Edie,' her dad retaliated irritably. 'I've got to be on me own to think.'

Lissie did not move a muscle until she heard the top stair creak as her mam went to bed, and then her dad in the next room raking the kitchen fire and throwing on more coal. She rolled over on to her back and stared at the darkness, too keyed up and wide awake to sleep. Why had that foreigner come to see her dad and what was it all about? After a while, her eyes began to close, but the next thing she knew she was being wakened by the sound of her dad's keys jangling in the dark.

She stayed absolutely still and opened her eyes slowly. As she got used to the moonlight coming in through the small window, Lissie made out the bulky figure of her father. He was unlocking the front of the old casement clock that didn't work. It stood in the back corner of the front room and Dad kept things in it that he never allowed her to see. He put some of those things in his pockets and then took out his big shotgun that he used for killing rabbits and wood pigeons in the back garden.

Lissie was puzzled. What was her dad doing, going out to shoot pigeons in the middle of the night? They didn't want any pigeons anyway. Dad only went out for pigeons when there was nothing else in to eat. And they still had loads of mutton left on the joint! Something was up. Something to do with that foreigner and Blake, his son. She crept back to the window and watched her dad walk down to the track. He had his gun under his arm and the barrels were set, ready to shoot.

Chapter 9

As Lissie watched her father disappear down the frozen woodland track, Blake and his father had reached the stone bridge over the canal. The moon was high and shone brightly through black leafless twigs, picking up sparkles of frost and the wing of a barn owl hunting for food. A single flare still burned by the lock gates and lamps glowed through the windows of the Navigator. Sensible cottagers had banked up their fires and shut their doors tightly against the promise of another freezing night.

'Dearne will not wait until midnight, I am sure. He, like me, will want this matter dealt with now,' Blake's father said to him. 'Go back to the inn. I shall stay here, on the edge of the woods. I do not want everyone at the Navigator knowing my business.'

'I want to be with you, Papa.'

'No, Blake. You saw how I handled him and you have no need to worry about your papa. I learned to fight well in the timber forests back home and I can beat a fat old man like Dearne any time. Tell Ephraim not to worry. I'll be back at the Navigator before midnight.'

Blake thought that Mr Ephraim might persuade his papa against this idea and said, 'At least come back with me to warm through, Papa. It is a cold night and you may have a long wait.'

But Papa was adamant. 'I know men like Dearne. He will not wait until morning. Besides, I need to cool my anger and the Navigator is not the place for me to do that. Do as I say and tell Ephraim everything is going well.'

'Leave it until the morning, Papa,' Blake pleaded. 'You'll freeze out here.'

His papa laughed. 'Not me, boy. I've endured worse than this in the Baltic. When Blake hesitated, he repeated firmly, 'Do as I say, Blake. Go back to the inn and tell Ephraim to go to his bed.'

Reluctantly, Blake did as his papa asked of him. He dawdled by the canal, watching the moonlight reflecting on shards of broken ice floating in the dark oily water. He strained his eyes to catch sight of the moving shadow of his papa as he retraced his steps to the woodland. The Navigator Inn was noisy with drinkers and the singing suddenly became louder when a door opened and two men fell out, hurrying through the icy air, home to their wives and beds.

Ale was flowing freely in the saloon as working men forgot how tired they were and thought only of their next drink. They clustered around the counter, talking and laughing loudly with the landlord, breaking into raucous singing and casting an occasional glance at the painted smiles and loosened bodices of the women who lingered with them.

Mr Ephraim was dozing alone by the fire. He ordered another brandy and a hot toddy for Blake.

'Your papa is a brave man,' he said. 'I hope he gets his money tonight. This is not a place for staying longer than we need to.'

Blake agreed. 'Why don't you take your brandy to your chamber?' he suggested.

'I cannot leave you alone down here.'

'Of course you can! No one will notice me in this dark corner. You are tired and should get some proper sleep.'

'Perhaps you are right. Your papa will not be long. I have seen him deal with strong young men, two at a time, on the dockside. He will be safe, I am sure.'

Mr Ephraim stood up and stretched. 'I need to rest.'

'I shall wait here for Papa,' Blake reassured him.

The burned-out logs on the fire fell with a hiss and Mickey Jackson came to replenish them. 'Your pa gone to his bed? Why don't you have a drop o' rum in your toddy?'

Blake shook his head and yawned, so Mickey returned to his cronies at the counter. Blake went out to the privy, next to the brew house across the backyard. The moon was high and frost already sparkled on the hard ground. As he came out of the privy, he saw Mickey Jackson leading a woman to a shadowy spot in the yard. He heard Mickey's rough voice and her girlish giggles.

Blake skirted the yard to avoid them. He heard muffled

protests from the girl, the tearing of fabric and then the rutting grunts of Mickey satisfying his lusts. He drew the collar of his coat up around his ears and shunned the warmth of the inn fireside to wait for his papa by the bridge.

The deep waters of the lock were still, the gates and sluices quiet. The silence unnerved Blake as he crossed the stone bridge. The only light was from the moon and a tiny glow that burned in the end-cottage window as he passed. Instinctively, Blake knew that something was wrong. The woodland was too quiet, as though all its creatures had gone to ground. There was no screech of a vixen or hoot of an owl, no scurrying of hedgehogs. The only sound was of his boots as he crunched through the ice and frozen leaves.

Halfway up the track, he heard the cracking of twigs and a weak human cry from among the trees. He stopped quite still and listened, following the sounds. He found his papa slumped against a fallen log, on the freezing ground. His right hand clutched at his thigh. Blake could smell the blood as he approached.

'Papa! Papa! What happened?'

'Blake! Is that you? Thank God, you are here. Help me – it's my leg – I can't stop the bleeding . . .' His voice trailed away and his face twisted in pain as he tried to shift his position.

'What happened? Who did this to you?'

His papa spoke breathlessly, 'He came after me as I guessed he would and we faced each other on the track. But when I saw he had a gun I had to run for it. I dodged into the trees, but he came after me.'

'Luther Dearne did this?'

'He was yelling at me, that I'd never get him and he'd kill me first. He meant it, son. He meant it.'

Blake had taken off his coat and jacket and was now removing his shirt and tearing it into broad strips. His hands shook as he bound the strips tightly around his papa's thigh.

'He's winged me, son, that's all. Caught me in the leg. I rolled into a ditch and under bracken. I had to bite on a twig to stop myself crying out with pain.'

Blake's hands were sticky with blood. He wiped them on the frozen bracken and shrugged into his jacket and coat. 'Where is Dearne now?'

'Gone. I heard him thrashing around until he gave up looking for me.'

There was blood everywhere. It had seeped through his papa's thick clothes and Blake could see the stain already spreading on his makeshift bindings. His papa tried to sit up but yelped with the pain. Gasping for breath, he went on, 'He walked right by me. But the gunshot had scattered the birds and foxes. The fool was distracted by their noises.'

'Hush, Papa. Be calm. How did you get to here?'

'I crawled out of the ditch. But I fear I have made the bleeding worse.' Exhausted, his head flopped forward.

'I must get you inside. You will die out here. Do you think you can stand? Here, Papa, put your arm round my shoulders.'

Blake gritted his teeth as he felt the heavy weight of his papa bearing down on his smaller frame. His father suppressed a cry and hobbled forward, uttering, 'You are stronger than you look, my boy. With you, I think I can make it to the inn.'

Blake almost collapsed himself as he half-carried, half-dragged his papa down the woodland towards the lock and the inn. 'We cannot cross the lock gates like this, they're not wide enough,' he muttered. Blake was exhausted but thinking fast. His papa was leaving a trail of blood and weakening by the minute. The bridge was fifty yards downstream. He might not make it to the inn. 'There is someone at home in the end cottage. I can see a light through the window.'

His papa nodded silently and his pasty face contorted as they fell with a thud against the cottage door.

Rosa was working by the light of her kitchen fire, melting beeswax with goose grease and eucalyptus oil to make green ointment. This salve was very popular with bargemen's wives for soothing cuts and burns. She hummed a tune quietly to herself as she stirred the mixture in a small saucepan. The thump at her door made her jump and she placed the pan carefully on the hearth before crossing the room to look out of the window.

'It's late,' she called. 'What do you want?'

'Help. Please help us. My papa is injured.'

Rosa opened her door a crack to see who it was. But the weight of Erik Svenson against it pushed it open wide. As soon as she smelled the blood, she stood back. Blake and his papa fell into her kitchen. 'What happened?' she demanded.

'Sh-shot. In . . . leg . . .' Erik groaned.

Rosa immediately pulled out a pallet from under her

dresser. Blake moved away a chair and between them they dragged his papa on to the makeshift bed.

'He isn't bound tight enough,' Rosa observed. 'The blood still flows. Fetch me that clean linen from under the mantelshelf.'

Blake obeyed instantly, shivering in spite of the warm fire. Rosa picked up a kitchen knife and began cutting through the blood-sodden wool of Erik's breeches. As she exposed his torn and bleeding flesh she realised that no amount of salve would heal this wound. Blood was seeping out in pulses and it showed no signs of abating. This man needed a surgeon. Even a surgeon might not save his leg, but he could at least save the man's life.

'Fetch me that pail of cold water from t' scullery, lad. I'll do what I can to stem the blood, but you'll have to go fer t' doctor from over Fordham.'

'Where's that?'

'Two mile upstream from t' lock. Get a horse from t' livery at t' inn. The marine sleeps over the stables.'

Blake nodded and Rosa continued, 'Light me that lamp first, and then hurry. When you come to t' next bridge, you'll see t' houses. The doctor's house is end-on to t' road an' built o' stone. Big 'un. Can't miss it, it has a brass plate on t' front wall. Tell him Rosa sent you.'

Blake stared anxiously at his papa's shredded, bleeding thigh. 'Papa, I don't want to leave you like this.'

His papa weakly waved an arm to dismiss him and croaked, 'Go.'

Blake dashed out into the frozen night. The stables by the Navigator were quiet, though a dim glow was visible through a crack in the wooden door. A lad of about his own age answered the thumping of his fists.

'I need a horse. A good one with a saddle.'

'Who . . . who are you?'

'I'm staying at the inn. My papa is badly hurt and needs a doctor.'

'Come inside. What's your name?'

'Blake.'

'I'm Peter. You're lucky I'm still awake. My horses are usually down for the night by now.'

'Quickly. My papa is bleeding.'

Peter Jackson crossed to one of his stalls. 'Take this one. He's the lightest and fastest I have – a thoroughbred carriage horse.'

Between them they saddled the horse and led him out into the cold night air.

Peter said, 'I'll wait up. It's not far. Follow the towpath to the next bridge. Good luck!' He slapped the horse on its rear and Blake galloped into the frosty darkness.

The doctor's house was in darkness but his rapping on the door was soon answered by a woman in her nightclothes. 'He's not here, lad,' she said. 'He's up at the Hall tending her Ladyship.'

'The Hall? Where? Where is it?' he demanded breathlessly.

'Nay, it's miles away from here, lad. Anyway, it's no good going for him. He won't leave her Ladyship, not in her condition.'

Blake was frantic. 'Is there another doctor?'

'Not round here, lad. But there's a woman who's good at tending t' sick down at t' lock.'

'Who? Where?'

'She lives in one of them woodmen's cottages down by Mexton Lock. Goes by the name of Rosa, I believe.'

Blake's shoulders sagged. 'Papa is with her now.'

'Then he's in the best hands round here.'

'But she says he needs a surgeon.'

'Been shot, you say? Step inside, lad. I'll give you some of the doctor's dressings for her. You can't do no better for him this night.'

The woman disappeared for a few minutes and returned with a package wrapped in calico. Blake offered her a coin.

'Nay, lad. T' doctor doesn't need that. Give it to Rosa. Not many folk have much time for her down at Mexton Lock, but if summat's up she'll allus do what she 'as to to help, like.'

'Thank you.'

The woman nodded. 'Best get off back now. Good luck.'

Papa was barely conscious when Blake returned. Rosa had built up the fire and lit more lamps. His leg was propped up with a bed bolster and Rosa was supporting his head as she tried to get him to drink.

Blake looked at the fresh wide binding on his leg and the red stain that continued to seep and spread. 'The . . . the doctor wasn't there. He's at the Hall somewhere.'

'Swinborough Hall, that'll be. 'Er Ladyship's with child. Must be 'aving trouble again,' Rosa observed.

'His housekeeper sent you these.' Blake dropped the calico parcel on Rosa's kitchen table.

'Well, I've done my best for 'im, lad.'

He stood in the centre of the room, watching helplessly. 'What can I do?'

'Here. Try and get him to drink. I'll fetch another blanket.'

Blake took over from Rosa and cradled his papa's head while he sipped a little more water.

'Blake? Is that you?' he breathed.

'Yes, Papa. It's me.'

'It's bad, my boy. Bad. The bleeding won't stop.'

'No, Papa, it will, it will. You'll get well again. You're strong. Your leg will heal.'

His papa moved his head very slightly from side to side. 'Dearne,' he whispered. 'It was Luther Dearne.' His eyes closed but a moment later he opened them and murmured, 'Look after your mama for me.' Then his eyes closed again and his head fell sideways.

Despair overtook Blake and he pleaded with Rosa. 'Help him! Rosa, for God's sake, help him!'

She covered his papa with another blanket. 'I can't do no more for 'im. The shot goes deep and his flesh is badly torn. I don't know if the surgeon could have done anything, anyroad. Let him sleep for now. We can only wait and see.'

Blake gently lowered his papa's head. 'He won't die, will he, Rosa?'

'Hush, boy. Morning will tell. Here, come and sit by the fire. I'll brew a concoction to calm us both down.'

It was a long night for Blake. He sat and watched his papa's breathing become slower and more laboured until it rattled weakly in his throat. He did not move a muscle as he watched. His mind and body were frozen, not from cold, but numb with shock.

This could not be happening. It was a nightmare, a demonic dream that he would soon wake from and all would be well. His papa would be whole and strong and – and – Luther Dearne would be dead. Luther Dearne dead, instead of his papa.

Rosa dozed in her chair by the fire. At daybreak, when the first barges came through, she went outside to pump fresh water. When she returned, Blake was still sitting in the exact same position that he had held all night, staring at the motionless body of his father.

Rosa placed a hand on Blake's shoulder and said quietly, 'I'm sorry, lad. I did all I could.'

Tears coursed down his tired, young face as he held his papa's large cold hand. 'No, Papa, no. Don't leave us. We need you. Mama and I need you.'

'You must try and be strong now, lad. For your mama's sake. Is she staying with you at the Navigator?'

'No, we – I have a friend there. Mr Ephraim's there.'

'You'd best go to 'im now, lad. You'll have to tell 'im. Make arrangements, like.'

Blake stared at the newly carved headstone and seethed through clenched teeth. 'He was murdered, Mama. He was not armed and he was shot!' His face was grim as he tried to control his simmering rage. His grief and anger had festered in the weeks since his papa's death. Neither his mama nor he wanted any of the lovely goose that Lucy had prepared for their Christmas dinner. Instead, they had walked together in silence to the churchyard.

'I know, my son, and I grieve for my beloved Erik as you do. Our lives will never be the same again, not for either of us.'

'Will you go back to Sweden, Mama?'

'Do you want to, Blake?'

'I shall go with you, Mama, if you wish.'

'I'd like to see my cousins again. But, you know, I like it here. It is not so cold in the winter. We have a lovely home and we still have our warehouse. You will soon be a man, Blake. Where do you want to make your future?'

'Without Papa, I don't know.'

'The warehouse will be yours when you are twenty-one. Ephraim and I can look after it until then, if you want.'

Blake nodded slowly. 'Can I leave school and work with Ephraim in the warehouse now?'

'You have to go to school for a few more years. There is still much for you to learn.'

'Schoolwork is boring, Mama. I want to be doing something more.'

He thought about the confines of the classroom. He could do the book work easily enough but preferred practical things and being outdoors. And he wanted to get even with Dearne!

'You will, Blake. When you are older.'

'Always it is when I am older, Mama!'

'Be patient—'

'How can I? When my father's murderer is free?'

'It is hard for me as well, Blake.'

'I'm sorry. It's just that I feel so . . . so helpless.'

He tidied away the last of the funeral tributes that lay

around the headstone and his mama laid a fresh wreath of evergreens and berries from their garden. She hooked her arm through his and leaned against him.

'If we stay,' he remarked, 'I would have to become part of life here, learn to be a Yorkshire man, live like one, ride and shoot, go hunting on the moors.'

'Your papa has found you a school where you can learn all those things. He understood you, Blake. You are like him.'

'And fight,' Blake continued. 'I want to learn to fight with my fists as Papa could. Real fighting, Mama. Like Papa did, like the prize-fighters do for money.'

His mama stumbled a little and he held her elbow until she recovered. Blake knew that she would not want this for him. But he was his father's son, and his mama knew that when he made his mind up to do something, he would do it.

'Would you leave me alone for a moment, Mama?'

'Of course.' She walked away towards the church.

Blake stood facing his father's grave and made him a promise. 'I shan't let him get away with this, Papa. You can rely on me.' And to himself, he vowed, 'You won't escape me, Luther Dearne. I'll kill you for this. I swear, I'll kill you.'

Chapter 10

Luther Dearne kept Lissie and her mam away from the lock after the fight. Lissie knew that something serious had gone on that night, something that had unsettled her dad. He was mad at the foreigners and the next morning was flushed and agitated. He had forbidden Lissie and her mam to go down to the lock until he said they could. The day after that, a stranger in a tall hat and dark coat with shiny buttons done up to the neck had come to see Dad and they went to talk in the front room.

The stranger wasn't expected, Lissie knew, because it was chilly outside and her mam hadn't told her to light the front-room fire. Mam went upstairs to put on her good dress and told Lissie to wear a clean apron and run a rag over her boots. Then Mam did something she'd never seen her do before. She stood on a chair to reach the top shelf of the kitchen cupboard and got down some little glasses that she rubbed up with a piece of old linen. Then she put them on the wooden tray with the bottle of sherry wine that her dad had brought back from Hull.

'Listen, you,' her mam hissed. 'We're going in there wi' this and you're not to say a word. Not one word or I'll thrash you wi'in an inch of your life. If 'e says owt to you, you just bob a curtsey and say "sir". And look down at your feet, d'you hear me?'

'Yes, Mam. Who is he? What's going on?'

Lissie's answer was a clip across her ear as her mam snapped, 'I said be quiet, di'n't I? Now open t' door for me.'

It was cold in the front room and the gentleman sat on the sofa with his hat beside him. He seemed very glad to have the wine and Mam refilled his glass twice. Lissie perched on the footstool by her mam who had settled in one of the high-backed chairs.

Her dad was in the other chair and he was saying, 'Aye, a foreigner did come to see me about putting some trade my way but I didn't know the gent and you can't be too careful wi' foreigners.' Dad gestured towards Lissie and her mam as he went on, 'I've got a wife and little girl to think of, so I sent him off sharpish, like.'

The visitor asked if there'd been a fight.

Her dad shook his head. 'Not wi' me, there weren't. I were too busy, I 'ad to get some supper in for the family. Just a few wood pigeons, like. You can see 'em roosting when the moon's up and the squire don't mind. He says shooting 'em keeps 'em off his corn.'

Everyone went quiet for a few minutes and then her dad took a deep breath and continued, 'If this foreigner were shot in the woods as you say, what was 'e doing creeping around that time o' night, I'd like to know? Up to no good, that's for sure. Well, I don't know nothing about no shooting, apart from the wood pigeons. And I bagged enough wi' just the one blast. Just the one.' He turned to Mam. 'They made a good supper, didn't they, Mrs Dearne?'

Mam nodded vigorously. 'They did that, Mr Dearne.' She put a bony hand across Lissie's shoulders and looked at the visitor. 'He's a good husband, sir. Always takes good care of us both. He came back real early and stayed in all night.'

The visitor sipped his sherry wine and looked around them. Their front room, he thought, was perishing cold without a fire this weather, but it was clean and tidy and he had been let in the house through the front door. Dearne, he decided, was a bit above your average canal trader, and he believed his story about the wood pigeons. More likely the foreigner had got into a fight with one of the rogues from the barges and they'd done him in. He got up, making comments about being satisfied, then took his leave. The landlord at the inn had told him that some travelling folk had followed the foreigner. He'd had trouble with them before and they must have shot him. Decent man, that landlord. He'd asked him back for his dinner. The visitor put on his tall hat and looked forward to some roast beef.

But Lissie noticed there were no smiles from anybody and she knew better than to ask any more questions. After the man had gone, Dad was very jumpy and short tempered and instead of going over to the Navigator, he spent quite a lot of time in the garden clearing out the brambles and ferns. Lissie wasn't allowed to go and see Miriam about school and even her mam couldn't go to Rosa's. Dad had forbidden it until all the tittle-tattle had stopped.

Lissie liked having her dad home all day and she helped him with tidying up their unruly garden. Even Mam pitched in with piling up the rubbish. Dad set light to it one afternoon and Lissie stayed outside until dusk watching the flames and warming her hands.

Not long after that, Mexton Lock was abuzz with tales of a bad accident where people had got killed on the new railway line yon side o' the Riding. The shooting was forgotten as canal folk nodded knowingly to each other and said that waterways were still the best way to get around. As the days grew shorter and Christmas was nigh, Dad started going to the Navigator again for his ale. They had a ham to eat that winter. Dad brought it in one night and hung it on the hook from the wooden cross beam in the scullery.

The shooting was forgotten and after Christmas he fetched Lissie some new boots to wear for going to school. Well, he swapped them for an iron cooking pot down by the canal wharf. They were not really new, but her dad rubbed beeswax in them until they were so shiny that they squeaked when she skipped about the house in them. They were too big for her now but she had her thick winter stockings to go inside them and she had put some screwed up rags in the toes to fill the space for this winter.

On her first morning at school, she laced them up

tightly and wrapped herself in her new cloak then scampered over the rough ground towards the lock. For the first week Dad had walked down with her and hung about the Navigator waiting for a free ride to the coast. He wanted to be off, away from here as soon as he could, he said.

He told Mam to take her to meet Miriam for school, but Lissie knew her mam never wanted to get up in the morning to go with her. She was glad to get away from Mam when Dad wasn't there. Anyroad, she had to rush. Lissie had to get to the Navigator early because Miriam wouldn't wait for her if she was late.

'It's bad enough 'aving to play nursemaid to you wi'out you slowing me down,' Miriam complained as they picked their way around the muddy puddles on the towpath.

Lissie knew they were supposed to walk together. Her sharp ears picked up most things in her mam and dad's conversations when they thought she was asleep by the fire. Miriam's dad didn't want her walking on the towpath on her own either. 'I'm not late,' Lissie protested. 'Anyroad, your dad says you have to wait for me and if you're not there I have to go into the Navvy and find you.'

Miriam grabbed her arm roughly and gave her a push. 'If you ever do that, I'll shove you in the water an' you'll die. You can catch me up, that's what you can do.'

Lissie stayed silent. Miriam was eleven, two years older than she was, and much bigger. The older girl wasn't a lot taller, but she had grown rounder this last year and was heavier. Lissie knew Miriam could and would carry out her threat, so she took to walking on the hedge side of the towpath. Miriam then took delight in stepping sideways and elbowing her into the brambles when she felt like it. Oh well, Lissie reasoned silently when she had to disentangle herself from the thorny branches, a few scratches were better than drowning. Luckily, she was faster on her feet than the older girl and was able to run ahead and avoid the worst. Miriam, she noticed, didn't chase her, and Lissie quickly learned how she could avoid the worst of Miriam's little tricks.

'Got any spice today?' Miriam asked her.

'No,' Lissie lied. She had a piece of pomfret cake wrapped up in a scrap of old muslin that she was saving until it was time to begin the walk back home at the end of the day. It was in a little pocket in her calico drawers and it would be nice and sticky and chewy when she sucked on it later in the day.

'Don't believe you.' Miriam gave her shove into the wet hedge. 'Your dad allus gives you some spice. Give it 'ere.'

'I 'aven't got any, I tell you!'

'You're a liar, Lissie Dearne. That's what you are! Where've you hidden it?'

Rain or no rain, the mud wouldn't stop Miriam knocking her to the ground and pulling up her skirts to search for the liquorice. She darted ahead, skipping with an agile grace over the smaller puddles. But the bigger, deeper ones slowed her down as they had to be negotiated right next to the deep water to avoid the wet hedges at the other side. Miriam caught her up easily.

'Give it 'ere or I'll push you in.'

Lissie really believed she would. She had watched Miriam's two older brothers dangle a young lad by his feet over the side of the lock and threaten to drop him in the water head first if he didn't give them the coppers he earned from running messages.

Well, Lissie thought, that was two against one and this is just me and her. The constant housework Lissie did every day for her mam when she got home from school had made her a strong little girl, a fact that was belied by her skinny appearance. She darted ahead again and waited further up the towpath for Miriam to reach her and carry on with her threats and demands. Then, quick as a flash, she pulled at the older girl's right arm, twisting it behind her back and pushing up the loose sleeve.

She grasped Miriam's wrist in her strong little hands and with a grip like tight iron bands twisted her hands in opposite directions as if she were wringing out a wet cloth. 'You're goin' to stop pushing me about, Miriam Jackson, d' you hear?'

'Ow! Ouch! Stop that, Lissie, stop it, it hurts!'

'It's meant to. Swear to me you'll stop.'

'All right, all right. I'll stop.'

Lissie loosened her grip but held on to the wrist. 'You 'ave to promise.'

Miriam scowled and stayed silent until Lissie tightened her grip again.

'Give over, Lissie. You're hurting me!' Miriam squealed.

Lissie gritted her teeth and doubled her effort. 'Not until you promise me you'll stop your little tricks. Just because you're bigger 'an me, doesn't mean I can't get you back!'

'Don't! It's burning me! Give over!'

'Promise me you'll stop! Promise?'

'I've already said I'll stop, 'aven't I?'

'Swear to me.'

'I swear on the Holy Bible.'

'Cross your heart and hope to die?'

'Cross my heart and hope to die,' Miriam replied miserably.

Lissie dropped Miriam's wrist abruptly. Miriam rubbed at the reddened skin on her forearm. 'I were on'y larking about. That hurt. Where'd you learn to do that?'

'Off your big brothers. I watched 'em try it on wi' one of the farm lads who came over looking for work. Soon sent 'im on his way, that did. And they tried it on wi' me once. But your mam saw 'em and stopped 'em. Gave 'em a right telling off, she did.'

'Yes, well, you wait till I tell 'em about this, they'll be after your blood again.'

Lissie frowned for a second, worried that Miriam might be right. But she knew that Miriam's mam could be as fiery as her dad and there was always hell to pay if the boys went anywhere near the two of them when they were playing by the lock.

'They wouldn't dare,' Lissie stated flatly. 'Your mam'd have their guts for garters.' Lissie had decided that she was no longer frightened of Miriam or her bullying brothers and her green eyes smouldered in defiance. The two girls stood face to face on the muddy towpath, neither sure whether they were friends or enemies.

Miriam pouted petulantly, thinking that this little gypsy from the woods was turning out to be more than she'd bargained for. But their dads were good mates so she supposed they'd better be as well. She said, 'Well, if you really 'a'n't got any spice you can 'ave one o' mine. They're barley sugar from the sweet shop in town.'

'Ta.' Lissie took the peace offering graciously and vowed to break her pomfret cake into two pieces to share on the way home. She'd have to save face with Miriam by 'finding' it in her things at school later though.

Miriam began to be much nicer to her from that day. She could be very nice when she wanted to be, Lissie realised, as they progressed through that first year walking the towpath together. At school, in her dad's inn and especially talking to the canal boatmen that summer, Miriam could be really nice to people when she wanted.

Lissie was at her happiest during those few years she spent at Miss Kirby's dame school. After two years, at eleven and thirteen, Lissie and Miriam were the oldest in the school, and they could mend and sew, cook and clean, and look after the little ones like their mothers did.

They spent hardly any time at all on letters and numbers, which pleased Miriam and disappointed Lissie. She liked reading and doing sums, and quickly progressed in both where her friend became bored. It was a long walk to school but one that Lissie would have done in bare feet in winter just to be able to read one of Miss Kirby's books! Sometimes she was allowed to read passages from the Bible to the whole class, or asked to write words and figures in Miss Kirby's big heavy accounting book that was kept locked away in a cupboard. She dreaded the day when she would have to leave school and go back to helping Mam in the house all week.

Mam seemed to despise her even more now that she went to school. When Dad was home Mam had to cook a tea every day and keep the house tidy without Lissie to help, so she was always in a bad temper by the end of the day. Even when Dad was back, Lissie dreaded going home from school and having to face her mam. But she was lithe and quick on her feet and, even as she grew taller, managed to dodge most of the cuffs and clips from Edie.

Dad didn't bring back many supplies when he came home these days as trade was going through a bad patch. This happened every now and then when one of the ironworks or foundries he dealt with went bankrupt, or a ship foundered at sea. On top of that, a new railway line had put a number of barges out of business. Lately, when Dad was home his days were passed more at the inn than at their house.

Mam snapped and sniped at Lissie all the time when she wasn't full of gin, and lashed out with her bony hands when she was. If Dad wasn't in when she got home from school Lissie disappeared fast to put on her old dress and weed the garden or clean up the scullery to keep out of Mam's way. And she always got up early, before Mam and Dad, so she had plenty of time to see to the fire, pump the water and set a kettle to boil before she went to meet Miriam at the Navigator.

That morning, Miriam's dad knew the boatman on a barge going upstream and he agreed to take them the two miles to Fordham, where their school was situated. It was a fine day and Miriam sat on the cabin roof, spread out her skirts and lifted her face to the sun. Lissie preferred to walk with the horse while the bargeman's son took a break. She loved the strong docile animal with his leather harnesses and polished brasses. But they dawdled and were late in arriving at school. They hurried into the dingy back rooms where Miss Kirby ran her dame school in the house that she shared with her brother.

'Line up!' Miss Kirby called in her high, trembling voice.

Her pupils scurried around until they stood shoulder to shoulder in front of her high wooden desk. Boys were on the right and girls on the left, with tall ones at the ends. Miss Kirby allocated tasks to her pupils according to their height. Quickly, the girls pushed their hair out of sight under bonnets and dusted down their pinafores with their hands. Miss Kirby walked up and down the row moving their positions until she was satisfied.

'Silence now,' she demanded, clapping her hands. 'Mr Kirby! We are ready for you.'

Miss Kirby's brother came down the dark passage from his study. He was dressed for town in a long coat and polished boots, with a proper top hat and a walking cane that he tapped on the brick floor as he inspected them.

'Boys! Outside!' he ordered.

'All of them, brother dear?' Miss Kirby asked timidly.

'Are you questioning my decision?'

You could have heard a pin drop, Lissie thought.

Miss Kirby stuttered a little. 'Th-the t-two new ones are very small. They cannot reach the workbench.'

He peered down at the smallest pupils in the middle of the row. 'Are they boys? Really, sister, why are they not wearing brown smocks?'

'Th-the g-girls will make them today.'

Mr Kirby ignored his sister and addressed the boys. 'George is waiting with the cart outside.'

They walked out silently, in single file, and climbed aboard the open farm cart that would take them to local workshops for the day.

Mr Kirby turned his attention to the girls, clothed in calico pinafores that covered their dresses and fastened at the back. Their bonnets were plain white and tied with tape under their chins. Mr Kirby was very strict about their pinnies and bonnets. The girls shuffled their feet and spread out so that he could walk round and inspect each one of them individually.

Lissie had some difficulty in keeping her thick black hair out of sight now that it had grown so long. She sensibly plaited it and wound it round her head to fit under her bonnet. Miriam just twisted and pinned hers into a loose knot so that honey-blonde tendrils kept escaping to frame her face.

Mr Kirby stood in front of the two of them with a stern expression on his long thin face. 'Sister, these girls are vain.' He glared at Lissie and Miriam. 'Vanity is a sin,' he declared. 'It leads us into temptation. You will both do extra Bible readings today. Sister, you will give these girls readings on the wages of sin.'

He lingered in front of Lissie and stared at her intently. 'This one, especially, is in grave danger of moral decay. You will see that she learns her Bible passages by heart. I shall listen to her recite them tomorrow at inspection.'

'Yes, brother dear,' Miss Kirby responded.

When he had gone, Miriam exploded. 'I'm glad that was you and not me! I'm hopeless at learning by heart.'

'Oh, I don't mind,' Lissie sighed, resigned to her task. 'He does pick on me though, doesn't he?'

Miriam shrugged. Lissie was growing up to look really pretty, but she wouldn't dream of telling her that. Mr Kirby was a regular chapel-goer and thought all pretty girls were 'in danger of moral decay'. He thought they should all look as plain and dull as his poor old sister!

'Where does he go all day?' Lissie asked as they set about organising the day's sewing.

'Business,' Miriam said importantly.

'My dad said the Kirby works had closed down.'

'They did, but he still goes into town every day.'

'What for?' asked Lissie.

'He wants to start the works up again, and—'

'And what?'

Miriam took on an air of superiority. 'I can't tell you. You're not old enough.'

'You always say that and I'm nearly as old as you.'

'No, you're not!'

Miss Kirby stood up at her high desk. 'Be quiet, you two, and get on with your work! Lissie, how dare you waste time chattering when you have Bible passages to learn for Mr Kirby.'

'Sorry, Miss Kirby.'

Miriam lowered her voice to a whisper. 'My mam says Mr Kirby's got a lady friend in town, and he goes to see her every afternoon. You think on that when you're reciting your Bible to him.'

Lissie didn't reckon there was anything wrong with Mr Kirby having a lady to court, but clearly Miriam thought otherwise. She wondered if he'd marry her and bring her to live here. Miss Kirby wouldn't like that, for sure!

The Kirbys' home was one in a collection of elegant houses in a small village, that had grown up around a track linking the turnpike to the canal. It was about three miles downstream from the Riding town and situated on the edge of a large landed estate, rich in coal and iron ore. The surrounding farmland was an attractive place to settle for enterprising men who had made their money from the manufactories of the South Riding, and who wanted their families to live away from the smoke and grime of the works.

Originally the turnpike had provided the only way into town, but later the canal and its tributary cuts opened up new transport links. Now there was talk of a railway to follow the waterways and keep the townsfolk of the South Riding supplied with all their needs.

Miss Kirby's dame school paid for the upkeep of the once elegant, but now run-down house that was her home. When her father and her dear mama were alive, her father's ironworks in the town had done well and her mama had employed an upstairs maid to help them dress in the morning and go to bed at night. It was such a trial for Miss Kirby now the ironworks had closed and she could no longer afford her own maid.

But her brother had kept on the elderly couple who

lived in the coach house at the far end of the garden. They slept in the upstairs room next to the hayloft and came into the kitchen for their meals. George had been her father's coachman and his wife Hannah her mama's cook. Now that Miss Kirby's brother kept only a pony and trap, as he could no longer afford a carriage, George did the gardening, looked after the orchard and fetched in the coals, while his wife stayed on as Miss Kirby's housekeeper.

It was a pleasant house to look at from the road, with large sash windows either side of a wide, panelled front door that carried a heavy brass knocker. Built at the end of the last century, before the days of the Regent, by Miss Kirby's uncle, it had been bequeathed first to Miss Kirby's father and then to her brother. In less than ten years, young Mr Kirby had shown that he was no iron master like his father or uncle, and had managed to bankrupt the small South Riding ironworks that his father had left to him.

He had kept the house, which had large rooms on two floors, spacious attics and a collection of store places and outhouses at the back. But it was too much work for one elderly housekeeper, even with help from one of the local village girls, and Miss Kirby was not gifted in any of the domestic arts.

She had been taught by her dear mama to read and write and do numbers but, unfortunately, did not care to pass her time with any of those pursuits. She could, however, play the piano and sing, and speak a little French, not that they were much use in her school. The parents of her pupils were not interested in their children learning those skills.

Miss Kirby was frequently irritated by her school but she tolerated it. It allowed her to buy silk for her Sunday dress and keep a good table for her brother. She looked after the young sons and daughters of local folk who had the means to pay her brother a small fee, called them her pupils, and had a ready supply of help for Hannah in the kitchen.

She relied heavily on bright energetic children like Lissie, who already knew how to clean and mend and could show the others for her. Without a talent for learning herself, Miss Kirby struggled hard to teach the children their letters and numbers and expected the older ones to learn more about housekeeping and cooking from the books and papers she kept in the house.

The schoolrooms were not proper living rooms but had been stores and pantries near to the kitchen at the back of the house. The windows were tiny which made the rooms dark, and the brick floors were damp and chilly in winter. When the weather was really cold Miss Kirby allowed her pupils to crowd into the warm kitchen across the passage. The older girls were usually baking bread and cooking broth for dinner and the smell was tantalising for hungry children who never seemed to get enough to eat.

Now it was summer, at least the schoolrooms were cool, but they were stuffy unless all the windows and doors stood open. The little ones were always restless and Miss Kirby kept discipline with a small leather horse-whip that she carried in her right hand all the time. Lissie had an advantage when she started school as she had already learned from living with her mam how to avoid grown-ups when they were angry, and Miss Kirby was no different.

But other pupils didn't fare so well and frequently sobbed into their mending. If their tiny fingers couldn't manage needles and threads they would be given cleaning to do, and Lissie knew from her own experience how depressingly awful scrubbing the brick floors could be.

One sunny morning, Lissie found the schoolrooms suffocating and oppressive. Miss Kirby came downstairs in her best sprigged muslin gown and in a bad mood. Lissie had heard raised voices from Miss Kirby and her brother in the adjoining room when the other pupils arrived for school that morning. She whispered to the young ones to get on with darning sheets and keep their heads well down. She waited until Miss Kirby had settled in her high chair at the front before venturing a question.

'Please, Miss Kirby, I was wondering if I could take the little ones outside today?'

'What on earth for, child?'

'They can start on their letters. If I take the slates we can sit in the orchard.'

'Nonsense! They're far too young for letters.'

'But some of them—'

'Do not answer back! Really! Why are you always so . . . so . . . argumentative?'

'Sorry, Miss Kirby. I thought—'

'Well don't! Sometimes I think you are too clever for your own good.'

The room fell silent. Only the sound of flies buzzing round the children could be heard until Miss Kirby continued, 'Miriam is my oldest pupil and therefore she will take the younger children today.'

Miss Kirby turned to her senior pupil and managed a smile. At thirteen years of age, it was high time the Jackson girl was off into service. A few months as a scullery maid in one of the big houses would soon knock some sense into her. But the girl's mother wanted better for her only daughter and life as a downstairs maid was not part of her future.

Neither was it to be back at the Navigator Inn helping her mother, which was just as well as the girl was useless in the kitchen. Fortunately, her father had money and had been persuaded that some extra learning and looking after the younger pupils might eventually get her a better position in service.

Lissie glanced at Miriam who preened her escaping tendrils of hair and smiled silently. Miriam taking the younger children for Miss Kirby? She had no patience with them at all, and poked them in the back if they didn't do things right. Lissie couldn't let it happen and exclaimed without thinking, 'But everyone knows Miriam hates looking after the little ones!'

'Lissie! I shall not tell you again.' Miss Kirby lashed her horsewhip against the chair leg. 'Sit down at once and hold your tongue.'

'Yes, Miss Kirby.' Dejected, Lissie resumed her place on a low wooden bench beside Miriam, who immediately stuck out her tongue at Lissie.

Miss Kirby clapped her hands together. 'Now, pupils. Miriam is in charge today while I accompany Mr Kirby into town. Everyone must do as she says and she will give me the name of anyone who disobeys.' She handed Miriam the horsewhip and swept out of the room.

Miriam stood in front of the group of wide-eyed children and smirked. As soon as she heard Mr Kirby's pony and trap outside, she took off her bonnet and pinny. Miss Kirby kept a small looking glass in her teacher's cupboard and she opened the door to search for it. The little children began to whisper and fidget on their wooden benches.

'Be quiet!' Miriam shouted with her head in the cupboard.

Lissie stood up and suggested, 'Why don't I get them started on the sewing?'

Miriam straightened up with the looking glass in her hand. 'Good idea. Right then, Lissie is taking the class and no one is to move from this room.'

'Where are you going, Miriam?' Lissie asked.

'For a look round upstairs, where do you think?' She twisted strands of hair around her finger and smiled at her image.

'What if Miss Kirby comes back?'

'She won't be back for ages. They've gone to see the manager at the bank in town. My dad says Mr Kirby's in queer street and Miss Kirby's on'y too pleased for me to stay on here as long as my dad pays up. Yours an' all.' She smoothed down her dress and went on, 'If old Hannah comes nosing, tell her I've gone to the privy.'

Lissie stared in disbelief. It didn't matter what Miriam did, she always seemed to get away with it. Fancy going in Miss Kirby's private rooms! No one was ever allowed to do that! Well, at least she would be out of the classroom and out of Lissie's hair. Lissie really looked forward to helping the little ones with their mending. And there would be time for the bigger ones to learn some letters.

'All right,' she replied. 'And I'll send two of them to the kitchen to help Hannah when she's ready.'

When Miriam had gone from the schoolroom with the looking glass in her hand, Lissie looked at the little faces in her class. They were smiling at her, some quite shyly and others more broadly. She heaved a sigh of relief and beamed back.

'Now, if you'll all get on quietly with your sewing, I'll read you a story.' As she turned to the cupboard to fetch a reading book she heard a whisper of pleasure ripple through the room and thought how much she enjoyed being there, helping the little ones, helping Miss Kirby, even helping Miriam with school work. Life was looking up for Lissie at last and she hoped her dad would let her stay.

Chapter 11

1842

'Do you have a name, boy?' Sir William demanded.

'Svenson, sir. Blake Svenson.'

Sir William raised his eyebrows slightly but did not comment as most South Riding folk did when they heard his family name. 'So you are young Svenson. Dan Sanders speaks highly of you,' he said and handed Blake his silver hip flask. 'Do you want to try some of this?'

Blake glanced at Dan and tipped the brandy to his lips, gagging slightly as it burned his throat.

Sir William watched, mildly amused. 'Well, Blake, you look like a boy who can take care of himself.'

'Thank you, sir.'

Blake flexed his shoulders, pleased with Sir William's observation. After two years at Grasse Fell school in the South Riding, he could shoot and ride as well as any of the other young gentlemen there. He attended his lessons and pleased his tutors, but the classroom stifled him and he lived for the outdoor life and sporting pursuits. Cross-country running and washing in ice-cold water from the pump were part of the school week, but on Wednesday afternoons a tutor came to help with extra sporting activities.

Dan Sanders was a burly, grizzled man of about forty years. He had Negro blood in him that showed in his large frame, broad nose and frizzy grey hair. His dark-brown skin and black eyes were unusual in the South Riding and he was well known among sporting men for his success in bare-knuckle fights when he was a younger man.

He worked the boys of Grasse Fell hard. In good weather they raced on the school field, lifting logs and running with them across their shoulders. On rainy days he taught them fist-fighting in the old buttery and they sparred with each other in a makeshift ring, protecting their young hands with mufflers brought in by Dan. Dan's visits quickly became the most important part of Blake's school week.

Blake had grown tall and broad with a long reach that gave him an advantage over boys his own age and Dan quickly noticed his potential. He gave Blake a series of exhausting tasks to build him up, most of which he repeated on his own when lessons were finished, using discarded logs on the cinder track outside the school stables. From there it had been a short step to persuade the headmaster and his mama to let him go to Dan's gymnastic rooms in town for extra coaching on Saturdays.

Blake had not seen Sir William there before. But then he was usually packed off back to school on the evening carrier, before the men arrived for their evening's entertainment. Tonight was different.

Sir William continued, 'Are you one of Dan's new fist-fighters?'

'No, sir,' he replied truthfully. 'I am at Grasse Fell.'

'Is that so? I know the headmaster there.'

'He knows that I am here, sir,' Blake explained.

Sir William laughed. 'Then he'll know you are in good company. Come and meet my friends.'

Dan's rooms were in a disused mill in a run-down part of town. He rented a storage house and loading area of Kirby's closed ironworks. Every Saturday after breakfast, Blake clambered into the back of a farm cart on its way to market to spend the day at Dan's. He had extra lessons from Dan, helped him set up his practice ring, and sparred with fist-fighters as they limbered up for their manly art of boxing.

He was matched with men his own size and sometimes heavier and stronger. His reaction to a beating was to learn to move faster and to ask Dan for more coaching. And with every winning punch he landed, he imagined his opponent was Luther Dearne. The more accurate he became with his fists, the more he planned his revenge.

Dan's Saturday-night fights had a small but regular following that included men from all classes of South Riding society. His orders from the headmaster were to make sure Blake returned to Grasse Fell on the afternoon carrier. This he did until one particular night, a week after Blake's fifteenth birthday, when he had arranged a fist-fight between one of his own men and a contester from the next town.

Blake was helping Dan set up the ring for the fighters and their handlers when Sir William and his party strolled in. They were well dressed and, to Blake, did not seem to be working men. He put down the water bucket and watched.

Sir William carried a silver-topped black cane that he waved as he came forward. 'Sanders, my man, how are you?'

'Good evening, Sir William. Have you come to watch the fight?'

'Depends. Is it London Prize Rules?'

Dan stood up straight in the large, double-roped square that was his ring. 'All my fights are London Rules now.'

'Excellent! Well, whatever your purse is, I'll double it.'

'That's very generous of you, Sir William,' Dan responded. 'I take it you've had a win at the races today?'

'You could say that,' he replied with a grin.

'Then, thank you. A good purse is sure to add more – er – interest. I expect you and your friends would like some refreshment?' Dan turned to Blake. 'Look after Sir William and his friends, lad. Get them anything they want from the back.' Dan gave him the key to the store cupboard in the room he called his office.

'Here, lad. Fill these.' Sir William and his friends handed Blake their pewter and silver hip flasks. He took them through to the back room and topped them up from a flagon of French brandy.

Sir William's friends were older than Blake, though not all gentry as Sir William was. One managed a local colliery and another worked his own forge. But he hoped they all shared Blake's liking for riding, hunting and fist-fighting. He grew excited by the prospect of an evening in their company and wondered what they were like.

The fight promised to be vicious and bloody, and the watching crowd was emotionally charged and loud. Dan's fighter and his contestant were well matched and each had brought in followers, mostly working men exhausted at the end of a day of physical labour but restored by ale or porter. Blake shinned up tall poles to set torches that lit the ring and threw the crowd into shadow. Then he joined his new friends to watch as the fighting began.

It started slowly. The fighters circled each other warily, throwing jabs punctuated by jeers from the floor. Then the blows came faster and heavier and the fighters began to sweat freely, their bare chests and backs glistening in the flickering light. Blood trickled down the face of Dan's fighter and smeared the knuckles of his opponent. From his privileged ring-side position, Blake could feel the heat radiating from their sweating, muscled bodies.

Blake joined in the chants and shouts with a racing heart. His face was flushed, his fists were clenched and his shoulders hunched as his body leaned and ducked, mimicking the blows, urging on the fighters. He glanced at Sir William, who seemed more controlled, and then at the others, whose blood was up as his was. Sir William smiled at him briefly then returned his attention to the fight.

The men from the next town cheered when their fighter knocked down Dan's man. The cheer rose to a roar as he staggered to his feet and retaliated with a vengeance, urged on by Dan and his supporters, raining blow after blow on his adversary. Both men were showing signs of exhaustion now, their knuckles skinned, their faces cut, swollen and bloody. Then Dan's fighter landed a strong, right-handed punch to his opponent's head and the man went down heavily with a thud, momentarily senseless.

Blake threw both his arms in the air, yelling as loud as he could. Someone grabbed him and hugged him, shouting in his ear. The noise was deafening as the local man was declared the winner. Supporters rushed to attend their precious injured fighters, the crowd cheered and jeered at the same time, coins and banknotes changed hands and arguments developed. Dan called Sir William into the ring to present the purse and raise the arm of the victor. He gave the loser, now back on his feet, words of encouragement and shook Dan's hand congratulating him on a good fight.

Blake watched with interest. Nobody commented to see a member of the local gentry shake a Negro's hand in front of a crowd. In this arena, where men were united by their shared passion for the sport, it seemed natural and he felt proud to be part of it. The crowd began to drift away, continuing their loud arguments as they re-enacted, indeed relived, every blow. Dan was beaming, clearly high on the success of the evening. He caught Blake's eye and called over, 'Good fight, eh, lad?'

'The best,' he replied. 'Shall I start to clear up?'

'No' tonight, lad. I've plenty of hands. You go off with Sir William and his party to celebrate. I've sent word to the school that you're with him. He'll make sure you're back by morning.'

'Morning? Where does he go to all night?'

'You'll find out, lad. Off you go now.'

'See you next week, then.' Blake shrugged and thought, Why not? Then joined his new friends in the cold night air.

The noise and arguments spilled out on to the street and into a nearby alehouse, disturbing the quiet stillness of the dark street. Sir William was in a good humour and he hailed Blake across the heads of his drinking companions.

'Are you coming with us, boy?'

Blake sprinted across the cobbles and clambered into the carriage with Sir William and two of his friends for the short journey to nearby supper rooms where they joined others from the fight to dine on Yorkshire puddings with roast beef and strong ale. As the hour grew late, Blake became caught up in the high spirits of his companions and he joined in their loud exchanges and laughter. A portfolio appeared from apparently nowhere and was given to Sir William to untie ceremoniously. The contents were passed around the table for all to see.

Blake was familiar with paintings of women in fine dresses and elaborate hats; he had seen them hanging on the walls at Grasse Fell and in the grand houses of school friends that he had visited. But he had not seen drawings like these before. These were Italian drawings, drawings of real women, women without their finery, showing the full curves of their bodies without dressing or cover. He stared at the likenesses, appreciating the skill of the artist, and listened to the comments of those around him.

The women in the drawings were beautiful, with handsome faces and voluptuous bodies. Simply looking at them stirred a masculine excitement in his groin and Blake understood the attraction of owning such likenesses, though, he acknowledged, they were not portraits to hang on the walls at home.

Sir William goaded him lightly. 'What do you think of these, Blake, my boy?'

Blake thought for a moment, aware that he was the youngest man in the party. 'Well, sir, I do not know the ladies so I cannot say whether they are good likenesses or not.'

A ripple of laughter ensued. 'But would you want to meet them, boy, to get to know them? Or maybe some – er – other ladies like them?' Sir William pressed.

'Yes, sir,' he replied smartly.

'Ha!' Sir William laughed. 'I knew it! Our young friend is one of us! Tell me, Blake, have you been with a woman yet?'

Blake knew what he meant but feigned an innocence. 'I'm not sure what you mean, sir.'

A voice from the end of the table called, 'I'll wager he hasn't. A guinea says he hasn't.'

'Keep your money for a real wager, Mr Kirby,' Sir William parried. 'The boy is just fifteen.'

'Time he tasted the real thing then,' someone else called.

A deeper voice added, 'A visit to Grace's, I think.'

There was a slight hush until someone said, 'Ask the lad, then.'

Sir William turned to Blake and said, 'Well? Are you

ready to learn about real pleasure from one of the ladies at Grace's, or do I send you back to school now?'

Blake had not heard of 'Grace's' before, but he had gained some knowledge of the kind of place it was sure to be from talking with other boys at school. He did not take any persuading. He was ready.

'Grace's,' he replied firmly.

There was more laughter and banter as the party began to split up. Some left for their homes and others went out to their carriages with Sir William and Blake. As Blake pulled on his cap, Sir William faced him squarely, tipped the brim back with the silver top of his cane and asked, 'Are you sure about this?'

In the light of the carriage lamp, Blake's clear blue eyes darkened and gleamed at the notion. 'Yes, sir.' He relished the thought of the pleasures to come. 'I am.'

Sir William gave him a brief nod. 'Yes, I do believe you are.'

Blake knew something of Sir William Swinborough as he was the biggest landowner in the Riding. A baronet of some forty years of age, his family held, and had held for generations, vast tracts of the South Riding. The land was good for farming and sheep thrived well on the wintry hills. Frequent rain produced soft spring water for making woollen cloth. But there were greater riches beneath the Riding soil. Ironstone and, especially, coal had made wealthy men of Sir William's father and grand-father. And Sir William had shouldered the responsibility of these new industries well. He was a fair landlord to the tenants and workers that tilled his soil, mined his coal and forged his iron.

Blake sat quietly in one corner of Sir William's carriage as it rattled its way through the dark cobbled streets. This would be the first time he had stayed in town past supper. Even with the backing of Sir William he would be in deep trouble at school. But he was finished with school now. In his heart he knew that he wanted to be out of it. Book work and a future at university rubbing shoulders with the sons of the English aristocracy was not for him.

Real life was what he wanted and he was about to start living it. His groin tingled with anticipation of a real woman, a proper woman, not a portrait or a drawing. He became nervous at the thought of experiencing real intimacy. What would he do? How would he do? A hand clutching a silver flask jutted in front of his face. He took it gratefully and swigged a mouthful quickly down his throat.

The carriage took them out of town, up the hill where a successful ironmaster was building a new home of local stone and best Welsh slate. Beyond lay farmland, and in the next valley a village by the river crossing. Before that was Grace's, the former home of a gentleman farmer, with its mellow stone walls and tall chimneys. The carriage stopped and, save for the snorting of the horses, there was silence. After the rowdiness of the fight and ensuing arguments over supper, Grace's seemed as hushed as a church.

Blake had expected an inn, or something resembling an inn. Once inside, he realised with a start that it reminded him of his own home, with an entrance hallway furnished as his mama's was. He saw a low table

supporting an oil lamp with a tall glass chimney, two
upholstered chairs and a looking glass in an ornate gilt
frame on the wall. They stood on a turkey carpet as
Grace appeared from the back of the house to greet
them. She seemed to be expecting Sir William and knew
his friends by name.

Sir William called him forward to meet her and he
saw that she was quite an old woman, with a worn, lined
face. She was dressed in grey silk with a lot of black lace
at her wrists and throat and a jet comb in her grey hair.

'We have a novice for you, Grace,' Sir William told
her lightly. 'He needs a lesson or two, don't y' know.'

Grace raised her pince-nez to her eyes and peered
closely at Blake. 'Handsome fellow, isn't he?' she mused.
'First timer, you say?'

Blake began to feel uncomfortable as he was scrutin-
ised by this older woman. She moved closer and addressed
him directly. 'Tell me, sir, what are you looking for? Dark
or fair? Or maybe—'

Sir William interrupted. 'How about a bit of a show,
Grace? We've not had one of those in a while.' A purse
of coins passed from Sir William to Grace and the older
man said to his companions, 'What d'you say to giving
the boy first pick? Just this once.'

Grace led the way into a large room, furnished and
lit like a private drawing room. She waved her arm
towards a decanter of port wine and glasses that stood
on the sideboard. 'Help yourselves, gentlemen, while I
organise my ladies.'

Blake declined the wine. He had drunk ale with his
supper and taken brandy in the carriage. His courage

was high and his nerves were already tingling in anticipation. The men settled comfortably in upholstered chairs
and sofas and waited.

Grace came back with a sheet of music and began
to play on a harpsichord. Her ladies entered the room
one by one, parading and twirling around the elegant
furniture. They were lovely, all of them, each one handsome in her own way. Soon they filled the room in
their fine, billowing silk dresses of pinks and reds and
greens. The air in the room was charged with desire.
The men became restless and moved about in their seats,
forgetting their wine and undoing the buttons of their
jackets.

And then the women began to, gradually, slowly, take
off their finery, helping each other with tapes and buttons
until their copious gowns and lace-edged petticoats were
abandoned, draped over sofas and tables, and they were
clad in only their stiffly boned corsets and ribbon-
trimmed under-drawers. There were six or seven of them,
smiling, twirling, bending forward to show the swelling
of their breasts and the roundness of their rumps. Blake
stared in awe. His heart was throbbing in his throat and
his body fired by an animal desire. Furtively, he glanced
at the other men and saw that, like him, they were
mesmerised by this show.

Blake had never in his life felt so excited. Never. Not
like this. These women were so desirable, so arousing, so
ready. His eager pulse raced and his immediate need to
possess one of them overwhelmed him. There were two
that he found especially irresistible. Both were mature,
rounded women of good stature. Their womanly curves

bulged from beneath their corsets. How he coveted an exploration of those curves!

Each had glossy dark hair dressed smoothly around her head in braids and swathes arranged to complement her smiling face. But, whereas one was from a southern climate with olive skin, abundant curls and smouldering brown eyes, the other had a northern pallor with ivory skin and light eyes, her long black hair coiled smoothly around her elegant head. When she circled in front of him for the second time he could barely restrain himself and his breeches bulged with desire. She looked straight into his eyes for a few seconds and they exchanged a steady level gaze.

And from that moment he was lost to her. He stood up and caught her hand to stop her moving on. She hesitated and looked about her. Blake saw her eyes meet Sir William's and watched as he rose to his feet quickly. The woman pulled at her hand to loosen it from Blake's grip, but he would not let her go. The music slowed and stopped as Sir William picked up his glass of port wine and crossed the room.

'Hah!' Sir William said. 'You have chosen Clara. You have good taste, my boy.' He swung round to face Clara squarely and asked, with an ironic twist to his lips, 'Tell me, Clara, do you choose him?'

Blake watched Clara frown silently and realised he had chosen badly. He had displeased Sir William. He let go of Clara's hand and stepped back, deferring to the older man. But Sir William surprised him by taking Clara's hand, kissing it lightly and handing it back to him, saying, 'Now, Clara, you take very good care of my young friend. I put my trust in you to teach him well.'

Clara looked mildly surprised but led Blake silently out of the drawing room and up the stairs.

Blake had seen a woman naked before, the only woman before this one to have stirred his sexual desires. That woman had been a relative of the school's head-master, a distant cousin of some sort who had stayed as a guest of his wife for several months. The summer that year was hot and he had seen her bathing in the forest stream as he crashed his way through the trees on a cross-country run.

He had slowed when he noticed the empty donkey-cart on the forest track, and crept through the undergrowth to where the stream fell into a wide rock pool before meandering on its way. She was a young woman with large drooping breasts and a round belly that other pupils had also noticed swelling under her skirts.

Her condition was the source of much dormitory snorting and giggling among the boys. When he had looked at her then, he thought she was beautiful. Her fair hair had been loosened from its pinning and she sat on a rock leaning back on her hands as though proud of her growing bulging belly.

Blake had crept away, aware of the masculine desires it had stirred in him, desires that were now repeated and burgeoning tenfold as he followed Clara up the wide, carpeted staircase. This was no hole-in-the-corner whorehouse as he might have expected, but quiet and well-furnished, as his own home was. With a shock, Blake realised that this familiarity added to the frisson of his arousal. The girl, no, the woman, closed the bedroom door and stood motionless in front of him, unashamed by her scant covering of frilled corset and drawers.

He realised now what he wanted in a woman, of all the women he'd seen that night and before. A woman of good proportions. Not a dainty and pretty little girl, but a handsome and comely woman with soft round curves. Like this woman. With light skin, like his and his people across the North Sea, yes, but with the drama of dark hair that made her skin look alabaster in contrast.

The room was lit by a subdued yellow glow from an oil lamp placed on a small table. A large bed made up with white linen and a red satin cover dominated the room and he began to feel nervous with anticipation. He pulled at his already loosened necktie and threw it to the floor, then began to fumble excitedly with the buttons on his shirt.

Clara came forward and stilled his hands. 'Wait. Wait a little. What shall I call you?'

'Blake. Blake Svenson.' Noticing her slightly raised eyebrows he added, 'It's Swedish.'

'Is that so? Yes, I see – the flaxen hair and blue eyes. Blue, like mine.' Clara's voice was soft and she spoke slowly. 'You must tell me more about your home country. But not now. Afterwards. We can talk afterwards. First, Blake, come closer to me and help me take off my corset.'

His fingers shook as he untied laces and ribbons and peeled down stockings to reveal soft white flesh that was cool and smooth and lightly scented. Her breasts were pale soft cushions, her belly gently curving and her rear as round and plump as a pudding. He wanted to devour

her, to dominate her and to possess her whole body with
his. But when her delicious body was fully exposed to
him and he could not stop himself from exploring the
contours of her velvet skin, she took his hands in hers,
telling him, again, to slow down and enjoy the waiting.

Yet, as she moved away from him she swayed and
pouted, and her smouldering eyes were sending Blake a
far different message. He growled, an unfamiliar low
groan, deep in his throat that he had not heard himself
utter before. He was, he realised, totally bewitched by
her. How long would she play this game with him?

Now she moved in closer to him, so that he could
feel her softness through his shirt, and began to unbutton
his breeches. With a practised skill she looked into his
eyes and smiled as she helped him with the fastenings
and peeled away his garments. She kissed his cheek and
whispered into his ear, 'Now your under-drawers, put
them over there on that chair and let me see what you're
really made of.'

When he turned back to face her she was stretched
out on the bed, completely naked, with her arms above
her head and her legs gently moving and swishing on
the shiny red cover. Her long black hair, now unpinned,
tumbled across the white linen pillow shams. She gazed
at him as he moved, naked, towards the bed, gave a gentle
nod, a tiny smile and she murmured softly, 'Well, now,
Blake, what do you want to do next?'

He could not contain himself. His throat closed as
every sinew in his body strained to take her for his own.
Involuntarily, he shook his head slightly, trying to deny
the power she held over him, the strength of this brutal

animal desire within him. Clara continued to smile gently, and now her whole body was moving and squirming over the slippery, sensuous satin. 'Blake,' she whispered, 'why do you hesitate? What are you waiting—'

Her whispers were stifled as his body covered hers and he drove relentlessly into hers, loosening his caged passions and giving himself up to his adolescent instincts and desires. Clara was the most beautiful creature he had ever seen. Her naked body, soft and white and yielding, was a symphony for all his senses. She smelled of a rose garden in full flower and tasted of fine French wine. Her soft murmurings, intent on soothing and calming his desperate passions, only served to inflame them further, and her velvet skin, moving in harmony with his urgent hunger, drove him wild with desire.

Young, strong and virile, he could not have enough of Clara's seductive body, he could not sate his passion. Once spent, he was quick to recover and take her again. And again. And when he was finally, finally exhausted, he slept.

But not for long. For Clara woke him and took his hands in hers again. 'Now, my young stallion, let me teach you a little about a woman's body. Let me show you how to tease and tempt a wife so that she will never look for pleasure outside your marriage bed. Such strong hands and searching lips must learn how to be gentle . . .'

That smile again and those wide bewitching eyes! How could he resist her? Slowly she guided his exploration and further discovery of her body into an adventure he found amazing and wondrous until – he did not know why or how or when exactly – he was aware that it was he and not Clara in control. She was lost in a writhing, whimpering submission, moving her body with his in a rhythmic joining together that enhanced the wonder of his newly discovered power.

Then Clara was panting, no, not panting, but giving out small harsh cries from the back of her throat, pulling her knees high and clasping her ankles around his sweating back. Her hands snaked over his damp skin, nails digging into his flesh, then her flat palms pressed against his muscled rump to urge him on to drive deeper into this most exquisite captivity.

Her body arched beneath him, surprising him with her strength. A prolonged strangled cry made him slow. Then she subsided and sank back on to the bed, sighing deeply. He stopped and rolled off her, seeing her face and body relax and flop. He lay beside and watched her in the lamp-light. She became tranquil and the lines of age etched about her eyes and mouth were softened and less obvious.

Her eyes opened suddenly and surprise creased her forehead. 'That should not have happened. My job is to . . .' Quickly, she glanced at him, lying full length on his side, his head resting on one hand. 'You didn't – finish. You must – you must carry on.' She reached out to pull him back across her, but he resisted.

'No. No, I said! Leave me be.' His desire for her was already subsiding. She had been a good teacher for him and had done her job well. And she was lovely, very lovely. But, he thought, she did this all the time, for Sir William, for other men perhaps, for her living. He sat up on the side of the bed and turned up the lamp.

'Why do you do this, Clara?' he asked.

'Why? Why?' She sounded irritated by his question. 'Why do you think?'

'But you are a beautiful woman and you have some wealthy and well-connected clients. Couldn't you get out of this and marry one of them? I'm sure you must have had offers.'

She sat up quickly, supporting her full breasts with an arm. 'You wouldn't understand. You're just a boy still.'

Blake twisted to face her and placed his hand between her thighs. 'Just a boy, am I?' He did not resist when she moved his hand away.

She answered, 'Well no, not now, maybe. You're a man and marriage is for men. They get the best deal out of any marriage.' She thought for a moment and added as an afterthought, 'Unless they are very lucky.'

'Has no one ever offered for you?'

'A few.'

'Well then?' He got up, passed her a shawl and pulled on his under-drawers.

Clara hugged the fine lacy wool about her shoulders and said bluntly, 'You don't know what marriage can mean for women – to – to be owned like a slave by some man. My father was a kind and gentle man but he died young when my sister and I were small children. And Mama had no means to carry on alone.'

'Ah, I see. Did your father not leave anything for her?'

'Our house and a small income; the reason why my stepfather married her.' She gave an involuntary shudder. 'He was a brutish man who beat us when we did not do as he demanded.'

Blake covered his eyes with his hand. He could never imagine beating a woman for any reason whatsoever. 'And you had no choice but to stay with him,' he stated quietly. 'I'm sorry.'

'Yes. So were we. Mama was older than he was, but he married her and then treated her as his housekeeper, and me and my sister as his – his servants.' Her voice faltered. 'He had women too, who visited the house to share his bed.'

'Oh, Clara, how awful for you.'

'It was so much worse for Mama,' she whispered. 'She challenged him one day and he beat her so badly that she never recovered. Her spirit was broken. She just took to her bed. And then, of course, without Mama to protect us, he began to take a carnal interest in my sister . . .' Clara choked on the words.

'You mean he violated her? His own stepdaughter?' Blake felt sick with anger.

Clara nodded briefly, biting her lower lip. 'When my turn came, I knew that I must leave him and Grace helped me. She had nursed my mother and when Mother died we both left. I would have starved if it hadn't been for Grace. Grace is good to her girls and being here is better than being a laundry-girl in the workhouse.'

'But what happened to your poor sister?'

'She escaped before I did, with a local farm hand. They married and took a sailing ship to the Americas.' Clara held her head high and continued, 'I am – now – quite alone in this world, and being here with Grace is my choice.'

'I see.'

'No, I do not think you do because you are a man. When women marry they become a chattel of their husbands, like a cooking pot or a plough.' Suddenly her frowning face relaxed and she smiled. 'Enough of this, I am beginning to sound like Grace.' She ran her fingers lightly down his naked spine. 'You are a fine young man, Blake. And I am sure you will find a lovely girl to marry and you will be kind to her.' She added lightly, 'If I were younger and if you asked me, I should marry you myself!'

He twisted round to kiss her perfumed hair. 'Can I come back and see you?'

'Can you pay my price?'

'I don't mean for this. I am planning on getting my own girl to love and marry one day. I mean to talk, as a friend.'

'A friend? Not likely, lad! Grace would soon see you off!'

'Then I shall just have to become Grace's friend too, shan't I?'

'Away with you! You have too much charm for your own good. Go on. Get dressed now. I have given you too much of my time. Sir William and his friends will be waiting for you downstairs.'

Blake kissed her again, this time on the cheek. 'Thank you, Clara. Thank you for everything.'

Dawn was breaking when Sir William and his party finally left Grace's. Blake gazed out of the carriage window for the first half-hour then slept soundly as it rattled its way across countryside and moor. The school was quiet as he climbed in through the buttery window and took a piece of cold pie from the pantry on his way to his cold, hard, dormitory bed.

In the weak morning light he looked about the building. It was too small, too confined a place for him now. He wanted to be out of it. He wanted freedom from book learning and neat suits of clothes. He wanted the open air, hard physical work and a girl of his own to love. Yes, a girl of his own to love. That's exactly what he wanted now.

'Mama.' He bent to kiss her on both cheeks and she looked up, momentarily startled.

'Blake! You're home so soon! The stagecoaches get faster and faster these days.'

'They do, Mama. We had a fine team of horses for most of the way, thank Heaven. It was hellish dusty and crowded.'

'Blake, your language! What have you been learning at that expensive school?'

Blake smiled to himself and was glad his mama did not know. 'How are you, Mama?'

School had finished for the summer and Blake knew that this was the last time he would be taking the stage home. The July sun was warm and his mother was sitting in the garden under the shade of a leafy walnut tree. As he'd walked across the grass to join her he'd thought how attractive she looked in a light printed-cotton dress trimmed with white lace.

Suddenly he felt fiercely protective of her. Somehow he would find Luther Dearne and make him pay for the murder of his father. He would see justice done, he would! If the constables and magistrates could not help him, then he must do it for himself, for himself and for his mama.

'Me? Bah! I am in fine health,' his mama replied. She was sitting at a small wickerwork table going through a substantial ledger and sipping a tall glass of iced tea. 'But let me look at you. It seems so long since I saw you last.' She tilted her head back to take in his full height, and studied him shrewdly for a moment. 'You are taller. And no longer a boy. No. You have grown manly like your papa in these past months.' She stood up to get the measure of him and lifted her arms to place her hands on his shoulders. 'My! What a fine man you have become. So tall and broad and strong – your father would be very proud of you.'

Blake took off his linen jacket and wide-brimmed straw hat and sat down, glancing at the open pages on the wicker table. 'What's this you're doing?'

'I'm looking after your papa's business for you.'

'Doesn't Mr Ephraim do that for us?'

'*Ja*. He manages the warehouse and office in Hull. And he does that very well. As good as when Papa was here.'

'So why do you have this ledger here?'

'Ah yes, the ledgers. I do as much for Ephraim as I did for your papa. Together we make sure we have no more fraud, *ja*? I look after the business for you.'

Blake laughed. 'The business belongs to you, Mama.'

'Only until you are twenty-one, and then it is yours. That is what your papa wished. By then you will have a university education and be a proper English gentlemen. *Ja*?'

Blake was silent for a while until his mama prompted him with another '*Ja?*'

'*Yes*, Mama. *Yes*. We are English now.'

Ingrid Svenson knew her only son, indeed her only child, well. 'What is it, Blake? You are not happy with what I have said? Shall I call Lucy for more tea?'

'No, Mama. No tea.' He flung himself down on the grass and looked up at her with a heavy sigh. 'I don't want to go to university. I want to – hell, I don't know what I want to do for sure yet, but I know it is not more studying. Book work is not for me, Mama.' There was a pleading tone in his voice. He knew this was going to be difficult.

'But you are so good at it. Your headmaster says so in his letters!'

'It isn't what I want to do, Mama,' he said simply.

'Oh, Blake, no. It would be such a waste.' His mama sounded disappointed at first but then she brightened. 'So, do you want to work in the warehouse? With Ephraim? That is good also, he will teach you instead of your schoolmasters. That is good.'

'Maybe,' he conceded, 'but later, when I'm older. I . . . I have things to do first.'

'What – things to do? What are you talking about?'

'I . . . I don't know, yet. Perhaps work on the keels in the Humber as I have done in the school holidays.' He paused before adding slowly, 'And go upstream, follow the canals through to the industrial towns in the South Riding. I have friends there now. Friends from school.'

'Upstream? Inland!' His mama raised her voice. 'You mean the towns near Mexton Lock, don't you? Where your papa was killed. Bah! Now I understand what you are saying. You wish for revenge. This is for revenge, isn't it?'

Blake grimaced. His mama was so perceptive. 'I have unfinished business there, Mama.'

'No, Blake, no! I will not allow you to do this. The waterways are dangerous. And that part of the canal is notorious for crime. There are so many thieves and vagabonds. That . . . that Dearne man had – has – many friends. They will kill you as well. No, I will not let you do this! I do not wish to lose my son as well as my husband.'

'And you won't, Mama. I promise. Look at me! I am a man now. I can take care of myself.'

'You are still a boy of sixteen even though you look like a man.'

They were both silent for a moment, then Blake spoke quietly. 'I have to do this, Mama,' he said.

She shook her head wearily. 'You are your father's son. But I worry so much for you.'

'You don't have to, Mama. I am strong and I can fight.'

'Blake! Blake! Please! No more fighting, please! I could not bear to lose you!'

'You won't lose me, Mama. I promise. Dearne may have his cronies at Mexton Lock but I too have my friends now. I have to find out what really happened to Papa and – and – and make Dearne pay for his crimes – one way or another.'

Ingrid groaned in despair. 'But we have tried! Ephraim did all he could. The constable would not listen to us. We are strangers, we are foreigners. They would not – will not – help us!'

Blake kept his voice low but the steeliness of his tone was evident as he responded, 'Then we shall have to help ourselves, shan't we?'

'Blake, do not do this! We cannot change the past now!'

His mama's anguish made him hesitate, and for a moment his shoulders sagged as he ran his hands through his thick fair hair. 'I have to know what really happened that night.'

His mama shook her head. 'I know. But it will do no good to anyone. I miss your father every waking minute of my life. But nothing is going to bring him back to us.'

Blake sprang to his feet, fired by the anger he felt every time he revisited the memory. 'He was murdered, Mama, and the constable did nothing. Nothing!'

'Blake, you cannot take the law into your own hands.'

'Why not? Dearne did!'

'It makes you as bad as – as he was.'

The anguish on his mama's face tore at his heart. 'Maybe I am, maybe I'm not, but Papa's death was no accident and we both know that. Yes, I want to kill that murderer Dearne for what he did to Papa. But first I want him to admit the truth about what happened that night – about the fraud and his fight with Papa and . . . and . . . yes, the shooting. I want him to admit to shooting Papa, and, by the devil, he shall!' He slammed his clenched fist on to the table, making the tea cup jump and rattle.

His mama stared at him silently for a long time. She knew now that she could not stop him. Finally, she spoke, choosing her words carefully. 'Then, my dearest son, my only son, you must do what you have to do. But I do not want to see you die like your father or be imprisoned because you could not control this anger of yours. Yes, I have anger like you have, but the years have helped me to deal with it and I have had the warehouse to occupy my thoughts. Your sporting activities in school have done the same for you, I know. Yes, you are strong and you can fight. But you must also have control. How will you control your anger, Blake, when you meet with Dearne face to face?'

'I don't know, Mama. But until then I'll labour like a man. Hard work will help to numb my pain. Try not to worry. Look at me! I am tall and strong and I know how to look after myself.' His voice took on a pleading tone. 'I have to do this. I owe it to Papa.'

'Yes, I know, and for that I love you dearly. But promise me that you will talk with Ephraim first. He hears news from the barges all the time.'

'I'll talk to Ephraim tomorrow. There is plenty of work on the canals. And in the South Riding there are coal-fields and ironworks—'

'Blake, does it have to be the South Riding? You do not have the safety of your school now. Look at you! You will stand out in the crowd. You are not one of them. The people there – they will remember you. They will ask about you and they will find out whose son you are. Bah! I have a bad feeling about this notion of yours!'

'Mama, calm yourself. No one will remember *me*—'

'They will! Your hair is so fair and your name—!'

'I was a skinny boy when Papa died and I am a grown

man now. My hair is not so flaxen. My skin will soon be as brown as a Negro's and I shall grow whiskers.'

'Bah!' Mama put her head on one side and studied his handsome, chiselled features. 'You have been thinking about this for a long time, haven't you?'

He nodded silently.

'So you really mean to go and find him?'

'Yes, Mama. I do.'

'And there's nothing more I can say to you to change your mind?'

'I'm sorry, Mama.'

'I am a mother and I have a son so I have to suffer. I have to let you go some time and watch you get yourself injured or worse. You promise me, Blake, you promise me that you will take care of yourself and that you won't forget about your dear mama?'

'As if I could! Mama, I am not crossing the sea. But this is something I . . . I have to do. I have to. I love you dearly, Mama, but now that I am grown I am my own man, and I have to make my own way in life.'

Chapter 12

Blake picked up a keel from the wharf at Goole. It was heading for Kingston upon Hull with a cargo of heavy metal axles for railway engines to be shipped down the east coast of England. The docks were busy, even busier than he remembered as a boy. He dodged and darted around mechanical hoists, wagons and horses, and heaps of coal and timber until he came to their warehouse and office.

Mr Ephraim was standing outside the wide open doors of their huge timber building, checking out a wagonload of raw pig iron that was to be loaded on to barges and hauled inland along the canals. He wore his usual sober suiting and polished black shoes, dusty from the warehouse floor, and carried, as always, a sheaf of papers. But as soon as he saw Blake approach, he waved away the wagon and a broad smile appeared from the depths of his straggly grey beard.

'How are you, Mr Ephraim?' Blake asked as the two

men shook hands cordially. 'And your dear wife and family, how are they?'

'I am well, my wife and family are healthy. The business is good. I am a happy man. And you – you are bigger than I am. A grown man. You must call me Ephraim now, like your mama does.'

'Thank you, I shall. Are you very busy? I'd like to talk if you can.'

'About the business? Of course! Come into the office.'

Blake followed him into a small room with a window that looked out on to the warehouse floor and two mahogany roll-top desks, one open for work and the other closed and locked. The walls were covered with mahogany cupboards which, Blake knew, contained shelves of precisely kept ledgers. They sat in leather upholstered, round-backed office chairs and Blake opened the conversation.

'I've decided not to go back to school, Ephraim.'

'Hah! And your mama does not approve so you have come to me to persuade her.'

'Not exactly. But you are right, Mama is not happy about it, although she accepts that there are other things I want to do.'

Ephraim nodded. 'You want to work in the business with me. Or perhaps instead of me?'

Blake laughed gently and shook his head. 'No, no. Never. I could never run it as well as you and Mama. But I do want to work.'

'Then work here. This is a good business, Blake, and it will need you one day.'

'I know, I know. And Mama is angry with me for not

wanting to do that. But this was Papa's dream. Not mine. I have my own dreams to follow.'

'Making your way in life is not a dream.' Ephraim sounded quite severe. 'In the future you will appreciate the fruits of your labour here.'

'Not my labour. Papa's labour, your labour, your fruits. And now Mama's. I want something different, something new.'

'And what is it that you want?'

'I don't know yet. That's why I need to go off and find out.' He turned suddenly to look out of the small window. The wharf was busy with men going about their business, unloading cargo, trading goods, shouting, sometimes fighting, but above all else they were living. Living. And his papa was not out there with them. He slammed his fist against the wooden panelling that lined their crowded office.

Ephraim nodded slowly. 'Ah, young Blake. My dear boy, you have this anger deep down. You need to work it out of your system, don't you?'

'Something like that, I suppose.'

'Yes, I see. You do not need my permission though.'

'No. But I need you to understand. Do you?'

'Yes, I do.'

'And I need your help to find work on the Humber.'

'Does your mama agree to this?'

Blake grimaced. 'Not exactly. I've tried to make her understand. I've tried, Ephraim, I've really tried!' He shrugged and his shoulders sagged. 'But she's my mama and I'm still her little boy.'

'Children! They always make us despair for them.'

There was a silence and then the older man asked quietly, 'You have made up your mind, haven't you?'

Blake looked directly into Ephraim's wise brown eyes and nodded, stating briefly, 'I have to do it.'

Ephraim thought for a moment. 'You could try the fly boats. They go by Thorne to the South Riding. A new carrier has set up taking fish and fresh vegetables from Lincolnshire through to the markets there. They haul non-stop for twenty-four hours and take two crews. It's hard work but as you can ride, the wages will be good—'

'Ride? Barges use heavy horses, don't they?'

'Not these! Fly boats are smaller and lighter than barges and they use Yorkshire Carriage horses. Thoroughbreds or near, fine bloodstock, I'm told, that haul for ten or twelve miles without stopping. The company keeps its own changes at horse marines on the way.'

'Yorkshire Carriages, you say? The same as those that pull the stagecoaches?'

'They're the best ones to keep up the pace. You drive them at a trot most of the time. But at night when the canal traffic stops you can ride them even faster. So they need men who can ride as well as being strong enough to labour.'

'A little different from the usual rough types on the barges, I'll wager,' Blake observed.

'Do not underestimate them, Blake. They are tough men who know their business. Manufacturing in the South Riding is expanding fast and the people there are hungry.'

A gleam came into Blake's eyes. Fly boats through to the busy towns in the South Riding! Fast, quiet and travelling at night. It would be a perfect cover for him to find out the lie of the land around Mexton Lock, to find out more about Luther Dearne and to work out how best to corner him and challenge him.

This is fate for me, Blake thought. Fate has presented me a way of confronting Dearne with my father's death and dealing with him once and for all. Luther Dearne is going to pay for what he did, and I shall not rest until he has.

Ephraim was right about the crews. They were strong men who rode well and worked hard and they expected the same from others in their teams. He passed easily for a local man now, thanks to his South Riding schooling. He knew the local dialect and geography. However, his arresting good looks ensured that he continued to stand out in any crowd.

Although his hair was no longer the flaxen blond of his boyhood, it had grown into a striking golden colour that took on lighter streaks in the summer sun. And it was still thick and silky so that it flopped over his brow if he didn't keep it cut. He covered it most of the time with a workman's cap. Now in his seventeenth year, he could labour as well as any man, and that summer he joined a crew of four that worked non-stop, two on, two off, through day and night carrying documents and cargo along the canal routes in the South Riding.

Sometimes they carried fresh fish rushed in from the North Sea, or picked up baskets of summer vegetables and salads that fetched a good price if they could get them into the early-morning markets. Return payloads were often small, honed-edge tools made by the Riding's numerous little mesters and bound for ships going to London or Newcastle.

His stamina was good, but not the same as the older, more experienced men who made up the crew. The hours were long and the work arduous and so for that first summer when he was not at the rudder or riding the horse, he was often sleeping in the small cabin off the rear cockpit. Timetables ruled his life and there was no respite for social visits to his friends.

They passed through Mexton Lock at night on the way into the towns, and it was often late evening before their return. The older men saw to changing the horse while he stayed at the rudder and there was little time to talk to anyone except the lock keeper. But he had not forgotten his quest and he watched and listened, biding his time as summer turned to autumn, and waiting for his chance.

Winter came early that year and a bout of fiercely cold weather well before Christmas froze several stretches of canal. The flyers were suspended and the company offered Blake work on coal barges for the winter. He would have taken it if he had not received a message from Ephraim, asking him to go home to see his mama.

He arrived in Goole expecting to hear bad news and feared the worst. His mama was in the kitchen helping Lucy make festive puddings for boiling. She was wearing a large white apron over her brown woollen day dress. He threw his hat and canvas kitbag on a nearby chair and hugged her, getting flour all over his jacket. She looked well, he thought, so what was wrong?

'Lucy,' Mama asked, 'would you make a start on plucking that goose in the scullery?'

Blake smiled at her as she bobbed a curtsey and disappeared. 'What is it, Mama?'

'Can we sit down first, Blake? Do you want some tea?'

He shook his head. 'I want to know what all this is about. Is something wrong?'

'Of course not! I just wanted to talk to you. I have made a decision.' She sat in the chair that Blake had pulled out for her.

'Well?'

She looked up into his eyes, narrowed by his furrowed brow. 'Don't be so worried, my dear. I have decided to go back to Sweden.'

Blake's jaw dropped and his eyes widened. 'I thought you liked it here?'

'I do, I do. But I want to see my cousins again. And their babies.'

Blake understood her need and his mind was in turmoil. This must be partly his fault. If he had been with her instead of following some crazed idea of his own, perhaps she would not feel the need to return to her distant relatives. 'Of course you do,' he said. 'I am so sorry, Mama. I should have stayed here with you, I didn't think—'

'Nonsense, Blake. You are young. You do not want to be looking after your mama.'

'You miss Papa very much, don't you?'

'Yes, I do.'

'So do I. Do you want me to go to Sweden with you?'

His mama shook her head slowly. 'No. Not unless you want to, dear. You have your life here.'

'You cannot travel all that way alone, Mama. I shall go with you.'

'I shall not be alone. Lucy will come with me.'

This was another surprise for Blake. 'Lucy is going to live in Sweden?'

'Oh, Blake! No, of course not. I am only going to *visit* my cousins. My home is here now and I shall come back.' She stretched out her hand to pat his comfortingly. 'You must stay in England and do what you have to do. But we have to talk about the warehouse, and what to do with this house while I am gone.'

'Will you be gone for long?'

'I do not know, dear. I will write to you from Sweden.'

'Have you spoken with Ephraim?'

She nodded. 'He manages our business so well now, and his eldest boy is a great help to him. We have no worries about that. But I want to know if you will be living here while I am away.'

'I . . . I wasn't planning on that, Mama,' he said cautiously.

She smiled. 'Just as I thought. I do not want to leave the house empty for so long a time. So, if you don't want to live here, I will make arrangements to let it. And if you do want to come back this way to work, you can lodge with Ephraim and his family until I return.'

Blake nodded in agreement. 'You have thought of everything, Mama.'

'Yes, I have been thinking of this visit since – well, since your papa died. You will promise to write to me, Blake?'

Blake got to his feet and bent to put his arms around her and kiss her. 'Of course I shall.'

So, early in the following spring, Ingrid Svenson and her maid Lucy sailed from Hull across the North Sea to Sweden. The flyer service on the canals started up again as soon as the hard frosts were over and Blake rejoined his old team as an experienced crew member. The waterways of the South Riding became his home and he came off the barge only when it was laid up for repairs, or a cargo had been delayed. Blake Svenson became a part of canal life; hard working, sometimes hard drinking, but all the time blending easily with others who made their living on the waterways of the South Riding.

Chapter 13

1844

Lissie Dearne, in her fourteenth year, feared she would have to leave Miss Kirby's soon to go and work all day in the kitchen of the Navigator Inn. Already, her evenings and Saturdays were spent there as a kitchen maid, leaving Sunday to clean up their own house for her mam.

Dad said Mickey Jackson paid part of Miss Kirby's school fee for Lissie so that she could work at the Navvy. She didn't mind. She knew her dad could not get much work nowadays and that money was short. But she did like going to school and would do anything to stay.

Miriam liked Lissie going to school as well because she helped her with the duties Miss Kirby gave her in the schoolroom. As the elder of her two senior pupils, Miriam was often asked to take over the schoolroom to give Miss Kirby a break. While Miriam enjoyed being left in charge, she needed Lissie to keep the children occupied, so their uneasy friendship continued.

As the days lengthened, they often dawdled along the

towpath, lingering at bridges, watching the water traffic and chattering to each other. They were enjoying the early morning sun on a farm bridge near to Fordham when they saw the flyer approaching fast.

'That's late today,' Lissie commented. 'It should be in town for the market by now.'

'Let's stay and watch,' Miriam decided, and leaned over the low stone wall, holding her bonnet on with her hand.

The rider was crouching over the neck of his horse, with his head well down as he slowed to a canter towards the bridge. Just before he disappeared underneath, he looked up at them and smiled.

'Did you see that?' Miriam said.

Both girls dashed across to the other side in time to see him emerge, sit up straight in his saddle, let go of the reins and raise his cap to them in salute. He raked back his floppy fair hair with his fingers and replaced his cap before urging on the horse. The small barge whooshed after him leaving a turbulent wake on the glassy brown water.

'I've not seen him before, 'ave you?' Miriam commented with wide eyes. 'He's younger than the others. Handsome too, from what I could see.'

Lissie stood rigidly beside her friend, staring after him. 'He's on'y a bargeman like all the others,' she managed to say at last.

He wore the same type of cap, with a soft crown and a peak to shade his eyes. Underneath it, his hair was the lightest she had seen in the South Riding, even at the front where it was darkened by sweat from his brow. But most of all she remembered the way he combed it with his fingers, taking it straight back from his forehead and replacing his cap firmly on top of it.

The memory jarred in her mind. She had been much younger then but she remembered that night. The night when her dad had seen his dad off. Well, his dad had knocked hers down, but he'd cleared off all the same.

He had been a boy then, one of the bigger boys, a stranger who had watched everything, as she had, Lissie recalled. She remembered that the constable had called at their house and Mam had given him sherry wine. And Dad stayed home so they had a bonfire in the garden and a ham for Christmas that had lasted to Twelfth Night.

Miriam's elbow in her back brought Lissie back to the present. 'Well? Don't you?'

'Don't I what?'

Miriam sighed irritably. 'Don't you think 'e's 'andsome?'

'Oh aye,' Lissie replied. 'He's handsome all right.'

It was that same lad, that foreigner she was sure, except that the lad was now a man. But he had the same features, like his dad had, noble-like, looking like one of those Greek statues pictured in Miss Kirby's books. And his skin wasn't pockmarked or craggy, it was smooth and a glowing light brown, not the mahogany wood colour usually found among the other barge folk on the canal.

'But 'e's not from round here,' Lissie added.

'Could be from one o' the ports on the coast,' Miriam conceded.

'Why don't you ask your brother about him?' Lissie suggested. 'He'll know. He knows all the horsemen on the canal.'

'No fear! My dad would skin me alive if he found out I'd been asking about one o' the bargemen.'

'We were only watching from the bridge. That's not doing any harm, is it?'

'You don't know my dad. He thinks all men are the same and he's not soft like yours.'

'My dad's not soft,' Lissie protested.

'He is – he's daft with you anyway. 'E thinks the sun shines out o' your backside.'

'Well 'e's me dad, isn't he?'

'That's all you know,' Miriam said archly.

'What d'you mean by that?'

Unusually for Miriam, she didn't snap back at her with a smarting reply. Instead, she took her eyes off the fly boat stern receding into the distance and turned round to face Lissie. 'They 'aven't told you, 'ave they?'

'Told me what? What are you going on about?'

'Not for me to say.'

Lissie stepped closer to her so-called friend. Although she was two years younger, she was as tall as Miriam now, though not as heavily built, because Miriam was buxom like her mam and at fifteen already looked like she was a proper woman.

Lissie was 'filling out nicely' as Miriam's dad had commented that morning, but her body was fine-boned and slender, so her budding breasts and rounding bottom were more noticeable. But although the heavy house-work she did for her mam after school had made her strong, Lissie knew there were other ways to influence her lazy friend.

'You'd better tell me, or else.'

'Or else what?' Miriam laughed.

'Or else I shan't help you with the little 'uns at school and you'll have to do it all on your own.'

'Oh, Lissie, you wouldn't! You know I'm no good with the little 'uns wi'out you.'

'Only because you're bone idle, Miriam Jackson! I've showed you what you can do and you just can't be bothered.'

'Well, you do it better than me.'

'Why don't you tell Miss Kirby that then, and we can do different jobs for a change?'

'Oh, I'd be even worse in the kitchen and I hate cooking even more than I hate the little 'uns!'

'So tell me what you meant and I'll keep on helping you,' Lissie answered sharply.

'All right, all right.' Miriam looked uncomfortable.

'Go on then, tell.'

'It's nothing. Well, everyone knows anyway. And you've only got to look at you to see—'

'See what?' There was a threatening tone in Lissie's voice. 'Tell me or I'll give you a Chinese burn again!'

Quickly Miriam said, 'Everybody says the gypsies left you on your mam and dad's doorstep.'

Lissie dropped her jaw, astounded. 'What?'

'You heard.'

'It's not true. I don't believe you.'

'Look in the glass, Lissie, at that black hair o' yours.'

Lissie knew her mam didn't like her black hair. It

was thick and glossy whereas Mam's was sparse and mousy-looking. Mam often called her a little gypsy when she was cross. She didn't look anything like her mam, either. Her mam had thin lips and a bump in her nose. Lissie was already taller than her mam, and Mam had really little hands and feet. Lissie's fingers were long and she was always needing new boots for her growing feet.

She shook her head, confused and angry. She was Lissie Dearne from Mexton Lock and nobody could say otherwise. 'I'm not a gypsy,' she protested. 'I'm not! I . . . I . . . I haven't got black eyes, have I? Or dark skin?'

Miriam shrugged. It was the only thing about Lissie that she envied. That delicate, pale complexion and those large, almond-shaped, smoky-green eyes were lovely by anybody's standards. Not that she'd ever tell her that. She grimaced and muttered, 'Maybe only half gypsy then.'

Maybe she could be, Lissie thought. Maybe her mam wasn't her real mam and her real mam had been a gypsy. That would explain why her mam never liked her. But Miriam had been talking about her dad. Her dad was her real dad. He had to be! She was his little darling, not his little gypsy. She wondered if she dared ask him about it. She thought not. Dad didn't hold with her asking questions like that. 'Be seen and not heard', was his usual reply.

Lissie looked silently at Miriam trying to be superior and putting her down all the time. It was all right for her, she was the spit of her mam and with her dad's hazel eyes. Everybody said so. Her two big brothers were just like their dad as well, though Peter, the youngest, was different. It was all very confusing! Even Miss Kirby and her brother had the same nose! And what a conk that was! It was just the same as the ones in the oil paintings on their stairway.

Lissie put her hand over her nose. It didn't have a bump and it was a lot smaller than her dad's nose. Well, she thought, you couldn't expect a girl to look like her dad anyway, could you?

She stated firmly, 'My dad is my dad and don't you say no different!'

'Suit yourself,' Miriam sneered. 'But you'd better learn summat more than a Chinese burn trick, because that won't save you when the gypsies come and get you. You want to watch your back, Lissie Dearne.'

This alarmed Lissie. If her mam wasn't her real mam, what if her real mam came back for her? She shrugged bravely and moved on from the bridge, saying, 'Gypsies don't come out this way. They camp near the towns where they can get tinkering work and sell their pegs in the streets. They couldn't have left me on the step, so there!' She was pleased with this and it seemed to quieten Miriam. Anyroad, she thought, even if Mam was not her real mam, her dad was definitely her dad and he loved her.

They watched the waves washing at the canal bank subside as the fly boat disappeared out of sight, but not out of Miriam's mind. She soon forgot her taunting game with Lissie in favour of a new interest in her life. 'That fly boat rider was 'andsome though, wasn't he? Don't you think so, Lissie?'

'Yes he was,' Lissie agreed. 'Very.'

She saw Miriam's head turn quickly to look at her. 'Well don't you go getting no ideas about him, Lissie Dearne, because I saw 'im first.'

No, you didn't, Lissie thought, but wisely kept silent.

'And anyway,' Miriam continued, 'you're not old enough yet.'

'Old enough for what?'

'Y'know. Courting. And getting wed.'

'I'm nearly fourteen!' Lissie protested. 'Eliza at the farm was wed at twelve!'

'On'y 'cos the farmer wanted a good dairymaid that didn't cost 'im owt.'

'Who told you that?'

'It's what me mam says. And she says fifteen is plenty soon enough for having babbies.'

When Lissie didn't reply, Miriam explained, 'You 'ave babbies when you get wed.'

'You don't allus have to have babbies. My mam on'y had me.'

'Aye, well, everybody knows about her. Sometimes it's like that. 'As yer mam told you about kissing yet?'

'Kissing? No, why should she?'

''Cos if you let a lad kiss you, you have a babby, that's why!'

'Don't be daft. Your dad is always kissing girls at the inn.'

'You watch your tongue, Lissie Dearne, or I'll thump you one.'

'Well, I've seen him do it! And they don't always have babbies.'

'That's different. I'm talking about the lads on the

canal. He kisses you and then he sticks 'is thing in you and then you 'ave a babby.'

'His thing?'

'You know – his thing.'

'What thing?'

'Oh, you know,' Miriam replied irritably. Then she paused. 'Well p'r'aps you don't 'cos you 'an't got any brothers like me. Miss Kirby's got a book about it. She keeps it in her top cupboard. I'll show you when we get to school, it's got long words in it and weird drawings and everything. You're good at reading so you can tell me what it says.'

'Why don't you just ask your mam?'

'She says I'll find out when I get wed. That's when you do it.'

'Do what?'

'Y'know. Like when we 'ave the stallion to the mares in the stable.'

'Oh, that.' Lissie blushed. If she accidentally caught sight of any of the animals coupling, her dad dragged her away and told her not to look. Maybe she would get down that book Miriam had seen and find out more.

From that day, Miriam was always anxious to get down to the towpath quickly after school, hoping to catch sight of the fly boat on its way downstream back to Thorne. Lissie was more wary. She remembered the night of the fight with her dad and thought that the lad might be a bad lot like his dad. But he was handsome all right, tall and straight-backed with muscled thighs you could see outlined through his riding breeches.

On one such day, a fine summer afternoon, there was

a bit of a commotion by the bridge and both girls gathered up their long skirts and broke into a run to see
what was going on. The horse reins were slack and the
fly boat was floating idly on the water. Two men were
on the bankside, their attention taken up completely by
their horse.

'What's up?' demanded Miriam as soon as they were
close enough to be heard.

The elder of the two men looked up. 'Mind your own
business,' he snapped, 'and clear off.'

Lissie hung back. The foreigner was there, half-hidden
by the front of the horse as he examined one of its
hooves. She heard his voice as he called to his mate.

'It's no good. He's lost a shoe. I'll have to walk him
on to the smithy at Mexton Lock. It's not far.'

His mate replied, 'You get off then. I'll wake the others
and we'll tow the boat after you.'

Miriam stepped forward importantly. 'My brother's the
smithy at Mexton.'

'I told you two to clear off,' the older man growled.

'Come on, Miriam, let's go,' Lissie begged, anxious to
avoid any trouble.

The foreigner straightened, patting the horse's neck
and whispering soothing words to him. Then he said to
Miriam, 'Walk with me, if you like.' He gave her a wide
smile and Miriam immediately swayed up to him and
replied, 'I don't mind if I do.'

Then he looked past her to Lissie and added, 'And
your friend? Will you walk with me too?'

Lissie hesitated. He hadn't seen her at all on the night
of the fight so he didn't even know she existed, but at

the same time her dad had told her not to talk to the bargemen. 'I . . . I don't know,' she hesitated.

'Oh come on, Lissie,' Miriam whined. 'It's on our way 'ome, i'n't it?'

'I . . . we . . . don't know him,' she hedged.

The foreigner smiled again and, keeping hold of the reins, took a couple of steps towards her. 'My name's Blake. And yours is Lissie. We're all walking the same way so why don't we keep each other company?'

Blake? Yes, she remembered that. His other name was foreign though. I expect that's why he doesn't say it, she thought. But he certainly didn't sound like a bargeman. He sounded more like Miss Kirby's brother. More like the gentry.

'You can lead the horse if you want,' he offered.

Lissie nodded her thanks. He seemed respectable enough, but you couldn't be too careful with bargemen, her dad had said. 'All right,' she agreed, taking hold of the long reins. She threw them over her back so she could walk closer to the horse's head. He was a fine beast, well groomed and strong but not as big as some of the old cart horses that hauled barges on the canal. 'What's his name?' she asked.

'Atlas.'

Blake was walking a few yards behind and Miriam fell into step with him and said, 'That's a funny sort o' name for a horse. My other brother's the horse marine at Mexton and I 'a'n't heard o' that one before,' she said.

'Oh, Miriam, don't you know anything?' Lissie replied over her shoulder. 'Atlas holds up the sky on his shoulders. I've seen it in one of Miss Kirby's books.'

'Books! Huh, that's all you think about. Wait till you're *fifteen* like me. You won't be reading books all the time then.' She turned her smiling face to her handsome companion and fingered the curls of hair escaping from her bonnet. Then she made a show of lifting the hem of her skirts away from the ground so that Blake could see her shapely, stockinged leg above her dusty boots. 'How old are you, Blake?'

'Older than you, miss,' he replied gravely.

Miriam persisted. 'You can call me Miriam, if you like. Can I ride Atlas?'

'Miriam!' Lissie held her breath while she waited for his reply. That girl had the cheek of the devil!

'I don't think so. Not today,' Blake said.

'Ah, go on,' Lissie heard Miriam's wheedling voice. 'You can lift me on to his back.'

'I said no.'

Good, thought Lissie. Miriam should know better than to ask, when the horse had lost one of its shoes. 'You can come and help me lead, if you want,' she offered. But her friend wasn't really interested in the horse. She was only interested in Blake.

Lissie wondered why he worked the fly boats. It was clear to her that he belonged more with people like the Kirbys or even landed folk. Miriam pranced around and prattled on about the Navigator and her brothers, and how Miss Kirby had put her in charge of the little ones at school. Blake said very little in response. In fact he was so quiet that Lissie thought he had dropped back to the barge for some reason and turned her head to look.

She was surprised at how close he was walking behind her, and for a few seconds her smoky-green eyes met his. His eyes were blue, a bright clear blue like the sky in summer, and she recoiled at the intensity of his stare. He smiled at her, a friendly grin that showed a set of good teeth. Lissie thought, for a fleeting moment, that he was the most beautiful man she had ever seen in her short life.

'Are you tired yet?' he asked her. 'Shall I take over?'

'No, thank you. I can handle him. He's a quiet beast and no trouble at all.' Lissie reached up to pat his neck as Atlas plodded on down the towpath. Glancing over to her friend, she noticed Miriam scowling, no doubt because Blake's attention was diverted from her. She turned her concentration back to the horse, not wanting to upset Miriam too much by encouraging Blake, but it made no difference.

He drew level with her and nodded in the direction of Atlas. 'He is obviously very happy with you leading him. Do you like him?'

'Oh yes, I love all the canal boat horses. They're so big and strong, but gentle at the same time.' She thought for a moment. 'Actually, your fly boat horses aren't that big, are they? What are they like to ride?'

'They're not racehorses, that's for sure. But they're fast for their size, and they have amazing stamina. That's why we use them.'

Miriam was not going to be left out of a conversation about horses and caught up with them, interrupting shrilly, 'My brother says they're carriage horses really, and pure bred, and that the fly boat company won't use any others.'

'That's right. He's a good horse marine, your brother. One of the best. Do you want a turn leading the horse?'

'No, ta. The reins'll dirty my dress.'

'Well, you could run ahead and ask your brother to get the fire hot in his forge. We haven't got time to waste.'

Miriam seized her chance. 'Lissie, why don't you do that? You're better at running than me.'

'Your ma says we should never leave each other on our own.'

'I won't be on my own. I'll be with Blake.'

'And your dad says you haven't to talk to any bargemen, 'cept the ones he knows.'

Miriam became irritated. 'Well my brother knows him, doesn't he? 'Cos he shoes the horses. That's just the same and—'

'You're doing just fine as you are, Lissie,' Blake interrupted. 'Unless you'd rather run on ahead.'

'No, thank you. This is fun.' Lissie continued with her task and smiled to herself as she imagined the scowl returning to Miriam's face. Do her good not to get her own way for a change, she thought. If she had offered to lead the horse, Lissie might have gone on ahead as she'd suggested.

But then, maybe not. She was beginning to like this foreigner. She liked the way he spoke now he was fully grown up. She liked the way he presented himself. He was a proper gentleman and he knew how to handle Miriam and her manipulative ways.

Yes, Lissie thought, she really liked him now. Well, she would always like the way he looked when he was riding a horse. Commanding. Yes, that was it. As though he was in charge of everything and gave the orders. And close up he looked even better. He was obviously tough and strong, all the fly boat men were. But he was tall with it, not like the stocky, thickset miners from around Mexton. He had a kind of presence in the way he walked, like he was proud of who he was, even if he was a foreigner, and he'd challenge any man who crossed his path. Looking at him gave her an unusual kind of thrill that she had not experienced before in all her thirteen and a half years.

'That's settled then,' Blake concluded. 'We'll all walk Atlas together. It's not much further now anyway.'

When they arrived at the smithy Miriam's brother yelled at her to stay out of the way and get inside the inn to help her ma. Petulantly she did as she was bid, pushing Lissie ahead of her. Lissie's dad was away on the canals at the time and had been gone for more than a week now, so her mam would be at Rosa's cottage. At least she would be in a good mood when she arrived home later today, Lissie thought.

'Thank you kindly for your help,' Blake said with a gentlemanly bow before the two girls walked on. He watched them hurrying towards the Navigator Inn and disappear round the back. Perhaps Lissie lodged at the inn with Miriam's family? Nice girl, he thought. A pleasant, uncomplicated country girl with the finest green eyes he had ever seen. And black hair too. He had noticed how dark her hair was as it escaped from her white cotton bonnet to frame her pretty face.

She was a few years younger than he was but he

hoped he'd see her again. That was something to look forward to, he thought, as he held on to Atlas's head, whispering gently to him while the new shoe was hammered into his hoof.

Miriam, the older girl, was a saucy young madam, he thought. Too pushy for her own good. Nothing like her young friend Lissie. Lissie was going to be a cracking woman when she was grown a bit more. She was a beautiful girl now, and one that greatly interested him. Her manner intrigued him. With her sharp wit and a wisdom beyond her years, she would be a woman to be reckoned with, he thought. He wanted to know her better. And he would, he decided. He had not worked out how he could accomplish this aim yet, but such practical details never worried Blake Svenson. He would find a way.

The fly boat, hauled by its crew, arrived shortly afterwards and they were soon on their way down to Thorne and the Trent, leaving the South Riding behind them until the next trip. Blake took a lasting image with him, an image of a young girl, with black hair, alabaster skin and an arresting pair of almond-shaped, smoky-green eyes.

He felt a thrill rising in his loins as he thought of her and he wondered how long it would be before he saw her again. She was young still, and so was he. But how much time did he have? She could be wed to some miner by this time next year! He could not, would not, let that happen!

Yet he had unfinished business to complete first. Business that must be dealt with before he could let any girl into his life to distract and cloud his judgement.

Business that would keep him working on this waterway until he had finished it, and finished with Dearne. Blake grew restless with impatience. He was eager to move on, to set himself up in the South Riding and be part of it. He knew where Dearne lived even though he was often away. Silently, he vowed to find out where Dearne was working and confront him soon, so that he could get on with his life.

Chapter 14

Quickly and quietly Blake slid down from the horse's back, released it from the harness and led it through the open door of the livery stable.

The horse marine was already waiting with a fresh horse. 'Where's Thomas?' he asked.

'Taking the rudder for a change. My name's Blake.'

The horse marine held out his hand. 'Peter Jackson. Call me Pete.'

Blake shook his hand. 'Do you live here?'

Pete nodded and raised his eyes to look at the ceiling. 'I sleep up there, next to the hayloft. My father owns the inn and my brother's the blacksmith.'

Blake nodded and yawned. The hours before dawn were the worst for staying awake, but he had volunteered to ride this stretch so that he would be the one to change the horse at Mexton. 'Pleased to meet you at last,' he said, yawning again. 'I am usually sleeping as we pass here.'

Pete grinned. 'You'll get used to it. I'll walk your fresh horse up the towpath if you like. You'll soon be through – the lock's emptying already.'

'Thanks.' Blake stroked and slapped the horse's glossy coat as they walked. 'Nice beast. Does he have a name?'

'This one's Titan. He'll see you right on to town and they'll look after him well there. Are you from these parts?'

'Further up-country. You?'

'Father's had the inn here since I were a nipper.'

So, thought Blake, this was the stable lad who had helped him on the night his papa was shot. He was the son of the landlord at the Navigator. But he did not appear to be a surly rogue like his father. Pete obviously loved his horses and didn't like them ill-treated or starved.

He stayed silent as Pete walked with him and talked about his stables, leading the horse, apparently relaxed in the stillness of the cool night air. He was not anything like his father, Blake decided, and wondered how much he knew about Dearne.

The gushing water escaping through the sluices of the lock gates slowed as they reached the far end, and Blake asked, 'Do you know anybody by the name of Dearne around here?'

'Luther Dearne? Aye, I know him. He lives yon side in the woods. What do you want with him?'

'I heard he does a bit of dealing up and down the canal.'

'I'd stay away from him if I were you. He's a bad lot.'

'Do you know where he is now?' Blake persisted.

'No idea. I don't think I'd tell you if I did. He's an out and out rogue, that man, even though he is a mate of my father's.'

'So, he's not there now then.'

Pete shook his head. 'He used to go downstream to the Humber a lot, but he gave that up a while back. He had a bit o' trouble wi' 'is dealers down that way. Now he goes upstream Sheffield way, I believe. I allus know the minute he's back though, because he calls in at the school on his way home. My sister's there and he brings them bolt ends of cloth for the sewing.'

'Your sister, eh? Where is this school, Pete?'

'I'm not sure I should tell you that. All those young girls and you such a virile young man . . .' Pete was grinning but he changed the subject and asked, 'Are you riding or Thomas?'

'I am, but only to the next village. There's a dairy there where we generally pick up some fresh milk and butter for the boat. Then we swap crews and I get some sleep.'

'That sounds like Fordham. Not far then.'

'Is there anything interesting at Fordham?'

'Nowt really, just a farm, a chapel and a collection of houses. Nice ones though. A doctor lives in one . . .'

I know, thought Blake, I even know which house. You told me all those years ago and you don't remember.

'. . . and that's where the school is,' Pete went on with a smile. 'It's a dame school at t' far end. A cut from the Swinborough estate joins the canal just past there. It carries coal from Sir William's mines down to the main canal for his ironworks in town. There's an alehouse too.

Started with a brewer selling to bargemen from his back door—'

Blake interrupted him. 'Sir William, did you say? Would that be Sir William Swinborough?'

'The same. You heard of him?'

Blake nodded and Pete went on, 'He's got coal and iron right under his feet. So 'e's got money, plenty o' money – the lucky bugger.' Pete fitted the heavy neck collar around Titan's thick neck. 'Whoa, fella. Steady now.'

Between them they tightened up the harness and saddle. 'There, Blake, he's ready. Thomas is just opening the lock gates. I'll pick up the tow ropes if you like.' Pete returned quickly and fixed the twin ropes to Titan's harness. He gave Blake a leg up into the saddle and the horse a friendly slap on his rear. 'Away you go.'

'Thanks. See you on the way back?'

'Not me. One o' my brothers, mebbe. I've 'ad enough o' working fo' me dad around here. I'm off to some stables near Donny to groom racehorses for the track. No more heavy horses for me,' Pete grinned.

Blake saw the excitement in his eyes and felt elated for him. 'Good luck, Pete,' he said. 'You deserve the best and I hope good fortune comes your way.' He flexed his shoulders and took up the reins, thinking that Pete was right to move on. He didn't fit in with the thuggish ways of his father and brothers. But he had given Blake some vital information about Dearne. Dearne had moved his crooked trading from the coast to the towns, and he had a customer at Fordham.

He rode on. They were behind schedule on this trip. Their milk and butter were in the shade of the small bridge at Fordham, waiting to be exchanged for a coin. But the farmer had taken his cows back to the fields after morning milking and the village was quiet. Blake's mind was full of plans as the sun crept into the cloudy sky in the east behind him. He kept riding. He was past his tiredness now and his mind was racing.

The waterways of the South Riding were full of contrasts, cutting through rural farms one minute then passing pit heads and furnaces the next. Dawn mists from the meadows swirled and mixed with smoke from the factory chimneys. Drystone walling and hedges gave way to rows and rows of brick cottages that housed miners and ironworkers and their families.

There was a future here for him, he thought. Furnaces and forges excited him and he wanted to be part of it. He could live here. He could mine the coal, or smelt the iron or hone the tools. This was more exciting than loading notes and ships' manifests. This was his future. But a future that could only be his after he had dealt with Dearne. First he had to confront his father's murderer. Fordham was where he needed to be. He had to find a way to get there.

As the sun rose on his back, canal traffic thickened and slowed until the flyer was forced to idle downstream of Tinsley for the morning. Bargemen were gathered in small groups on the bank and word spread quickly of a breakdown up ahead. A winching crane had jammed the previous day and the wharf was thick with heavy barges waiting to unload. Blake moored the boat, fed Titan, then joined the others already slaking their thirsts at a nearby alehouse.

Thomas shoved a tankard in his direction. 'No point in waiting. That lot in front'll be all day an' we got fish on board. We got t' get the fish off to market.'

'Can't we get through at all?' asked Blake. 'We don't need winches to unload.'

'It's chaos down there today. I've bin talking to t' land-lord here and 'e's got us a couple o' carrier carts. We'll leave the boat 'ere and take what we can by road.'

'What about the return load?'

'I dunno what it is till we get to the Tinsley office.'

Thomas, a brawny ex-sailor with a wife and family back home in Hull, had already finished his ale. 'Blake, you come wi' me, lad, and you two tek t'other cart. Mek sure you tek plenty o' ice wi' t' fish. If we've got good 'osses we'll get it to market in time.'

Blake gulped down his tankard of ale and followed. After loading the carts, he took the reins of a pair of heavy draught horses.

'Want some o' this, lad?' Thomas offered him some tobacco to chew.

He shook his head. 'D'you know around these parts, Tom?'

'Aye, a bit. What you looking for?'

'I came to a fight here once. Big crowd.'

'Oh aye, they likes their fights round here.' He gave Blake a searching look. 'You done any fighting yerssen?'

'A bit. Sparring, mainly. For Dan Sanders.'

'I've 'eard of 'im. Negro, i'n't 'e? Used to t' be a prize fighter hissen.'

'That's him.' Blake paused. 'We went on to a – a country house after. You know, men only.'

'Whorehouse, you mean?'

'Yes, I suppose it was. For men of means though. You know, gentry and the like.'

'Did it have a name?'

'Grace's. They just called it Grace's.'

'Never 'eard of it. Ask in the office, it's not far now. Keep them 'osses going – we don't want t' sun on this fish.'

The wharf side was in as much chaos as the canal. Loads coming in by the new railway for shipping to the coast by barge were already queuing and they were turning away all smaller traffic until the following day.

Tom came out of the company office with a smile on his face. 'No payload until t' morrer. I'm back to the flyer to get some sleep. The rest on yer can do what yer like as long as y're back 'ere by six in t' morning.'

Blake set off to explore some old haunts. He hitched a lift on a carrier heading towards the fringe of town and from there walked to Grace's. The terrain became familiar and he recognised landmarks from his previous visit when he made an early morning exit with Sir William in his carriage.

He grinned, as he had done before, when he caught a glimpse of Swinborough Folly, a tall stone tower standing proud in the landscape, built to celebrate the defeat of Napoleon. It was not that long ago he'd been here, but it seemed a lifetime. He was just a schoolboy then, but now he was a working man.

There were not many factories out here and the houses were bigger. They were quite close together but some had tracks around them, leading to carriage houses. It was after lunch when he arrived at Grace's. The canvas bag slung over his shoulder was heavy and ice-cold water was dripping from it down his back. Grace's would be quiet, he reckoned, but somebody would be up and about. He whistled cheerily as he went round to the back door.

'Who are you? What d'you want?' A young girl, wearing an old work dress and grubby cotton smock, was carrying a bucket of ashes across the backyard.

'Urgent delivery for Grace. It won't keep. I've got to get it in some cold water.'

'There's a pump at the sink in the scullery.' The girl tossed her head in the direction of an open door.

Blake tipped the slippery fish out of his bag and into the deep stone sink. Some of the ice was still there under its calico wrapping. Huge chunks of it had been packed around the boxes in the hold of the flyer. It had stayed cold enough down there during the journey but under the hot sun it had melted fast.

The young girl returned with an empty bucket. 'Pooh! What's that when it's at 'ome?'

'Cod. Best fish in the sea. Ever tasted it?'

She shook her head and peered in the sink. 'Don't think so. Ugly, i'n't it?'

Blake began to pump fresh cold water over it. The sound of leather shoes on the flags behind him made him stop.

'What is going on in here? I heard a man's voice.'

'Clara?' He didn't have to look round. He remembered her soft husky tones.

'Yes. Who are you?'

He turned. She was wearing a light-grey print cotton dress and a white lace cap. Just as handsome as before, but in the light of day through the open doorway he was reminded sharply of the age gap between them.

'Blake? Blake!' she laughed. 'Yes, it is you, isn't it? Well, I don't believe my eyes! You're so much bigger, and broader – and – and – well, you're a full-grown man now, aren't you?'

He grinned. 'I am. I'd give you a hug but I'm a bit – er . . .'

Clara wrinkled her nose. 'Yes, you are. What is that smell?'

'This fellow.' He gestured towards the sink. 'It's a present for Grace. Is she well?'

Before Clara could reply, another, older voice interrupted. 'Yes she is, thank you. Quite well.' All three turned to see Grace who had joined them in the scullery. She was wearing a plain black silk afternoon dress that rustled as she moved. Her gnarled hands were covered by black lace mittens and she held a gold framed pince-nez that she used to peer into the sink.

'Is that a cod? A whole cod? I haven't seen a whole one o' those since . . .' Grace paused for a moment, remembering younger days on the east coast of Yorkshire when – well, it must be nigh on fifteen years ago – when little Lissie was born. 'Is it for us?'

'For you, ma'am,' Blake replied smartly.

'From whom?' she demanded.

'From me, of course.'

'And who, young man, are you?'

Clara exchanged glances with Blake and explained,

'He's a friend, Grace. He came to – er – see us with Sir William two years ago and – er – since then he's—'

'Do you mean he is a client?' Grace's voice had risen an octave. 'What is he doing in the scullery and why do I not know him, Clara? What has been going on?'

'Nothing, ma'am,' Blake broke in. 'Truly. I used to be at Grasse Fell school.'

Grace gave him a cold silent stare.

Clara added, 'He came to us with Sir William once. Just the once—'

'And Clara, well, Clara's was – is – we're just friends. Almost a sister to me, aren't you, Clara?' he added hastily.

'A sister, eh?' Grace examined Blake closely through her pince-nez. 'What is your name, sir?'

When Grace was satisfied he was telling her the truth, she thanked him, quite sincerely, for the cod and retreated to her upstairs parlour. Clara breathed a sigh of relief and took Blake's hand in hers.

'I warned you not to call. Grace doesn't allow gentlemen callers if they're not clients. She's very strict about it. But it is good to see you. I want to know everything you have been doing since you left Grasse Fell. Come into the kitchen, there's some game pie left over from luncheon.'

They sat at the corner of a large pinewood kitchen table and talked while the kitchen maid put on a clean apron and prepared tea for Grace's household. Blake told her about leaving school and starting on the fly boats. He also talked of his mama going to Sweden and that led to questions about his papa. So, after some hesitation on his part, and persuasion from Clara, he told her about the murder and the injustice of it all.

'You're very angry, aren't you?' Clara commented when he stopped talking to draw breath.

'Wouldn't you be?'

'Well yes, I would. But try not to let it eat at your heart so. You cannot bring him back and you have to put this search for vengeance behind you.'

'I cannot. Not until I have confronted Dearne and got the truth out of him.'

Grace's kitchen maid slid a tray across the table carrying tea to drink, sandwiches and scones. Clara poured the strong brown liquid into china cups with matching saucers. 'Do you know where he is?'

'Around here somewhere. Have you heard of a place called Fordham?'

'Of course. It's on the edge of Sir William's estates.'

'Who lives there?'

'I don't know exactly. There's a dairy farm and a chapel. The old doctor lives there and there's a dame school . . .'

'Do you know anything about the school?' Blake asked.

'The house belongs to an ironmaster who went bankrupt. Kirby Ironworks, if I remember rightly. He rented out some of his factory storerooms when the furnaces closed. His sister runs the school and he – er – he comes into town quite frequently.' Clara stopped talking abruptly.

Blake raised his eyebrows. 'I remember Kirby! From that night?'

Clara's face remained expressionless.

Realisation dawned on Blake and he laughed. 'No! Do you mean he comes here?'

'Regularly. Most afternoons. He has quite an appetite, I am told. He sits on the management board of the Mechanics Institute and he spends his mornings there.'

'The Institute? Where's that?'

'In town. It's very popular with all the furnace workers and forge masters round here. Sir William's a trustee of the Institute, I believe.'

An idea began to germinate in Blake's mind. An idea for his future. 'Clara, you're a wonderful woman and I love you,' he exclaimed.

'That's what they all say,' she replied with a grin and sat back to drink her tea. She watched him eating and drinking for a few minutes then asked, 'Have you found yourself a girl yet?'

Blake thought of Lissie and how she had often been in his mind since he met her on the towpath when the flyer's horse lost a shoe. 'Maybe,' he murmured.

'Only maybe? If it's only maybe, she's not the one—'

'She is!' he interrupted fiercely. Then added more calmly, 'She is young, that's all. I should wait until she's older.'

'Well, don't wait too long. If she's caught your eye, she will have others interested as well.'

'You're right, she will,' he realised. 'She is a real beauty and might not wait, and I have things to do first.'

They both heard the casement clock out in the front hall strike the hour and Clara stood up abruptly. 'So have I,' she exclaimed. 'I must go and help the others get ready.' She stood up to face him and added, 'Come and visit us again soon and do take good care of yourself, Blake.'

'Don't worry about me.' He grinned and kissed Clara's cheek. 'You make sure you keep yourself well. Grace too.'

She walked with him through the back door and round to the front of the house, then waved as he took his leave. He strode away, fortified by friendship and food, and planning the downfall of Luther Dearne, his courtship of Lissie and his future.

Chapter 15

'I've got a secret,' Miriam announced. She licked a finger and curled a strand of hair around it.

Lissie followed her along the path from the canal to school, swinging her bonnet by its tapes. It was summer and silky red poppies were blossoming in the surrounding cornfields. Lissie trailed her free hand through the long grass by the path and said, 'Knowing you, you won't have it for long. Are you going to tell us?'

'I can tell you – er – *part* of it,' Miriam decided.

'Go on then, tell. We'll be at school soon.'

'It's about Miss Kirby's. Of course, you know, I should have left school by now for a *po-sition*.' Miriam's emphasis made it sound very important.

Lissie shrugged. Miss Kirby did not want either of them to leave because they did all the work in the school-room while she was 'at home' in her drawing room or returning the visits. But pupils left all the time if they

were needed in their own families or could get a job in
service. 'So what?' she asked. 'Is that all?'

'Don't you want to know what's going to happen?'

Lissie resigned herself to Miriam's game. 'Are you
leaving then?' she ventured. 'To help your mam and dad
at the inn?'

'No, no, no! My mam and dad say they won't have
me working at the inn. I've got to do something more
befitting.'

'Befitting what?' Lissie asked.

'Just befitting,' explained Miriam. 'My dad's got
money, you know, so I can do what I want.'

'What d'you mean, do what you want?'

'Well.' Miriam took a deep breath and launched into a
speech. 'My mam says she doesn't want me to marry any
of the lads from round here and that I'd be better off doing
a ladylike kind of job until somebody suitable for me comes
along. She doesn't want me to go back and work at the
Navigator. She says I can do better than that, I can.'

'Get you, Miriam Jackson! You mean you're going
into service!'

'Better than that and it costs a lot of money, Miss
Kirby says! Your mam and dad 'as to be able to buy the
stuff to make your dresses. You have to 'ave dresses for
winter and summer, with collars and cuffs and caps to
match. Three of everything, Miss Kirby says, one on, one
in the wash and one ironed and waiting.'

Lissie was impressed. This sounded more exciting than
blackleading coal grates and scrubbing cooking pots at
the Navigator all day. 'What are you going to do then?'
she asked.

'Can't tell you.'

'Don't you know?'

'I told you — it's a secret.'

'Well, where are you going then?' Lissie persisted.

'That's a secret an' all.'

Lissie kicked at loose stones on the dusty path. If Miriam left school she'd most likely have to go as well. Her dad had said as much to Mam the other night. Money was short and now she was nearly fourteen she'd have to start earning her keep. Most girls her age had been earning for two years or more. Oh, but she did like going to school. Not that she'd ever let Miriam Jackson know how she felt about it. 'Well I don't care,' she lied, with a shrug of her slender shoulders.

'Oh, you will when you hear. I'm fifteen now and I'm going to have a proper *po-sition*. You'll find out soon enough. I won't have to wear a pinafore or take a turn in the kitchen like you. And my mam says I can have a new gown for Sundays, after the harvest is in, Mam says.' Miriam looked sideways at Lissie and gave a smirk. 'Then you'll have to be nice to me all the time, Lissie Dearne.'

Only if you're nice back to me, Lissie thought. But she wondered what was going on. Her dad had already said that there was no more money for school and that they were lucky the railways were not built on this side of the Riding yet so he could still pick up a bit of work from the canal trade.

'Well, I don't suppose I'll be at Miss Kirby's much longer, either,' Lissie responded defiantly. 'I'll be leaving school an' all soon. My dad says it's time I went out to work, but my mam says she doesn't want me to go away because she likes me at home with her.'

'Well, my mam'll be wanting more help at the Navvy when I'm not at home. You can go and work there,' suggested Miriam. 'Come on, let's run. We're goin' t' be late!'

But Lissie didn't run. She jammed her bonnet down over the thick black braids coiled around her head and kicked the loose stones on the path angrily. It wasn't fair that she'd have to leave school. Miss Kirby was a mean old maid but she let Lissie read her books and always asked her to help with the accounting in the big ledger. A life of scrubbing pots and floors at the Navvy and living with her mam just didn't bear thinking about.

'I tell yer, trade's bad, Mickey.' Luther leaned on the counter at the Navigator and nursed his tankard of ale. 'If it's not them canal companies it's the railways tekking it all. There's not much left over for me these days.'

'Aye, well, that's not my fault and I can't do nowt about it.' Mickey's eyes hardened. 'You owe me, Luther, and I wants paying.'

'I 'a'n't got no money.'

'Well, you'll 'ave ter get some. I wants me dues. My Annie's got her heart set on some o' that fancy satin stuff for our Miriam's new Sunday doings.'

'That costs a lot, that does.'

'Aye, I know. Tell you what – you get me some of it and we'll call it quits. Decent stuff, mind. Fit for a lady.'

Luther considered Mickey's offer. It would be easy enough for him to filch a bolt end of calico. There was so much of it about that warehouse place, it would hardly be missed. But fancy stuff was different. He looked across the counter at Mickey's face, staring at him, hard like. Mickey had offered him a deal because they were mates. He'd be setting his lads on anybody else.

Luther took a swallow of his ale. 'I'll 'ave ter go over to Sheffield fer that.' He could go and see that widow woman he had met. She knew where the best stock from Manchester went and she did not mind a bit of knocked-off stuff for herself. This cheered him and he finished his tankard. 'You're on, Mickey.'

'See to it then,' Mickey growled, and added, 'Your Edie gunna stay away from 'ere while you're gone?'

'She bin mekking a nuisance of herssenn again?'

'Not right in the 'ead, if yer ask me. Allus round 'ere asking folk for gin. Our Annie 'ad to fetch that Rosa woman to tek her home last time.'

'I'll gi' 'er another belting. Don't seem to make no difference though.'

'You want ter try some o' that tincture from the 'pothecary. That'll calm 'er down.'

Luther thought about this and murmured, 'Aye. I might do that.'

He'd have to do something about Edie. He did not have the money to keep buying her gin these days. He relied on Lissie to cook him a dinner and keep the house straight. She was a good little lass, but she would have to start earning proper now. He did not want her working here at the Navvy. Not with Mickey and his lads around. Maybe he could get her a place in service? Edie would just have to put up with it if she did not like it. She spent most of her time with Rosa when he was gone anyway.

He had a good idea what they got up to in that smelly little cottage down by the wood mill, but did not really care any more. Edie did nothing for him now and he couldn't even rise to her in the bedchamber. He got all he wanted from that widow woman over Sheffield way. Bit of all right, she was. Knew what to do to him and enjoyed it as much as he did. The first time she'd sat on top of him in her bed and done all the work he nearly cried. All those years he'd wasted on Edie! He washed his hands of her. Rosa could have her for all he cared!

Lissie's school routine went on as usual for another month. When they arrived, Miriam, as Miss Kirby's oldest pupil, was asked to supervise the little ones for morning sewing. Lissie loved to look after the little ones because she liked showing them how to do different stitches, whereas Miriam simply prodded them with the blackboard pointer when they stopped to rest their little fingers.

But Miriam's news, when she thought about it, cheered Lissie. If Miriam was leaving to go into service, then Miss Kirby might ask her to take over! Oh, that would be lovely! She'd like nothing more than to be able to take over teaching the little ones, instead of being sent to help Hannah in the kitchen!

'Miriam,' whispered Lissie before they went into their groups, 'tell her you don't want to take the little 'uns today.'

'Why should I?'

'Because you don't! You haven't got any patience with them. And I have. You know I have.'

'That's where you're wrong,' replied Miriam smugly. 'I'm going to be taking them every day from now on.'

'What? You? Give over, you can't stand them.'

Miss Kirby interrupted their hurried conversation. 'What are you two girls whispering about?'

Miriam got in first. 'Nothing, Miss Kirby. Lissie was saying how much she will miss my help with her lessons. When I start my *po-sition*.'

Lissie gave Miriam a sharp kick under the desk as Miss Kirby smiled benignly at her eldest pupil and said, 'Yes, indeed, I'm sure *all* the older pupils will miss your help. But you are old enough now to move on and you are very fortunate that your father has seen fit to let you learn by my example. Most girls . . .' Miss Kirby gave her class a pitiful look '. . . most girls would have left home and been in service for several years by your age, so think Miriam, how lucky you are to be able to stay near to your dear mother and father and find an occupation here.'

'What!' Lissie's jaw dropped open and there were mutterings among other girls in the class.

'Silence!' Miss Kirby snapped the class to attention by striking a heavy book on her high teacher's desk. 'Your mothers and fathers already know this, so it is fitting that I tell you all now. The school will be expanding from Michaelmas. I shall be taking boarding pupils and Miriam will be my new pupil teacher for the younger ones. I, of course, shall continue to be in charge.'

'What?' Lissie repeated, flabbergasted and wondering

what would happen to her. Her dad couldn't afford to pay Miss Kirby for any more schooling, let alone any bond as a pupil teacher or anything else for that matter. So that was Miriam's secret! She was bound to be even more superior in her ways now, going on and on about her new *po-sition*.

'Lissie,' Miss Kirby snapped again, 'do stop saying "what". You heard perfectly well. Now, on your feet, girl. Hannah is not at all well today and she needs you in the kitchen. Take two of the others with you and start the broth for dinner.'

Lissie's heart sank. No one would want to work in the kitchen on a hot day like today and whoever she chose would be sullen and fractious. She thought quickly and, with one eye on the horsewhip, asked, 'Miss Kirby, can we fetch the vegetables in ourselves? Save old George's back a bit?'

The older woman levelled a glare at Lissie, who kept a lively enquiring expression on her face. 'Very well, Lissie. Tell George I sent you and ask him to chop some wood and bring more coals in for the kitchen fire. Now, who wants to help Lissie this morning?'

Six hands shot up which Miss Kirby ignored and instead she chose two who would have preferred to stay and sew.

Lissie fixed a blackened cauldron over the kitchen fire and set the bones to boil. Not much meat on them today. She'd have to crack them and get the marrow out to get any kind of nourishment into the broth. There was no sign of Hannah so Lissie put the flour and barm for the bread in a crock under a cloth by the hearth to warm and found a couple of garden baskets for her helpers.

The old man that Miss Kirby's brother kept to help with their outside work was well past it now, she thought. Time they got someone younger to do the garden.

In Miss Kirby's father's day they could afford their own coach and four, as well as indoor and outdoor servants. But George did everything now and he was probably very glad of the home and few shillings that Mr Kirby paid him to do the outside jobs and look after the pony and trap.

His wife, Hannah, was as ancient as he was, and with a back just as bent. She had to do all the work round the house, including the cooking, and Miss Kirby never volunteered any assistance. Mind, Lissie thought, it was going to be different now, what with boarders and everything. It was going to be far too much work for old Hannah.

The Kirbys had an outside pump for water, and a trough big enough for the horses to drink. Lissie organised her helpers into washing the onions, potatoes and carrots, then carrying fresh water into the kitchen. The pump water was cold and crystal clear and she drank a tankard of it while she kneaded the bread dough. Miss Kirby came through to check up on them as she usually did, but this time, instead of walking briskly around and poking her nose into all the pots and pans, she sat in one of the kitchen chairs and watched Lissie at work.

'Lissie.'

Lissie jumped. What now, she thought?

'Yes, Miss Kirby.'

'Has your father spoken to you?'

'What about, Miss Kirby?'

'A position, girl!' Miss Kirby sounded irritable and raised her voice, repeating, 'A position for you.'

'Oh that.' Lissie guessed that she'd have to leave, especially now that Miriam was starting as pupil teacher.

'Well?'

'He hasn't said for definite. But he told me he couldn't pay you any more. And I do like coming here, Miss Kirby.'

'Of course you do, child. Any girl of your background would be very grateful for the schooling that your father has provided for you.'

Miss Kirby paused and thought. Mr Dearne was a rough one to be sure. He didn't have access to the means that his friend Mr Jackson did, but he brought her good calico on a regular basis and for a knock-down price. Both the men were of dubious character though and she fervently hoped that her new boarders would come from better families.

But of the two men, she preferred Mr Dearne. She didn't like the way Mr Jackson looked at the older girls on the occasions when he called at her school. It sent a shiver right down her back. Nevertheless, he was prepared to pay for a bond for his daughter to learn to be a teacher, which meant less time in the classroom for herself.

Mr Dearne was not a man of means and he had driven a much harder bargain. But Lissie was by far the brightest and most hardworking of the two girls and Miss Kirby did not want to lose her. Mr Kirby was very pleased with his plans for the school expansion, but she was not very happy about all the extra work. Thank goodness she had been able to strike a deal for both girls.

She managed a smile at her young pupil and said, 'Well, now you are nearly fourteen and quite full grown, your father has decided you must leave school this summer.'

'Yes, Miss Kirby.' Lissie had thought this might happen. But she wished she could stay on like Miriam and learn how to teach the little ones.

Miss Kirby became agitated as she talked. 'I don't know what will become of us all, I'm sure.' Lissie resigned herself to a lecture as Miss Kirby went off on one of her rants. 'Taking boarders is Mr Kirby's idea. He says there are lots of these new tradespeople in the towns who want their boys and girls away from the manufactories. Can't say I blame them. The smoke and grime from the ironworks in these parts is too thick even to breathe. A bit of country air will be very good for their young girls.' Miss Kirby shook her head and sucked her teeth in disapproval. 'But these new railways will be everywhere before long, bringing more smoke and grime.'

Lissie hadn't seen any railways yet but she thought they sounded exciting and something to look forward to. The railways were making changes to trading all over the Riding, she'd heard her dad say, but they hadn't come as far as this side of town yet, and the Kirbys, like all the folk down at Mexton Lock, still relied on the canal and the turnpike for getting around.

Wisely, Lissie kept quiet about her views and

continued to pound the bread dough. The Kirbys had
nothing to complain about, she thought. They had this
big house and more money to spend than most folk
round here. But Mr Kirby was known for being mean
with his money and Lissie had heard them arguing earlier
in the morning room, so she guessed it was about Miss
Kirby's allowance and the new boarders. And, no doubt,
about who was going to do all the work!

'So you see, Lissie,' Miss Kirby continued, 'I shall be
turning the attics into dormitories for the extra pupils
and it will be far too much work for my housekeeper.'

Housekeeper? Lissie thought. She meant Hannah of
course, already bent double from a life of toiling for the
Kirbys. Poor dear, how would she cope with an attic full
of school pupils? Perhaps Miriam would be living in to
keep an eye on them?

'I am taking on a maid of all work to help my housekeeper and,' Miss Kirby seemed quite proud of her next
statement as she gave that simpering little smile she
normally saved for other gentry like herself, 'and,' she
continued, 'I shall have a laundry woman to come in
once a month.'

No laundry maid job for me, then, thought Lissie, as
she cut up her bread dough into even-sized lumps. That
would have suited her, tucked away in the wash house
out the back, away from Miss Kirby's prying eyes and
her little horsewhip. She'd often been sent to help
Hannah in the wash house.

'Of course,' Miss Kirby went on, 'I shall have plenty
of pupils to keep the schoolroom clean and cook their
food, but my dear brother and I shall need someone to

do the cooking and cleaning for us, as well as supervise the pupils when they are doing their domestic training.' Miss Kirby stopped talking, then added, 'Well?'

Lissie eyes widened. Well, what? She hadn't been listening properly. What should she say in reply? She repeated the word, adding a slightly incredulous note and brief shrug.

Miss Kirby's eyes narrowed. 'Aren't you pleased, girl? That your father has agreed to this? That you will be that lucky girl?'

Lissie's jaw dropped in amazement. *She* was going to be the Kirbys' maid of all work? Her! All she could think of was that she wouldn't have to work at the Navvy and have Miriam's dad and brothers leering at her scrubbing the kitchen floor.

She said, 'Oh! Oh yes, Miss Kirby, I am very pleased.'

Fortunately Miss Kirby took the surprise in her voice for delight. But Lissie wasn't surprised that Dad had agreed to it, because he'd already told her she would have to leave school. She was surprised that Miss Kirby wanted her of all people. Miss Kirby always favoured the girls who came from better-off families than she did.

She continued shaping dough into bread cakes for the oven and added in her most humble voice, 'Thank you, Miss Kirby. Does that mean I shall be living here?'

'Yes it does. And you will do well to remember how very fortunate you are that I have chosen *you* from all my pupils. You have shown great promise in your domestic ability, and Mr Kirby prefers your bread to anyone else's.' She stood and put on her sternest glare.

'But you must learn to curb your tongue. And you will learn, Lissie. You will learn to curb that tongue of yours.'

Miss Kirby swished her horsewhip against the table leg to emphasise her point and continued, 'Your father will receive a remuneration for your services and he has promised to provide you with new boots. Board and lodging will be deducted from your wages, of course, and,' Miss Kirby hesitated as though she found the words hard to say, 'and I shall provide the stuff for your aprons and caps.'

Lissie suppressed a smile and kept her head down, pretending to concentrate on the bread cakes so Miss Kirby wouldn't see her mouth twitch. Good old Dad! He must have driven a really hard bargain with mean old Miss Kirby to get her to pay for the uniforms. Dad would know that the cheap calico cloth he brought her from town was sold at a profit to her pupils for their smocks and pinafores.

This news, and the realisation that she wouldn't have to live at home with Mam any more, or suffer her drunken tantrums and frequent clips round her ears, cheered Lissie. Of course she'd miss her dad. Though knowing him, he'd stop off to see her at Miss Kirby's every time he passed by on the canal.

She wondered what it would be like living here with the Kirbys all the time. It was a nice house, she thought, with big airy rooms at the front, and it had a lovely garden that grew scented roses in the summer. There was also a big vegetable patch with gooseberry bushes and an apple and pear orchard right at the bottom next to the coach house. Fordham was nice too. It wasn't rough like Mexton Lock and it had a chapel that everybody went to on a Sunday. She might not be a pupil teacher like Miriam, but this was definitely better than being at the Navvy.

Lissie remained composed as she made the last of the bread into a cottage loaf and pushed a floured finger down the middle to stick the small ball of dough on top of the big one. 'Thank you, Miss Kirby,' she repeated. 'When do you want me to start?'

'Why, right this minute, girl! My pupils will be off to help out on the farms soon and you have the attics to get ready as well as your uniforms to make. Mr Kirby has a man coming in to clear out the old storerooms at the back for a new schoolroom. There will be plenty of cleaning for you to do. Oh, and remember, from today you are no longer a pupil here. You are a servant in this house so you must address me as "ma'am" and Mr Kirby as "sir".'

'Yes, Miss K— I mean, yes, ma'am,' Lissie replied dutifully.

Miss Kirby gave her an approving look, adding, 'And of course, you will address Miriam as Miss Jackson in front of the pupils.'

Lissie groaned inwardly. Miriam would treat her like a servant now. Still, her friend had told her she wouldn't be starting as pupil teacher until Michaelmas and there was the rest of the summer between now and then. Her cheer was short-lived though as Miss Kirby added, 'Miss Jackson will be here after the harvest, helping me to get the new schoolroom ready.'

'Will she be moving in as well, then?'

'Er – er – well no, she will be lodging in the village. There is not enough space in the attics as you will be sleeping on the landing up there.'

'With the new pupils, ma'am?'

'From Michaelmas, yes. Hurry up with that bread. Then find yourself an old smock to wear because it's very dusty up there and you need to get a bed ready for yourself for tonight.'

'Tonight?'

'Of course tonight, girl. You have a position now. You father will bring your box tomorrow.'

And so Lissie did not go back into the schoolroom that day, but spent the afternoon scrubbing out the landing at the very top of the house and searching the dark cobwebby attics for something to sleep on. She found an old feather mattress stuffed into an even older wooden box and some pieces of rough woollen fabric for blankets. By the time it grew dark she was very grubby and very hungry, having missed her tea as no one thought to call her to come and eat. She crept down to the kitchen. No one was there and the house was quiet. The Kirbys were probably in the drawing room or their bedchambers and she had not seen Hannah all day.

She cleaned herself up under the outside pump making her dress very wet in the process and then tackled the pile of dirty pots and pans left, obviously for her, in the scullery sink. All the food had been locked away in the pantry except for a tin plate on the kitchen table with some bread and cheese.

Lissie scrubbed down the table and fetched herself a

tankard of fresh cool water from the pump to wash down her simple, but very welcome, meal. She found a stub of candle in the cupboard by the range and lit it from the dying fire with a taper.

She didn't like the attic landing. Isolated at the top of the narrow back stairs, she felt cut off from the rest of the house. There were draughts from the skylight over her head and scuffling noises of mice – or rats – from the closed doors to the attic rooms. But she cheered herself up by thinking of her dad who would be coming to see her the next day. Tired out from all the work, Lissie blew out the candle and was soon fast asleep in her makeshift bed.

Chapter 16

'Why don't you let me do that for you?' Lissie asked.

Hannah continued to cough – a cough that made Lissie grimace with distaste. Lissie took the heavy break-fast tray from her and put it back on the kitchen table. She led Hannah to a chair and sat her down, rubbing her bent old back. The coughing eased and was replaced by hoarse, wheezing breaths. Lissie measured a spoonful of doctor's linctus and tipped it down her throat.

'You sit there for a few minutes and I'll take Mr Kirby's tray in.'

Hannah did not protest as Lissie carried the kidneys and bacon, and freshly made coffee, down the passage to Miss Kirby's morning room. Her boots left footprints in the lime dust and Lissie looked forward to another day of washing floors. Raking ashes and cleaning fire grates was nothing compared with the muck in the new schoolroom from Mr Kirby's builder!

Mr Kirby was alone in the morning room. His sister

had decamped to stay with cousins as she could not abide the upset in her household. Before she left she had supervised Lissie as she covered all the furniture in her dining and drawing rooms at the front of the house. Then she had locked them up and departed. The only downstairs rooms in use were Mr Kirby's study and the morning room, apart from all the domestic offices and schoolrooms down the passage at the back.

'Where is Hannah?' Mr Kirby demanded. He was sitting at the small table reading a newspaper.

'Hannah is not at all well, sir,' Lissie explained as she finished serving his breakfast. 'It's the dust, sir. It makes her cough.'

It makes us all cough, she thought. It got everywhere and it was difficult to shift, leaving grey smears all over despite her scrubbing. Every day it floated up the back stairs to the attics that she was trying to clean up for the new pupils. And it made her hands so sore! She had taken to smearing lard on them at night and sleeping in old gloves.

He was watching her again. Lissie didn't dare look at Mr Kirby, but she knew he was. She felt his beady brown eyes on her every move and his stare made her nervous. She had thought at first her cap was skew-whiff or her apron had a mark on it. But he was always the same. Normally she didn't see much of him as she spent most of her time in the back rooms. She didn't go into the front rooms to clean until after he had left for town.

'Will that be all, sir?'

'Tell Hannah she must serve lunch. I do not want to see you in here again.'

'Sir.' She bobbed a curtsey and left.

Hannah had recovered from her coughing, but she was still sitting on the kitchen chair, with a vacant look in her rheumy old eyes.

'I'll do the cooking today,' Lissie volunteered. 'You just sit at the table and do the fruit and vegetables.'

While the builder was knocking down walls in the old stores, Mr Kirby stayed at home. But he never set foot in the kitchen. He spent the morning in his study or outside giving orders to his builder and to George.

Lissie raced around doing as much as she could of the cleaning and laid the table in the morning room for lunch. She placed the tureen of vegetable soup on a tray and said, 'Can you take this in, Hannah? Mr Kirby wants you to serve him, not me.'

Lissie held open the passage door for her then hurried to the scullery to make a start on the pots. She was heaving up a pitcher of hot water when she heard the crash. She dashed through to the passage and found Hannah sprawled on the flags, surrounded by broken china and a pool of steaming vegetable soup. Mr Kirby stood at the open door of the morning room.

'You clumsy woman! You will pay for the china out of your wages.' He glared at Lissie as though it was her fault. 'Fetch me some more soup.'

'I think she has fainted, sir,' Lissie said.

He stepped forward and peered down at the still form of his housekeeper.

'Find George,' he ordered, adding, 'Get my soup first.'

Lissie scurried away to change her apron and serve up more soup. She tried to make Hannah more comfortable with her shawl and some kitchen cloths, then went out for George who carried his wife down the garden to their bedroom over the stables.

Fortunately, summer pudding was Mr Kirby's favourite and he brightened when Lissie presented it to him. 'Is Hannah not recovered yet?' he asked.

'No, sir. George has put her to bed.'

'This is not good enough. My sister would soon have her to rights.'

Lissie bit her tongue to prevent herself shouting at him that Hannah was very old and very poorly and did he want to work her to death? She was resigned to thinking that, yes, he probably did.

'I have no instructions for supper, sir.'

Mr Kirby tutted and shook his head. 'Really, I should not have to speak to a kitchen maid,' he answered irritably. 'I shall dine at the Manse tonight.'

Lissie cleaned up the passage and washed the cooking pots and china, then cleared and cleaned the morning room and Mr Kirby's study and bedchamber, emptied his chamber pot and swept down the stairs, scrubbed the front steps and polished the brass doorknocker, emptied the ashes from the kitchen range and scrubbed the kitchen table and floor, then thought about tea for George and Hannah – and herself.

She prepared beef tea with toasted bread for Hannah, and cold cuts and pickles for George. Exhausted and thirsty, she quaffed a tankard of ale left over from lunch and immediately felt better. More lime dust was beginning to settle as she heard the builder stop his bashing at the old brick walls and go home.

She felt sticky, dirty and tired. After George had taken their tea to the coach house, she was alone in the house. So she banked up the kitchen fire, shifted the damper to heat water in the side boiler and took down the tin bath in the scullery.

It was bliss, sheer bliss! She wallowed in hot water scented with refreshing sprigs of rosemary and washed herself with her own soft soap that she had made over the kitchen fire. Her dusty dress had had a beating on the line outside and her chemise, bodice and drawers were rinsed out and pegged alongside it.

She poured another jug of water over her head and began to pull a comb through her long black hair. It was dark in the windowless scullery and dusk had closed in while she bathed. She began to hum a tune to herself and sing the words of hymns that she knew.

As the water cooled she climbed out and reached for a square of linen to dry herself. A sharp intake of breath caused a soft scream in her throat. Mr Kirby was standing in the doorway to the kitchen.

'Sir!' She held the linen cloth in front of her.

He was finely dressed in evening clothes with a starched white shirt and a silk tie around his neck. He had a silver hip flask in his gloved hand and he tipped it to his lips.

'Sir?'

'Carry on.' He waved the hip flask in her direction, took another swig and swayed against the door jamb.

'I shall not, sir. You will be good enough to leave.'

He gave a low laugh. 'Wilful little trollop, aren't you? I said carry on.'

'No.'

He strolled towards her and snatched away the cloth. She slouched forward to cover herself with her hands and arms.

'Stand up straight when I'm talking to you!'

Reluctantly, she dropped her arms to her sides and straightened her back and shoulders. She stood stock still, tense and frightened, an ivory statue lit by a rising moon coming through the kitchen windows and doorway.

He walked all around her, inspecting her as he used to when she was a pupil. He was very close to her and she could hear his heavy laboured breathing and smell strong drink on his breath. He stood behind her and leaned forward to whisper in her ear. She felt his suiting brush against her damp skin.

'Harlot,' he whispered.

She heard him take another drink and then felt a gloved finger trail over her bottom and around her waist to the soft swell of her young breasts. As he circled each breast in turn she winced and tried to think of a way out. Duck and run up to the attic? No, there were no locks on the attic doors. Down the garden to the coach house? Yes, she would be safer with George and Hannah. But she had no clothes or boots to hand. Perhaps she would have time to drag them off the line before he caught up with her? Perhaps not, she realised.

'Harlot,' he repeated. He pushed one of her breasts upwards with his hand.

Evil man, she thought, he had no shame. She said, 'I'm sure Miss Kirby would not want to know of this.'

He stopped and removed his hand abruptly. 'And who would believe a cheap little slut from Mexton Lock?'

But he must have thought better of his actions for he hit her sharply across the face, just once, and barked, 'You will not speak of this.' She fell sideways against the stone sink and when she had recovered he was gone. She heard him shouting at George to harness the pony and trap as he was going into town.

'Well now, Lissie,' Miss Kirby said, in the New Year. 'You are fourteen and quite a grown woman. How would you like to be my housekeeper?' She did not wait for, or expect, an answer, and went on, 'I shall hold the keys to the pantries and as soon as Mr Kirby has left for town each morning you will give me your list for the day.'

Considering she had been doing the work of housekeeper since Hannah collapsed last summer, Lissie thought she would like the position very much. Hannah had died before Michaelmas and Lissie had coped single-handed until the pupils returned from the harvest. Now she had as many willing helpers as she needed and those that cared for domestic work took to Lissie easily.

The folk in Fordham had done well this year because the harvest was good. But Lissie knew that her dad had hardly done any work this winter and her mam couldn't get out of bed without her gin, so money was still short down at Mexton. She considered Miss Kirby's offer silently.

'Well? Have you nothing to say?' Miss Kirby demanded.

'Er – Miss Kirby, ma'am. Will I be getting more pay?' Lissie asked. There. She had said it.

Miss Kirby frowned at her angrily. 'It is not your place to ask for such things.'

Lissie kept a bright smile on her lips and responded quickly, 'What did my father say when you discussed it with him?' Dad had not said anything to her about this last time he visited.

Miss Kirby shuddered. The idea of *discussing* anything with that dreadful ruffian from Mexton Lock made her skin crawl. 'Oh, you are such a tiresome girl,' she muttered.

Lissie drove home her point. 'I am only paid as a kitchen maid, ma'am.' And, she thought, You've been getting a housekeeper on the cheap for nearly half a year. I deserve more wages and my dad needs the money at home.

Lissie was worried about home. Her mam didn't do anything to look after Dad and spent most of her day sleeping off the drink, or whining at Dad to get her more of her gin. Dad had started taking her a tincture instead. It calmed her down, he said, and the apothecary in town had said that a lot of women took it.

Lissie only saw her on her half-day, which was one Sunday afternoon a month. But she thought better of asking Miss Kirby for more time off as well. This was a good position and she needed it.

The only regular money going into home was her wage. Miss Kirby paid it quarterly to Dad, but it never lasted the quarter and, if he didn't get any work, there was nothing else when it had gone. At least this position gave Lissie food and shelter and a supply of calico to make her drawers!

Miss Kirby tutted and muttered indecisively until she said, 'Well, I suppose you do the domestic training for my pupils too.' She heaved a sigh and finished, 'I . . . I shall talk to your father next time he visits. Now put on your bonnet, it is time for chapel. Have you laid out the sherry wine in my morning room?'

'Yes, ma'am.'

She added water to the stew for the pupils and checked on the joint of beef for Miss Kirby and her brother. It was roasting on an iron grid in the big oven by the fire, with a dish of potatoes underneath to bake in the drippings.

'Come on, Lissie,' Miriam called from the passage. 'We're waiting for you.'

She grabbed her wool shawl and filed out with the pupils, following Miss Kirby and her brother to the chapel. Lissie avoided Mr Kirby these days and when they did come face to face he gazed straight through her as if she did not exist.

No one from Mexton Lock ever went to chapel but Fordham folk gathered there on a Sunday. The Kirbys sat in the front pew with the old doctor and two local farmers. Other families sat together behind them. Miriam and Lissie with Miss Kirby's boarding pupils in their clean caps and pinnies were at the back.

'I see the alehouse keeper and his wife are not here again,' Miriam smirked.

'And a few of the farm labourers, keeping him company in the tap room,' Lissie giggled. 'Oh good, here's Eliza. Move up so she can sit by me.'

'Where's Job?' Lissie whispered to Eliza.

'One of his cows is off-colour, so he's stayed with her. He's not fond of chapel anyroad.'

'Shame,' Lissie responded, disappointed. 'We'll miss him singing.'

'We can make up for him, can't we?' Eliza smiled.

The three girls and dozen pupils sang their hymns gustily. The louder the organ played, the louder they sang. Miss Kirby looked round once at them and Lissie beamed back at her. Her pupils were enjoying the freedom and Miriam was there to shush them up during prayers.

'What's he going on about?' Eliza whispered once the sermon had started.

'Search me!' Lissie answered. 'But I like watching him, don't you?'

Eliza nodded and grinned. The preacher became red in the face, waved his arms around and his voice rose to a crescendo. Lissie recognised his Bible references but was lost when he alluded to goings-on nowadays. It was interesting to watch, though, especially when she noticed the back of Mr Kirby's neck go red.

Lissie was flattered that Eliza had made a friend of her. Eliza was eighteen and married to a dairyman with his own land and herd. He was a lot older than she was but they rubbed along well enough, as far as Lissie could make out. Eliza was well known as the best dairymaid in this part of the Riding. Her butter tasted better than any that came from the market in town.

After the service they spilled out into the chilly damp graveyard that surrounded the chapel building.

'I wish we had more time to chat,' Eliza said.

'Me too. But you know what Miss Kirby's like. No slacking!'

Eliza giggled. 'My Job has just arranged to supply your school with butter and cheese. And fresh milk, if you collect it.'

'Ooh, that'll be nice.'

'I'll put a pailful aside from the morning milking. What time do you get up?'

'Oh, early. I have to get the range going for hot water and for cooking breakfast.'

'Come down while it's drawing. There'll be nobody about then and we can have a chinwag.'

'You're on!'

Early morning was Lissie's favourite time of day. As winter receded and streaks of dawn lit the bridge and canal, she watched the countryside emerge from its hibernation. She carried the empty pail down to Eliza's dairy just in time to see Job herding his cows over the little bridge to taste the first juicy grass of spring. Eliza met her on the bridge with two tankards of rich, creamy milk, still warm from the cow.

A tandem of narrow boats laden with coal came down the private Swinborough cut and glided into the main navigation. They were hauled by a yoked pair of carthorses that plodded diligently on towards the ironworks in town.

Lissie looked back down the canal towards Mexton. 'I think the flyers have started up again,' she commented. 'There's one coming up fast now.'

'Well, he'll 'ave to look out, the coal's not straightened up yet.'

Lissie's heart began to thump as the flyer approached. The horse rider was a man she didn't recognise, dark skinned and swarthy-looking. The helmsman, too, was unfamiliar. She wondered if Blake was still working on this flyer and imagined, if he was, that he was sleeping below, his eyes closed and his floppy fair hair tangled.

His features were still vivid in her mind and she thought how much she would like to see him again. She hoped the coal barges would get stuck on the turn and slow down the flyer. But they didn't and the flyer was soon on its way and overtaking the slower tandem.

'Come on, Lissie,' Eliza reminded her. 'Time to get back to work.'

The following week there was an unseasonable warm spell of weather that caused early morning mist to rise from the fields by the canal.

'Shall we walk a little this morning?' Eliza suggested when Lissie called for the milk.

'I like sitting on the bridge,' Lissie responded, and thought, I might see the flyer again.

Eliza put her head on one side. 'All right then.'

They sat on the low stone wall in silence while they drank their milk.

'Here it comes,' Eliza said suddenly.

'What?'

'The flyer, of course. What else are we here for?'

Lissie twisted her head. Her heart turned over. The rider was approaching fast and she realised, with a start that, this time, she recognised him. She stood up, flustered. The rider slowed down to go under the bridge and stopped altogether when the barge was past them.

Blake swung down from the saddle, fixed a nose can on his horse, and called to Thomas at the helm who passed him a tin jug, a plate and a coin.

Lissie stood rooted to the spot on the bridge.

Eliza commented. 'It looks as though they want something. I hope it's a regular order like last year.'

Blake sprinted down the towpath and on to the bridge. He gave them both a smile and a short bow and Lissie felt a strange nervousness course through her veins.

'A fine morning, ladies,' he said, handing over the containers to Eliza. 'A quart of milk, if you please, and some butter.'

Eliza took the utensils and money and went off in the direction of her dairy. 'I won't be long,' she called to Lissie. 'Wait for me.'

He turned to Lissie. 'Well, this is a pleasant turn of events. How are you?'

Momentarily tongue-tied, she acknowledged him with a brief nod of her head. It must be nigh on a year since she saw him last. He looked tired. There were dark shadows under his eyes and his face appeared strained. He wore riding boots that came up to his knees and they were worn and scuffed and dusty. As were his moleskin breeches and dark riding jacket.

But she still thought he was the tallest, strongest, handsomest man that she had ever seen. He took off his jacket and flexed his neck and shoulders. If anything, his shoulders were broader than she remembered. His forearms, visible below rolled up shirtsleeves, were tanned and sinewy and his hands looked strong and capable.

She found her voice eventually, but 'I am very well,

thank you' was all that she could think of to say. After
a brief silence she added, 'And you, are you well?'

'In excellent health, I am pleased to say, Lissie.'

He remembered my name! With an inner thrill, she
thought: He remembered my name, and gave him a small
smile.

Blake suddenly felt weak all over. He put it down to
a hard night's riding. But he thought, She is so lovely, I
want to hold her and kiss her and . . . He felt a stirring
in his loins and pulled himself together quickly, trying
to control this most basic of instincts that he felt for her
at that moment.

Lissie marvelled at how white his teeth looked against
his tanned skin. He had a good growth of beard around
his chin, she noticed. It gave him an untidy, ravaged
appearance that she found surprisingly attractive. She was
aware of a new sensation, a kind of yearning that she
felt low down in her stomach. She tensed to make it go
away.

After a pause, he added, 'Canal life suits me.' He
continued to gaze at her, taking in her increased height
and developed figure. Under her dark shawl she wore a
plain grey cotton dress with lace edged collar and cuffs.
Most of her full skirt was covered by a starched white
apron and her beautiful black hair was tucked away out
of sight under a white mob cap. He saw a clean, fresh
and very lovely young woman with alabaster skin and
wide green eyes, and he coveted what he saw.

'Shall we walk awhile?' he suggested, gesturing to the
footpath by the field. 'Tell me what you have been doing
this past year.'

Lissie hesitated for a moment. He began to loosen his neckerchief and undo a few of his shirt buttons to wipe away the sweat from his throat. She was mesmerised by these movements and the glimpse of his chest beneath his clothes. A small amount of springy hair, darkened and dampened by sweat, appeared and then disappeared as he re-buttoned his shirt.

When she didn't move he raised his eyebrows and asked, 'Shall we sit then? Are you working at the dairy?'

She shook her head. 'Oh no. I just came down for the morning milk.'

He sat on the wall, stretched out his long legs and yawned. 'Well, I'm just finishing my night's riding, so I don't mind if we sit. Will you not join me?'

Lissie felt the odd stirring in her nether parts again. She wanted to move closer to him, to sit beside him, but her instinctive caution would not let her.

This man was a bargeman, on the elite flyers, yes, and he spoke well – like a gentleman – but he was still a bargeman and, therefore, one to be avoided. Yet at the same time he had this manly presence that thrilled and attracted her.

'I . . . er . . . I . . . yes, of course.' She backed away and sat on the opposite wall, facing him. Sitting primly upright, she straightened her long skirts around her, allowing her shawl to fall away from her shoulders.

Blake felt his heart begin to beat faster. He realised that she was totally unaware of how perfect she looked to him, and of how much he wanted to kiss her pretty mouth. Indeed he had been unaware of how strong these feelings were himself until now. He had conceded from their last meeting on the towpath that he was attracted to her, and convinced himself that it was her good nature and pleasant disposition that he liked.

But that was a whole year ago and she had grown into a handsome woman since then. As he sat there in the early morning light watching the mist burn off the surrounding meadows, he forgot what he was doing on that stretch of the canal. His mind filled with thoughts of the beautiful creature in front of him, who had been too young for his serious interest when he last saw her, and who had now blossomed into a fine young woman and was sitting just a few feet away from him.

He swallowed and took a breath. 'You have a position here?' he asked.

Lissie began to relax a little and nodded. 'At the school.' She sat up even straighter, and, proud of her new title, added, 'I am the housekeeper.' It was the first time she had described herself as such and she took pleasure in it, raising a smile and placing her hands, neatly clasped, on her lap.

It was her innocent pride that fired him and how he controlled himself at that moment he would never know. Blake had had a long arduous night on the canal and was all but dead on his feet. He had been doing most of the riding as they were missing one of their crew until they reached Tinsley. Yet he could have taken her in his arms and ravished her right there on the bridge, tired as he was. He managed to keep his voice steady and asked, 'Is the school far from here?'

Lissie nodded towards the main street. 'Oh no, not far. It's the big house at the end.'

'Do you like it there?'

'Oh yes, the pupils are always nice to me.'

'And so they should be! What is the name of this school of yours?'

'Oh it's not mine, it's Miss Kirby's . . .' Lissie stopped as she blushed and looked down, feeling foolish.

He was so – so strong, she thought, and his natural easiness was drawing her closer to him. She wanted to touch his face to see if it was real. Her heart began to beat in her throat and her stomach felt a little queasy.

Blake would have liked that moment to go on for ever. He had a desperate urge to take her in his arms and to love her with a passion. At eighteen, he thought of himself as a man. Lissie, he saw, was a woman now, no longer too young to court. And he wanted to claim her as his own, before any local miner or farmer's boy turned her head.

With a sudden nervous gesture, he took off his cap, ran his fingers through his damp sweaty hair and tried to stay rational. 'Ah yes,' he replied. 'I know Mr Kirby. He gives talks at the Institute in town.'

Lissie had seen him rake back his hair like that before and watching him do it again only served to remind her of those times. Down by the lock that night, at the fight between his dad and hers, riding by on the flyer and then during that walk along the towpath last year. He remembered her from the latter but she remembered them all. Who was he really? She took a deep breath to calm her churning stomach and said conversationally, 'Miss Kirby is his sister.'

'And do you help to teach the younger ones? I should

imagine you would be very good with them, very patient.'

Lissie thought again how much she would have liked to do that. But Miriam had been the lucky one there. 'Oh no,' she said. 'My friend Miriam does that. She is a pupil teacher now.'

Blake, desperately trying to retrieve his normal composure, picked up this line of conversation. 'That would be Miriam from the Navigator at Mexton Lock? Her brother, Peter, used to be the horse marine there . . .'

As he talked of Peter and the smithy at Mexton, Blake began to feel in control of himself again. Soon he would be free of company timetables and living properly in the South Riding. He was getting closer to Fordham, closer to the school and closer to that scoundrel Dearne.

He was near to catching up with him and then he could get on with his life. A life, he realised with some satisfaction, that would include this delightful young woman sitting sedately on a small stone bridge by an English meadow.

Lissie was aware that something in the conversation had changed his countenance and inwardly groaned. It was when she mentioned Miriam. Miriam! It was always Miriam! She seemed to have this effect on grown men. They were always interested in her and her coquettish ways. Even the preacher in chapel was taken in by her preening and twittering. And here was another one just like him!

Lissie sighed, gathered up the folds of her skirt and stood up. 'There's Eliza with the milk. The pupils will be wanting their breakfast.'

'No, wait! Don't go yet, Lissie. Stay and talk a little longer. Please?'

Lissie was shaking her head and muttering 'I can't, I have to get back' when a loud voice from the water interrupted them both.

'Hey! Blake! What a' you playing at there? Get back 'ere wi' that milk.' Thomas had mounted the horse and was ready to move on. 'You don't get paid to go courting, lad. You'll 'ave plenty o' time for that when we gets to Tinsley.'

Blake grimaced and got to his feet. 'It seems I cannot stay either. I must say goodbye for now, Lissie, but I'll look out for you as we pass. Shall you look out for me?' He raised an eyebrow in query before replacing his cap, turning towards the canal and calling, 'I hear you well enough, Thomas, I hear you.

'Until the next time we meet?' He gave her a friendly salute and hurried away, collecting the milk and butter from Eliza before sprinting back over the bridge.

'When will that be, I wonder,' Lissie whispered softly to herself, watching him stride down the towpath. He scrambled aboard and took the helm as Thomas urged the horse forward. She watched the flyer gliding slowly through the water, gathering speed until it disappeared from her sight, hidden by a curve in the bank and the bushes lining the fields.

'D'you want this milk for the school today or not?' Eliza called from the track.

Lissie jumped and turned round. 'Yes. Yes, thank you, Eliza. I was just enjoying the morning air.'

'Mmm, if you say so. I saw you from the dairy. Found yourself a sweetheart, have you?'

'No, I have not,' Lissie protested with a blush.

'Well, if you haven't, I reckon he has. Believe me, Lissie, that one has taken a bit of a fancy to you. You want to watch them bargeboys. They don't call 'em fly-by-nights for nothing. You'd better not let Miss Kirby see you wi' a follower or she'll have you out on your ear as soon as look at you.'

'We were only talking, Eliza,' Lissie said.

Eliza smiled knowingly. 'And I were only watching you,' she said archly.

Nonplussed by this reply, Lissie simply shrugged and picked up the heavy pail. 'Thanks for the milk, Eliza. See you tomorrow, then.'

Eliza grinned and shook her head as Lissie walked away. But Lissie was thinking, It wasn't me that he was interested in. It's never me. It's always Miriam where men are concerned. Lissie grew angry as she stomped back up the dirt road to Miss Kirby's. Miriam didn't deserve him! And he deserved better than Miriam! She was saucy and flighty with every man she met and Blake would be no different. Well, if he was taken in by her wily ways she could have him, and good luck to him!

Chapter 17

'Dad! Dad!' Lissie waved her cloth at him as he walked up the road with a package under his arm. It was after luncheon and she was washing the half-landing window that looked out over the front door. She finished the window quickly and hurried down to the kitchen.

'Come in, Dad. Oh, it is nice to see you.'

He was puffing and panting and immediately sat down to get his breath back. The kitchen chair creaked under his weight and he said, 'It's a bit of a pull up that hill for me now.'

'I'll get you some water,' Lissie volunteered.

''A'n't you got any ale, lass?'

Lissie went to the pantry and drew a jug of George's brew from the barrel. She poured them each a tankardful. 'What have you got there?'

He winked at her and unwrapped two or three layers of muslin to reveal the end of a bolt of cream-coloured silk.

Lissie fingered the fabric gently. 'Oh, that's beautiful, Dad. Where did you get it?'

He took another swig of ale. 'Well, Lissie, lass, there's this widder over Sheffield way and she's a right good seamstress—'

'Dad!'

'You don't mind, do you, lass? Me and yer mam, well, yo' know what she's like. She's gone from me now, and a man needs his comforts.'

Lissie had suspected that this was going on and sighed. 'I know, Dad. I wish I could get home more to help.'

'Nay, lass. You're better off 'ere. You've got a good carry on 'ere. Anyroad, this widder, like, she's got her own workshop, but no fella to look out for 'er, and she 'as some right good customers. Rich folk from the manufactories, not wi' a lot o' land like round 'ere, but they live in big 'ouses all the same.'

Lissie was still fingering the silk. 'She gave you this?'

'I done a few jobs for 'er, round the 'ouse, like. It were left over from a bride's doings.'

'A trousseau?'

'Aye, that were it.'

'Ooh, Dad, it's lovely. Is some of it for me?'

Her dad grimaced and took some more ale. 'There's on'y a few yards left and I reckon Miss Kirby'll give me a good price for that, lass. I need the money for the . . . for yer mam's medicine, see.'

Lissie was disappointed but understood about the money. 'Miss Kirby's having one of her quiet rests in the drawing room. I'll tell her you're here when I take her tea in.'

'You 'a'n't got owt t' eat, 'ave yer, lass?'

Lissie cut him some bread and the end of a collar of bacon that she had boiled. She knew it was his favourite. She placed a jar of mustard pickle on the table and he helped himself, topping up his ale at the same time.

Later that day, after her dad had left with his profits, Lissie was sitting in the back garden shelling peas for supper when she heard the trap arrive and saw old George lumbering up the drive to see to the horse. Miss Kirby, flushed and excited, called Lissie into the kitchen.

'There will be three for supper tonight,' she said, inspecting the dinner already simmering on the hob. 'Put out the best table linen and make sure you have a clean apron. I shall need you to serve.'

'What's going on?' Miriam asked when she brought the pots back from the boarders' tea in the schoolroom.

'A guest. You will have to watch the pupils doing the washing up tonight. I'm busy.'

'There's no need to go all lah-de-dah on me just because you've been made up to housekeeper,' Miriam responded loftily.

'Oh, Miriam,' Lissie sighed, 'just watch that they don't break anything.'

Lissie tied a fresh, lace-trimmed apron over her grey afternoon dress and put on a matching cap. She took a tureen of pea soup to the dining room, where she left it on the mahogany table next to a cottage loaf. After standing back to satisfy herself that the silver and china settings looked their best, she went to the drawing room to announce supper.

Three heads turned towards her. She opened her

mouth to speak but nothing came out. He was here. Blake was here. In Miss Kirby's drawing room. His long, booted legs were stretched out across the hearth. His black coat looked new and he was wearing a neck tie, a proper neck tie, over a white shirt.

If he was surprised to see her he did not show it. Perhaps he wasn't, for he knew she was the housekeeper here. He sat there and smiled at her, making her knees go weak and shaky. They all waited for her to say something. She swallowed but still no sound came out.

'Yes? What is it, Lissie?' Miss Kirby said eventually.

She found her voice at last. 'Supper, ma'am. It's ready.'

Her hands were shaking as she dished up jugged hare, greens and carrots. She sat on a kitchen chair waiting for the dining-room bell. Blake! Here! He certainly looked different from when she had last seen him by the canal. In fact, he looked quite the gentleman in light-coloured breeches and polished leather riding boots. What was he doing here, of all places? She hoped fervently that he had not told Miss Kirby that he knew her, otherwise she would be in trouble.

She jumped when the little brass bell high on the kitchen wall jangled. Usually, Lissie removed the soup dishes, took in the meat course and went straight back to the kitchen. But when they had visitors, she stayed to serve, taking round the plates and then offering the vegetables.

As she approached Blake's chair, she thought she would drop the dish, her hands were shaking so much. Only when he had taken his vegetables did he turn his head and look directly at her. His face was expressionless apart from the eyes, which were like the clear blue sky on a summer day. His eyes smiled, briefly, at her, but that was all. She moved on to Miss Kirby and the gentlemen resumed their conversation.

Blake had been warned by Kirby not to talk about Sir William's parties. As far as his sister was concerned, they had met at the Institute.

'I tell you, Mr Kirby,' Blake said, 'the future is steel — carbon steel. It's more versatile for all manner of things.'

'Not as strong as iron though,' the older man pondered. 'It's no use for the railways.'

'No. I grant you that. It's a different metal for a different job. You can roll it thinner and make all manner of things that are lighter and cheaper to transport.'

Lissie shrank back against the wall behind him. His broad shoulders strained the seams of his jacket as he stretched to pass the breadboard to his host.

'Have you been in Yorkshire for long, Mr Svenson?' Miss Kirby asked.

'A few years now.' He hesitated. 'I was at Grasse Fell school.'

This information impressed Miss Kirby. 'Does your family come from the South Riding?' she asked.

'East Coast, ma'am. The Humber. My late father had business there.'

'Late father, eh?' Miss Kirby murmured. 'And your mother? Does she still live there?'

'She is in her home country at present.'

'Oh? Home country? Where—?'

'Sister, dear,' Mr Kirby interrupted. 'Do stop quizzing our guest like this. Why don't you tell us about your own little school?' Mr Kirby gave his sister one of his glares.

Miss Kirby took a deep breath. 'My school? Yes. I . . . I have two classes now, you know, and my own pupil teacher for the little ones. Her name is – er – Miss Jackson. You . . . you must meet her, Mr Svenson—'

'Sister,' Mr Kirby warned.

Miss Kirby blushed. 'Oh! Of course I did not mean to say – er – only that all my pupils adore her, and . . . and, well, brother dearest, she *is* one of the prettiest girls in the parish.'

Mr Kirby took over the conversation. 'Do you have brothers and sisters, Mr Svenson?'

Lissie quietly collected the empty dishes and returned to the haven of her kitchen. She sat at the table and stared at her gooseberry flummery for a long time. She had made little almond biscuits to go with the flummery and she arranged them prettily on a porcelain plate. An extra batch was finishing off in the oven.

Why was it that Miriam always cropped up in the conversation? she thought. Perhaps that's why he was here? To meet Miriam. Well, that wouldn't be tonight because she had already sent the pupils to bed and left for her lodgings in the village.

The bell went for pudding and Lissie carried it through. She tried not to look at him, and when she furtively glanced in his direction his eyes were firmly fixed on the tablecloth. She stacked the plates and tureens wondering how much longer he could pretend that he did not know her.

As she carried a pile of dishes out of the room, she

heard Blake raise his voice and say, 'This is really a very delicious meal, Miss Kirby. You have an excellent cook and I can see that I shall enjoy my stay here.'

His stay here? *Here?* Perhaps she had heard wrongly. Surely he was not *staying* here? The Kirbys entertained guests for supper quite often these days and occasionally, they did not go back to town until the following morning. Lissie kept the two spare bedrooms at the back clean and aired for just such occasions. But they didn't *stay*.

She tackled the pile of washing up in the scullery with vigour, only breaking off when the bell went for her to clear the pudding plates and add to the pile. Mr Kirby was pouring port and talking heatedly to Blake about the price of things. Miss Kirby had left for the drawing room, where Lissie had left a small pot of coffee and the best tiny china cups.

Lissie could go to bed when she had finished all the pots and pans, and put everything safely away. She took her biscuits out of the bottom oven and left them to cool on the freshly scrubbed kitchen table. It was a hot sticky evening and the airless scullery was stifling. The attic would be even hotter and stickier, so she wandered down to the orchard to cool off before going to her bed.

The orchard was her own private place after dark. No one else went there and she sat under the trees to enjoy the silence. She leaned against the fissured trunk of an old, gnarled pear tree and took off her boots and stockings to enjoy the cool fresh grass between her toes. It was a clear night, with bright stars and a half moon.

She thought that Blake would probably not mention to the Kirbys that he knew her or Miriam. His appearance was that of a young gentleman now, so, Lissie reckoned, he would not want the Kirbys to know that he had been working on the canals until recently.

The back of the house was now in darkness, except for a tiny yellow glow of a candle stub through the attic skylight. It was late. She would have to go inside soon.

Another yellow glow appeared in one of the back bedrooms, then it disappeared and reappeared a few minutes later in the kitchen. The door opened quietly and she glimpsed a white shirt in the darkness. It must be Blake. Mr Kirby did not come into the garden except to talk to George. And George had gone to his bed.

He strolled down the path to the horse trough and scooped up a handful of water that he threw over his face, spreading it through his hair and round the back of his neck with his fingers.

Lissie held her breath in case he heard her. Though why she was worried about that she did not know. She had as much reason to be out here as he had. He meandered along the rows of vegetables and fruit bushes and eventually sat down on a stone garden bench at the edge of the orchard. Lissie would have to walk by him to go back into the house.

Well, she couldn't stay here all night. As she scrambled to her feet her starched cotton petticoats and full skirts rustled in the quiet of the night. He turned his head to listen.

'Who's there?' he called.

She stayed silent, not sure what to do.

'Is that you, Lissie?'

Still she did not reply.

'Are you going to hide in the orchard all night? Why don't you come and sit by me? The honeysuckle smells particularly sweet in this corner of the garden.'

She walked slowly towards the stone bench, carrying her boots and stockings in her hand.

'Good evening,' he said politely. 'How are you?'

'I'm well, thank you. Are you?'

He murmured something in response and she stopped walking, keeping what she considered to be a safe distance from him. 'What are you doing here?' she asked.

'I'm trying to cool off. The house is very warm tonight.'

'I mean what are you doing staying here? What do you want?' she asked bluntly.

'I want you to come and sit by me. And to talk to me.'

'What about?'

'About you. Tell me, is Lissie your proper name?'

'Yes.'

'Lissie, short for . . . ?'

'Short for nothing. Just Lissie.'

He stood up and she took a step back.

He said, 'Look, I'll move to one end of the seat and you can have the other.' He sat down again. 'There. Is that far enough away for you?'

She sat on the bench and pushed her feet into her stockings.

'Mr Svenson—' she began.

'My name is Blake. You know that.'

'Miss Kirby would never allow me to call you that here.'

'Miss Kirby is probably fast asleep in bed by now.'

They sat in silence for a while, then Lissie asked, 'Have you given up the fly boats?'

'I have. I have been going to classes at the Institute in town. That is where I met Mr Kirby.'

'He often talks of the Institute. What is it, exactly?'

'A school. Like this one. Well, not quite like this one. It's for men to learn how to be engineers and manu-facturers.'

'How do you learn about that?'

'By reading books.'

'Oh, I love reading books. Miss Kirby lets me read all her books.'

'Do you like your position here?'

She thought for a few seconds and then replied frankly. 'Yes. But I wouldn't like it half so much without Miss Kirby's books to read.'

'What kind of books do you like?'

'Oh, all of them.' Her stockings were around her ankles and she wondered if, in the darkness, it would be all right to lift her skirt hem so that she could secure her garters. She decided not and folded her stockings over instead. Then she pushed her feet into her boots and stood up.

He got up quickly and caught her hand. 'Don't go yet.'

She should have shaken off his hand and gone into the house that minute. But she didn't. She allowed him to pull her closer and bend his head to hers. She allowed him to kiss her and it was the most wonderful feeling in the whole wide world. He held her tightly against him as his lips searched hers for a response. A response that came from her slowly at first, and then more passionately as her heart began to thump uncontrollably.

She put her arms around his neck, feeling the cool dampness of his skin and hair, grasping his head with her hands so as not to let him go. Her body moulded into his and his hands roamed her back and waist and hips, searching through the folds of her skirt. A strange uneasy flutter spread through her legs and stomach and she wanted him to go on like this, to go on for ever and ever. But suddenly he stopped. He took her hands from around his neck and placed them by her sides.

'Lissie, Lissie,' he groaned.

'What is it? What's wrong?' He does not like me after all, she thought.

'I did not wish for this to happen.'

'Oh.'

He was shaking his head. 'You don't understand, I should not have done that.'

Lissie's heart plummeted. 'But you did.'

'I know. I am sorry. I—'

'I see.' She was right. He did not like her. She turned to walk away.

'No you don't see!' He caught hold of her hand again, but this time she shook it off. She remembered what Eliza had said to her. *You want to watch them bargeboys. They don't call 'em fly-by-nights for nothing.*

'Good night, Mr Svenson,' she said. She gathered up her skirts so that she could escape from him as quickly as possible. How could he? How could he take her in his arms like that and then reject her? The man was a fraud. A foreigner masquerading as a gentleman! She hoped he would not be staying long at the Kirbys.

A lamp was on the kitchen table, turned down low. Her little almond biscuits were now quite cold on their baking tray. There were two tiny gaps where someone – Blake, it must have been Blake – had sampled them. She could not understand why this made her so angry, so – so beside herself with vexation. She tipped the remaining biscuits on to a tin plate and carried them upstairs.

The dormitories were quiet, although Lissie knew the older pupils were still awake. She put her finger to her lips and went round with the biscuits, leaving one by the pillow for those who were asleep. Finally, she shushed the whispering and flopped on to her own bed, trying to understand why her body felt so shaky.

Hurt and confused, she fretted about the kiss. She hadn't asked him to do it. Welcomed it, yes, but he had stolen it from her. And then pushed her away. He was cruel and she did not like him for that.

Tired, upset and increasingly perplexed, she eventually fell into a restless sleep. She heard the early morning rooster crow, and an ox-cart rumbling along the road, then realisation dawned. Of course. It was Miriam he wanted. He had come here to court Miriam.

Chapter 18

'Have you heard the latest? Miss Kirby is taking a lodger.'
Miriam came into the kitchen as soon as she arrived for
school the following morning. She was wearing one of
her best dresses. A pretty blue cotton one, too new for
the schoolroom.

'Who told you that?' Lissie asked. She was sitting at
the table writing her list for Miss Kirby.

'I heard it at my lodgings. Mr Kirby brought a
gentleman from town home in the trap yesterday.'

'Yes, he did.'

Miriam's eyes widened. 'Did you see him? Who is he?
What's he like?'

'Oh, I don't think he'll be staying. Not when Miss
Kirby finds out who he really is.'

Intrigued, Miriam sat down at the table. 'What d' you
mean, Lissie? Do you know him?'

Lissie kept her eyes on her list as she replied. 'He's
that horseman from the flyer. The one whose horse lost

a shoe. I bet he hasn't told Mr Kirby he used to work on the barges.'

'Oh, I remember him,' Miriam breathed, excited by this news. 'He was real handsome, he was.'

'He still is, if you like that sort,' Lissie replied shortly.

'You wouldn't tell on him, would you, Lissie?'

'No I wouldn't. Would you?' She stopped writing and put down her pencil, then finished cutting slices of bread and spreading it with dripping for Miriam's pupils. 'There, you can take that lot in for their breakfast.'

Miriam picked up a piece of bread and dripping for herself. 'Bring me a mug of tea in the schoolroom? Please, Lissie. You know I'm stuck in there all morning.'

Lissie sighed and shook her head. Miss Kirby did not allow tea in the schoolroom, but if Lissie didn't take her some, Miriam would land her with pupils who were hopeless in the kitchen and then Miss Kirby would blame Lissie for getting behind with her work.

When she took in the tea the schoolroom was a mess as Miriam had not tidied away last night's sewing before she had left the previous day.

'Miriam, get a move on! Miss Kirby will be in here soon and she'll be furious if she sees it like this.'

'You do it for me, Lissie. Go on, you're much quicker at these things.'

Lissie sighed. 'Are you sure you really want to be a teacher, Miriam?'

'Oh yes. It's better than working for me mam at the Navvy.'

'But you're no good at it!'

'I know,' her friend wailed. 'That's why I want you to 'elp me.'

Reluctantly, Lissie lined up all the pupils on one side of the room and gave the bigger girls brooms to sweep the floor then asked the smaller ones to pick up cutting-out debris from the worktable. Lissie was on her knees behind the tall teacher's desk when the door to the schoolroom opened. Oh no! Not Miss Kirby already! She held her breath and waited for Miriam to get rid of her, desperately thinking about what she would say if Miss Kirby found her there.

'Oh! G-Good morning.' Even in those short words Lissie could hear Miriam's demeanour change. It was as though someone had turned a key in her back. There was no whining, no pleading, as she went on, 'Can I help you, er – sir?'

Slowly, Lissie sat back on her heels and watched as Miriam got down from the high teacher's chair and saun-tered towards Blake at the door.

He was dressed for town in his high boots and long black coat and was carrying a tall black hat and gloves. 'I heard voices,' he said. 'This must be the schoolroom.' He looked around with interest.

'They can be untidy little b-blighters sometimes,' Miriam explained. 'Lissie was just giving me a hand.'

'Lissie? Is Lissie in here?' Blake stepped forward into the room and let the door close behind him.

'She was just leaving. Weren't you, Lissie?' Miriam directed.

'Yes. Gladly.' Lissie got up off her knees and dusted down her calico apron with her hands. 'Good morning,

Mr Svenson,' she said and bustled past him with her head held high.

He didn't answer but stepped aside and let her pass.

Lissie fumed silently in the kitchen and kicked the big iron fender in frustration. Infuriating man! Miriam had looked really pretty this morning in her blue cotton dress with lace at the cuffs and throat, and with her honey-blonde curls escaping and mingling with her cap strings.

She fingered the plain brown twill of her morning work dress and wondered if she should curl her hair. One thing was certain, if she did, Miss Kirby would not like to see tendrils of black hair showing beneath her cap when she was in the kitchen. She went to clear the dining room and saw Mr Kirby in his pony and trap outside the front of the house. Blake dashed out of the front door, climbed up beside him and they left for town.

Miss Kirby did not allow pupils in the front rooms of her house, so Lissie set them to work in her kitchen and started on the cleaning herself. She left Blake's bedchamber until last. He was tidy, she noticed. He had made the bed and left his nightshirt neatly folded on the pillow. She picked it up and hugged it to her breast, burying her face deep in the folds of cotton. She wished it was him. She wished he was here, in the room with her, alone with her, kissing her again.

He had books in his room. They were stacked on the mantelshelf and she lingered, looking at the titles. There was a horsehair armchair by the fireplace and she sat down for a moment to flick through one of his books. It was all about how to make things from iron and other metals and it had drawings in it with numbers and letters on them. Still nursing his nightshirt, she stroked the pages, imagining him reading the book and writing a note on the small table by his right arm.

She felt rather than heard Miss Kirby enter the room, and when she looked up, Miss Kirby's fury was obvious.

'What do you think you are doing?'

'I . . . I was just looking, ma'am.'

'How . . . how dare you? Give me that nightshirt this instant! Mr Svenson is a guest in this house and a gentleman. You are here to look after him, not pry into his private papers.'

'No . . . I . . . er . . . I wasn't, I mean, I was only—'

'Prying. You were prying. I should dismiss you this minute.'

'No, no please, ma'am, please don't send me back home.'

'I shall not discuss it now. Finish here immediately and go down to the schoolroom. One of the children is ill.'

Miriam was in a panic because one of the new boarding pupils had been sick on the schoolroom floor. Lissie cleaned up the mess and took the little girl outside. She sat her in the shade and pumped some fresh water for her to drink. Miss Kirby came out and decided that the pupil could lie down for the rest of the day and the crisis was over.

'I shall see you in the morning room now,' she said to Lissie.

Lissie stood in the middle of the small room and waited for her employer to speak.

'You have disappointed me, Lissie. Going through a gentleman's possessions indeed! What have you got to say for yourself?' Miss Kirby was very angry.

'I . . . I was only reading one of his books, ma'am.'

Miss Kirby had learned how to glare like her brother did. She had the same beady brown eyes and they stared unblinkingly at her.

'I . . . I'm sorry, ma'am. It won't happen again.'

There was another silence.

'Very well. You will forfeit your next half day and will clean every knife in the house before you go to bed tonight. That is all, you may go.'

Dejected, Lissie went back to her work, wondering how she would tell her dad that she could not come home this month. By good fortune, Miss Kirby did not want a cooked tea that evening. Her brother and his guest were staying in town for an evening lecture at the Institute and she had asked for a light supper on a tray in her morning room. Lissie spent the afternoon cleaning kitchen knives with an old cork and some sand. She hated knife cleaning as it made her finger ends so sore.

By evening she was tired and missing the sleep she did not get the night before. Her last duty was to leave out the gentlemen's late supper in the dining room. She arranged cold cuts of pickled tongue, Yorkshire cured ham, plum relish and fresh-pulled lettuce hearts under muslin cages on the table. She had made a cherry pie especially and left it with a bowl of fresh clotted cream from Eliza's dairy. Miriam came into the kitchen for some bread and cheese before she went back to her lodgings.

'Are they all in bed?' Lissie asked.

'They should be. I sent 'em up there half an hour ago.'

'Haven't you been up to check?'

'No point. You'll be going up soon. I've not seen George with the trap yet. Where's Mr Kirby tonight?'

'You mean where is Blake. They are at a lecture in town until late.'

'Oh. I'll get off then.' Miriam cut another piece of bread and cheese, wrapped them in her handkerchief and left.

In the attic most of the little ones were asleep with their day clothes heaped on their boxes. It was a long day for them and they were always tired out by nightfall. A few older girls were whispering and giggling and one was systematically folding all the discarded pinafores and dresses. Lissie broke up two who were squabbling about where the candle should be.

Luckily, the sick child had improved, but she complained of being thirsty so Lissie poured her some water from the washstand ewer. She closed the dormitory doors thankfully, put on her own nightgown and brushed out her long black hair. A light breeze came in through the attic window that she propped open permanently in summer, and she heard the pony and trap coming down the drive.

Tired as she was, Lissie lay on her back with her eyes wide open, imagining Blake and Mr Kirby in the dining room enjoying their supper. She hoped they – he – would like her cherry pie and then chided herself for being foolish. The house went quiet. She got out of bed

to check that the candles in the dormitories had been
blown out.

The sick girl, like her, was wide-eyed and restless. 'I'm
not sleepy now, miss,' she said.

'Hush. You'll wake the others. Would you like some
more water?'

'I'm hungry, miss.'

'Did you eat some tea?' Lissie whispered.

'No, miss. Miss Jackson didn't bring me any.'

'Do you mean you haven't eaten since dinner?'

'I didn't have any dinner neither. I didn't feel like any
then. I'm hungry, miss.'

Lissie put her fingers to her lips. 'You must be very
quiet. Go and climb into my bed on the landing and
I'll fetch you something from the kitchen.'

'Some bread and dripping, please, miss,' the girl said
immediately.

'Not dripping, not after you've been sick. How about
some bread and honey?'

'Yes, please, miss.'

'As long as you are very quiet.'

Lissie pulled on felt slippers that she had made herself,
took her lamp and crept down the back stairs to the
kitchen. Some of the empty dishes from the dining room
had been placed on the kitchen table. She could smell
cigar smoke and realised that one of the gentlemen had
carried them through. Mr Kirby had not done anything
like that in the past. She jumped, startled, as the door to
the garden opened.

'I saw the lamp.' Blake stood in the open doorway.
He was not wearing a jacket and his shirt was open at

the neck. 'I've been down to the orchard. You were not there tonight.'

She went into the scullery immediately to fetch her shawl from the nail behind the door and wrapped it around her thin cotton nightgown. 'One of the pupils has been poorly,' she muttered as she sat down to prepare the food.

'May I talk to you while you work?' he asked.

'What about?'

'You. Why are you being like this with me?'

'Like what?'

'Ignoring me.'

'I'm not ignoring you. I'm busy.'

'Lissie, you are not busy now!' he exclaimed. 'For heaven's sake! It's the middle of the night!'

'So go to bed then.'

He walked across the room, took the bread knife from her hand and placed it carefully on the table. 'Stop and listen to me for a minute. Please?'

She pulled her shawl tighter around her nightgown. 'What do you want?'

'You, Lissie. I want you. I wasn't going to tell you. I was going to wait until you were older and I had proper work in the Riding. But I can't. I can't wait for you.'

She forgot the bread and honey, and the poor child waiting hungrily in the attic. 'B–but you pushed me away.'

'I told you. I planned to wait.' He took both her hands and pulled her gently to her feet. Her shawl fell away. He pushed his fingers through the long silky curtain of her hair and let it fall gracefully on to her thinly clad shoulders.

She was shaking. She could not believe this. He was saying he wanted her. *Her*. Not Miriam after all.

He held her chin lightly and traced the contours of her eyes, nose and mouth with his fingers. His thumb lingered on her lips and she parted them and nibbled at it, ever so slowly, with her teeth. In the glow of the lamp his face looked dark and stormy – no, not stormy, hungry – his face looked hungry.

She twined her hands around his neck and stretched up to kiss him. Her lips parted and his mouth and tongue searched hers with a passion that she returned. His arms snaked around her. His hands were all over her body and her blood was pounding in her head. She tottered backwards and he clasped her tighter, closer. She was acutely aware of his hard body against hers, of his muscled thighs, his rising manhood and his firm chest against her softness. Together, they pushed against the table, rattling crockery and dislodging a dish that fell to the stone flags and shattered.

He stopped kissing her for a moment and simply held her close, her head pressed against his chest, whispering breathlessly, 'I want you, Lissie. I need you. Tell me you feel the same.'

Every inch of her skin was alive with a passion that left her speechless. She was in a turmoil, drawn into a vortex of desire that she could not understand, let alone control. She had no resistance when his hands searched under the thin cotton of her nightgown for her soft, yielding flesh. Or when his lips lowered to her throat, and then to her breasts . . .

'*Stop this at once!*'

They froze. Slowly, Blake disentangled himself from Lissie's nightgown, picked up her shawl and wrapped it around her.

Mr Kirby, clothed in his dressing robe, stepped into the kitchen. His sister hovered behind him in the passage. The ensuing silence lengthened.

Finally, Blake swallowed and said, 'I am the cause of this, sir. This is my doing.'

'Be quiet, Mr Svenson. Lissie, I am ashamed to have you in my house. My sister has told me of your behaviour in Mr Svenson's bedchamber today. You are dismissed. You will pay for the broken china out of your wages. Pack your box in the morning and leave.'

Blake took a step forward. 'No, Mr Kirby, do not do this. Sir, this is all my fault. You cannot blame Lissie. She is innocent here.'

'I asked you to be quiet, Mr Svenson!'

'No, sir. I shall not stand by and let this blameless young woman suffer for my weakness.' Blake hesitated for a moment before going on, 'You are a man yourself, sir, and you know of men's urges . . .'

'How – how *dare* you speak of such things before my sister!' His face was so flushed that Lissie thought Mr Kirby was going to explode.

'But, sir, I know you understand these things, you—'

Mr Kirby raised his arm to strike Blake, but Miss Kirby stilled it from behind with her hand and said, 'No, brother, dear. That is not so wise.'

Lissie saw that Blake's fists were clenching and unclenching by his side.

Mr Kirby dropped his arm and said, 'I am shocked,

deeply shocked, by your behaviour, Mr Svenson. I invited you into my home as a guest and this is how I am repaid!'

'It's . . . it's not his fault, sir,' Lissie stammered. 'I came down for—'

Mr Kirby's fury was rekindled. 'I think I know very well what you came down for! I warned my dear sister not to employ you . . . you . . . you . . . it is very clear to me what kind of woman you are!'

'No, sir. You are wrong!' Blake protested. But he knew that Kirby was not a man that he could reason with, especially after wine and port.

'And you, Mr Svenson, should know better than to give in to the temptation of . . . of *harlots*. I will not have you under my roof. Leave this house immediately!'

'Now, sir? In the middle of the night?'

Mr Kirby waved his arms around and shouted, 'Get out of my house! Get out, I say!'

Blake glanced at Lissie with naked despair in his eyes then left. Lissie moved to follow him into the garden.

'Stay where you are, you little trollop! Sister, fetch my cane.'

Luckily for Lissie, Miss Kirby came forward and calmed her brother with entreaties not to wake her pupils and to save any punishment until morning. However, she was just as angry as he was and said, 'Lissie, go back upstairs this minute.'

Lissie, her head now as cold and clear as day, obeyed instantly. She picked up the bread and honey and folded the pieces together.

'Leave that where it is!' Miss Kirby snapped.

'It's . . . it's for the sick pupil, she—'

Miss Kirby glared at her. 'Very well, take it. Go now.'

As she hurried into the passage and up the back stairs, Miss Kirby added, 'You will have your box ready to leave before breakfast.'

'I am sorry, Lissie, love,' Eliza said. 'It was that lad off the flyer, wasn't it? I saw him leave with Mr Kirby in the trap yesterday morning. I was just taking milk to the doctor's house when they went off. I tell you, he was a bit of a surprise to me, he was, because he looked quite the gentleman, all dressed up for town.'

Lissie sat in silence on the stone steps of the dairy. She was thinking of those stolen moments in Blake's arms last night and how much she wanted to repeat them, and how she did not regret her actions for one minute. She hoped, desperately, that she would see him before she left Fordham for good.

She had sent a message to her dad and he might be back on a barge this afternoon, someone had said. She had not seen anything of Blake this morning. Unable to sleep, she had carried her box down from the attic herself and left it outside the kitchen door before daybreak.

Eliza was sympathetic and went on, 'You can stay with us at the farm. For as long as you like. You know that, don't you?'

'Thanks, Eliza. But I'll have to go home with my dad when he gets here. I expect I'll find work at the Navigator.'

'Look, why don't you leave your things in the dairy and come back to the farmhouse with me? I'll leave word at the alehouse where you are. If your dad – er – or that lad – comes looking for you, they'll know where to find you.'

'What will your husband say?'

'You leave him to me. He'll not cause any bother.'

'Thanks, Eliza.'

Chapter 19

Luther Dearne's first stop when he climbed off the barge at Fordham was the alehouse, where he heard all about the to-do at the school the night before. He hurried up to the school hoping to talk Miss Kirby round with a few yards of Nottingham lace. He was not even allowed in the kitchen door. Old George came outside and told him firmly to take Lissie's box and leave or Mr Kirby would send for the constable.

Luther retreated to the alehouse.

Blake slept in the trap at the coach house. George went in the house to pack his belongings and agreed to keep them until he found somewhere to stay nearby. Finding lodgings was not easy for Blake as word had spread quickly and no one wanted to upset Mr Kirby by taking him in. All he thought of was Lissie and what he would say to her when he found her. Where was she?

His mind was distracted when he saw Luther Dearne

going into the alehouse. He recognised him straight away. He had seen him from a distance at the wharf in town, and a local bargeman that Blake knew had confirmed his identity. His blood began to pound in his head. All the frustration and anger that he had for Mr Kirby and his imperious manner was suddenly refocused on this ghost from his past.

His deep-rooted grief bubbled to the surface. Everything was Dearne's fault! It all went back to his crooked dealings that had led, ultimately, to his father's death. His rage focused on this man who had murdered his father and got away with it. Well, not for much longer, he resolved. He was never more ready than now to confront him. Blake wanted his revenge more than ever as he followed Luther Dearne to the alehouse.

Luther was thinking about where he would get the rent at quarter day, now that Lissie had lost her position. He was already up to his eyeballs in debt and Lissie would not be able to earn the same skivvying for Annie Jackson at the Navigator.

It sounded to him as if his little girl had grown up faster than he had realised. He didn't think she was interested in lads. And she was a bonny lass. All the fellas at the Navvy said so. But she was a good girl and did as she was told when it came to staying away from the bargeboys and such. She never encouraged them like that Miriam did. And they knew better than to mess with the Jackson lass, or her little friend. Mickey saw to that.

Well, at least his little Lissie wasn't turning out to be a dried-up old prune like Edie! Still, the tincture was doing the trick for Edie. It quietened her and it was cheaper than gin. But she was no use to man or beast these days. If his Lissie came back home he could kick out Edie and she could go and live with that Rosa woman.

Thick as thieves those two were. If you asked him, Luther thought that Rosa was a witch, and she was only tolerated at Mexton Lock because she was good with the sick. Like Edie, in a way. Folk only put up with her loony ways because she was Luther's wife. Well, he didn't care about her any more, but he reckoned his Lissie wouldn't let him kick her out.

Where the hell was he going to get the rent? A bolt of cloth might pay Mickey his dues for drink and food, but it was not enough for rent. Perhaps he could find a husband for Lissie? He had been prepared to pay a good price for her as a babby. There must be some barge owner around looking for a woman. A widower would do. With a few shillings to spare to keep his pretty young wife's parents off the streets.

Luther thought this was one of his better ideas and he slapped a coin on the alehouse counter. 'A pint of your best, landlord,' he said.

He was staring at his half-empty tankard when Blake walked in. Blake bought himself a pint and retired to an opposite corner where he could watch Luther's drinking and movements. A group of farm labourers came in from the fields to slake their thirsts and blocked his line of vision.

Blake decided it would be best to tackle Luther outside. He finished his ale, slipped out through the back door and surveyed the cobbled yard at the back. It was almost totally enclosed by stone walls and outhouses on each side. But, like the much bigger Navigator Inn at Mexton, it had a privy opposite, across the cobbles. He stepped into the shade, leaned against the wall, and waited.

After the evening milking, one of the milkmaids came to tell Lissie that her dad was in the alehouse and she hurried to find him. The day was overcast and dark grey rain clouds were blowing up from the west. Luther was on his third pint when she sat down beside him.

'Dad, Dad! Have they told you what happened? Oh Dad, I'm ever so sorry!'

'Nay, lass. It can't be 'elped. Did he do owt to you though? Tell me if he did and I'll kill him, I will.'

'No, Dad, he didn't. He didn't do anything wrong, honest.'

'Mr Kirby thinks 'e did, or 'e wouldn't have kicked the both of you out like that!'

'We had a kiss, that's all. You know what Mr Kirby's like! He's a chapel-goer and he doesn't hold with that sort of thing.'

'It were just a kiss, then?'

'Honest it was. We were in the kitchen.'

'Well, whoever 'e was, 'e seems to 'ave scarpered now.'

Lissie sighed, feeling dejected. Where had Blake gone? She didn't want to go off home with her dad without talking to Blake first.

'You'll 'ave to get work somewhere, lass,' her dad said. 'Trade's real bad fer me nowadays.'

'I could go into town and find something. You must know people there, Dad.'

'Aye, I do that. But I'll not have yer working in town. It's too far away from me and yer mam. She's allus said 'ow much she wants yer back home.'

'But I won't be earning if I'm at home with Mam.'

'There's work at the Navigator for now. Summat else'll come along. Your old dad'll see to that.'

Just as she thought. Lissie sighed again. 'How is me mam?'

'Same as always. No use to anybody. You'll have to cook t' dinner for us when we get back. I've time for another pint afore we go though.'

After his fourth pint, Luther pushed his way through the throng of thirsty farm workers to find the privy across the yard. He stumbled about in the gloom until he had relieved himself, then made his way outside to go back to his ale.

He came face to face with a young, well-built fellow whose piercing stare left him feeling cold. His heart seemed to flutter in his chest, then it missed a beat and he panicked silently. Luther had done enough dodgy dealing in his life to be very wary of strangers who took an interest in him. There was another man in the privy, but only the two of them in the yard.

He glanced around. Behind him was the stinking privy and a stone wall. On either side of the yard the stone-built stores were locked and barred. His only way out was across the yard down a narrow alley and he'd have to get past this young tyke to get there.

Luther became anxious. This man was tall, with broad shoulders and big fists already tightly clenched by his sides. He looked as though he meant business, business

that Luther didn't want to get involved in. He noticed
he was dressed smart, for town. He wouldn't want a fight,
would he? He wouldn't want to muck up those nice
clothes, would he?

Luther stepped briskly to one side with a casual
remark, 'It's the door behind me, squire, but you'll need
to hold your nose as well as your cock.'

Blake covered his escape route with one easy stride.

'Look here,' spluttered Luther, 'I don't know who you
are, but—'

'Svenson. My name is Svenson.'

Luther felt his heart turn over again and he began to
sweat. Svenson! Bugger! It must be nearly six years since
he'd seen off old Svenson, but it still worried him from
time to time. Who was *this* Svenson then? Surely not
that skinny kid? Nay, it couldn't be!

'Never 'eard of yer, mate,' Luther grunted as he tried,
again, to push by. Bloody hell, the fellow was rock solid!
He thought he saw a movement at the back door of the
alehouse and swivelled his glance. But if anyone was
there they had melted back into the shadows. Luther
raised his voice, just in case. 'Out of my way, man. I have
no business with you.'

A strong arm barred his escape route. 'I have business
with you, Dearne. You murdered my father. You shot him
in cold blood to cover your thieving ways and now you
are going to pay for it.'

'Not me, mate. I don't know what you're talking
about.'

One of those large fists gripped his shoulder and
pushed him backwards, throwing him against the rough

stone wall. Luther's hands were clammy and he could feel the sweat trickle down the sides of his face. Yet he felt strangely cold, as cold as ice, and reality seemed to be slipping away from him.

A voice, strangely disembodied to his ears, sent the chill deeper into his head. 'I have searched and watched and waited for you. You're a murderer, Dearne, and if the magistrates won't make you admit it, then I shall.'

Luther was winded. His arm was hurting where he had banged it against the wall. What was happening to him? He felt pain grip him like a tight belt around his chest. The fellow must have struck him right in his guts. He hadn't felt it in the guts, it was his arm, his arm . . . His knees buckled beneath him and he choked for air. The belt around his chest became tighter, as if he was being throttled, he couldn't breathe, he couldn't see, he couldn't hear . . .

It all happened much more quickly than Blake had planned. His words were strong, but when he saw the older man close up, Blake could see that there would be no contest in a fight. The man was heavy with belly, not muscle, and his face was jowly and florid. Blake had pushed him against the wall and threatened him, raising his fist. When he saw the fear in Dearne's eyes, he pulled his punch and was sure that he had not struck him. But Luther Dearne went down before him, clutching his arm, spluttering and choking.

This was not how Blake had planned it at all. He had planned to overpower him, yes, then march him down to the canal, to a more isolated spot where he would extricate the truth about his father's murder. Maybe he would have to rough him up a bit, but not enough to floor the man.

Blake stood over Luther with his shoulders hunched and fists clenched. Luther, helpless on his back, gurgled like a baby. One of the farm labourers came out of the privy door, with his eyes wary and wide, and edged cautiously around Luther's motionless bulk.

Lissie had pushed through the men in the alehouse, ignoring their coarse remarks about her sullied reputation. If she waylaid her dad in the yard, she might persuade him not to go back into the alehouse and they could set off for home. She heard raised voices from the direction of the privy and slowed her pace. If drunken men were arguing, she had best stay out of it.

But from the shadow of the open doorway she was shocked to recognise the voices and figures of Blake and her dad across the yard. Blake had his back towards her. Dad had his back to the stone wall. She thought she saw another figure in the gloom at the entrance to the privy.

She inhaled sharply. Dad had found out it was Blake at the Kirbys last night and was going to thump him! She must stop him! Her dad was no match for Blake – Blake would kill him! She was too late. She saw Blake's clenched fist raised in anger. She heard her dad's strangled cry and saw him sink to the ground.

'Stop! Stop it! Get away from him!' she cried. She picked up a piece of wood and ran across the cobbles. 'Get away from him! What have you done to him?' She hit Blake across his body again and again with the wood.

'Lissie!' His surprise to see her there was mingled with

confusion as he tried to dodge the blows. 'What are you doing?'

'Leave him alone, you brute!'

He caught hold of the end of the wood and wrenched it from her grasp, protesting, 'Stop this, Lissie. It's nothing to do with you!'

'You hit him! You knocked him down!' she accused shrilly.

'No! I didn't touch him!'

'Liar! You're a liar! I saw you!' She fell to her knees on the cobbles. Her dad lay motionless on his back. His eyes were closed and a choking, gurgling sound came from his throat. She took hold of his shoulders and shook them vigorously, crying, 'Wake up, Dad! It's me, it's Lissie! Wake up! Wake up!' But the gurgling was fading and his corpulent body lay still. His right arm fell from across his chest to the ground. Lissie's heart missed a beat and her throat closed as she realised what had happened.

Blake's face was stony and his eyes wide. He stared at the scene before him, unable to believe this was happening. Lissie had called this man 'Dad'.

'No, no, don't die, please don't die,' she whimpered to the twisted purple face of her darling dad. What had Blake done to him? Kneeling beside his still form, she continued to shake his shoulders. 'Open your eyes, Dad. Open your eyes for me. It's Lissie, your Lissie. Don't leave me. Not now. I couldn't bear to lose you now!'

But she knew that it was too late. Her anguish and grief spilled over and she turned her head to look up at Blake and screamed, 'Murderer! Murderer! You've killed him!' She began to sob, cradling her dad's lifeless head in her arms, rocking backwards and forwards as she knelt beside him. 'You killed him, you killed him,' she choked. 'You've killed my dad.'

Blake continued to stare uncomprehendingly at the scene. He was frowning and shaking his head. This couldn't be true. How could this be? When he found his voice again it was a hoarse whisper in his throat. 'I don't understand, Lissie. Is this man your father? But he can't be. He can't be! He murd . . .' He stopped talking, horrified by this realisation. No, he did not believe it. This man was his father's murderer. He was nothing to do with his beloved Lissie. He couldn't be!

'Of course he's my dad,' she sobbed. 'My darling, darling dad. And you've killed him! You've killed my dad.' She was weeping now, her shoulders sagged and shook as she whispered, 'How could you do this? I loved you. I would have done anything for you.' She inhaled raggedly, her grief and anger mingling uncontrollably. 'You'll pay for this. I'll make you pay for this. I'll see you hang for what you've done.'

Blake's anguish mixed with an increasing bewilderment. 'Lissie – no. Listen to me,' he begged, 'I didn't touch him. I swear I didn't. He can't be dead, he can't be!'

Two men from the alehouse had come out to investigate the commotion and as they drew near, Lissie replied angrily, 'I saw you. I saw you hit him with your fist, and then . . . and then he went down, he fell down at your feet. I saw it all. I did.' She turned her head to the two men. 'Did you hear me? I saw him murder my dad. Fetch the constable.'

Blake protested, 'No, Lissie, no, you've got this wrong.'

One of the men came forward and took Blake's arm. 'Best come with us, lad, until the constable gets here.'

'Let go of me!' Blake stepped back and out of his grasp, but the other one barred his way. 'It's young Svenson, isn't it? The one who's come to lodge at the schoolhouse?'

The other man added, 'Oh yes, I 'eard about him. The young gentleman who's bin taking liberties with the girls there.'

'Yes, that's him,' Lissie interrupted shrilly. 'But he's not a gentleman. He's a bargeman off the flyers!' She turned her grief on Blake and cried, 'You're a liar and a fraud! You come here, all dressed up in your fancy gentleman's clothes, with your fancy way of talking and you're nothing but a common bargeman. A common *murdering* bargeman!' She choked and spluttered on her words but she meant every one of them. 'I hope they hang you for this.'

The two men closed in on him, one for each arm. Blake was too quick for them. He elbowed one in the stomach and winded the other with his fist, then turned smartly and disappeared down the narrow alley at the side of the alehouse. He sprinted along the street, over a low stone wall and into the woodland beyond. He moved so quickly that neither Lissie nor the two men realised what was happening until it was too late and he had gone.

'Don't worry m'dear,' one said to Lissie. 'The constable's men'll catch up with him tomorrow. He won't get far once word gets round.'

Lissie didn't care any more. Her whole world had fallen apart. Nothing would bring back her dad. And Blake? She had thought she'd found a friend in Blake, and a man that she could love. She had thought he cared for her. He said he did. But it was all a pretence.

Why had he done this to her beloved dad? Her dad was an old man and Blake was young and strong. He was no gentleman. He was just a thug like Mickey Jackson and his lads at the Navigator. How could she have thought she loved him? Blake Svenson was nothing more than a cold-blooded killer and she hoped he'd rot in hell.

Chapter 20

Blake moved quietly, hacking his way through the scrubby undergrowth that grew thickly in the woods surrounding Fordham. His lack of confidence in the local constable and magistrate ran deep, and had done so since the injustice of his papa's death. If the constable caught up with him he would be doomed. He was known as a bargeman. Even worse, he was a foreigner.

Had Lissie known all along who he was, who his father was? Had her father put her up to this charade? Had she deliberately led him into a trap that would end with him in the hands of the constable? No, she would not have wanted her father to die. That part, he was sure, was not planned.

But if he were in jail, Luther Dearne would be free for ever! Had Lissie been deceiving him all this time? Oh God, he thought. She was Dearne's daughter. His flesh and blood. His beautiful Lissie was the daughter of a murderer. His father's murderer.

He was breathing heavily and his heart was thumping when he reached the waterway. It was a dark, dank night and he was frightened. If the constable's men caught up with him he would be locked up, with no chance to prove his innocence, to find out what had really happened.

A ghostly silence blanketed the canal. Tethered horses stood quietly on the towpath and a string of sleeping barges lined the bank. He stared at the still, black water and wondered, fleetingly, how cold it was and how long it would take him to die. Dying was better than rotting in an English jail until he was hanged for a murder he did not commit!

But giving up was not his way. He was Blake Svenson and proud to be him. He was a fighter and a survivor, and he was innocent. He had not killed Luther Dearne. He was certain of that. However Dearne had died, it had not been his doing. Even so, the man was dead and his darling Lissie hated him with a vengeance for it.

Blake anguished, wrestling with his conscience. He had wanted Dearne dead. He had lain in wait for him. He had prepared to fight him and then drag a confession out of him, so that the magistrates would hang him for his papa's murder.

What should he do now? Flee downstream to the coast? He could be on a ship to Sweden within the week. He could start a new life. His mother had cousins there, he would not be alone. But he would have to leave England for good. Leave the South Riding and above all, leave Lissie for ever.

His head was in turmoil. The shock of realising his

lovely Lissie was the daughter of Luther Dearne was too much for him to bear. How could such a dear, sweet creature be the offspring of that vicious manipulative crook? It didn't make sense. A growling groan escaped from his throat as he sank to his knees beside the inky water.

How could she continue to want him, thinking that he had killed her father? Lissie hated and despised him. She wanted him dead. She wanted him incarcerated and hanged. He had to get away from here, but where could he go?

Blake staggered to his feet and set off. He walked through the night, following the waterways upstream towards town and then he waited under a bridge for the flyer to come by. The horseman knew him and Thomas was resting in the cockpit, so they welcomed him as a passenger without question. His physical exhaustion ensured that sleep quickly overtook him.

But not for long. His mind continued to churn with bad dreams of Lissie tempting him into her bedchamber and then transforming herself into a hooded hangman. He even felt the rope around his neck when he woke from his nightmares, anxious and sweating, and grateful to continue his journey.

He left the fly boat before it reached Tinsley and walked cross-country, skirting the ironworks and terraces of labourers' houses in the town. He knew the landscape and travelled with a purpose, avoiding known roadways and farms. He knew where he was going. He was going to a place of refuge away from prying eyes, where everyone was always discreet. Always.

He reached Grace's late, as nightfall approached, after walking since dawn. His shirt was grubby and his coat and boots scuffed and dusty. He was exhausted, hungry and, most of all, thirsty.

'Let me in.' He rapped on the scullery door of Grace's and whispered as loudly as he dared, 'It's Blake. Open the door, quickly.'

A young female voice whispered back, 'Go away. It's all locked up back here. You can't come in.'

'Who are you?'

'Why do you want to know?'

'I won't harm you, I promise. But please, please let me in. I must see Clara tonight.'

There was a short silence, then the young voice replied more loudly, 'Gentlemen callers round the front, if you please, or I'll have to get madam.'

'Do that then! Call her, you silly girl!' Blake stopped and took a deep breath. 'I'm sorry,' he went on. 'It's just that I am so very tired. Madam Grace knows me and I don't want any of Clara's services. I just need to . . . to talk to her.' He slumped against the door, almost fainting with thirst and fatigue. 'Please . . .' he begged.

He must have closed his eyes or fainted, or he simply fell asleep on the back step. The next thing he knew he was falling over on to the quarry-tiled floor as the scullery door swung back.

He heard a distant voice say, 'It's him all right. Looks as if he's walked across the Pennines. Mary, pull the day bed out in the kitchen and fetch some coals for the range. Then get yourself off upstairs till morning. Go on, girl, you can sleep in my bed. Get on with it!'

Blake prised open his eyes. 'Clara? Is that you, Clara?'

'It is that, my lad. And what have you been up to since I last set eyes on you?'

'It's a long story . . .' His voice faded. 'Can I have some water?'

Clara went to the scullery sink and started pumping. When he had drunk a tankardful she said, 'I think you had best get some sleep first. Can you stand? There's a bed in the kitchen and a drop o' brandy in the cupboard if you need it. Come on, lad, on your feet now.'

The water and brandy revived him. 'Thanks,' he murmured. 'Stay with me, Clara. Please. I need to talk — I'm in a bit of trouble.'

'I guessed as much. Why would you be here looking like this if you weren't? You're not going anywhere else tonight, that's for sure, so we'll talk when you are properly rested.'

The welcoming warmth of the kitchen range soon took over and he collapsed gratefully on to his makeshift bed. It was pitch dark when he woke. For a second he wondered where he was, and then the memories rushed into his mind and he knew why he was here. A fire glowed across the room and there was an oil lamp on the dresser behind him. The bed was little more than a pallet pulled out from the bottom of a cupboard. But there was plenty of padding underneath him, even if his feet did hang over the end. He pushed away a rough woollen blanket that was keeping him warm.

Someone was moving around, over by the range, and he heard the heavy clunk of a drinking mug. He craned his neck to see around the table legs. 'Clara. Is that you?'

'Blake! You're awake. Well, this is a fine carry on, isn't it? I expect you'd like something hot to drink. It's just mashed.'

Her level, matter-of-fact tone reassured him. He would be safe here.

'What time is it?'

'Four o'clock. The last client has just left. We have had some good spenders in tonight. Grace is really happy, which is just as well for you. Are you getting up for this tea? There's bread and cheese as well.'

Blake realised how starving hungry he was. When the bread and cheese was gone Clara fetched the remains of a plum pie from the pantry and he demolished that with some thick cream.

'Another brew?' Clara asked as he finished.

Blake nodded. 'Thanks.'

Clara set the refilled mug in front of him and asked, 'What happened?'

He shook his head slowly. 'I don't know. I don't know how everything went so wrong.'

'Surely things can't be that bad,' Clara smiled optimistically.

Yes they can, he thought miserably.

Clara waited a few minutes then prompted him. 'I heard you were doing all right for yourself on the fly boats. What went wrong?'

'Nothing really. I came off them and went to the Institute and . . . and . . .' Oh God, his life was such a mess! He changed the subject. 'How is Grace keeping?'

Clara went along with him, thinking that things were probably worse than she realised. She replied, 'Grace is in fine fettle. She had a nasty fever last winter, but pulled through all right and she'll be with us for a good few years yet. Tough as old boots is our Grace.'

Blake raised a smile at last. 'I'm pleased to hear that. And you, Clara, how have you been?'

'Oh, you know, surviving.'

'Are you happy?'

'Sometimes.'

'Aren't you ready to do something different? You must have a bit put by.'

'It's a good living,' she replied sharply. 'Besides, I do what Grace wants to do. I wouldn't go off and leave her now. I'd be dead if it wasn't for her. I'd have starved to death on the streets. And . . . and . . . well, she is getting on in years a bit and she kind of thinks of me as a daughter, you know.'

'Does she have no family of her own?'

'I don't think so. She was brought up in the work-house and married a sailor who was lost at Trafalgar. Mind, she may have had a baby once, one that died, I think. She says she's never had any, but sometimes she talks about how she got out of service and she talks about a baby. And then she shuts up and asks for some brandy.' Clara paused and sipped her tea. 'Have you been to see your own mother lately?'

'She went back to Sweden to see her cousins. I had a letter from her. She had it delivered to our warehouse on the Humber and Ephraim, who runs the business for us, sent it to the flyer office for me.'

'Is she well?'

'The crossing was rough, but she says she has recovered.

Lucy, her maid, is with her. She writes cheerfully, considering . . .'

'I am sure that she misses you very much. I would if you were mine. Have you written to her?'

'Twice. The last time just recently when I came off the flyers and enrolled at the Mechanics Institute. I know that will please her. But now . . . this . . . she cannot know about this.'

'I don't see what can be so wrong that you cannot tell your own mother!'

Blake, revived by the hot drink and food, took a deep breath and began, 'I'm in a bit of trouble, Clara. I just need to disappear for a while.'

'I guessed as much. Sweden seems as good a place as any.'

'No. I've got to stay and clear my name somehow. I didn't do it, I swear. And there's this girl I told you about. Oh, Clara, you should meet her. Her name is Lissie and she is such a darling. She sparkles like the stars in the night sky and . . . and . . . now she thinks I killed her father. I . . . I . . .' He gave an exhausted sigh.

Clara got up to put more coal on the fire. 'You'd better tell me all about it.'

Blake floundered, his emotions churning again. 'I . . . I don't know where to start.'

'Try the beginning.'

The beginning – where was that? All those years ago when Dearne shot his father? Or, more recently, when he had searched out Kirby at the Institute to effect an introduction to his home?

'I . . . she . . .' he began. 'Do you remember when I

told you about my father's death? Her father was his murderer. He was a liar and a cheat and a thief. And he shot my father.' Blake ran his fingers through his hair and his shoulders sagged. 'How could that ruffian produce such a bright, beautiful girl like Lissie? How, Clara? How?'

Clara stretched her arm across the table to hold his hand and listened to his tale. It was breaking dawn when he finished talking. Luckily the household did not stir until later when Mary got up to see to the range and get the hot water going. Grace stayed in bed until noon and Clara dealt with the household's affairs until teatime, when Grace would be dressed and ready to receive her visitors.

Clara was a good woman, Blake reflected. She deserved better than this for her life. But it was what she wanted. If he had loved her he would have taken her away from here and not worried about the difference in their years. But he did not love her, not in that man and woman way. Clara was a friend. And Blake desperately needed a friend.

'But you can't stay here, Blake!' Clara protested. 'Some of our clients are well-known townsmen. They guard their reputations and Grace guarantees them absolute discretion. If you were seen and – God help us – recognised as a wanted fugitive, there would be hell to pay. Are you sure that Sweden is not the best place for you until it all blows over?'

'That was my first instinct. But they will be looking for me on the waterways down to the coast. And . . . and I really do not want anyone over there to know.' He ran his fingers agitatedly through his thick hair. 'If my mother finds out, it will break her heart.'

'But you didn't kill that man! You told me you didn't do it!'

'I was there though. And everybody thinks I did! Clara, you have to help me, I don't know what to do. I didn't kill him, I swear I didn't. But he did die. He died before my eyes − he just crumpled up and fell to the ground. I don't understand it, I pushed him back against the wall. That's all I did. I didn't punch him, I didn't!'

'Well, you are a strong man, Blake. And you're a good fighter, I'm told. How well known was Dearne anyway?'

'He had friends up and down the canals. Been around for years, but was known to be crooked and untrustworthy.'

'There you are then. The magistrate will understand.'

'Understand what? That I killed him?'

'No. They'll see that he had it coming to him.'

'So you *do* think I killed him.'

'No, Blake. You're twisting my words. You know what I mean.'

'Well the magistrate doesn't know what happened either. He only knows what others tell them. I'm worried, Clara. Luther Dearne had a lot of local friends.'

'Where is he from then?'

'Mexton Lock. He is as thick as thieves with the landlord of the inn there.'

Clara stared at him in horror. 'Not the Jacksons from the Navigator? You don't want to make enemies of them.'

'Too late. I already have. They are not all bad though,' he added, thinking of Pete, the horse marine.

'If you say so.'

There was something in Clara's tone that made him pause and he glanced at her face. 'They don't come here, do they?'

'Of course not! Grace wouldn't allow that sort over the threshold. No, it's not that, though they do come into town fairly regularly – especially the father and his eldest son.'

'And?'

Clara faltered, as if she regretted opening this line of conversation. 'He's . . . he's well known for being brutal with his women.'

Blake's eyes rounded. 'With you? Mickey Jackson has attacked you?'

'No, I've never met him, but I know his reputation. He . . . he, well, my stepfather was like him. The local street girls all stay well clear of him.' Clara choked slightly on her words. 'But I expect he finds his pleasure somewhere else now, with some poor unfortunate . . .'

Blake came over to comfort her. 'I'm sorry. Don't upset yourself. I've heard tales of the two older boys being like their father, but the youngest works with horses and he is kindness itself. And his girl, Miriam, well she is wayward but she is settled as a pupil teacher now. She's a cocky wench to be sure, who'll get herself into trouble before long, but I don't think she has suffered like you did. Her mother got her away from the inn.'

Clara recovered. 'You know quite a lot about them.'

'I've been asking around.' Blake thought for a second. 'I can't do that any more. That's why I need you.'

Clara heaved a sigh. 'It's no good. Grace will not let

you stay here. What if someone like Sir William found out?' There was another short silence, then Clara went on, 'Of course, Sir William might help.'

'I haven't had contact with him since – since that first night I came here.'

'But he has news of you! He knew you were on the flyers and that you had been at the Institute. He took a liking to you that night.'

'How do you know that?'

Clara gave him a long, steady gaze. Finally she rose to her feet and picked up the tray before her. 'I'll just take this tea upstairs for Grace. She'll be awake now. Why don't you have a wash in the scullery and then we'll toast some bread by the fire?'

Refreshed by cold water, Blake's head cleared and he was sitting by the glowing coals when Clara came back. The morning was dark and damp with a cold rain lashing at the windows. Blake handed the toasted bread to Clara who spread it with butter and honey. She brought more cushions to sit by him in front of the range.

'Grace agrees with me. I'll ask Sir William's advice.'

'I shouldn't think he would want to get involved.'

'Oh, he doesn't like crooks any more than you or I. But I won't say why you want to go to ground. He's a man of the world and he'll accept that you have a good reason.'

'But I have only met him the once—'

'He remembers you and . . . and . . . well, he knows that you have called here.'

'How is that, Clara?'

'I tell him everything.'

'Everything? You mean about your clients?'

'Oh, Blake, for a man of your education you can be very slow about some things.'

'What on earth do you mean?'

'Sir William *is* my only client. He pays well to keep it that way.'

'Then, I – er – we . . .'

She nodded. 'You did not realise how privileged you were that night. You . . . I . . . we needed his permission.'

'Yes, I remember.'

'He once said that he wished he had a son like you, a son with your spirit and courage.'

'Well, well. But he is married, is he not? Does he not have any sons?'

'He has no children at all – it is his greatest sadness.'

'Yes, I can understand that.'

'There is a persistent rumour about a bastard that he fathered when he was a young man. It caused quite a scandal at the time. He has always been a man full of life and ideas. Grace's provides a discreet outlet for his energy.'

'But his wife, Lady Swinborough – does she know about you?'

'I believe so, and by all accounts she turns a blind eye to his visits. She is an invalid, you see, worn out by too many miscarriages and stillborn births. They were slowly killing her and the doctor advised no more. People have to deal with their lives as best they can. It is no good being too idealistic, is it, Blake?' Clara gave a wry grimace. 'Don't judge him too harshly. His wife has the best doctor he could find. He always hoped for an answer but she is too old now. Sir William still loves her. Maybe you'll understand when you're older.'

He was beginning to understand something. To understand what it was like to want someone so much that it hurt. And then to have your belief in them, and theirs in you, shattered. Was this the answer? To seek solace elsewhere as Sir William had?

Not for Blake it wasn't. He still held a memory of Lissie. A painful memory. A memory of her body close to his, and his desire to possess her made him ache with longing. How could this have happened to him? He had had everything to live for, and it had all been snatched from his grasp. Now, all he could hope for was jail at best and the gallows at worst.

In despair, he covered his face with his hands and wept silently. Clara held him close until his grief eased for the present. When he was more composed he continued, 'You must believe me, Clara. I didn't want Luther Dearne to die by my hand. I only wanted him to admit what he had done to my father. I only wanted the truth!'

'I do believe you, Blake. Now calm yourself. What is done is done and we have to make the best of it.'

But he wasn't listening. Consumed by despair, he was reliving all the grief of his childhood. It was tearing his heart out and he couldn't stop himself. He began to talk again, to ramble. 'I tried to get a doctor for my father. Peter Jackson was just a boy like me, but he helped. He lent me a horse and I rode over to Fordham. But the doctor was not there. His housekeeper said he was at Swinborough Hall and wouldn't leave. I might have saved him if only I could have brought the doctor!'

'You did your best.'

'My father died, Clara! My father died because I failed!'

'It wasn't your fault. You must stop blaming yourself! It is eating away at you and that is why you wanted this revenge. Well, you have what you wanted. Luther Dearne is dead. You can move on now.'

'To where? What can I do?'

'I don't know and neither do you. But we have to get you away from here, so that you can lie low until they stop looking for you.'

'Why would they stop?'

'We'll put out word that you have gone back to Sweden. That will satisfy the constable. Now, have you ever worked down the pit?'

'Down the pit?'

'Yes. Down a coal mine. Or any sort of mine?'

'No, but I'm willing to try it.'

'Sir William's estate is vast and he has some drift mines in the hills. There are no deep shafts. They are safe and the teams are reliable. The coal keeps the furnaces going in Sir William's ironworks.'

'Where are these pits?'

'They are well away from town, and from the canal. All the coal is brought down in narrow boats on a private cut that links to the canal. So you'll be able to lie low until the panic dies down.'

'Where would I live?'

'Sir William is a good landlord. He has built rows of cottages near the pits for the colliers and their families and you'll easily find lodging with one of them.'

'Sounds perfect for me.'

'Well, we'll have to get Sir William to take you on, but I'm sure he will when I ask him.'

'Thanks, Clara. You're a true friend.' He reached out for her hand. 'I have to prove that I didn't kill him and I don't know how. Help me, Clara. Please. Help me to prove my innocence.'

Chapter 21

'Dad, oh Dad,' Lissie sobbed. 'What'll I do now? What'll I do without you?'

It was a week after he'd been killed and, still numb with shock, Lissie stood outside the stables at the Navigator and listened to the hammering as the lid on her dad's coffin was secured in place.

Somebody came and helped her into the back of the cart where the coffin rested. She rode with it over the stone bridge and along the woodland track to home. The day went by in a blur, just as all the other days had since her journey from Fordham with her dad's body.

They had left him in the stables until the coffin was ready. Miriam's dad from the Navigator took charge of everything. Lissie had never been very much aware of him as he was usually in the saloon of his inn. But now he was organising things and he kept asking her if she was all right.

Lissie did not answer. She had no words to say. She

had lost her bonnet and her hair was tumbled. Her dress needed mending, but she no longer cared. All she wanted was her dad back. They placed the coffin in their front room, resting it across their two best chairs with one end on the horsehair sofa. He was a big man, her dad, and it took three of them to carry him.

Someone shoved a little glass of spirits into her hand. She didn't see who. She didn't see anything. The next thing she knew Miriam's dad was stroking her hair and saying to her, 'You tell your mam not to worry. Mickey will take care of everything.'

Lissie wondered why he couldn't tell her mam himself as he was there, in the house. Then she realised that her mam was already dead drunk and fast asleep by the cold ashes in the grate. Lissie stood there, lost, in the untidy kitchen and wondered how she would cope with her mam now her dad was gone.

Mickey lingered a moment, looking at her. 'You've grown up proper while you've been working at that school. Your ma'll be pleased to 'ave you 'ome again. Tell 'er I'll call back tomorrer.'

He seemed not to want to leave. He stared at her and Lissie just stared back at him blankly, unaware of time or feeling. Then Mickey said more briskly, 'Yes, tomorrer. I'll drop by tomorrer.'

Lissie climbed the stairs, took off her boots and crawled fully clothed under the bedcovers. She sobbed herself into an eventual sleep.

Mickey Jackson continued his unusual half-friendly behaviour after the funeral. Edie always made him welcome because he brought her bottles of gin from the

Navigator. Edie liked the tincture from the apothecary as well though, and she told Lissie to go and ask Rosa to get some.

'I'll have to pay for it, Mam,' Lissie said, holding out her palm.

'Tek 'er yer dad's timepiece chain from the cupboard. It's gold so she'll get a good bit for that in town.'

'But it was me dad's! You can't sell it!'

'I've no use fer it and he sold his timepiece months ago.'

Lissie did not know that things had got so bad at home. She did as her mam asked and Rosa was very kind about it all. She gave her two bottles of Mam's tincture saying, 'It's laudanum, lass. It's like medicine for 'er now. Gi' her a few drops in a glass of wine, if yer 'ave it. I'll get as much as I can fer the chain. 'Ow is she?'

'Same as always. Mickey Jackson seems to be taking care of most things. Why don't you come and see her, Rosa? Mam would like that.'

Rosa shook her head. 'Better not. Not while Mickey's around. Treating you all right, is he?'

'Oh yes,' Lissie replied, thinking of the gin.

'You tell yer ma from me that she can allus come here if things get bad.'

'Thanks, Rosa. We'll be all right though, as soon as I get some work.'

But Rosa did go to see Edie. On the day that Mickey went off with his eldest lad to see Peter and go to the races at Doncaster. They set off early and were gone all day. Lissie took her chance and went over to the Navigator to ask Annie for a day's work in exchange for

some meat trimmings and drink for Edie. Rosa saw her
go by, reached for her shawl and went off to see her
friend.

'Edie, ducks, 'ow are yer doing?'

'Oh, Rosa, I'm right glad to see you. Come and sit
by the fire. Our Lissie made it up wi' a log from the
wood afore she went.'

'I've brought yer some o' yer medicine.' Rosa placed
the small brown bottle of laudanum by Edie's tin mug
on the hearth.

'Put some in there fer me, will yer?'

Rosa picked up the mug. 'It's empty. 'A'n't yer got
owt to drink?'

'Not till our Lissie gets back from the Navvy.'

'Not even any ale?'

Edie shook her head.

'I thought Mickey Jackson were looking after you?'

'Last time he called he said I had to pay 'im 'is dues
somehow.'

'Can't your Lissie earn it at the Navvy?'

'If their Annie'll 'ave her there. She says it'll encourage
me to go over and cause trouble.'

'Aye, well, me ducks, she might be right there. Is there
any hot water in this?' Rosa lifted the blackened kettle
off the swing hob, poured some water into Edie's mug
and added a few drops of her laudanum. She looked
around her as Edie drank and said, 'Nice little house this,
it'd be a pity to lose it. You'll 'ave to give Mickey what
'e wants.'

'Oh aye? How?'

'Oh, Edie, you know 'ow 'e likes women. Save 'im

going inter town if 'e can come 'ere fer it. Do you want some o' my henna fer yer 'air?'

'Oh not that, Rosa. I couldn't stand that wi' Luther, let alone Mickey.'

'Yer just shut yer eyes and do it. Wi' men like 'im, yer don't even 'ave to tek off yer drawers.'

'Eh?'

'Yer do it wi' yer 'ands. Or yer gob.'

'Me gob?'

'Well, not yer gob wi' 'im. I heard tell that he 'as a right big 'un and nearly choked one of the lasses in town.'

Edie's voice rose to a squeak. ''Ow d'yer know that?'

'Edie, ducks, 'ow d'yer think I get me rent on quarter day?'

'Yer go to t' market and sells yer salve, don't you?'

'That on'y buys me flour and lard. I 'ave to do a bit of whoring fer the rent.'

'But yer told me yer di'n't like doin' it wi' men!'

'I don't. That makes it easier fer me to charge 'em. Anyroad, like I said, I do it wi' me hands or me gob. You could give it a try.'

'Oh I don't know. Perhaps I could ask the parish to pay me rent.'

'Yer don't want them poking their noses inter everything!' Rosa protested. Edie had been a good friend to her over the years, sharing any coppers Luther left behind when he went on the canals. She liked Edie and Edie liked her. Rosa continued, 'They'll find out what we get up to together and they won't like it.'

'Oh, Rosa, they wouldn't stop us, would they?'

'Oh aye. I'd rather pay me own rent and do what I want.'

Edie didn't reply. She swallowed the rest of her warm water and laudanum and fell silent.

Lissie found her dozing by the fire, tucked up in Lissie's old school cloak. She saw the laudanum bottle and guessed Rosa had called. It was a relief to her that Mam was asleep because Annie had not given her any work. Instead she had told her to stay away, on their own side of the canal, and not to talk to their Miriam again.

But she had calmed down a bit when her lad, who was minding the inn for Mickey, went to check on his beer in the outhouse, and added, 'I'm sorry about yer dad, lass. Tek this bacon knuckle fer yer mam. There's a bit o' meat left on it.'

Lissie had hurried home. She cut off the meat and boiled up the bone with some barley and vegetables from the garden. They had a feast for dinner that day and her mam was quite placid now she had her medicine.

'I'll try further afield for work, Mam,' she said after they had eaten.

'No,' her mam replied. 'Get this place clean an' tidy fer when Mickey calls. I wants ter keep 'im sweet.'

'How long has Mickey Jackson been coming over here?' she asked.

'It were when yer dad couldn't get work and had nowt to spend at the Navvy. He took to coming over wi' a few bottles or a jug o' draught. And a drop o' gin fer me.'

Lissie realised that this was where all the money had gone, because Mickey would want paying one way or another. She wondered how Mam was going to afford her gin, now there was nothing coming in.

'Mam, why can't I go out to work somewhere?' she pleaded.

'I want you 'ere,' her mam whined. 'I needs looking after now.'

That was true. But she needed her laudanum now as well. As long as she had that, Lissie realised, her mam didn't complain. It could have been anybody banking up the fire and cooking the dinner for her. Lissie got the house and bit of garden organised, but they needed coal, and flour for bread.

'Haven't you got any coppers anywhere?' she asked.

'No. I told you we 'a'n't got no money,' her mam scowled. 'Yer dad left nowt except debts.'

'Then let me go and earn some money by working!'

'Nay, lass. Mickey says yer don't have ter. He says – he says yer can stay and look after yer old ma.'

'What on earth has it got to do with him?' Lissie demanded.

''E owns the 'ouse now.'

'What? This house? Dad left him our house?'

'Nayow! It were already 'is. He bought it off yer dad years ago, when the canal trade was bad and yer dad got into a bit o' bother. Kept him outta prison, Mickey did. We paid 'im rent, like. But we 'a'n't got no money now yer dad's gone.'

Lissie became even more anxious. 'But it's past quarter day and we haven't paid any rent! I'll have to go out and work for it!'

'Yer don't listen ter me, do yer?' Mam cried. 'Yer never

listen! That's what I'm saying. You don't 'ave to go out ter work. You can stay 'ere, Mickey says.'

'Mam! Mickey Jackson won't let us live here rent-free, believe me. He'll turn us out. We'll be in the work-house.'

'Mickey won't let that happen.'

'You seem very sure of him, Mam.'

'I've bin thinking.'

'About what?'

'Things. Just things.'

Lissie could get no more sense out of her. The house was growing cold and there was no more food apart from vegetables from the garden. To lose their house Dad must have borrowed heavily from Mickey during hard times and not paid it back when trade was good. Edie always had her gin and Lissie had never wanted for boots or a working dress. But now Mickey Jackson seemed to own everything about them.

'Mickey's been good to us,' Mam told her.

'Well he's not being very good now,' Lissie remarked pointedly. 'Is he going to turn us out or what? We'll end up on the streets!'

''E promised it wouldn't come to that. 'E promised me.'

Lissie shrugged. Mickey and her dad had been as thick as thieves for years. There would be things she didn't know, and most likely her mam wouldn't know either. Mam had never questioned Dad about where the money and the gin came from.

Lissie looked at her steadily. Her mam had aged in the few years she had been at the Kirbys. She looked old and worn out, and her skin was shrivelling on her bones. But she was her mam and Lissie knew what her duty was. She would have to look after her, whatever happened.

'I'll take the rugs out and beat them, Mam; I need something to keep me busy now the funeral and mourning is over and done with. But we can't live on fresh air.'

'We won't 'ave to.'

'Then where is the money coming from?' Lissie wailed.

'Mickey allus said ter me he'd help out, if I were nice to him. Rosa's told me what he means. He'll likely bring some meat wi' 'im next time he calls and he can 'ave 'is dinner wi' us. Can you cook a dinner fer us, love?'

'Doesn't he eat Annie's dinner at the Navigator?'

'He likes to get away from there sometimes. You know, into town and that.'

'Well, coming here isn't going into town! Still, if he brings us some meat, I'll cook it for us.'

'You're a good lass, love.'

As Lissie scrubbed and polished, she realised that was the first time her mam had ever called her 'love'. Maybe she was softening in her old age.

If she scrubbed by day, Lissie cried by night. She grieved for her dad, and anguished over Blake. She heard from the Navigator that he had disappeared. The constable's men did not catch him and they said he had left the country.

Well good riddance, she thought. But she grieved for him also. She *had* loved him. And now he was gone there was just an emptiness inside her, a void where her love for him should be.

Her mam was unreliable so it was up to Lissie to keep body and soul together. Mickey was probably only being nice to them because her dad had been a good friend of his. He had a reputation for being rough and tough though, so she did not expect his good nature to last. Even so, he sent round some flour and pig fat, and a couple of pheasants for dinner. Lissie found vegetables to go with them, and there was some fruit on the trees in the garden.

'What's he coming for, Mam?' she asked as she rolled out suet pastry for a pudding.

'To see 'ow we're getting on, o' course.'

'But why?'

'Well, he's our landlord now an' 'e wants to see we keep the place nice an' that. So we 'as to be nice back to him.'

And he brings you gin, Lissie thought. Mickey must have taken a shine to her mam when he was visiting her dad. Mam seemed to be happy with the arrangement so who was Lissie to question it?

'He likes you then, Mam?' Lissie queried.

'Well, I wouldn't say that exactly.'

'What then?'

'Come on, Lissie. You know what I mean. You're a grown woman now. I 'eard the stories about you and that lodger at the Kirbys.'

'You mean the one that killed dad?'

'That's the one. Miriam told her ma that you'd been found in his bedchamber in on'y yer nightgown. Miriam said you knew, all right, what men wanted.'

'It's not true. Not like that, anyway.'

'But Mr Kirby did catch you in bed wi' the lodger, didn't he?'

'No, Mam. I wasn't in bed with him. I was kissing him, that's all.'

'Oh! That's not what I 'eard. Anyroad, you know what it's all about now, don't you?' Her mam sounded irritated by her denial.

'Yes, Mam,' Lissie sighed. 'I know what you mean.'

So that was how her mam paid for her gin. In that brief moment Lissie felt sorry for her. From things her dad had said, Mam didn't like the bedchamber side of being wed and never had. So providing those kind of favours for Mickey Jackson must be hard on her. But she needed her gin every day, she couldn't live without it, so perhaps Mam was grateful that Mickey had taken a shine to her.

Lissie wondered if Mickey's wife knew about this arrangement. Miriam's mum had been like Miriam when she was younger, but she had grown stout during her years working in the kitchen at the Navigator. Perhaps Mickey had tired of her and preferred his women skinny like her mam.

When Mickey came for his dinner it was just like the old days. Just like when Lissie lived at home and dad was alive. There were pot-roasted pheasants, done slowly with celery and herbs in the bake oven, and Mam's favourite apple pudding to follow, all served up in the kitchen at the scrubbed wooden table.

Mickey was a big man like her dad, but he hadn't run to fat. He was broad and muscular, from a family of strong, labouring men who had built the canals years ago. When he arrived he gave Mam her gin and had a present for Lissie, just like her dad used to. It was wrapped up in old calico and he said, 'It's not new, but it's made o' good stuff. Used to belong to the missus, on'y she's too big for it now. Go on, try it on.'

'It's a dress, Mam,' Lissie squealed in surprise as she opened the parcel. 'Oh, it's really pretty, and just look at this lace!'

Her mam came over to feel the material. 'Oh aye. That is a nice bit o' stuff. Go on then, lass. Put it on.'

'What? Now?'

'Aye,' her mam nodded. 'It's all right. I'll see to t' cooking.'

The dress material was a beautiful, soft, floral sprigged cotton, with lace trims at the neckline, sleeves and hem. It fitted her well at the waist and billowed out over her boots to skim the floor. The bodice was a bit tight, but the shoulders were fine. She pulled at the lace to cover where she was bulging out of the low neckline. She wondered if she dare go to the Navigator in it after tea. Mickey and her mam were sure to want her out of the house.

Mam shouted upstairs. 'Tea's on t' table. Let's be having you.'

Lissie felt like a real lady for the very first time in her life. If only her dad could see her, he'd be so proud. She clattered down the stairs and floated into the kitchen, holding her skirts off the floor as she came into the room.

Mam looked at her, nodded briefly, and said, 'Very nice. Sit down and eat up then.'

Mickey stared at her for a bit then poured her some ale from the bottles he'd brought with him without saying a word. He pushed a glass across to her.

'Drink up, lass.'

She took a sip and he repeated, 'I *said* drink up.'

'Do as he says, love,' her mam added, finishing off her own drink.

Lissie emptied her glass and he refilled it immediately.

When he'd finished his meal, he belched loudly and said, 'That were a tasty bit o' pheasant, Edie. I'll just have a pipe and another tankard.'

Lissie picked up the hint and volunteered, 'Shall I go out? I could go to the Navigator if you like.'

'Nay, lass,' her mam said quickly. 'Go and sit in t' front room. I'll clear the table. You wouldn't want to dirty that dress, would you?'

'No, Mam. If you're sure . . .' It wasn't like her mam to be so nice. Must be because Mickey was here.

It was chilly in the front room and Lissie sat on the old horsehair sofa and pretended she had rung for a maid to bring her some tea. She thought that this was a nice way to carry on and maybe things might get better with Mickey around. She was just beginning to wonder if her mam and Mickey would be going upstairs when Mickey came into the room.

'Well, Lissie, my lass. You look a pretty picture sitting there in that fine dress.'

Lissie smiled and said, 'Thank you ever so much, Mr Jackson. It's lovely.'

He lumbered over, took hold of her hand and pulled her to her feet. She slammed into his chest, which smelled of stale ale and kitchen grease. Then, as his other arm held her jaw, he pressed his foul, slobbering mouth over hers.

She squealed and struggled to get away but he held on to her firmly.

'Stop wriggling, lass. It's time for a proper thank you now. Come on.' Mickey dragged her across the room and into the tiny hall. 'Get up those stairs and look sharp about it.'

Shocked and frightened, Lissie yelled, 'No, I won't! What are you doing?'

He gave her a painful shove from behind. 'Don't start playing about now.'

'No, no, not me! It's my mam you want! Mam! Mam! Where are you, Mam?'

Edie's flushed face appeared at the kitchen door. Mickey turned his head and said, 'You told her, Edie, didn't you?'

''Course I did. She knows what to do.'

'Mam, what? What did you tell me?'

'Y'know. About what men want.'

'B-but I thought that was you. I thought it was you he wanted!'

'Don't be daft.' Mickey pushed her again and she fell up the first few stairs. 'What would a red-blooded man like me want with a wizen old crow like Edie? Gerrup there and tek that dress off.'

'Mam! No! No, Mam, I can't. I won't. You can't make me.'

'Can't I?' Mickey growled.

Edie frowned. 'I don't know, Mickey. If she don't want to . . .'

'Oh she does, all right. You can see just by looking at this one that she does. Besides, I like 'em spirited. You leave her to me, Edie. She'll come round.'

'She's on'y a young 'un, Mickey . . .'

'I like 'em young. You should know that by now.' Mickey gave Lissie another hard push up the stairs. 'Come on, lass, let's try out the goods.'

One of his arms circled her waist easily and he lifted her bodily off the stairs to drag her the rest of the way. Ignoring her kicking and protesting, he threw her into the front bedchamber where her mam and dad had slept and slammed the door shut behind him. There was no key in the lock so he dragged their heavy oak chest across the door.

'Now then, lass, let's you and me have a bit o' fun.'

Horrified, Lissie scrambled to the window, but she knew before trying that it would not open. The wood had swollen and warped over the years and it did not budge.

Mickey laughed and made an animal-like growling noise in his throat. 'Go on then, lass, gi' us a bit of a fight. I like a bit of a fight. It makes it all the sweeter in the end.'

She shook her head, so frightened that she was unable to speak and cowered against the wall until he said, 'What are you waiting for? Get that dress off.'

When she did not move he took off his leather belt and flicked the end at her, whipping her arm. She flinched at the stinging pain and rubbed the spot with her other hand. He flicked the belt again, catching the back of her hand and she let out a cry.

'All right!'

Her fingers fumbled with the tiny buttons at the front of her bodice. Whenever she stopped undressing he flicked her again with the belt until the dress and her petticoats had dropped to the floor.

Then he threw down the belt and tore away the rest of her flimsy undergarments until she stood completely naked by the bed.

'Please don't do this,' she whimpered, but he seemed not to hear her.

He pushed her roughly on to the bed. When she tried to cover herself with the blanket, he took both her hands in one fist and lifted them above her head so that every inch of her unclothed body was exposed to him. He stared at her for a long time.

And then he smiled, showing his broken, stained teeth. He let her go and she thought he had changed his mind. Weak with relief, she tried to roll from the bed, away from him. But he clawed her back and hit her hard across the face.

'Stay where you are,' he growled.

He had stopped only so that he could take off his own clothes and as he pressed his coarse swarthy body on hers he snarled like a starved, caged animal.

He terrified her. 'Please don't,' she begged. 'I . . . I haven't done this before.'

'That's not what I 'eard. I 'eard you've bin goin' wi' one o' the bargemen.'

'It's not true,' she croaked.

She pushed at his body and tried to wriggle out from under him. This only served to inflame him further and he slapped her hard with the flat of his hand, knocking her almost senseless. Her defeated, flaccid body flopped back on to the ticking mattress.

Then his coarse hands and foul mouth were all over her, pinching, prodding and poking, and then he drove into her again and again, forcing her flesh apart and covering her mouth with his to stifle her screams.

She must have fainted at that point because the next thing she knew he was holding her head and telling her to take a drink. The brandy trickled into her mouth and revived her. She wished it had not, for that was only the first of several attacks on her that night.

When she struggled against him he became on fire. His eyes burned and his nostrils flared as his brutal assault overcame her weakening resistance. If she tried to escape in the quiet interludes when he was recovering his strength, he hit her.

Eventually, he became exhausted by his efforts and fell into a noisy slumber. Lissie thought that he had had enough of her and would let her leave. Cautiously, she slid away from him in the tumbled bed. But the pain and stiffness, and exhaustion of her bruised, aching body, made her groan involuntarily as she moved, and he woke up.

He revived quickly and began the kissing and stroking again. Except that it wasn't stroking, it was grasping and kneading, then nipping with his teeth at her most sensitive parts. She yelped instinctively, tried to push him off her and then cringed, waiting for the blows.

He grunted. 'You're a strong young wench, I'll gi' yer

that. Don't fight me so much, then I'll not 'ave to hurt yer.'

Already she could feel his arousal pushing at her side and managed to croak, 'Please, no more. It hurts so much and I am so sore . . .'

He growled into her breasts. 'Aye well, if as you say it's t' first time, it will 'urt. It allus 'urts t' first time. You'll start to enjoy it now . . . I told yer not to fight too much, di'n't I?'

His swarthy heavy body was over her again, stabbing at her, tearing her flesh, again and again. This time it seemed to go on for ever, until the sweat ran off him on to her face, filling her nostrils with the stale stench of his body and the ale on his breath.

After that, he became too exhausted to throw his hairy body across hers, so he took her hands and guided them to his private parts.

'Come on, lass. Play wi' 'im. He needs a bit o' coaxing now. Put a bit o' life back inter 'im.'

She recoiled in disgust as her fingers tangled with his sticky, matted body hair and warm quivering flesh. She felt sick at the thought. Then he put a large calloused hand around the back of her head and pushed it down towards his feeble arousal.

Oh God, she thought, did he expect her to kiss it?

'Open your gob, love,' he ordered. 'Put him in yer gob and gi' 'im a good suck.'

Not in her mouth, surely? She gagged at the thought and when he shoved her face over it she felt the bile rise in her throat and she retched. She would have vomited over him if he had not yanked back her head.

'Not ready for that yet, lass? Ee lass, tha's got t' learn a bit more if yer wants to keep yer ma's rent paid. I 'ope yer not goin' to be like yer ma in the bedroom. Like a dead crow she was, just a bag o' bones and no idea at all. A man likes a bit o' playing around in the bedchamber. Aye, a bit o' playing around. I reckon thee an' me can have a good bit o' fun together, once yer know what to do, like.'

She lay there, the taste of vomit in her throat and thought, So this is what hell is like.

It was still dark when she woke again. Every muscle and bone in her body ached and screeched at her as she moved. The sheets were damp and smelly where they had lain. She tasted blood on her lips and hoped some of it was Mickey's, from where she had bitten him. But she guessed that it was hers, and that the dragging pain deep within her stomach had been caused by Mickey's relentless assault.

She felt dirty, soiled and ashamed. Ashamed that she had let this happen, that she did not fight harder. She remembered how Blake had held her in his arms, how his hands had been so gentle, and how he had controlled his urges during that first kiss in the orchard. She thought of what might have been with Blake and she wept.

Dawn was breaking and a candle flickered on the oak chest that was still in place across the door. A bottle of brandy and a glass stood on the mantelshelf and beside it a phial of her mam's laudanum. Mickey snored loudly as she crept out of bed as quickly as she dared.

He stirred and snorted. 'Get back in 'ere, now,' he yawned.

'Just getting a drop of brandy,' she replied. 'I thought it might revive me.'

She picked up the bottle. 'Why don't you have a drop? To get your strength up, eh?' She tried to sound coquettish and persuasive and it worked.

He leered at her. 'Don't mind if I do.'

Her hands shook as she poured out the brandy and then added what was left of her mam's laudanum, stirring it round with her finger before she turned towards him. She kept a fixed smile on her face until he had drained the glass and fallen back on to the pillow. It was easy for her to sit quite still on the bed while the laudanum took effect and his snoring returned.

Ignoring her aches and pains, she heaved back the oak chest inch by inch. It scraped along the floorboards but Mickey did not wake up. Downstairs was quiet too. She gathered up what was left of her clothes and crept across the landing to dress.

Mam had raked out the ashes and left them on the hearth plate for Lissie to take outside. She must have been downstairs all night for the fire was going and there was a full kettle on the hob. Now Mam was nodding off in her chair with a tin mug by her side. And another bottle of laudanum, Lissie noticed. No wonder they had no money for food! Lissie stole quietly across the kitchen.

'Is that you, Lissie?'

'Yes, Mam.'

'You're up early. Mek us a brew, will yer?'

Mam did not even ask how she was or if she wanted

hot water for a wash. Lissie waited until she saw her eyelids droop again, then dropped some of her laudanum into her tin mug and topped it up with gin.

'You have another drink, Mam,' she said. 'And a nice rest. I'm just having a wash in the scullery.' She handed the mug to her mam and hovered behind her chair as she drank.

Then she took the kettle, poured some hot water into a tin bowl, stripped off her clothes and washed herself all over, standing on an old sack at the stone sink. Every part of her felt bruised and tender and there was blood coming out of her as if her bleeding had started early that month. Her insides hurt and she felt as if she was being torn in two. From the kitchen cupboard she fetched the strips of linen that she used to line her under-drawers and pulled on her brown work dress and shawl.

Then she took her dad's old leather hunting bag from the front room and began systematically to pack a few clothes and some bread and cheese. As she moved around she felt the bleeding again. With some satisfaction, she tore up the pretty dress that Mickey had brought for her. The plain underskirts would do for more padding to stem the blood. The soft cotton felt comforting in her under-drawers but the aching and tearing still dragged at her insides. She wondered, briefly, how long the pain would take to go away and, on impulse, took the laudanum bottle as well.

Feeling exhausted and weak, she took a draught of water and chewed on a heel of bread. Hopefully that would revive her enough to put a safe distance between her and Mickey Jackson before he came round. The laudanum was safely tucked away in her bag, along with a few coins that Mickey had left to buy more flour and lard. She put on her old comfy boots that were kept for the garden and tied her new ones by the laces to the broad leather shoulder strap of the hunting bag. The bag felt heavy and it hurt her shoulder as she slung it across her bruised and battered body.

When she was ready she filled her pockets with good apples from the outhouse and left. This had been her home but she felt no remorse. She did not belong here. Miriam had been right all along. Her mam wasn't really her mam and even if her dad was her own dad he was gone now. Gone for ever.

And Blake? She tried to push all thoughts of him from her mind. He had had no right to kill her dad in cold blood like that. She had hoped the constable's men would catch up with him and that he would hang for his evil deed. But he had been too wily for them and had escaped to his native Sweden where he belonged.

When Lissie thought of him a void opened in her body, a cold emptiness that ached with yearning for him. It reinforced her pain and made her despise him more for doing this to her. She took one last look at the little house and the untidy garden that had been her home. It held nothing for her now. Nothing. Whatever unknown lay in store for her, it had to be better than a life as Mickey Jackson's whore.

The tears streamed down her face as she resolutely put one foot in front of the other, forcing herself to move on. She would survive this, she would! There had to be something better for her somewhere. She could live with hardship and was not afraid of work. There had to be a way for her.

Her instinct was to take the track down to the canal and reach the towns from the towpath. But Mickey or one of his boys might see her and bring her back. So instead, Lissie disappeared into the woods at the end of the garden, putting as much distance as she could between her, the canal and the Navigator Inn.

She knew the woods well and soon found a pathway through the undergrowth to where the turnpike skirted the trees. The turnpike was the safest route; most of the people who knew her used the cheaper canals and cuts for getting about. Travellers on the turnpike were noisier too. She was bound to hear horse riders approaching, and carriages if anyone came after her. Traps and hand-carts were quieter, but they were slower and she'd be able to see them coming in time to leave the road and hide in the trees or fields that lay on either side.

But as she trudged through the trees, hardly recognising the path as tears blurred her eyes, her aching became a nagging pain again and the increasing stickiness between her legs warned her that the bleeding had not stopped.

She must reach the turnpike! If she could get to the turnpike before she rested she might take a sip of the laudanum to ease the pain. Perhaps not though, for she had to push on and get further away from Mexton Lock before nightfall. Her dad had often said a man could lose himself in the towns, and that nobody would find him if he didn't want them to. Well, perhaps a woman could lose herself as well.

No, she would not rest, she would stand the pain and save the laudanum for night when it would deaden the cold as well as the pain and let her sleep. She only had to reach the turnpike . . .

As her bruised and torn body protested, her mind became numb and her thoughts were frozen. She had no idea of where she would go or what she would do, only that she had to get away from Mickey Jackson. She knew that she had to survive.

She had bread, cheese and apples for two days and could get fresh water from springs and horse troughs by the road. An isolated barn or cowshed would give her shelter for the night, hopefully with some straw to warm her.

Also, she had a little money now. She felt sick to her stomach as she reasoned that she had earned it. But she would need it when she reached the towns. The knowledge of it there, secreted away in a small drawstring pouch, gave her a feeling of security and determination that urged her battered body forwards.

She had nothing else in this world, save the things she carried with her. She was alone and frightened, frightened of what might happen to her, of who would come after her to drag her back to a life of violation and servitude. She had no notion of what might happen to her in the future but she knew she had had to make a choice, to stay for Mickey Jackson's pleasure or leave the woman who called herself her mam. A woman who had sold her to their landlord for the price of the rent and a bottle of gin.

Lissie knew that whether she lived or died now was

down to her and her alone. What happened to her in the future would be because of what she had chosen to do. This was not her mam's choice, or Miss Kirby's, or Mickey Jackson's. It was hers. Her choice.

But could she survive? She knew she was injured and realised, too late, that she should have gone to Rosa's first, for help. But there had not been enough time. The bleeding was getting worse and she was beginning to feel faint. The pain in the pit of her stomach was increasing and walking seemed to be pulling her apart.

What should she do now? Lie down in a ditch, give up and die? Or stay alive? Stay alive by moving on? Keep going, keep putting one foot in front of the other as each step would put a greater distance between her and a life she had to escape.

She had to block it out of her mind. It never happened. It had been a bad dream and she would wake up soon to hear her dad whistling his way up from the canal carrying a sack over his shoulder and calling for her to come and see what he'd brought her . . .

Chapter 22

Lissie thought she must have fallen as she could not remember leaving the woods. The trees had thinned and now only thick hedges and drystone walls edged the turn-pike. She was in the ditch beside the road, her back against the loose stones of the wall. Through a gap she could see that the fields behind had been harvested and the rooks were down, feeding on the gleanings. Nearby, at the edge of the road, a lone carrion crow tore at a dead rabbit knocked senseless by the hooves of carriage horses.

Perhaps she had thrown herself into this ditch to avoid an express stage coach? She was so thirsty. And so cold. Thankfully, the sun had not set and there was still warmth in its rays. The bottom of the ditch was damp and chilly, but she didn't want to move. It hurt so much to move. But she knew that if she stayed and let herself slip into a faint again she would die. She clawed at the grass, hauled herself out of the ditch and forced herself onward.

The turnpike was nearing the track that led down to Fordham, and Miss Kirby's school. Lissie had been at her happiest there, helping to look after the pupils, going to chapel and, most of all, meeting Eliza. She choked back a sob as she realised that she would never see Eliza and Job again.

Nervously, she drank from the stone trough at the top of the rise and moved on. The clear cold water revived her and she was able to push herself more, biting on the leather strap of her bag when the pain became too much to bear. She stumbled along the turnpike ruts until her hunger and weakness melded with pain and exhaustion. A break in the endless drystone walls let her into a field of springy turf that smelled clean and fresh. She ate some bread and cheese, then pushed her best boots beneath her head and allowed herself to sleep.

Her slumbers were short-lived as she was aroused by raucous laughter and the creaking and clattering of a cart on the flinty surface of the turnpike. She heard two men shouting, worse for drink she guessed, as they stopped to feed their horse. Lissie froze and shrank back against the stone wall, listening to their coarse language.

Eventually they quietened and when she heard a snore she stretched her neck to see over the wall. The heavy draught horse was chomping from a nosebag and the men – no, not men, for they were just boys really – were out cold, sprawled on the road beside a brownstone ale flagon, on its side and empty. The cart was loaded with straw, warm dry straw, destined for winter bedding at some farm along the way.

Lissie saw her chance and took it. Ignoring the pain and bleeding, she clambered on to the back of the cart and buried herself in the straw. It warmed her stiffening joints and the cart would take her further from Mexton Lock than her weary legs ever could . . .

Later she was vaguely aware of the cart moving. She heard the boys urgently gee-up the horse. But they were quieter now, having slept off their youthful inebriation. If they found her, she would explain to them how . . . why she was here . . . Warmed by the straw and exhausted by her fight to keep going, she gave in to sleep.

It was dark when she woke up. The cart was turning and it jolted dangerously as it hit a rock in the road. Lissie pushed the straw aside and saw the turnpike receding into the distance as the cart bumped its way down a narrow farm track. She would be discovered! The straw would be forked out into stables or the like and those two coarse and vulgar youths would find her! Terrified of what they might do to her she gathered together her meagre possessions and slid silently off the straw, a bent, shadowy figure clutching the ache in her stomach. Slowly and painfully she retraced the track back to the highway.

She had no idea where she was, only that she was off the turnpike. This highway was smaller and without deep ruts from coaches. Tracks and byways criss-crossed the South Riding as far as Sheffield and beyond. The dark eerie silence was broken by a night rider and the thumping of horse's hooves as he galloped by. She was damp all over from the dank night air and chilled to the bone. Frightened, she tried to quicken her pace so that she would warm up a little, but within yards had keeled over, groaning with weakness and pain. Her toes would not move inside her boots and her fingers did not have the strength to grip the buckle of her bag and open it. She rubbed them frantically and blew on them to get them moving. She must keep going otherwise she might fall into a faint and freeze to death!

As she began her weary trudge onward, Lissie realised it was not the night air that was icy, it was only her own body that was getting colder and colder as it slowed down in its fight to keep going. She must find shelter and warmth where she could rest safely for the remainder of the night. There was no moon or stars that night to light her way and the countryside was not familiar. She must find water to drink. She was so thirsty . . . all the time, so thirsty . . .

There was a fork in the road. The highway stretched in front of her, but to one side lay a track through sparsely wooded land that sloped down from the road, and, hopefully, hopefully, a sleeping farm with barns for shelter. She sat on a tree stump for a long time to gather her strength. In the darkness, she made out a cottage, a large one, built of stone with a slate roof. It had a well-kept garden and cinder paths. The track continued past the cottage and disappeared into more woodland beyond. A vixen screeched and an owl hooted but no sounds came from the cottage, no light burned in its windows.

At one side, there was a long, low building of the sort that houses animals. It was also stone built and in good repair, but firmly shut, its stout wooden doors padlocked against intruders. But, Lissie knew, animals needed water and she crept around until she found a water butt at the back.

Water gave her a second wind and she thought she might climb in through one of the high windows and bed down with the animals. But as she clambered on to a grassy stone and then the damp wooden lid of the butt she felt her flesh tearing again and the familiar warm stickiness of fresh blood between her legs.

Her head felt light and dizzy and she stumbled, falling from the water butt and crying out in pain. Her shawl snagged and tore and her bag fell open, spilling out its meagre contents. From inside the barn she heard a horse whinny and fret at the commotion. She leaned motionless against the rough stone wall and sank slowly to the cold wet ground. The laudanum bottle rolled at her feet. Laudanum! The laudanum would help. It would take the pain away, take the cold away, take the world away.

Just one small sip, that's all, to help her through the night. She winced at the bitterness from the one sip, but gradually her damp and chilly corner seemed a better place. Her aches and pains drifted away and her bleeding seemed to ease. A warm feeling seeped through her veins and her eyelids drooped. She sank further into the ground and drifted into her own oblivion.

She was aroused at dawn by the sound of a horse and cart on the cinder path. She caught a glimpse of it disappearing towards the highway, laden with baskets of livestock and sacks. A man and woman sat upfront, hunched against a chilly wind.

There was a strange tinny taste in her mouth and she

was thirsty again. She was stiff with cold and unable to move her limbs until an early morning sun shed its warmth. Her legs felt like lead weights and her head was feverish and befuddled as she staggered towards the cottage. It had a long covered porch, standing proud of the front door. The porch was well built of old oak posts, with a roof to keep off the winter hail and snow. The door itself looked heavy and was patterned with iron-work studs.

She had to get inside, to warmth, shelter and food, or she would die. She did not want to die. The cottage was quiet and the dawn sun was now hidden by dark clouds that were banking up from the west. She fell with both hands against the stout wooden door and tried to raise a cry or two. No one was home. No one heard her beat the wood with her hands and plead for some help. She trudged silently back to the water butt to drink. The effort made her almost faint and her legs buckled under her. There was no help for her here. She had to move on.

Desperately she tried to focus her eyes on the track. Why did her head feel so light and her legs so heavy? A steady drizzle wet her through and made her already damaged body chilled and even weaker. She couldn't go on, she knew she couldn't. But if she lay down here she might die from the cold and wet. Yet she must rest, other-wise she would bleed to death.

Her head was spinning, the trees were swimming around and the ground kept coming up to meet her and then receding. She felt dizzy. Sick and dizzy. She clung on to an oak post for support. She was back at the cottage, under the porch. Her feet had carried her down the track instead of up towards the highway. It was meant to be, to rest here. Just a short while until her strength returned again . . . The cottage would have a fire . . . a warm fire . . . and perhaps some bread and milk . . . She had money . . . she could pay . . . if only they would let her stay by their fire . . . until the rain eased . . . then she would be on her way . . .

The post was slipping away from her, she couldn't hold on any more. She was mumbling to herself, garbled words that tumbled out. Yes, I have a long way to go . . . right on into town to find work . . . Yes, I am a good worker . . . I have worked in a school . . . I can read and write . . . Please let me in . . . just for a few minutes to warm myself by the fire . . . please . . .

But nobody came as she muttered her pleas through the thick wooden door and beat her hands helplessly against the studded oak. Her back was racked with pain and her life blood was ebbing away into the makeshift bandages between her legs. She began to shiver uncontrollably and her eyes blurred, making her unable to see properly.

She fumbled in her bag for the laudanum and took a sip, then another and another slipped easily down the back of her throat before the small brown bottle slid from her fingers. Her legs buckled beneath her and a cloud of oblivion enveloped her bruised and battered body and soul.

She remembered the pain easing. And then the rain, the ceaseless, soaking rain, and the wind blowing puddles on to the draughty porch, making the fired clay tiles so muddy and slippery that she could not get back on her feet. She remembered the reddish-brown hue of the tiles, and, as the rain seeped through her clothes, the same reddish-brown of her blood as it smeared its way down her legs and spread through her skirts. And then she remembered nothing, only a welcoming blackness releasing her from her suffering.

After the blackness came the horror. Her dad was here, her beloved dad was holding her and kissing her cheeks and hair. But when she looked at his face it wasn't her dad, it was Mickey Jackson and he was laughing at her. Her mam was here too, laughing with Mickey and drinking his gin. Then someone knocked the bottle out of her hand and started beating Mickey with his fists until Mickey fell in a senseless heap on the floor, and when Lissie ran over to look, it was Blake standing there and the man on the floor was her dad and he was dead. Dead. And then she was screaming and yelling at Blake, 'Murderer! Murderer!' over and over again until she floated away.

She felt hot. She was burning alive. Water. She needed water from the pump. Fetch water from the pump. More water. More water. And then there was water all over her and she was icy, icy cold. She must be in her grave, in the cold, cold earth. She was dead. This is what it was like to be dead. Cold and more cold all around her.

Her hands and feet were pinched and nithered and there was no fire because she hadn't cleaned the grate and Miss Kirby was shouting at her to get the fire going. But it wouldn't light and her fingers were too numb to strike the flint. There was a heavy weight on her chest

that felt so tight she couldn't breathe. She was suffocating. She was in her coffin, suffocating.

She beat her fists against the sides and they yielded,
strangely soft, letting in more cold wet air. She was
fighting, fighting for air. She wanted to breathe. She didn't
want to die. She wouldn't die. She wouldn't. Somebody
help me. Take my hand. Somebody, take my hand, don't
let me die.

And in her fever someone did take her hand and held
on to it, dragging her back from the brink of death,
holding on to her, keeping her safe. The heavy weight
bearing down upon her chest eased and she could breathe
again. Roused from her delirium, she felt the softness of
a feather bed and pillows beneath her.

This must be Heaven, she thought, as someone raised
her head and gently offered a cup of water to her parched
lips. She drank, then sank back into the gentle haze of
garden lavender beneath her head. And in her new found
comfort, at last, she slumbered peacefully.

She woke up facing a small window that looked out
on to a grey sky. It had proper curtains made of some
heavy, green material. They were pulled back now to let
in daylight. The room was small but it had a chair and
a washstand holding folded linen and torn strips next to
a row of small pots and bottles. She could smell the salve,
the strong odour of wintergreen overpowered her
lavender pillow.

There was a fireplace with cupboards fitted into
alcoves on either side. A fire burned in the grate and an
earthenware pitcher stood on the hearth. The bed was
wide and very soft. Lissie fingered the sheets. They were

old, but made of linen, like Miss Kirby's sheets, and the bedcover was made up of the same stuff as the curtains. The wooden bedstead creaked as Lissie tried to sit up. Shortly afterwards she heard footsteps on the stairs and the bedroom door opened.

'Well, well, you pulled through after all. You've had me fair worried these past few days.'

A large-boned woman with greying brown hair under a lace cap and wearing a coarse-textured grey work dress stood in the doorway. She had striking features and held herself well, giving an overall effect of being handsome rather than beautiful. Her expression was a mixture of curiosity and anxiety as she looked critically at Lissie.

Lissie tried again to lever herself up into a sitting position. 'Who . . . who are you? Where am I?' she croaked. Her throat was parched.

'Don't try and get up, you're too weak still. You've been very ill and you must rest.'

'How did I get here? I can't remember . . .'

'You will in time. Don't fret yourself, you're safe here.'

Safe? Suddenly, Lissie was stricken by panic and her eyes widened in alarm. 'Has he found me? Where is he? Has he been here? Don't let him in! Please don't let him . . .' She tried to turn back the covers. 'I should go, move away from here . . .' But her arms weren't strong enough to shift the heavy blankets and her legs would not move.

The woman came forward quickly and placed her hand over Lissie's as it clutched the bedcovers. 'Stay calm. You have to stay calm to get better.'

Her quiet insistence was reassuring and Lissie fell back against the pillows.

'You'll be in bed a while yet, my girl. It was touch and go for some time.'

'How long? How long have I been here?'

'There'll be plenty of time for questions when you're better. You have to concentrate on getting your strength back for now.'

'But what happened to me?'

The older woman grimaced sympathetically. 'You'll remember when you're ready to. And I'll be here for you.' She hesitated, before adding, 'You lost a lot of blood and then you caught a raging fever. But you're over it now and you'll get well again.' The grimace turned into a smile. 'You will get well, I promise you, if you try. But only if you try. You will try, won't you?'

Lissie nodded. Snatches of her nightmares pushed themselves forward in her head. 'It was raining, I remember it was raining . . . and . . .' As the memories flooded back, tears welled up in her eyes.

Again the woman held her hand. 'Don't dwell on it now. It's over and you're on the mend. Your body will heal and you must be strong in yourself to help it along.' After a minute or two she added briskly, 'Now, I'll bring you some beef tea and bread to begin with – er – what do I call you, what's your name?'

'Lissie. Lissie D— Er – just Lissie.'

'Well, I suppose that "just Lissie" will have to do for now. I'm Martha. Martha Thorogood.'

'Thank you, Mrs Thorogood.' Her voice croaked again and she coughed.

'Call me Martha. Please. We don't stand on ceremony at this farm.' She frowned slightly. The girl was still very weak. 'You rest now. I'll fetch your soup.'

'I can come downstairs,' Lissie volunteered. 'I don't want to trouble you.' She made a supreme effort to sit up and realised that every part of her body hurt and her insides felt as though they were being mangled. She fell back. Martha was right, she had no strength.

'It's no trouble. And if you move around you'll start the bleeding again so it's best for you to stay put.' Martha gave her another reassuring smile. 'You've a long way to go yet, lass, before you can get up.'

Lissie again allowed herself to sink back into the feather pillows and mattress. She remained there, motionless, until Martha returned. Looking around the room at the linen and salves, she realised that Martha had taken very good care of her. Her nightgown was beautifully soft and white, with lots of smocking, drawn-thread work on the sleeves and ribbon ties at the neck.

She pushed back the gathered cuffs to expose her wrists and forearms and noticed with a shock how thin and bony they had become. And pale. Her skin was so white it looked like marble.

Martha came back with her beef tea and some toasted bread on a wooden tray that had large handles at either side. She put the tray on a wooden chest at the foot of the bed while she helped Lissie sit up, stuffing more soft pillows behind her so that she felt comfortable. Then she placed the tray across her knees and said, 'If you can take some of the toast, soaked in beef tea, it will help you get stronger. And there's warm milk and honey in the tankard.'

Lissie realised she had little appetite for any food. However, she knew that she must try otherwise she'd just waste away. She picked up the spoon. The beef tea was surprisingly good and the delicate savoury taste perked up her palate. She took another spoonful and a little of the soaked toast. 'Thank you, Martha. You have been so kind to me. Why would you be so good to a total stranger?'

Martha moved a pile of clean linen to the wooden box and drew up the only chair nearer to the bed. 'Ee, lass! I couldn't let you die on my doorstep. When I got back from market that day I thought you were already gone. You were just a soggy wet heap on my front porch. And there was blood all over, where the rain had spread it through your clothes and over my tiles.'

'I'm sorry . . . I . . . I . . . don't know what happened to me. I think I fainted.'

'Fainted? You were in a stupor for days. No blood left in your veins at all to be sure. I think it was all soaked into your clothes instead. It took a while to get out, but it's not too bad now, just a dark patch here and there. Doesn't show too much on that brown dress of yours.' Martha tossed her head, indicating the alcoves behind her. 'All your things are safe and sound in the cupboard there. I cleaned up what I could.'

Lissie felt Martha's keen brown eyes watching her as she spoke. She remembered it all now. Mickey Jackson, the attack and feeling so soiled, so dirty and ashamed, and walking out on her mam. She prayed that she would never have to see Mickey Jackson again. Ever.

'I . . . I can't go back. I can't,' she stammered.

'No, I expect not. But you didn't do yourself any good being on the road, walking and out in all that rain. And I didn't know how much of that laudanum stuff you'd taken – I found an empty bottle on the porch. You were very weak from the bleeding – and then you caught a fever, a nasty one, which had me very worried. I didn't know whether you'd have enough strength left to fight it.'

'I was in a lot of pain. The laudanum helped. It just took it away so I felt I could go on.'

'Oh aye, it does that all right. But it cannot stop you catching the fever. You had to ride out the fever yourself. And being in a weakened state, taking no nourishment, it was touch and go for a while.' Martha watched quietly for a few moments as Lissie took her beef tea and toast and then added, 'You must be a strong young woman underneath to come through this like you have. I've seen women die of much less.'

Lissie laid down her spoon. 'I am so grateful to you, Martha. I had nowhere to go. But, believe me, nowhere was better than staying where I was. I can't thank you enough for taking me in.'

The older woman smiled. 'I don't know what you're running from, but I've been looking after you for two weeks now and I've seen the bruising and the tearing so I know more or less what's happened to you. How old are you?'

'Nearly sixteen.'

'And you've no wedding ring, so the man that did this to you was not your husband. Well, I'll not ask you to relive it, but if you want to tell me, I'll listen.'

Lissie felt mortified with shame at the memory. 'I can't . . . I can't talk about it. It's too painful, too awful . . .'

'Aye well, then it's best forgot if you can. I'll leave you to finish your beef tea and get some more rest. That's the best medicine for you now.'

Alone with her thoughts Lissie ate as much as she could manage and took a little of the milk and honey. Within minutes she felt exhausted again and her eyelids drooped. Half-asleep, she thought she heard doors opening and closing downstairs and the clatter of crockery. An aroma of meat stew drifted up the stairs and under her bedroom door.

The house was unusually quiet. No voices, no family – just Martha perhaps? But she had seen a man, hadn't she? A big man, driving the farm cart off to market that day. He was a fair bit younger than Martha. Maybe her son? Or just a farm hand? She couldn't tell. Nervously, she wondered where he was now and what would happen if he came upstairs when she was alone.

Martha tended to her needs well and Lissie grew stronger by the day. She worried for the older woman constantly climbing up and down the stairs for her and begged to come downstairs. But Martha would hear none of it.

'You can get down all right but you would do yourself some damage climbing back up the stairs to be sure. You don't want to set off the bleeding all over again.'

'How bad am I, Martha? You know, inside me?'

'Hard to tell, really. It looked worse than anything I've seen before. But you are young and young bodies mend better than old ones.' She hesitated before continuing, 'Your flesh was badly torn and I don't know how much you were damaged right inside. I'll be right in thinking you've not had any babies yet?'

Lissie shook her head. 'I'd never been with a man before. Not like that – and he was so . . . so brutal . . .' She choked on the memory.

'Aye well, it was painful for you because you were still a maid. You are a pretty one though. And men do like to bed pretty maids.'

'I tried to fight him off.'

'That would've made it worse for you, but you weren't to know. Your flesh will heal with time, and we shall have to wait and see about a baby.'

Lissie's mouth dropped open. 'A baby?'

'Aye, lass. It does happen when you lie with a man. You could be with child. His child.'

'No! No, I can't be! I didn't want to do it! He made me do it! He forced me!'

'Makes no difference to God's will. If God wants you to have a baby then you'll have one. But you need not fret so. In my experience it's unlikely you'll have kept it, what with all that bleeding going on and you being so ill with the fever. You never can tell though. You've got a strong heart underneath that pallid skin, and you're healing well.'

Martha thought for a moment, then went on. 'I suppose you could try coming downstairs awhile. If you did, John could carry you back upstairs.'

Lissie clutched the bedding and drew it up to her throat.

'Who is John? Is he your husband?'

'Nay, lass,' Martha laughed. 'My husband is long gone to his grave. John is my son and he works the farm for me. He lives with me here but spends most of his time outdoors. He loves the outdoors does my John, like his father before him I suppose.'

Her face softened and she smiled. 'John won't do you any harm, my dear, though he does sometimes lose his rag when things go wrong. He's a gentle giant. But he can't speak like you or me. He was born like it. I had a putrid fever when he were in the womb and they say that caused it. He's stone deaf, you see. So he never learned to talk right.

'He has good eyes though,' Martha continued, 'and he's quick on the uptake. You only have to show him something once and away he goes. And strong. Like his father. His father was a big strong man. But he was old when John was born so he never really saw him grow up. Gone to his grave now, God rest his soul.'

She gently unclasped Lissie's hands from the bunched up bedding. 'John won't hurt you, love. He wouldn't hurt a fly.'

Lissie smoothed down the sheets and Martha asked, 'This man, the one that did this to you, who was he?'

Lissie considered lying. It would be so much easier to say he was a stranger who had attacked her on the road. But Martha deserved the truth, Lissie decided and so she said, 'He was someone my mam and dad knew. Mam said – I thought she said – she said he was going to look after us.'

Martha gazed at Lissie steadily for a long time before

she went on. 'When you had the fever, you were delirious and you talked. You said things.'

'What things?'

'Most of the time it made no sense, but, well,' Martha heaved a sigh, 'you talked about a killing, a murder. Did you kill him, Lissie? I have to know. Did you kill the man who did this to you?'

'No.' Her answer came out with a long sigh. 'I wish I had. Him and my mam together. The pair of them are evil and I hate them both.'

'Your mam? You wished you'd killed your mam? Did your dad kill him, then?'

Lissie shook her head and the tears welled in her large green eyes. 'No, nothing like that. No. It's my dad who is dead. All this would not have happened if my dad had still been alive. He was murdered, you see. It was my dad who was murdered.'

'Your dad. I see. By this man? Did this man kill your dad?'

Lissie's heart turned over as she thought: No, my dad was murdered by someone else. By a man I thought I loved. But he was a fraud and a liar and just using me to get at my dad. How could I have been taken in by Blake? she thought. He seemed so genuine. Best forget I ever met him. If I can.

She stared at the lime-washed plaster walls and said, 'No, it's just that when my dad was killed we had no money and my mam said I had to . . .' she choked on the words '. . . to go with him to pay the rent.'

'Your own mam. Oh, I'm so sorry, Lissie.'

She began to cry. 'She was at her wits' end and she

needed her gin and she said I wasn't to work at the inn.' It was the first time she had cried about the attack and her tears began to flow freely down her face. 'He bought me a dress and I thought he was being nice to me because he wanted my mam. But all the time it was me he wanted. And Mam said she'd explained it to me but she hadn't really. And he dragged me up the stairs and pulled the chest across the door so I couldn't get out.'

The sobs were rattling from her throat in shudders as she relived the horror. Martha held her until she calmed and Lissie carried on, her voice wavering with hiccups. 'She – she's not my real mam. She never wanted me, I can see that now. I . . . I don't know who my real mam is. Nobody does, but my dad has always looked after me and he was nice to me. He let me go to school when he had the money, but it ran out and then I worked there in the kitchen and seeing to the house for the schoolmistress and her brother.' She heaved in a noisy breath. 'They were strict about everything but it was a nice house. Like this one.'

'Hush, now. Talk about it if you must, but you don't have to tell me if you don't want to.'

Lissie's grief spilled out. 'Bl . . . Bla . . . this friend of Mr Kirby's came to stay and I had met him before and I liked him a lot. I thought he liked me as well but it turned out that he was putting on an act. He was after my dad and he killed him in a fight.' She wiped her eyes with the back of her hand and inhaled shakily. 'After that, Mam had no money for the rent. The man that – that did this to me had bought our house off Dad years ago when the canal trade was bad. So it was him, you see, and we had to pay him his dues . . .' The memories were too vivid. Her words stuck in her throat and she gave herself up to her tears.

Martha's soothing voice interrupted her, 'And that's enough for the moment. You're too upset and I see why now. It's too much for a body to deal with. You have to take your mind off what's happened, otherwise you'll not get better. You can come down for your dinner today and John will bring you back up afterwards. Wrap yourself in my big shawl and put these goatskin slippers on your feet.'

Chapter 23

Lissie's recovery was slow and steady, and soon she was pulling a skirt on over her nightgown and tying a shawl round her shoulders so that she could stay downstairs for dinner and tea.

'You must remember that John can't hear you,' Martha explained. 'And try not to rile him because he can go off in a tantrum sometimes. He sees really well, so if you want his attention, wave one of these calico cloths outside. He can catch sight of it from as far away as the top pasture.'

She looked at the young woman sitting in her rocking chair by the kitchen range and was pleased with the improvement in her colour. 'Well, now you are feeling stronger, we'll kill a fowl for dinner. I've got two of them not laying and I reckon one of them can go in the pot.'

Lissie thought that Martha's husband must have been fairly well off for a tenant farmer. Farmers in the South Riding were usually tenants if they were not gentry. It was good land by all accounts, just at the edge of a big estate and only a few miles from the ironworks towns in the valley.

As Lissie's strength returned, she was able to help Martha run the farmhouse. There was always a good fire and Martha was a capable housekeeper. Her high tea of home-cured ham and new-laid eggs marked the end of the working day for John and he came in, ruddy from the fresh air, and, as always, hungry and thirsty. Martha made real tea to go with the meal every day and they drank it with fresh-baked bread or scones, and jam made from the orchard fruit.

The autumn evening closed in chilly as Martha mulled a tankard of ale for John and put out cold pie for his supper. Although he could not speak, Lissie could tell from his face how he was feeling. He was cheerful tonight, but yesterday he had been frustrated about something out on the farm and had made angry noises in his throat to try and tell them about it. He had thumped the table making the knives jump and rattle. Martha became cross with him in turn and shouted at him to stop. Even though he could not hear her, he knew from her countenance that she was angry.

Lissie realised then that his frustration was not about the farm. He had been angry with himself for not being able to speak.

'Martha?' Lissie asked.

'What now, lass? I'm a bit tired tonight.'

'Have you got a slate and some soft chalkstone?'

'Yes, I have. I use them for the prices when we go to market. They're in the cart in the barn.'

'I think I'll just go out and fetch them.'

'Not in this cold wind, you're not. You'll catch your death,' Martha protested.

'I was fine tying up raspberry canes in the garden this morning.'

'You're always the same when you get a bee in your bonnet! Well, take my big shawl. And John, to hold the lamp.'

They were soon back in the kitchen, at the scrubbed wooden table with slates and chalk. Lissie drew a picture of a pig and showed it to John. Then she chalked the word 'pig' underneath and got him to copy the letters on his slate. She did the same for a cow. He laughed about her drawing but knew what it was.

'What are you two doing over there?' Martha asked.

'I'm teaching him to read,' Lissie replied. 'If he can read and write he can as good as talk to us, and then he won't lose his temper. He only loses it when he gets frustrated.'

'Do you think he will be able to learn though?'

'Oh yes, Martha. I am sure he will. I know he can't speak, but he can think all right.'

'Well, would you believe it! After all these years!'

'Martha, he will be able to do his numbers as well,' Lissie added excitedly. 'I know he will!'

'Well, this is the best news I have ever heard!' Martha exclaimed. 'If he can do all that I shall be able to make over the farm to him properly. My husband only left it to me because of John's affliction.'

Martha watched Lissie teaching her adult son to read. She was so much better now. This was just what she wanted to take her mind off her ordeal. But the girl also needed something to take her outside of the farm and meet up with other folk.

Lissie looked up and saw Martha staring. They exchanged easy, comforting smiles and Martha thought that she would not want Lissie to leave them.

John learned quickly during the dark evenings of that winter, and soon moved on from slate and chalk. However, when spring arrived, his work on the farm soon took him away from his lessons. One evening the following autumn, he was writing something on paper that Martha had brought in from her bureau in the front parlour. Sitting at the kitchen table he bent over his task, concentrating hard, dipping his quill frequently in the inkpot and scratching away at the paper.

'Don't you be spilling any ink on that fresh-scrubbed table, my lad,' Martha warned. 'I have to knead the bread on there.'

'I'll get him to fashion a board to write on,' Lissie suggested. 'He needs a writing slope anyway because he is too big to sit hunched up here. Miss Kirby had one at the school. If I draw what I mean on a slate, he'll make it in no time.'

Lissie and Martha were sitting by the fire at the end of their working day. It had been a particularly busy day for all of them as tomorrow was market day and they had been loading the farm cart to take into town at first light. As usual there was plenty of produce to sell, vegetables that they could spare from the garden and some apples off the trees. Martha's chickens had bred well that year and she had surplus hens and cocks, which always fetched a good price.

But this time they had something different to offer. It had been Lissie's idea. As she regained her strength she wanted to help out Martha and John in any way she could. Martha had said it was enough teaching John to read and write, but Lissie could only do this at the end of the day when he came in from the fields. Even then, he was sometimes too tired to do much.

So she needed something to occupy her during the day. There was planting and hoeing to be done in the vegetable patch when John was busy on the farm. She had also helped Martha with preserving and storing her fruit and vegetables to see them through the winter months. And there was always bread to bake, meals to prepare and rooms to clean, an aspect of life at which both Lissie and Martha excelled.

But it was not enough for Lissie just to earn her keep. She wanted to give more to the woman who had saved her life. Martha needed a new woollen dress before the winter set in and Lissie planned to earn enough to buy some good cloth for both of them.

'What is John doing at the table? I thought he'd be too tired for any book work tonight,' Martha commented as she threw another log on to the range.

'I don't know, but he'll show us when he's done.'

It didn't take long before he brought the single sheet of paper over to Martha. On it he had written, in beautiful copperplate script, the word 'Mother' and underneath 'I love you'. Tears came into her eyes as she nodded her appreciation to him and he went back to the table.

A few minutes later he returned to the fireside, this time to show Lissie his work. Again a sheet of paper, this time with her name and underneath 'I love you'.

Lissie was slightly taken aback, but John was grinning and holding up his left hand to signal her to wait. He went back to the table and wrote some more before showing her the paper again. Now it read 'Lissie. I love your pies.' Lissie giggled and passed the paper across to Martha.

'Yes well,' Martha smiled, 'you do make a tasty pie, I'll give you that. And my John knows a good pie when it's about.'

'Let's hope the townsfolk think the same.'

'Oh, I think they will,' Martha responded. 'They work hard in the furnaces and forges in town and they do like to fill their bellies. The womenfolk are always looking for something tasty for tea.'

Lissie's expression was a cross between pleasure and pensiveness. She'd loved making her pies but couldn't believe anyone would be paying good money for them when they could just as easily bake them themselves.

Martha, with her wisdom gained from years of selling produce in the town market, knew different. She was convinced Lissie's pies would sell. She had already cleared the front parlour table to make up the wool into new dresses.

That night Lissie slept well, having had a hard day baking. She dreamed of making raised pie crust and boiling pigs' trotters for jelly. It was a relief to wake up and know that her pies were cooked and cold now, and wrapped in calico cloths in baskets already on the cart in the barn.

Today, for the first time, Lissie would go with Martha and John to town for the market. Town! She had heard so much about life in town, but Fordham had been the nearest she had ventured and that had only been one street of big houses with side roads of cottages. Town! And with her own pork pies to sell in the market square!

They left at dawn and the early-morning mist had cleared by the time their farm cart reached the top of the final hill before town. Already the factory chimneys were smoking and plumes were swirling about the rooftops. Town had its own smell too, that was different from the farm; a stench of decaying animal and vegetable waste mixed with chimney smoke from coal fires was overlaid by a thicker acrid atmosphere belched out by the works. It rose up the hill to meet them, making Lissie catch her breath and cough.

'It's a clear day,' Martha commented as they rode side by side next to John urging on their horse, 'and once we're down in town we'll be out of this smoke. It's bad when it rains though. The clouds bring the smoke down on you and you can't breathe then.'

Lissie had never in her life seen so many houses all at once. Rows and rows of them, mostly brick and slate and not like the warm stone of the villages that she knew. And so many people too, out early, going to labour in the ironworks, pits and forges, or going to market as they were.

They approached the centre of town and the noise became louder for the road was cobbled. Horses and carts rattled along and the boots of so many people clacked and clattered after them. The market square was already busy when they arrived, with fretting livestock unsettled by their journey and penned in by unfamiliar hurdles.

John drew up on the edge of the town square, where another road came in from the other side of town, and set up their pitch. He gave their horse a nosebag and let down the back of the cart, taking out two empty barrels across which he stretched planks of wood. On top of this he heaved down the baskets filled with Lissie's pies and she began to unpack them.

She had little ones for selling whole, and bigger round ones for cutting into wedges with Martha's sharpened kitchen knife. Martha stacked her apples and garden vegetables next to them. Her chickens were kept in wicker-work baskets on the cart. John went off to look at the stock pens, his familiar face soon recognised by old friends who slapped him on the back and muttered things he couldn't hear.

There were people all over, more than Lissie had ever seen in her life before. And they kept coming; talking, laughing, shouting, arguing and sometimes fighting, especially around the two alehouses that fronted the square. Someone started playing a flute and a few men, influenced by drink, began dancing, their boots ringing on the cobbles. Lissie chalked on a slate that she propped up by her basket, *Pork Pies. Best in the South Riding*.

She had sold out before midday. Most of the garden produce had gone as well, and all of Martha's chickens. Lissie was amazed. She could have sold her pies all over again. Easily! There were so many people with money to spend!

'They've got families to feed and no farm like we have,' Martha explained. 'And there are inns and boarding houses in town. Innkeepers like a decent chicken for the pot when they can get one. There's an even bigger town past Tinsley, right at the end of the canal. They make knives and tools and stuff that goes all the way to London to be sold. But this place is big enough for us.'

'I'll say,' Lissie enthused. 'Look how much we've got to buy our cloth.'

'Aye, you've done well. At this rate we'll be buying silk next time instead of wool. The draper will stay open late today, so why don't you have a stroll round the market and town for an hour or so. Then we'll have our bread and cheese afore we do our own marketing.'

Lissie wandered about looking at other wares and listening to the auctioneer shouting the bids as the stock pens emptied and new owners led their animals away. She ventured down a side street or two but found them unsavoury places, especially around the inns and going down to the canal.

There was a big dirty ironworks on an island there, where the river went one side and a canal had been cut the other side for the barges. The barges brought the iron ore in and took bar iron out to forges where it was worked into axles for railway engines and the like. There were some forges nearby, and the slamming of drop hammers made her head rattle when she got too close!

There were women too. She had seen the women in the square early on and knew what they were about. They pulled down the necks of their bodices and took out any lace or muslin to expose their throats and swelling breasts. One had hitched up one side of her long skirts to show off a shapely ankle and slender leg as she waited.

They loitered for men to come out of the alehouses, flushed with drink and, hopefully, with money still in their pockets. Then the two of them would disappear down an alley for their own special bit of marketing.

Lissie recognised one of them with a start as she realised how far from home the woman was. She had put some stuff on her hair to make sure that she was noticed. It was gaudy, Lissie thought, more like the colour of Martha's copper kitchen pans, than hair. She watched her for a while, fascinated by her appearance, then approached her.

'Rosa? It is Rosa, isn't it?' she asked tentatively.

The older woman turned slowly to face her, her eyes unusually bright and her lips red with French rouge. 'What?' she said abruptly. 'What do you want? This is my patch. Clear off.'

'It's Lissie. You must remember me. Edie's girl.'

Rosa blinked and looked her up and down. 'What? Lissie Dearne? Little Lissie Dearne? So it is. Not so little now, are yo'? You come to work 'ere an' all?'

'No . . . I . . . er . . . I wondered how . . . how Mam was getting on?'

'As if you care! She could be dead and gone for all you know. Some lass you turned out to be, deserting your dear old mam in her hour of need, wi' your poor ol' dad hardly cold in the ground. It's lucky she had me to look out for her, else she'd 'a' bin in the workhouse long ago.'

'How is she, Rosa?'

'She i'n't that well. What do you think I'm here fo'? She needs her medicine and it costs money. Now, if you're here to work an' all, I'll thank you to clear off to your own patch.'

A brawny man in dirty breeches and a greasy coat came out of the inn and saw the two women together. He obviously knew Rosa and came right up to them both.

'Well, well. You got an apprentice now, Rosie? How much for the young 'un?'

Quick as a flash Rosa replied, 'A guinea.'

'Don't be daft!'

'You can afford it, Jethro Baines, and you can have her for the night for that.'

His eyes lit up. 'What? Tek her home wi' me?' Then his face fell. 'What'd the missus say?'

'Lucky bugger, probably,' Rosa sneered. 'Are you buying or not?'

'Only the young 'un.'

'I'm not for sale,' Lissie broke in firmly.

'Oooh! Hoity-toity an' all! I'll gi' thee a shilling. Tek it or leave it.'

'I *said* I'm not for sale.' Lissie turned to walk away but Rosa gripped her arm with a surprising strength and stopped her.

'You 'eard the lass,' Rosa added. 'Clear off, Jethro.'

'Huh. Some company you keep these days, Rosie me girl. I'll find missenn a decent tart down by the cut.' He went off with a jaunty stride, whistling to himself.

Rosa was still holding on to Lissie's arm. 'We thought you were dead,' she said. 'Going off like that and never coming back. Why did y' do that to yer old mam?'

'She didn't tell you then?'

'Tell me what? That you didn't want to work for your keep? We all 'as to work for our keep and if you 'a'n't got no man to fend fo' you, you 'as to find summat.'

Lissie realised that without money for rent, Mickey Jackson would have turned her mam out. 'I . . . I didn't know what else to do. I couldn't . . .' She choked on the words, unable, even after all this time, to talk about that dreadful night. 'Where is she now?'

'She's wi' me o' course. Where else would she be? We allus looked after each other an' I i'n't gi'ing up on 'er now.'

'How bad is she, Rosa?'

'She's got no strength, but I reckon there's a year or two left in her yet. She talks about yer sometimes. She says your name. Why don't you come and see her for yerssenn? You'd better make it soon though, if you wants 'er to talk any sense.'

The parish clock struck the hour and Lissie realised Martha and John would be waiting for her. 'I've got to go now, Rosa. Will you tell Mam I'll come and see her? Before Christmastide, if the snows keep away.'

Rosa looked doubtful and said, 'I'm not saying owt to 'er if yer don't mean it.'

'I do mean it. I promise.'

'All right then. Clear off now and let me get on wi' me business.'

Lissie retraced her steps back to the market square. She wondered how far it was from Martha's farm to Mexton Lock. Maybe a day's journey if she took a carrier along the turnpike and walked down through the wood.

But her inner journey, she thought, would be the longest one of her life.

She discussed it with Martha a few days later. 'I want to see her, Martha. For all her faults she was the mam that brought me up. And I did walk out and leave her.'

'Well, if you have the strength to go, you must do it,' Martha advised, keeping her eyes on the sewing in her hands.

'I am frightened though,' Lissie admitted.

'What of? Your mam?'

'No. Him. You know, the one that . . .'

'Do you think he'll try it again?'

'Well no. Mam's living with her friend Rosa now, so she's not beholden to him any more. He generally picks his women from the ones that hang around the Navigator.'

'Best stay away from there, then. Will Rosa be able to put you up?'

Lissie thought she would. 'I'll stay on the woodland side of Mexton Lock while I'm there.'

'Maybe John should go with you and take the cart?'

'Oh no, I couldn't ask him to do that,' Lissie replied. 'He's needed for the ploughing before the winter frosts set in. Mind, he could take me as far as the turnpike where I can get the morning carrier.'

Martha sighed. 'Well, if you are set on it you'd better not delay. T' weather can easily turn nasty at this time of year.' She gave a small smile at last. 'I'll make up your new winter dress while you're gone. It'll be something to bring you back to me.'

Lissie detected a wistful tone in Martha's voice and

looked at her sharply. 'But of course I'll come back to you, Martha,' she said. 'Do you think I won't? There is nothing for me now at Mexton Lock. The house is gone and Mam has never wanted me. My true family, the one that I love, is here.'

Martha's eyes glistened with tears. 'Just make sure you do, lass.'

Lissie walked over to her chair and put her arm around Martha's shoulders. 'I wouldn't leave you and John. You're all I have.'

Martha put down her sewing and took a deep breath. 'Well, as long as that's settled, I'll get on and make some beef tea for you to take to your mam. And fetch in some new laid eggs and butter for her. And how about one of your pies for Rosa?'

'Oh, Martha, you are so good to me. I do love you.'

Then Martha did something she had never done before. She took Lissie in her arms and gave her a long lingering hug. Her voice was squeaky and hoarse as she whispered, 'Just make sure you come back to us safe and sound. All right?'

'I'll be back, I promise you, Martha. And don't you go fretting about me, I'll be all right. I will.'

Chapter 24

Retracing that journey, now a lifetime away for Lissie, affected her more than she had thought it would. It started as soon as she reached the turnpike and waved goodbye to John. The jolting carrier cart brought back memories of the straw wagon, the cold, the pain and the bleeding. The memories worsened as she passed the wall where she had hidden and waited for the two lads to fall asleep after their flagon of ale. They became even worse when she approached the familiar woods, pulled her box down from the carrier, and searched for the track down to the canal.

The track was wider now, and the trees thinner as more lumber had been cut in her absence. The walk seemed shorter and the woods smaller than she remembered. Her world had grown in the time she had been away. She realised that she had grown in her worldliness as well. She had had a woman's body then, but without a woman's wisdom. Now she had the benefit of Martha's wise counsel. She hoped that it would help her to survive this visit.

As the track passed her former home she shivered at the memory of her last night under that roof. She had pushed all those dark thoughts to the back of her mind. She had locked them away in a box in her head for good. But her body shuddered as she hurried by.

The house was occupied. There was clean washing on a line strung out between two of the apple trees in the back garden. Small clothes and bedsheets blew about in the breeze. She recognised a pretty woman with frizzy carroty hair tending the vegetable patch. As she straightened, rubbing her back, Lissie saw she was with child. She had been walking out with Mickey's eldest two years ago. They must be married now and living in the house. She hoped the woman had not seen her and scuttled on, the dragging weight of her box pulling her down.

The lock looked exactly the same. Why should it look any different, Lissie thought? Still the piles of coals and heaps of logs. Still the Navigator Inn and its surrounding buildings over on the other side. Still the slow steady progress of the barges through the lock, filling and emptying, filling and emptying, as it had always done. Over the sound of water rushing through the sluices she could hear the ringing of the blacksmith's hammer on his anvil as he worked. Nothing had changed. Why should it? Why should it have changed just because she had gone away?

Rosa was surprised to see her, but welcomed her, and seemed genuinely pleased with the beef tea and food from the dairy. There was broth on the hob and Lissie sat down gratefully to a steaming bowlful of it with a heel from a stale loaf. She broke up the bread and dropped a piece in the broth to soak.

'How is my mam?' Lissie asked.

'Fair. She talks about yer sometimes. Well, mostly rambles on these days, but she keeps saying yer name. And she goes on about Luther.' Rosa paused. 'She says you were his and not really hers.'

'Well, I sort of knew that anyway. She always told me when I was naughty that she'd sell me back to the gypsies.'

'Aye well, y' 'ave that look about yer. She knows more than that though. After Luther died and . . . and then yer cleared off, she 'ad to sell his things to try and pay t' rent – most of t' furniture, his garden spade an' fork. An' his gun.'

Lissie looked down. If only her mam had talked to her earlier about paying the rent, she might have thought of that herself. The gun alone would have fetched enough to keep them going for quite a while.

'It weren't enough for Mickey Jackson,' Rosa continued. 'He wanted that house for his eldest lad and . . . and, well, your mam spent all her money on gin anyroad. She moved in 'ere wi' me and my earnings from t' herbals kept us going for a bit. But even that's not enough for yer ma's laudanum. She gets through quite a bit o' that nowadays. Still, I goes to market day in town every now and then,' she shot a sideways glance at Lissie, 'as yer know. Usually at quarter day when t' rent's due, and we manage.'

'You do that for my mam?'

'We go back a long way, me and yer mam. She were

allus a good friend to me and I'd do owt for her. It's no skin off my nose. Men are all the same anyroad, an' I can tek 'em or leave 'em. Me and yer mam get along fine. Leastways we did till she took poorly this summer. She's lost a lot o' her strength now, but she rallies every now and then and comes downstairs.'

'She should have told me about Mickey.'

'She said she did.'

'I didn't realise what she meant. I could have found another way.'

'Oh aye? 'Ow? 'E allus gets what he wants. 'E wanted you, not 'er.'

Lissie accepted that this was true and tried to calm down. 'Well, I was mad with her.'

'She were mad wi' you an' all.'

'Will she want to see me after all this time?'

'Oh aye, she'll see yer. She been asking for yer since she cleared out o' t' house. She found some bits and pieces o' Luther's, along wi' 'is gun in the old clock. From yer real ma, she says.'

Lissie felt suddenly weak and shaky. She had not expected this. Maybe her dad had been married before and he'd held on to a few keepsakes. Dad had been soft like that, she recalled, more so than her mam.

The beef tea was sizzling in a small copper pan on the hob. Rosa stirred it and said, 'I'll tek this upstairs and tell 'er yer 'ere. Come upstairs in a bit and she'll be all right to talk. Five minutes only. She 'a'n't got much attention now.'

Lissie was shocked by Edie's appearance. Her tiny, bird-like frame was now just a bag of bones held together by her sagging, yellowing skin. Her eyes were sunk deep into their sockets and circled by dark brown shadows. The bedding was old and the sheets grey, and the room was filled with an unsavoury smell of sickness and the chamber pot.

Lissie gagged as she entered. It brought back stark memories of her own near demise at Martha's, except that her mam's room did not have that underlying salty smell of blood-soaked rags.

There was a table near the bed, covered in tiny bottles and pots of potions and salves that were Rosa's stock-in-trade. Lissie noticed that the empty ones were mostly brown laudanum containers from the apothecary, and not gin. Rosa was sitting on a rickety wooden chair, coaxing the beef tea down her mam's throat.

'Come on, Edie, ducks, try this for me. Just a few spoonfuls for yer old Rosie. Yer got a visitor today. Your Lissie's 'ere. 'Ow 'bout that then? She 'eard y' were poorly, like, an' 'as come to see yer.'

A spoonful of the beef tea gurgled in Edie's throat and eventually slid down.

'Lissie? Our Lissie's 'ere?' Edie wheezed.

'Aye. D'yer want to see 'er?'

'Must tell 'er. Luther. Luther said . . .'

'Take yer time, Edie, love. Here, sit up a bit now. I've got this cushion fo' yer back.'

Rosa made Edie as comfy as she could and then nodded to Lissie to move closer to the bed.

'Lissie? It is you, i'n't it?'

'Yes, Mam. I'm sorry you're poorly.'

'Left me all on me own, you did. Wi' that mate o'

yer dad's. He were a wrong 'un, he were. Still is. I 'ad nowt left, y'know. Nowt.' Her eyes had an artificial brightness as they darted about, taking in Lissie's appearance. 'Still an 'andsome lass, I see,' she went on. 'Always were an 'andsome lass. 'Ave yer brought some more o' me medicine?'

Lissie glanced at Rosa who nodded towards the table. 'Put a few drops o' that laudanum in that glass o' water. She'll drink it down herssenn.'

After a few minutes, Edie continued. 'Luther said 'e'd tell you when you were grown up, but 'e never did. 'E were drunk when he told me. 'E said your real mam were a proper lady.' Edie made a grunting noise from the back of her throat. 'One o' the gentry, he said.'

'Mam? Are you sure about this?'

'I never believed him, o' course. Allus coming home telling tales, were yer dad. But after he were gone an' we 'ad to sell 'is stuff I found yer bits and pieces in t' old clock. And she said we 'ad to keep 'em for you.'

Lissie flashed a grateful smile at Rosa. Edie, calmed by her medicine, took another sip and lay back on the pillows. 'Fancy that. Fancy yer real mam being a lady. Fancy that, eh?'

'Mam? Did Dad say who she was?'

Edie sighed, her eyes were glazed and she was smiling a secretive little smile to herself.

Lissie persisted. 'Did he say, Mam? Did Dad say who my real mam was?'

Rosa came forward. 'Edie, love, tell 'er what Luther told yer about where he got 'er from.' Rosa turned to Lissie. 'She's often said it.'

Edie wheezed again. 'Bought you from some woman, 'e said—'

'*Bought me, did you say?*' Lissie's voice came out as a hoarse whisper. Her dad had bought her? Paid somebody money for her? Someone – her mother – oh God, please no, not her real mother – had *sold* her? Please God, don't let her say my real mother did not want me either. She coughed a little and asked, 'Rosa, could I sit in that chair awhile, please?'

Rosa shifted the tin soup bowl and old tray, saying, 'Bit of a shock is it, lass? Yer could 'a' done a lot worse, yer know.'

Edie muttered on. 'Bought you, 'e said. When 'e were down t' canals on t' coast. Good days they were. Plenty o' money. Plenty o' coal fer t' fire. He came back wi' you one day. Pleased as punch he were. Pleased as punch. Some right pretty things you 'ad wi' yer an' all. Bonnet and shawl like a proper gentry babby. I suppose if yer mam were a lady, then—'

Rosa broke into Edie's ramblings. 'She said Luther told 'er 'e'd bought yer from a woman staying at an inn over on the Humber. An' when we found yer things, it seemed he'd been telling t' truth all along. I'll show you.'

It was a pouch made of oiled cloth and inside was a wooden cigar box, old and with the label worn away. The box contained an empty silver locket on a delicate neck chain and a silver picture case with a likeness inside. There was also some fine lacework and a piece of paper, a billhead for the North Star, in Hull. And a date. Several months after her birthday. A date on a bill for staying and eating at the inn and written in Luther's hand was a sum of money and *For Lissie*. On the back was scrawled *Mrs Beighton* and *Saltby*.

Lissie stared at the contents. 'Do you think Mrs Beighton was my real mam?'

Rosa placed a comforting hand on her shoulder. 'If she were a lady then it's more than likely Mrs Beighton were 'er nursemaid who looked after you.'

Lissie opened the picture case again. 'Is this my real mam, then?'

'She looks like a lady ter me,' Rosa speculated. 'Young though. T' likeness is yer mam, all right. You got her black hair and big eyes an' all.'

Lissie let out an exhausted sigh. This was too much to take in. Her real mam was a lady. A lady who was not able to keep her. Lissie guessed the reason. Not wed and probably disowned by her family, Lissie was lucky that she hadn't ended up in the workhouse! What would she have done if Mickey Jackson had left her with child?

As Lissie examined the likeness, Edie rallied and wheezed, 'She died. Luther said she died, yer mam, when she 'ad you.'

Lissie suddenly felt very sad, for a lost life, for her mother and – and – for herself. A realisation dawned on her that, if her dad had bought her, he wasn't her real father either.

'Mam?' she asked quietly. 'Did Dad say who my proper father was?'

'It wa'n't him. I were wrong there,' Edie replied.

'Who then?'

Rosa answered. 'Luther di'n't know.'

'Maybe this Mrs Beighton did?' Lissie suggested.

'Where's Saltby?' Her mother's family may not have wanted her but her father might! Did she have a proper father somewhere? Maybe uncles and aunts too? Where are they? she wondered. In Saltby?

Rosa put a hand on hers and answered, 'Lissie, ducks. Like as not 'e never knew nowt about yer. Them secrets are best kept quiet. You wer all right wi' Luther, weren't yer?'

'Yes. He was a good dad to me,' Lissie conceded.

Rosa was right. No one had wanted her when she was born. But to be sold as an infant, like a hireling on market day! She could never have done that to a tiny baby, whatever the circumstances. She would have found a way! She would!

Her head drooped. Not wanted by her real family, or even by her mam here. The only dad she had ever known was dead, murdered by a man she thought she loved. Lissie had never felt so alone.

She fingered the few trinkets feeling her sadness wash over her. 'Can I keep these, Mam?'

Her mam nodded and Rosa spoke for her. 'Oh aye. That's why yer ma wanted to see yer. They're yorn anyroad.'

'Thank you. Both of you. I know how difficult things have been, and – and – well, you could have sold them.'

'Ee lass, even if yer'd come 'ere dripping gold you couldn't do much to help yer mam now. It's just t' laudanum that keeps 'er going and I can earn enough for that.'

'You're a true friend to her, Rosa.'

'She were allus good to me when Luther were flushed wi' money.'

'Yes. It was like that with Dad. Either plenty or a famine. But he was generous when he had it. And he did his best for me, with sending me to Miss Kirby's and getting the position there. I'll always be grateful for that.'

'Aye, well, 'e's gone now, God rest his soul.'

Lissie swallowed hard before her next question. 'Do you know – I mean, did they ever find him – his murderer, that is?'

'Didn't you 'ear, lass?' Rosa exclaimed. 'That foreign lad never touched 'im. A bloke coming out o' t' privy saw it all. They di'n't find no bruises or nowt on Luther. He just died. T'old doctor said it were a seizure, like. Nay, they stopped looking for that foreigner ages ago, but I 'eard 'e'd gone back to 'is home country anyroad.'

Lissie covered her eyes with her hand. *Blake. Blake. He didn't do it. Blake didn't kill my father. And now he's gone. Gone away. Across the seas. I've lost him. Lost him for ever. Help! Oh help me, someone! This is too much to take in. Too much.*

Rosa continued, 'If you'd 'a' stayed around a bit longer, you'd 'a' known that.'

Lissie nodded silently and sagged weakly against the bed.

'You all right, ducks?' Rosa asked.

'Yes, thanks. Well no, not really. All this about my mother . . . and Luther buying me, it's . . . it's unsettling. And now this about the way Dad died . . . I . . . I hadn't heard anything where I was.'

'You found somewhere ter live, then?' Rosa asked.

'On a farm over Swinborough way. I help keep the place going and make pies to sell on market day.'

'Oh. Is that what yer were doin' there that day in town?'

Lissie nodded. 'I'm happy there, Rosa. I promised I'd go back. But if you need help with Mam, I can stay for a bit.'

'Nay, lass. Yer ma's no trouble ter me. Stay on fer a bit if yer want. But I can allus send for yer if she teks a turn for the worse. Look, she's dropped off ter sleep now. Shall we go down and have ussenns a drink?'

Rosa brewed up one of her garden-herb mixtures that tasted slightly bitter. She sweetened it with honey and they drank it out of bowls in Rosa's cluttered kitchen. Lissie found it reviving and calming at the same time.

'Will you be staying 'ere, or a' yer goin' t' tek a room at t' Navvy?' Rosa asked.

'No! Not the Navigator! I can't stay there!' Lissie exclaimed. 'I . . . I mean . . . I . . . I don't want to stay there. Can I stay here, Rosa? I'll sleep in the chair by the fire if you've got a spare blanket.'

Rosa raised her eyebrows. 'Still worried about Mickey, are yer? 'E'll 'ave moved on from you by now. 'E's got brass in 'is pocket, so there's plenty willin' ter go wi' 'im fer that. Mind, they're not as young and 'andsome as you, me duck.'

Lissie preferred not to risk it. 'I'd much rather stay this side of the canal if I can. It was always nicer on this side.'

'You're right there, lass. You're right there.'

'Who's the horse marine these days?'

'T' old fella's back. Young Peter Jackson went off ter some fancy racing stables near Donnie. An' Mickey's eldest lives in Edie's old house now, wi' his missus and babby.'

'Yes, I saw her on my way down. Another one on the way.'

'Middle lad is still working for his dad. Good brewer, 'e is. Folk wh' 'as got t' money comes from all ovver fer a keg or two fer their own cellars. Brews a good tankard o' ale, 'e does.'

The evening closed in and they sat by the light of the kitchen fire. A copper kettle rumbled on the swing hob and a blackened pot hung from a hook over the coals.

'That broth I had earlier was tasty, Edie,' Lissie commented.

'Aye. I boiled up a bacon hock and some barley.'

'Shall I make a bacon pudding with the meat?'

'Go on, then. Put some cabbage in wi' it.'

Lissie cleared a space on Rosa's rickety table and set to work. When the pudding wrapped in greased calico, and the cabbage stuffed into a net were simmering in the pot, Lissie asked, 'Is Miriam still at the school?'

'Miriam? Oh 'er! Right little madam she turned out t' be! She left soon after you went. She go' a position as a nursemaid at a big 'ouse in Derbyshire. Never comes 'ome ter see her mam at all now. Just writes letters saying 'ow grand everything is.'

'But I thought her dad had a bond for her at the Kirbys?'

'There were a bit of a to-do wi' followers,' Rosa explained. 'An' after all that wi' you and that lad off the barges, ol' man Kirby got rid.'

Lissie sighed. 'Poor Miriam. The Kirbys were very strict though.'

'*He* were!' Rosa scoffed. 'Two-faced bugger, if yer ask me!'

'What do you mean?'

'We-e-e-ll,' Rosa scorned, 'he reckoned he were a chapel man an' all that, but I know different. Allus in the Lion drinking, and gamblin' at t' races wi' all the gentry. And women!'

'Women?' Lissie queried.

'Oh aye, 'e likes 'is women does ol' man Kirby.'

Lissie remembered that night at the school, when Mr Kirby had had a builder doing out the new schoolroom, and she had bathed in the scullery. She remembered the way he'd looked at her, all over, as she stood dripping wet and naked on the stone scullery floor. He had called her a harlot, and pawed at her breasts, and she remembered being frightened of what he might do next. But, fortunately for her, he went off into town, presumably to one of his women.

'He never brought any lady friends to meet his sister,' Lissie said.

'Like I say,' Rosa sneered, 'two-faced.'

Lissie made herself as comfortable as she was able for the night by the fire in Rosa's small kitchen. Her limbs and body ached from the journey and from the tension that was gradually spreading through her veins. She must have dozed from time to time but her mind was too full to sleep.

She had more or less known that Edie wasn't her real mother, but had never dreamed she had been a lady. She wondered again who her real father was and whether he had been told about her. It would be nice to know. But not if he had been the one to sell her! Rosa was right. She had been lucky. She had been sold to Luther. He had been a good dad to her and she wouldn't have changed that.

The loneliness and emptiness crept over her as Rosa's kitchen fire died down and the air became chilled. She missed Martha's wise counsel and John's good humour. They would have helped her cope with all this. Martha had warned she might find it difficult to return here, and Lissie had ignored her. She thought she was strong enough to deal with it. But she had reckoned without all this about her birth. She wished Luther was still alive so she could ask him all the questions buzzing about in her head.

The hardest part to take in was finding out that her dad had not been murdered after all. Not murdered! Blake was innocent. She had accused him of murder and he was innocent. No wonder he had taken off like that! She had called for the constable's men to take him away. It was her fault. Her fault that he had left.

She rocked backwards and forwards in Rosa's kitchen chair, aching with misery. She had shut him from her mind, told herself she could not love a liar and a murderer. And since then she had been trying to close the void it left inside her. She had not been successful. She knew that now. It was as though all her efforts had been in vain and this awful, awful emptiness was consuming her. She folded her arms across her body as she rocked but the void remained. A void, she knew, that only Blake could fill.

If only she had known before that he was innocent! Now it was too late. He had gone from her life. He was the only thing, *the only thing*, she wanted from her past. Even worse, she had been the cause of his disappearance. What had she done? Her life was in pieces and it was her own doing.

'Blake. Blake.' She whispered his name over and over again. 'Where have you gone? I need you so much. Where are you?'

As she tormented herself with these feelings of remorse, she wondered if he ever thought of her.

Chapter 25

Blake racked his brain to work out a way of proving his innocence. Who would believe him? His fists had been ready to fight. Witnesses had heard him and Luther Dearne shouting at each other in the alehouse yard. And they had seen Dearne fall senseless to the ground! On top of all that, Lissie was Dearne's daughter! How come? he asked himself. How come that lovely girl is the daughter of a murderer?

'Get a move on, Blake!'

'Just waiting for young Eddie to catch up!' Blake called in return.

The two latecomers hurried forward to join big Eddie and his mates for their day at the coalface. Their metal-tipped clogs crunched and rang on the rocky surface as they made their way down the slope of Kimberhill drift, steadily descending into blackness.

'I didn't know the Swinborough estates stretched this far out,' Blake commented to Eddie as they walked.

'Swinboroughs have owned all this part o' t' South Riding for generations. Used to be iron an' all but most o' the best ore is worked out now,' Eddie replied.

'Good coal round 'ere though, an' it's everywhere. Coal seams like Kimberhill's fair jump outta t' ground. Old Swinborough only had to dig down into the hill-sides and carry it away!'

'He owns ironworks in town as well, doesn't he?'

Eddie clicked his teeth and jerked his head to one side. 'Shrewd man is Sir William. All t' coal we mine goes down t' cut to t' furnaces. His grandfather dug t' cut when t' main canal were built.'

'I met Sir William once,' Blake said. 'At a prize fight.'

'You a fist-fighter?'

'Not really. I did some sparring once.'

'Hear that, lads?' Eddie shouted. 'This 'un 's done some bare-knuckle scrapping. We'd better watch out then, 'a'n't we?'

A ripple of laughter ran through the men as they followed wagon rail tracks down the long black slope to their labour. Blake laughed with them as they trudged.

After a year or more with this gang, he was pleased that he fitted in now. They were suspicious of him at first, wary of the way he spoke, and they kept their distance from him. But he lodged with Eddie, his wife and young Eddie, just fourteen, and the men respected Eddie, so Blake was accepted.

'Your cottage looks fairly new to me,' Blake continued.

'Aye. Sir William built 'em so we w'u'n't have to walk as far to t' pit. Now t' word's got around, everybody wants to work at Kimberhill so they can 'ave one o' t' cottages. Womenfolk like 'em, y' see. They got indoor pumps fo' t' watter and new ranges in t' kitchen. And cellars fo' t' coal.'

'That steam engine back there must have cost him.'

Eddie nodded. 'We 'ad pit ponies pulling t' wagons afore that. But t' coalface is a long way down now, so 'e 'ad t' engine put in. Goes for owt new, does Sir William. You bin on one o' them railways yet?'

'No, not yet.'

'Well, they'll be ovver this way soon, they say.'

The gang reached the bottom of the slope and set up their lamps. A train of wagons stood empty, waiting to be filled with coal dug out by pick and shovel and the sweat of a man's back.

'Get stuck in, lads! It's already raining outside!'

Blake welcomed the labour. It took his mind off the outside world and the fact that he was a wanted man. He was eternally grateful to Clara for using her influence with Sir William and locating this place for him. It was a good choice, well out of the way of town folk. She had promised to find out what she could about the search for him, and to get word to him somehow. The only person he could trust was Clara. She would never betray him.

He thought a great deal about Lissie and Luther Dearne, his own actions on that day and how he had messed up his life for good. He was well rid of them both! A cold-blooded killer whose blood ran in the veins of his lovely daughter! She was a siren, a temptress, and he was glad that he had found out sooner rather than later. Even so, at times he wished he could go and find

Lissie and explain that he wasn't a murderer like her father. Foolish thoughts! He was a wanted fugitive and the constable's men would be waiting on every corner for him!

Blake considered himself to be a strong man. Working on the fly boats had given him stamina. But, he swiftly realised at Kimberhill drift, he was nothing compared to the strength and stamina of his fellow colliers.

The top ones were stocky men, short and thickset, with huge, muscled arms and even brawnier legs. They kept going in the worst of conditions for long, long hours. They toiled on when they were worn out, in the heat or in the cold, in the dark and in the wet.

The older ones were best, they had courage, and a determination that kept them strong, with some to spare for the younger, inexperienced men who became angry with their tools when they were exhausted at the end of their day. They looked out for each other at all times, as Eddie did for Blake.

Blake was taller than the others, and agile with a good reach. His suppleness in cramped conditions made up for his inconvenient height, and his quick thinking and speedy reactions made up for his inexperience.

Coal mining was dangerous work. The men at Kimberhill drift knew the main risk was flood; when the rain seeped in all over, an icy enemy, making your clothes wet and your tools rusty. The soil above their heads became clogged and the wooden pit props creaked. The coal became heavier to haul and the air dank and suffocating. Experienced colliers were seasoned weather-watchers and knew before they went down when the day would be short and the steam whistle would call them out early.

They had to be quick to hitch the wagons before they were hauled away, screeching and rumbling up the metal tracks, drowning out any conversation between the men. With their heads well down and their bodies bowed in the small space, the gang followed their wagons, planning what they could do with the rest of the day as they toiled back to the surface.

On that day a coupling pin was loose. In their haste the last wagon had not been properly hitched and, as the steam-driven pulleys dragged the train to the surface, it suddenly broke free, fully loaded, and rumbled back down the slope to the men trudging wearily in its wake. There was not much room in the tunnel. As soon as Blake realised what was happening, he yelled a warning, pushing his mates out of the way with his elbows and his legs. But young Eddie was in front of him and he froze as the wagon gathered speed.

He didn't move a muscle. Perhaps he couldn't.

Blake yelled again. 'Jump, Eddie, for God's sake, jump!'

Blake darted forward, grabbed the lad by the waist, twisting his body to protect him, and leaped sideways with all the strength his legs could muster. The loaded wagon rumbled past them, gathering speed, crumpling and crushing hastily discarded tools until a mesh of picks and shovels locked the wheels on one side and with a screech and a thunder, it toppled, spilling its load and raising a choking, blinding fog of coal dust.

Then everything was quiet except for the distant chugging of the steam engine winding the remaining wagons to the surface. One by one the men called each other's names and, between the coughing and the groaning, one by one, they answered.

'Harry?'

''Ere.'

'Ezra?'

'Right.'

'George?'

'Aye.'

'Eddie?'

'That's me.'

'Young Eddie?'

Silence.

'Young Eddie?' The second time his father called him there was fear in his voice.

Then Eddie heard his son cough and reply, 'I'm over here, Dad. I'm all right. I hurt a bit where I fell but I'm all right. It's Blake though. He's sort of laid on top o' me and he i'n't moving.'

'You stay where you are, lad, till I get to you. D' yo' 'ear me? You keep still now.'

'Yes, Dad.'

Slowly, gradually, the dust settled and the air cleared. A single lamp, miraculously, still glowed. The men moved cautiously, shaken, bruised and cut, but alive and able to walk. All except Blake, who lay motionless where the wagon had clipped his outstretched foot, throwing him off-balance and head-first against the solid, rocky wall.

Blood trickled from his temple and his left foot lay at an awkward angle. Rain was already seeping through the seam and it ran in rivulets down the walls of the mine and coursed away to the coalface. Soon the icy water would be ankle-deep and rising.

'Where's Joe?'

''E's gone for the medicine box. No need to panic, lads. They'll 'ave 'eard what's 'appened on t' surface.'

It was a half-hour trek to the surface, but on the way out there was an alcove carved out for housing tools and drinking water to supplement their cans of cold tea. They also kept poles and canvas for splinting limbs and carrying back injured men. Mining, as they knew, was a dangerous calling.

Joe was a bone-setter and he came back with the tools of his trade. He'd learned about bones from his dad who'd learned it from his dad.

'Let the dog see the rabbit,' he ordered gruffly as he set about his task of feeling and prodding and straightening, and then splinting Blake's foot and strapping him to the canvas stretched between two poles.

'He's a long 'un, to be sure,' Joe said, rolling him over on to his makeshift stretcher.

Blake groaned and his eyelids flickered in the dim glow of the mining lamp. 'Good sign,' muttered Joe, 'but keep 'im as still as you can, lads. Best get moving. Water's rising fast.'

They carried him out through the pouring rain to Eddie's small terraced cottage, and, somehow, got him up the narrow stairs to his bed. Eddie cleaned him up while his wife saw to the cuts and bruises on their son. Young Eddie would be all right after a drink of negus and a long sleep.

His mother made the negus with port wine, honey

and hot water and it always worked for her children. She was used to tending cuts and bruises and knew her menfolk were tough. This young lodger was a different breed though. Strong enough and a good worker by all accounts, but not from real mining stock, she thought. You 'ad to 'ave it in your blood to survive working in the pits.

Eddie sighed wearily and watched his wife clear up the bowl of water and bloody rags. 'Joe says he'll be up there a while, lass. Broke his ankle and taken a knock to the 'ead. Can you manage all right?'

'Oh aye. Joe's wife 'll come round to lend a hand if needs be. I've seen a lot worse.'

'Aye, me too.'

He listened to the ceaseless rain coming down in torrents. 'Reckon we'll be rained off for a week at this rate. We got plenty o' coal in?'

'Cellar's full. Bank up the fire and get them wet clothes off. You'll catch your death.'

The heavy rain continued and Kimberhill mine was flooded for more than a month. The men walked five miles morning and night to another pit for work while they waited for the water to go down. Blake drifted in and out of consciousness for several days until one morning, when he opened his eyes and saw young Eddie staring at him from the bedroom doorway.

'Dad! Dad! He's woke up! Blake's woke up, Dad!'

Blake frowned as he collected his thoughts. He had been vaguely aware of pain and of people fussing round him and, as he lay there feeling too exhausted to move, he remembered the accident. His head was thumping and his ankle hurt. He tried to move it and it hurt even more. He fingered his head where it was sore and tender. He'd taken a fair crack and there was a swelling to show for it and, he guessed, a deep cut and some colourful bruising.

His ankle was bound, done up with plastered bandages from calf to toes, and propped up on a bolster at the bottom of the bed. His toes felt cold but he could wiggle them all right. Damn! He was going to be like this for a long time while it mended. Well, at least young Eddie was all right. He hoped the others were too.

Young Eddie came back with his dad. Eddie's hands were dirty with soil from his garden at the back. It must be a Sunday. Young Eddie put some coal on the fire from a bucket on the hearth. His dad splayed his hands to show the soil still on them.

'Just digging a few parsnips to go round t' meat. By gum, I'm right pleased you've come round. 'Ow you feeling now?'

'My leg hurts a bit and my head's thumping like mad.'

Eddie poured some water into a tin mug from a can on the mantelpiece. 'Drink some water. Your leg's not too bad. It's t' ankle, Joe said. It'll be as good as new once it's mended, if you can keep off it, like. Heads are funny though. Can you see all right?'

'If that's young Eddie by the fire there, then yes, I can.'

'That's good. Thanks for what you did for our Eddie.'

Young Eddie jumped forward. 'Yes. Thanks, Blake. You saved my life.'

'Off you go now, lad. Fetch those parsnips in for your

mam.' Eddie sat on the only chair in the room. A heavy, wide, wooden thing that had seen better days. 'We're missing you in our gang but it can't be helped. You have to stay off that ankle if it's to mend proper, like. You'll be laid off a good few weeks and then we'll be into winter.'

'What does that mean?'

'Kimberhill drift floods a lot more in winter. Most of us goes off to other pits. Pit manager's dropping by to say hello after chapel today. Then we'll 'ave us dinner. You hungry?'

'I could eat a horse.'

Eddie grinned. 'That's a good sign. I reckon you'll do. You'll 'ave to stay up here a while, but you'll do all right. Joe'll bring round a crutch for you to get about and you'll be able to shuffle down the stairs on yer backside soon.'

He stood up and turned round, lifting the wooden seat of his chair to reveal a chipped chamber pot. 'Talking o' backsides, Joe's missus sent this round for you to use, and she says if you 'as trouble going she's got something in her cupboard for you.'

'I'll bet she has,' Blake replied ruefully. 'When's Joe coming round with the crutch? I'll go mad cooped up here all the time.'

The rains continued for several weeks, causing major problems at Kimberhill drift. Blake followed Joe's advice and his injuries healed well. He helped out around the house and Eddie's garden where he could, and spent much of his time reading. Eventually, he was able to get out using the crutch and made his way to the offices at the mine.

'Come in and sit down, lad. How's the ankle now?'

Blake hobbled into the pit manager's small office, grimy with ingrained coal dust. He carried a well-thumbed book in his free hand, which he placed on the manager's worn and grubby desk.

'It's coming on nicely, sir. Joe says I'll be putting my full weight on it soon.'

Blake had met this man only once before. He was one of the gaffers who travelled around on horseback, checking up on Sir William's various works, sorting out problems and feeding through information. He'd been to the pit to see about the accident and had already had a chat with Blake. That was how he knew about Blake's interest in steel and how he had come to lend him the book.

The manager was a brisk, no nonsense man, a bit like Sir William, Blake thought. He nodded briefly, seemingly satisfied with Blake's response.

'Thanks for the loan of the book,' Blake went on. 'We do need to keep producing iron to forge, but I've always thought there was a future for steel as well.'

'So I believe. You've spoken of it to others. How did you learn about it?'

'From the Institute. When I came off the flyers I did some classes there and went to some lectures.'

'Why the interest in iron and steel?'

'I reckon it's in my blood. My great-grandfather dug iron ore out of the mountainside in Sweden. My grandfather smelted it and hauled it. My father shipped pig iron over here. I want to be part of its future.'

'I would have thought that shipping iron, like your father, would be a better line of work for an educated man like you. It's clean and it's profitable.'

'It's not for me. I'm no clerk.'

'You're no collier either, lad!' The manager got to his feet to emphasise his point.

Blake put his hands on the chair arms to lever himself up and then thought better of it. 'You're not laying me off because of one lousy accident, surely?' he protested. 'I'm a good worker, ask any of my mates.'

'Oh aye, I have already. And they all speak very highly of you. But you can do better than this.'

'What do you mean? Mining coal is good work and it pays well. Besides, I like hard graft. Always have. I want to stay down the mine.'

'Yes, that's what your mates say too.' The manager came round his desk to face him and leaned back against it. 'Come on, lad. You're educated! You've been to school and you can read. Not just the news-sheets, but proper books about new processes and materials. You're wasted down the pit!'

'I want to stay. I have my reasons.'

'Well I have my reasons for shifting you,' the manager snapped. 'We mine this coal here to keep the furnaces going in the valley. And we can't keep 'em going wi'out getting the coals down there. I can use a decent man like you, one who knows what he's doing.'

'I thought production at Kimberhill had stopped.'

'D' yo' think I don't know that! Since the big flood at Kimberhill I've been bringing coals over from Mexton. I can't get Kimberhill back to full production until Sir

William has installed a bigger steam engine to pump out the water. I've got empty barges standing idle, and furnaces cooling off for lack o' coals!'

Blake grimaced and sighed.

The manager continued, 'As soon as you're walking proper again I'm putting you on the narrow boats bringing the coals from Mexton down to the works.'

Blake scowled as he realised there was no choice for him. The irony was, he thought bitterly, he *wanted* to be out of the pits, back on the canals or working on a furnace in the ironworks. But he dare not risk it. Not yet. There could be a drawing of him as a wanted man on every street corner in town. He'd be better off staying here, well out of the town.

The manager was staring hard at him, expecting an answer. 'Look, lad, you came here with a nod from Sir William and I never asked no questions. So why don't you tell me the real reason you came to Kimberhill drift. I may be able to help. You can't spend the rest of your life holed up here. Besides, I want men like you in the ironworks. You'll have to live in town then.'

When Blake did not respond he tried again. 'I heard you had a sweetheart down Fordham way. Still waiting for you, is she? You could wed her and be living in a manager's house before long, if you'd only listen to what I'm saying.'

Blake covered his face with his hands and heaved a sigh. If only, he thought, if only. He looked up and said frankly, 'I killed a man.'

Visibly shocked, the manager went back to his chair behind the desk. 'God no. Nob'dy said it were that serious. You'd better tell me about it.'

Blake did. All of it. The truth about his own father, the Kirbys and Lissie, and how Lissie's father had died. The manager listened to him in silence, pursing his lips as the story unfolded. Finally, Blake shrugged, saying, 'A friend of Sir William's told me about Kimberhill drift and I wanted to keep away from town and lie low.'

'For how long though?'

'I don't know,' Blake groaned. 'Oh God, I don't know.' He watched as the manager gave a weary sigh and chewed at his lip, pulling his mouth sideways.

'I'll do anything to stay—' Blake continued.

'Shut up, I'm thinking!'

Blake looked down at his hands, worker's hands with scars and calluses. They were not a clerk's hands. They were hands that he was proud of.

The silence lengthened until the manager broke it by saying briskly, 'Right. Two things. I've not heard about this murder of Luther Dearne and, believe me, I know most that goes on in these parts. We've had no constable's men around the works or the pits asking questions. I would know if they were looking for you, lad. And they're not. Still, I'll find out what I can for you.'

Surprised at this response, Blake muttered, 'Th-thanks – er – thank you, sir. And the other thing? You said there were two things.'

'The other? Oh yes. I already said it. I need a capable man like you on the Mexton run. The sooner, the better. So when do yo' think you'll be fit enough to handle a narrow boat?'

Chapter 26

At Mexton Lock, Lissie was staring at her mam's tray on Rosa's rickety kitchen table. A glass of port wine with a few drops of laudanum helped her mam sleep. She gazed at the small brown bottle and wondered how many more sleepless nights she could take.

Rosa's horsehair chair was comfy enough, and she had a stool for her feet. But the memories kept coming back – painful recollections that pushed at the lid of the sealed black box in her mind.

Rosa had not asked Lissie to go over to the Navigator for anything, not even when their ale ran low. The older woman carried the cans over the bridge and back by herself. Lissie was grateful for that. Instead, she borrowed a sacking apron and with Rosa's approval, set about cleaning her small cottage.

This morning she had pumped water at the trough behind the row of woodmen's cottages and filled the boiler at the side of Rosa's kitchen fire. When the water was hot she carried it in a bucket through to a tub in the scullery and washed all the linen she could find in hot water and real soap. Then she took Rosa's rag rugs outside, draped them over tree branches and bushes and beat them clean for all she was worth.

It was while she was doing this that she saw Mickey Jackson go by. He was carrying a jute tool bag. She guessed he was going to see his daughter-in-law and grandchild. She held her breath and her heart stopped as she watched him and prayed that he would not turn and see her. He didn't and she breathed out raggedly as he disappeared up the track through the woods.

But her stomach churned. Fear and loathing rose in her gullet and she gagged at the bitter gall in her throat as she remembered the smell of him and the feel of his gross swarthy body invading hers.

As she retched she realised how much she still hated him, how much she had pushed the bad memories to the back of her mind and imagined him dead and gone from this world. But he wasn't. He was carrying on as if nothing had happened, visiting his family, probably mending the window in the very same room he had degraded and defiled her.

She retched again and hated herself for the continuing effect he had on her. She leaned over and pumped cold fresh water over her face to wash away the bile. Her dress became wet and she went inside to dry out, sitting very still, alone by the fire, saying nothing, watching the daylight fade through Rosa's small kitchen window.

Why hadn't she thought before of how much

returning here would bring back that dreadful, dreadful time? What could she do to take away the memory, to forget how loathsome he had been and what he had done to her?

The battered wooden tray was on the table, ready for Rosa to take up to her mam. Lissie stared at the small brown bottle on the tray. She had taken laudanum when she fled from here. Martha had also given her a little to help the pain of her injuries after the attack. She remembered the blissful floating euphoria that helped her survive the hurt and humiliation. Just a few drops in a glass of wine, she thought, would be enough to dull her mind, enough to blot out this resurrected hell that threatened to blight her life for ever.

She stood up and moved towards the table. The evening was drawing in. Another long, dark and sleepless night lay ahead of her, reliving the torment. How long would the memory take to fade again? Maybe she would be all right tomorrow? Perhaps she just needed to get through this night? Just a few drops would help, she was sure. She picked up the small brown bottle and took out the cork.

'Nay, lass, it's too early for that! Yer mam won't be awake for her supper if yer gi'es it 'er now.' Rosa burst in the door with a can of ale and two bottles of porter. 'By gum, them cans get heavier.' She flopped down on to her fireside chair, rubbing her shoulder.

Lissie's hand shook as she pushed back the cork and replaced the bottle on the tray. 'I – er, I haven't started to cook anything yet.'

'Aye, well, yer don't have ter tonight. Annie Jackson

wants some o' me green salve for her hands and she were roasting mutton for t' inn so I did a deal wi' 'er.'

Lissie pushed her shaking hands behind her back and asked sharply, 'What sort of deal?'

'Two pots o' salve fo' three roast dinners! What do yer think o' that then?'

Lissie moved away from the table, trying to sound normal. 'That sounds like a good deal, Rosa.'

'Aye. She wants to send some to their Miriam.' Rosa smiled and added, 'Yer mam likes a slice o' roast mutton wi' a 'tater.'

'You are good with her, Rosa.'

'I do me best. Mind you, I'm tired out tonight. Been up and down them stairs all day. And this shoulder's playing up again. Can you tek the salve over to the Navvy for us? And tek a tin fo' t' dinners?'

Lissie closed her eyes and swallowed. *No! Please no, not tonight. Just not tonight.*

'Yer'll be all right,' Rosa prompted. 'Mickey'll be serving ale in the saloon. Yer on'y 'as ter nip in and outta t' kitchen. Won't tek yer a minute.'

Lissie inhaled deeply. She had to go over there some-time. Just as long as she could keep away from Mickey Jackson! She said, 'Of course. I'll get my shawl.'

It was twilight, early evening, with only half a moon and no one had lit any flares. A couple of working men were busy marshalling a train of narrow boats slowly through the lock. They were loaded with coal and pulled by a brace of heavy horses. As she crossed the bridge and looked upstream her eyes grew accustomed to the gloom.

She frowned. It was the way he moved. There was a man, a tall man, commanding another of the narrow boats and organising the horses beyond the lock gates. She watched him cross the far set of lock gates and talk to the lock keeper. A flare was lit. There was a train of three barges to get through the lock that evening.

At first she was sure it was him, the man she once thought that she loved, the man she believed had killed her dad. Then she shook her head and moved on. Her mind was playing tricks on her. He had gone away she had heard, out of the country. Since seeing Mickey Jackson all her thoughts were befuddled by bad memories. This man too was a bad memory now.

She went round the back of the inn to avoid going through the saloon where Mickey would be. The meat and potatoes were not quite ready. Annie was busy and said, 'Why don't you go into the saloon for a tankard while you wait?'

'No thank you, Mrs Jackson. I'll stay in the kitchen.'

'Well, I can't be doing with you! I've a group of travellers in tonight, all baying for their food. Go and stand out there.'

Lissie hovered outside the kitchen, on the cobbled yard that led to the brew house. A light glowed through the half-open door. After a few minutes two men came out, one carrying a lamp, and walked across the yard to the kitchen. Lissie recognised them and shrank back into the shadows.

'Well, well, well. Look 'ere, lad. Look who we' got 'ere.' Mickey Jackson held up the lamp to see her face.

'It's Edie Dearne's lass. Come back to say sorry to me and yer old ma, 'ave yer?'

Lissie pressed her back against the rough stone wall. 'Keep away from me,' she said.

'Or what?' Mickey moved closer, slowly lowering and raising the lamp. 'Still a fine-looking lass, I see. Always was a fine-looking lass, was our Lissie.'

'I'm not your Lissie.'

'No? Your ma said you were, and you owe me summat from then, lass.' He pushed his grimy fingers through the folds of her skirt to between her thighs. 'Some more o' that,' he sneered.

He stood so close to her that she could smell the ale and tobacco on his breath and feel the heat of the lantern against her cheeks. His bloodshot eyes and flushed unshaven face leered at her in the yellow glow. Coils of lank greying hair hung greasily from under his grubby cap. The stench of stale sweat in her nostrils overtook the yeasty fumes from the brew house.

Suddenly he swung the lantern to one side and barked, 'Here, tek this inside, son, and see to t' men in t' saloon. I've got some unfinished business 'ere.'

Mickey's son disappeared fast, leaving Mickey standing in front of her. He was breathing deeply, and he placed a hand on the stone wall each side of her head. 'Still got that fight in yer, 'ave yer? Or 'as some young stallion knocked it out o' yer yet?'

Lissie's throat closed with fear. Her stomach knotted and, again, she felt the bile rise in her gullet. 'Keep your filthy hands away from me, you evil man!' she hissed.

He smiled. It was a crooked, lopsided grin that showed

his stained and broken teeth. 'That's my girl,' he whispered, as his foul breath closed in on her mouth.

She lifted her knee as hard as she could into his groin and pushed him away with her hands. Her effect on him was minimal but she realised that she had startled him, and quickly she ducked under his arms to escape. As she struggled to break free he caught hold of the fabric of her gown and she heard it tear as she pulled away from him. She gathered up her skirts and ran as fast as she could around the corner of the inn towards the canal and the bridge.

But the back of her skirt, torn away from the waist as it was, trailed on the ground behind her. In the darkness she missed her footing, caught the heel of her boot in the fabric and fell, winded, on the bank side.

Mickey Jackson was right behind her, grabbing the back of her skirt, ripping it away and pinning her down on the ground with his body. He pushed her face into the soggy soil, tainted with coal dust and machine oil, and she felt his hand fumbling with the buttoning of his breeches.

She twisted her neck, scratching her face in the gritty sludge and yelled as loud as she could, 'Help me! Somebody, please help me!' Through the darkness she made out the top of a laden narrow barge in the lock, the last one waiting for the sluices to be opened and empty the lock. Someone must be around! The lock keeper might hear her. 'Help!' she cried. 'Please help!'

But her words were lost as Mickey shoved her head further into the mud. His body was a dead weight on top of her. He had torn away the back of her drawers and she felt his hardened arousal press into the soft flesh of her rump. He pushed one of his hands under her stomach to lift her rear away from the ground. Desperately, *desperately*, she clenched her muscles and tried to squirm away from him.

The scream in her throat spluttered out through coal grit and soil, but she kept trying. She struggled with all her ebbing strength to heave him off her back, twisting her body this way and that, but he was too heavy, too strong and too inflamed with his greedy needs to stop now.

Then suddenly, quite suddenly, she was free.

'Get away from her, you animal, or so help me, I'll kill you!'

His heavy weight was lifted from her back. Cold air breezed across the naked flesh of her bottom and legs. She heard the thud of fists on flesh and the cries and groans of fighting men. She rolled over in the sludge to see who it was.

It *was* Blake! No, it couldn't be! Not him. Here? At Mexton Lock? She must have knocked her head when she fell. She must be hallucinating.

But no, she wasn't, her head was clear and it *was* him! He had freed her from this vile beast and was making a good job of knocking Mickey senseless.

She sat up and pulled the fabric of her torn skirt around her. Blake was dusting himself down with his hands and walking over to where Mickey was flat on his back and groaning.

But as she sat up two figures loomed out of the darkness and punched Blake low in the back. His knees buckled and he staggered but did not fall. Mickey's sons set about Blake with a vengeance, throwing punches and kicks indiscriminately. Lissie watched in horror as he cowered against the blows with his arms encircling his head.

Then Blake retaliated. He had the advantage of height and reach. He placed his punches accurately and knocked down first one brother and then the other. But they were also young, strong men and they each recovered in turn to fight back. The blacksmith landed a heavy blow to the side of Blake's head that sent him reeling. The younger son grabbed his arm and quickly the other arm was seized in a vice-like grip by the blacksmith. Blake struggled at first but they held on to his arms tightly and eventually he stopped.

Mickey clambered slowly to his feet and Lissie, behind him by the edge of the canal, saw him approach Blake with his raised clenched fists. Mickey would kill him! Blake had no chance against him with his arms pinioned by the Jackson brothers! She stood up and cast about looking for a weapon. Her boot struck a discarded winding handle used for raising and lowering the sluices in the lock gates.

She bent to pick it up. It was an old one, made of rusting iron and heavy in her hand. No one was looking at her. She took it in both her hands, not caring that her skirt fell away and her drawers were torn, and using all her might, swung it round to strike Mickey's head.

He let out an animal howl and turned, startled, but did not fall. She had missed and struck his shoulder rather than his head or neck. He swayed, recovered, and then began to approach her again. She had not even winded him.

Blake yelled, 'No, leave her alone.' He was struggling again to free himself and crying, 'Run! Run for it!'

She could not. Her legs wouldn't move. Fear froze her to the spot.

Mickey was just a few yards away and she heard a growl in his throat as he lumbered towards her. His breeches were still undone and his hands were already pulling the buttons aside to expose his renewed arousal. She took a step backwards, glancing nervously over her shoulder at the nearness of the oily dark water. At that split second, the cold deep water was preferable to whatever Mickey Jackson had in mind for her.

Blake yelled again, 'Keep away from her, you animal! Leave her . . .' His words were lost in a strangled groan as he was punched into silence.

Lissie's instinct for survival took over. She had nearly died because of what this man had done to her in the past. She remembered the belt. And the tearing injuries to her insides. Injuries that were worse because she had tried to fight him. She still had the winding handle in her hands, but it had been no good to her and Mickey could easily wrench it off her and use it on her in his anger.

Her head cleared and she knew what she had to do. She looked at him and she smiled. She held the iron handle at arm's length and dropped it into the lock, listening for a thud as it landed on a loaded coal barge or a splash if it hit the water. She heard a splash. The narrow barge had drifted to the far side of the lock.

She was ready for him. She smiled again. She tore away the remainder of her skirt to expose the front of her drawers and placed both her hands in the waistband to push them down and offer him what he wanted.

He growled again and lurched forward. He would have fallen against her if she had not stepped smartly to one side. Mickey realised his mistake and arched his back, flinging his arms over his head. But he was too late. He carried too much weight, too much momentum, and could not stop himself from moving forward that extra step, the step that took him over the edge.

Lissie watched him as he tottered, desperately trying to fling himself backwards. It seemed a long time to her as he wavered like a tree in the wind, until, eventually, he toppled forward into the lock and, after a second, hit the black water beneath.

It all happened very slowly and she watched every second of it. A muscled, heavy man, he made a big splash in the lock, causing waves that hit the stone-built sides. The stern of the coal-laden narrow barge hit the wall and bounced very slowly away from the far side.

Mickey coughed and spluttered and yelped as the water soaked into his clothes and dragged him down. There was an iron ladder cut into the lock wall and he struck out for it as best he could. The second he disappeared over the side, his sons dropped their grip on Blake's arms and rushed to the lock side.

'Fetch a rope,' one yelled. 'I'll go down the ladder.'

Mickey thrashed and splashed in desperation to reach the ladder. The stern of the heavy boat, glistening blackly in the moonlight, bounced gracefully away from the far side of the lock and swung slowly towards Mickey. Nothing and no one could deter its gentle drift until it connected with Mickey's screaming, heaving bulk and crushed him against the wall. Mickey's son stopped his descent as he realised that he too might be crushed.

Mickey's agonised screams echoed through the night. Lissie choked with horror. Tons of floating coal were grinding against the stone wall of the lock and squeezing the life out of Mickey Jackson, leaving his anguished haunting cries a mere gurgle in the water.

Lissie stared as the wayward barge slowly recoiled and released Mickey's crushed and lifeless body, a body that sank silently beneath the water's undulating surface.

It was over. Finished. She had wanted to kill him and she had.

She began to cry. Tears of relief ran down her cheeks. He was dead. Mickey Jackson was dead. Someone had retrieved the torn skirt of her dress and was wrapping it around her. He turned her round to face him, gathering up the fabric and knotting it firmly in place.

'Lissie?' he said. 'It *is* you!'

'Blake?' she said vacantly, her senses dulled by shock. 'You're in Sweden, aren't you?'

He shook his head silently.

'M-Mickey J-Jackson, he fell. He just fell,' she muttered. What was Blake doing here?

'I know. I saw him.' Blake took off his corduroy working jacket and placed it around her shoulders.

'I didn't kill your father,' he said. Even though he shot mine, he thought. How could he look at her and not remember that?

She pulled the coat around her trembling shoulders. 'I know. Rosa told me. She told me lots of things.' Lissie let out a long shuddering sigh. 'He wasn't my real father anyway. I didn't know that until yesterday. He bought me. When I was a baby. Who would want to sell their own baby? Any baby?'

'I'm sorry your father died.' Blake realised that he meant it. And, though he still grieved for his own father, revenge no longer simmered in his breast. He had worked out his vengeance with the coal he had mined at Kimberhill. Did it matter any more, he thought? Did anything matter except that he had found his Lissie again, and she was safe. She was the same Lissie to him, whoever her father was and whatever he had done.

After a second she added, 'He was the only father I ever knew and I loved him. I didn't want him to die.'

But I did at the time, thought Blake. And Lissie knows that. Will she ever forgive me?

Someone lit flares. Rosa came over the bridge to find her, saw the commotion and retreated to her cottage. Drinkers came out of the Navigator to find out what was going on. Lissie recognised Eliza from the dairy farm at Fordham. She was arm in arm with her husband Job.

'Lissie? Is it you, Lissie?' Eliza came forward, concerned. 'Oh, what has happened to you, you poor love?' She looked up at Blake's bruised, bleeding face and torn clothing. 'This isn't your doing, is it?'

'N-No, Eliza,' Lissie said. She was feeling strange, chilled and shivery and numb. It took a huge effort for her to add, 'The Jacksons beat him up. He was – he was trying to protect me.'

Eliza put her arms around both of them. 'Come home with us,' she said.

Job added, 'I've got our farm cart round the back of the Navigator – if you don't mind sharing it with a keg of ale and some straw?'

Lissie nodded, too exhausted to speak. Her face was scratched and sore. She was feeling very cold and starting to shiver.

Blake lifted her on to the straw bedding in the cart and climbed in beside her.

'It's not far,' Eliza called over her shoulder as the horse pulled them forwards.

The farm cart rumbled through the night air, following rutted tracks to the dairy at Fordham. Lissie, wrapped in Blake's heavy jacket, curled up and shivered in spite of the warmth of the soft barley straw around her.

Blake stretched out beside her, and placed an arm above her head. 'Let me hold you. The heat from my body will warm you.'

'No!' It was the first syllable she had uttered since the shivering started. It came out as a strangled whisper, forced through her closed throat. She turned away from him, curled her body tighter and pulled the jacket closer in a vain attempt to shield herself.

Blake lifted his arm away and covered his eyes with his hand. Rejection. Was that all he could hope for? He could not blame her. She had come through a dreadful ordeal. But he did want to hold her, to warm her, to make her well again. Her shivering was becoming worse. He could hear her teeth chattering. He took off his flannel work shirt and draped it over her.

He wondered how he looked. His jaw felt swollen and he had a cut over one eye. There were livid patches and grazes on his arms. No doubt there would be more hidden beneath his undershirt. The bruises from his beating were already stiffening up into nagging aches. He was tough though, he would recover. But Lissie, she was not so strong. She had been running away from Mickey Jackson and he had no idea what Mickey had done to her before he heard her cries.

'Is it much further, Mr Dacre?' Blake twisted his neck to speak to Job.

'No, lad. Just down by the big field and over t' canal bridge an' we'll be 'ome. You two all right back there?'

'Lissie's very cold. She can't stop shivering.'

Eliza pressed her husband's arm gently. 'Can you go a bit faster, Job? Lissie's had a really bad time.'

'Hold on tight then. Not far now.' He flicked the reins and his dappled grey mare broke into a trot.

Lissie clenched her jaw in a vain attempt to stop her teeth chattering. She was unable to think straight, unable to talk and hardly able to breathe. Her breath came in short rasps and she felt that she could not fill her lungs with air no matter how hard she tried. She curled up tighter and felt another covering drop over her. The extra warmth was no help. She could not stop the shivering.

It was Blake who had rescued her. She had not been imagining it when she had seen his silhouette in the light of the flare by the lock gates. He had been there all the time during her ordeal, marshalling coal barges through the lock. Her spirits had lifted when he loomed out of the darkness to tackle her attacker.

Now, in the aftermath, her fighting spirit had deserted her. A numbness of body crept over her and she struggled to arrange her thoughts in her mind. She felt detached from the world, closed off from reality. It's easier to let go, she thought. If she let go, the shivering would stop and the pain would go away. Yes . . . the . . . pain . . . will . . . go . . . away . . . Lissie thought idly as she slipped silently into a faint.

Blake carried her from the cart into Job and Eliza's low, stone-built farmhouse and gently lowered her on to the parlour couch. He winced as he straightened. Those Jackson thugs had cracked a rib or two, no doubt. He was bruised and cut but he'd suffered worse in the past and right now he was more worried about Lissie. Her beautiful black hair was tumbled and knotted, and the delicate skin of her face had been bruised and cut during her attack. Now Blake was alarmed by her pallor under the streaks of dried sludge and coal dust.

'Have you got another blanket for her, Eliza?' he asked. 'Her skin is icy cold.'

Eliza took charge of the situation and despatched her husband to open the damper and draw the kitchen fire, light oil lamps and fill a warming pan with coals for the spare bed upstairs.

'Here, put this over her,' Eliza suggested, handing Blake a thick woollen rug. 'A drop of brandy might help. You look as if you could do with one yourself.'

'Yes, I could.'

'In the dresser cupboard.' Eliza nodded in the direction of a large oak sideboard displaying a variety of plates and pots. 'Me and Job'll have one an' all.'

Blake sat beside Lissie and supported her head while he coaxed brandy through her pallid lips. She coughed and spluttered but revived and managed to swallow some of it. Warmth began to course through her veins and her shivering eased.

'Th-thank you,' she muttered. 'I . . . I don't know what came over me.'

'It's only to be expected after what you've been through,' Eliza replied in her usual common sense way. 'You'll stay with us tonight. Blake, you can have the couch if you like.'

Blake ran his fingers through his coal-streaked fair hair. 'I wish I could stay. I was taking a train of coal barges through the lock when I heard Lissie's cries for help. I've left them with a young lad. He's only a nipper. He won't be able to manage them on his own, not with two Cleveland Bays hauling.'

'You'd best get off, then. I'll look after Lissie,' Eliza responded.

Lissie made a huge effort to speak. 'Will you . . . will you come back?' she croaked.

He hated leaving her like this. His heart ached to hold her close and make her well again. His throat closed and he simply nodded, whispering, 'If you want me to.' He bent over to kiss the top of her head, blocking the light from the lamp.

The shadow of his broad shoulders covered her face and Lissie smelled the coal grit on his clothes. She tasted again the wet gritty dust in her mouth and she relived the horror of her attack, her face being pushed into the black sludge and the weight of Mickey Jackson squeezing the breath out of her body.

'No!' She recoiled from Blake's lips, pressing her back

in to the couch and, helpless with distress, saw the surprise, the anguish and then the naked hurt in his eyes.

Job came forward with another lamp, illuminating the panic in Lissie's frightened eyes. He placed a gentle hand on Blake's shoulder. 'Leave her be, for now. Give her some time. The lass was all but raped and . . . and . . . well, she saw the man perish. Nasty way to go, being slowly crushed by a coal barge. That sort o' thing is hard for a young 'un to deal with.'

Eliza echoed her husband's wisdom. 'We'll look after her well, Blake. You can rely on us. Come and see how she is on Sunday, if you can.'

Blake straightened up. The pain from his bruised ribs was nothing compared to the pain in his heart. Lissie could not bear him even to touch her. His blue eyes were bright with tears as he stepped out into the cold night air.

When he left the mine at Kimberhill he had harboured hopes of finding Lissie at Mexton Lock. The lock keeper had told him that she had gone away after her father died and the house had changed hands. No one knew where she was, but her mother was still around, living with Rosa in Woodmill Row.

He remembered Rosa. She had helped him when his father was shot. Maybe Lissie had found a position in service somewhere and come back to Mexton to see her mother?

Blake hoped, desperately, that Lissie was going to be all right. She had been cruelly attacked by that rogue. Men like that deserved everything they got! But Mickey Jackson's death had been particularly nasty. It was one of Blake's barges that had crushed him to death. He shivered at the memory of the man's screams. He was glad that young Eddie had been up stream from the lock with the horses and not seen what had happened.

Young Eddie would be wondering where he was. It was late. Painfully, he broke into a run on the towpath until he had sight of his horses tethered and waiting, munching slowly from their nose cans.

'Am I glad to see you,' Eddie exclaimed. 'The lock keeper gave me a hand with this last barge. He said you were in a fight. And t' inn keeper drowned in t' lock! Flipping 'eck! Did you knock 'im down, Blake?'

'No I did not. He fell. It was an accident.'

'Oh.' Young Eddie sounded disappointed.

'Have they taken his body out yet?'

'Aye. We had to wait till he were out afore we could shift t' last barge. I watched 'em fish 'im out. The lock keeper had to fetch a winch from t' mill and they hooked him up just like a big fat pike. Wait till I tell me dad about this!'

'That's enough, Eddie,' Blake snapped. 'Get the harnesses on the horses while I check the tow ropes. We've lost too much time already!'

'All right! Keep your 'air on!'

Normally sure-footed, Blake winced in pain as he clambered from one barge to another on the string of three, and misjudged his footing twice. After hearing a second curse from Blake, Eddie called, 'I can do that fo' you, if you like.'

'I told you to look to the horses, Eddie. Make sure the harness is secure.'

'Yeh, yeh. Did yo' know that girl then, Blake? The one he were after?'

'I said drop it, Eddie! We have no time for gossip. This coal has to be in the works by morning.'

The heavy horses moved on and their floating cargo edged forwards into the night. As they glided past the dairy at Fordham, Blake hoped and prayed that Lissie would be all right.

The farmhouse was quiet when Lissie woke the next morning after her brandy-induced slumber. Job and Eliza were long gone to milk their cows. She felt as though she would break in two if someone pushed her, and climbed out of her big feather bed carefully.

Eliza had draped clean clothes over the wooden bedstead for her to dress. The sun was already high in the sky as she pulled back the shutters. Her bedchamber overlooked a backyard, where chickens scratched and a few geese cropped the grass. She sat on the edge of the bed with sagging shoulders and a drooping head.

Mickey Jackson was dead. She was rid of him at last. Or would this image of his evil crooked face be for ever etched in her mind? It had seemed a lifetime since he had raped her, until last night. Now she felt as if it had happened all over again. Last night's attack had resurrected the memories, just as vivid and just as horrific. But she had come through it, and now she was over the shock she felt stronger.

Blake only knew of last night's attack. He did not know about her earlier ordeal. Would he still be interested in her as a woman if he did? She remembered that look in his eyes last night when he had turned away from her, confused, unsure about her, and who would not be? In despair, she poured water from the ewer into a bowl on the washstand. She did not allow her mind to dwell on the past or what the future might hold for her. It would take all her courage to face the day.

Eliza came back to their farmhouse for breakfast. Lissie cut bread and butter and mashed tea and found more strength in the daily routine.

Eliza fried eggs on an iron griddle over the fire and commented, 'Job's brought one of the cows in for the night. He's out there with her now.'

'Shall I call him in for you? You look exhausted.'

'I'm used to it, dairy folk always have early starts. I often go to bed soon after tea.'

'Let me help you with the chores. Tell me what you want doing for dinner.'

'No, you rest up for a few days and get yourself back to normal.'

'Thanks, Eliza, but I need to be up and doing. Otherwise I shall dwell too much on last night.'

'Oh! All right, if you say so,' Eliza replied. 'As long as you don't go wearing yourself out.'

'It will help me to sleep,' Lissie said simply.

'Well, if you're sure. The brewer at the alehouse in Fordham killed a pig t' other day and a quarter of it is ours. Tastes good an' all, because he feeds it on the butter-milk left over from my churning. There's a nice piece of the belly in the larder. It's my Job's favourite, he says it's the sweetest o' the lot. We can have it for dinner if you set it to roast in the slow oven. Job likes his crackling really crisp.'

'You've got some apples ready on your tree out there, I'll make some sauce to go with it,' suggested Lissie. 'You have a sit down. The dairy is a lot of work for just the two of you.'

Eliza agreed. 'I had an old woman from the village to help me in the farmhouse until she died, bless 'er. I think I can manage through this winter on my own, but after calving next spring Job is giving me a proper dairymaid. Mind you, she'll take some getting used to, I've been working the dairy on my own since I were knee-high.'

'Well, you can show her what to do. I was showing young 'uns what to do all the time when I worked at the school. Were you born on this farm, Eliza?'

'No. My mam came here as dairymaid after my father was killed in the pit. I was a babe in arms then, but she was a good dairymaid, my mam. She married the farmer, old Mr Dacre, when I was about eight. Then one winter him and my mam caught a fever that took them both so I was left on my own. I was twelve by then, but I'd been working in the dairy with my mam since I could walk, so I knew what to do.'

'Everybody says you're the best dairymaid around here.'

Eliza smiled, proud of her achievement. 'I try to keep it as my mam did.'

'But you wouldn't have been able to look after the cows as well, not on your own,' Lissie commented.

'No, well, what happened was that old Mr Dacre had wanted to leave the farm to my mam and my mam had wanted me to have it, and everybody thought that would happen when they died.'

'Do you mean the farm is yours, not Job's?' Lissie exclaimed.

'No, there was some family will that entailed the land. My Job is a cousin to old Mr Dacre, and it came to him. He was a tenant farmer before and very pleased to have his own land. But when he found out about me he said he couldn't let me stay.'

'He turned you out? Job turned you out?'

'Heavens no! I had nowhere to go. What he was saying was that I could only stay if we got wed. We could not live on the farm together unless we were wed. So I became Mrs Dacre. I've been Mrs Dacre for eight years now.'

'Do you like being Mrs Dacre?' Lissie asked.

'I do. My Job is the kindest, gentlest man I know and I love him dearly. He was insistent that he would not take me into his bed until I was older. And even then he said I had to want to, like, y' know, want him as my husband.' Eliza blushed and glanced at her friend. 'I am sorry, I should not be talking of such things.'

Lissie stopped cutting bread and gazed vacantly at the slices in front of her. Her heart cried for what she had lost. She had not experienced such compassion at her own introduction to the desires of men. Her initiation had been brutal and painful, wrenched from her unprepared body as she was beaten into submission.

The fear that Mickey Jackson would repeat his attack last night had terrified her so much that she was not sorry he was dead! But his death could not take away the wretched memory. Or give her back what she had lost.

She remembered when Blake had first held her in his arms, in the orchard at Miss Kirby's house. He had said he wanted her when Mr Kirby had caught them kissing in the kitchen.

But there were things that Blake did not know about her, things that had happened to her in the time between. Would he still want her if he knew? And what of her? Could she ever let a man near her after her experiences at the hands of Mickey Jackson? Any man? Even Blake?

Chapter 27

The following Sunday dawned bright and sunny. A day to lift the heart, Eliza thought as they walked back for breakfast after morning milking. 'Are you coming to chapel with us?' she asked her husband.

'You know what I think about chapel.'

'But you enjoy the hymns. And you've got a good voice on you.'

'Aye, I like the singing all right.'

'Well then?'

'It's that preacher. He goes on and on about the alehouse. I don't like it. Farming is thirsty work and a man likes a drink after a hard day's labouring.'

'I know. But he'll be going on about something different this week I expect,' Eliza replied. 'I think it might do Lissie some good if she went.'

'Raise her spirits a bit, you mean?'

'Yes. Give her an appetite for her dinner.'

'Go on then. I'll wash off the cow muck and put on my Sunday suit for the pair of you.'

Lissie wasn't keen on the idea. But she managed a smile and hadn't the heart to refuse Eliza. Her friend had done so much for her and, yes, they both liked going to chapel. It cheered them up.

They set off in a buoyant mood to walk the short distance along Fordham's main thoroughfare to chapel. Lissie looked well in Eliza's second-best dress. It was a sage green colour that matched her eyes and she wore a pretty bonnet trimmed to go with it. Lissie noticed a few dark glances cast in her direction and the small congregation were whispering between hymns more than usual. They all fell silent for the sermon as the preacher climbed up the steps of his plain wooden pulpit.

He started quietly as he always did. Job looked down at his hymn book for most of the sermon. Eliza and Lissie liked to watch his performance. He was a man of middle years with a round florid face and unruly coppery hair that flopped about as he became more animated.

It was when the preacher made a reference to the *carnal* attractions of alehouses that Job raised his head. This was a new slant on an old argument, he thought. Lissie stared straight ahead. She recognised the backs of two people in the front pew. Miss Kirby and her brother, sitting side by side in their Sunday finery.

The preacher was raising his voice . . . *the harlots who frequent these places and bring down decent hardworking men* . . .

Job stole a glance at his wife who raised her eyebrows.

. . . the sins that belong to Jezebel who flaunts her temptation . . .

Eliza, sitting between her husband and her friend, turned her head towards Lissie, whose expression had frozen on her face. She reached across to hold her friend's hand.

. . . that a man should die while this temptress moves among us . . .

Job leaned over to whisper in his wife's ear. 'I've heard enough of this. We're going.' He put his hand under her elbow.

'We can't walk out in the middle,' Eliza replied quietly.

'Yes we can.'

'What about Lissie? It'll make it worse for her. Everybody will look at her.'

'No they won't. They're all watching the preacher.'

'They'll hear us.' One or two of the congregation had already turned round, scowling, to see who was whispering. 'Sshh, Job. He's nearly finished.'

Lissie was mortified. Frozen to the hard wooden pew, she continued to stare blankly ahead. The preacher blamed her. They all blamed her for what had happened. Men were men, and decent women should not put temptation in their way. It was her fault that Mickey Jackson had died.

Eliza held both their hands tightly and whispered, 'Sit still and don't say anything. We won't move until everyone else has gone.'

The small congregation filed out. A few ignored them, but most looked pointedly in their direction, shook their heads and tutted at each other.

The Kirbys were the last to leave. They stood up slowly and paced down the stone flagged aisle. Miss Kirby was dressed in a plain gown made of delicately printed challis that looked new. She wore a small bonnet tied with silk ribbons and walked deferentially behind her brother. She hovered by his shoulder, with a cross expression on her face, when Mr Kirby stopped to address Job.

Mr Kirby's coat looked new as well, and he had a fine tweed waistcoat underneath with a heavy gold watch chain across it. He was carrying a tall hat and some kidskin gloves. The pair of them certainly looked better off than when Lissie had worked at their school.

'I expected better of you, Job Dacre,' Mr Kirby began. 'When you took over the Dacre farm you did right by your young wife, and our small community has held you in good esteem. But her youthful ways have turned your head and it is a man's duty to see that his wife keeps good company.'

Lissie knew that Mr Kirby would brook no argument about her. As a child in school he had identified her to be in danger of moral decay. And her behaviour with Blake had served to reinforce this opinion.

All three kept their eyes firmly fixed on the pulpit at the front. Eliza held on to her husband's and her friend's hands and squeezed them again.

Mr Kirby continued, 'This village does not want,' he sneered with distaste, 'does not want . . . that sort of woman in its midst, the kind that lusts after men and leads them into temptation without restraint or shame. These are evil, wicked women, who bring down the good name of decent men. You were a respected man in this village until you offered shelter to . . . to . . . that *Jezebel.*' His face was going red and he fingered his tight Sunday collar. 'I am sure your good wife, young as she is, does not wish for such a temptress under her roof. Perhaps she, too, has been bewitched by the harlot's ways.'

He stopped, expecting a grovelling assurance that Lissie would be cast out from his home. When Job remained silent, Mr Kirby went on, 'Yes, I see she has already worked her evil spell on you. Well, if that is the case, we shall not be needing any of your supplies from your dairy to the schoolhouse while that . . . that woman . . . is lodging beneath your roof. You will find that others in this village will follow my example. Do I make myself clear?'

He marched off, not waiting for a reply. Miss Kirby, unable to add to her brother's tirade, uttered just one word as she passed their pew. 'Harlot!' she breathed, then hurried after her brother.

Only Eliza saw Job's eyes narrow with anger. She squeezed his hand hard and he remained silent.

Lissie stared straight ahead, her eyes glassy with unshed tears. It was her fault that Mickey Jackson had died. She had tempted him and as a result he was dead. She was a killer as well as a harlot. And now her friends would lose their livelihood. Everyone had to suffer because of her. They would all be better off if she just went away.

The thunder of hooves outside her front-room window made Eliza look up from her sewing. She got up and crossed to the window. It was nightfall and Job was out in the cowshed with his sick cow.

Blake had come to see Lissie as he'd promised. He was riding a glossy chestnut hunter and dismounted quickly. He held on to the reins and met Eliza at her front door.

'She isn't here, Blake. We tried to stop her leaving, but she would have none of it. It was Mr Kirby, you see. He has set everybody against her.'

'That damned hypocrite!' Blake exploded. 'No wonder he lost his ironworks!' He took a deep breath. 'Sorry, Eliza. I didn't mean to curse. I got here as soon as I could. When did she leave?'

'After we got back from chapel this morning. She wouldn't even stay for her dinner.'

'Do you know where she went?'

'Back to Rosa's, she said.'

'Thanks, Eliza.'

He re-mounted and galloped off over the small stone bridge and down the towpath to Mexton Lock. He was not going to let her get away from him this time! Since moving down from Kimberhill, Blake's life had taken a turn for the better. He lodged with Sir William's works' manager in their neat house, a little way out of town on the valley road. It was brick built with a single attic room for servants, a young couple who looked after the manager, his wife, three children, a horse, and now Blake.

Blake had written immediately to his mama and to Ephraim. He had taken both letters down to the flyer office and found a small dusty packet waiting for him. It contained a letter from his mama and two from Ephraim, the last one pleading for a reply with his where-abouts. Ingrid Svenson and her maid Lucy were coming home the following summer, and bringing two of his cousins to visit.

To have found Lissie again had made his life perfect. He could not wait to see her and he spurred on the hunter. The horse was sweating when he arrived at Rosa's cottage and rapped at the door.

Rosa glanced through the window, straightened her apron and patted her hair. Thoroughbred horses were rare on this side of the canal. She answered the door and put on her best voice. 'Can I help you, sir?'

'Is Lissie Dearne here? I need to talk to her.'

'Lissie Dearne? Well, who shall I say is asking for her?'

'Tell her it's Blake. Blake Svenson.'

Rosa stared at him. She had a good memory for names, especially unusual ones. It was a Svenson that Luther Dearne had shot all those years ago. What did he want with Lissie? She had enough on her plate already!

Blake noticed the stare. He cocked his head to one side. 'You have met me before, when I was a boy. You took in and cared for my father when he had been shot.'

Rosa frowned. She did not want any trouble. 'I remember. What would you be wanting with Luther Dearne's daughter?'

'I mean her no harm!' Blake's patience was running out. 'Just let me see her. Please.'

Rosa was thinking, My God is this that little boy? He has grown into a fine handsome fellow. He had been here the other night, at the fight, when Mickey Jackson drowned in the lock. Lissie seemed to know him, all right, and they had gone off together with Job and Eliza Dacre. Good people, were the Dacres.

'Rosa! Please?' Blake repeated impatiently.

'Are you a friend of Lissie's, then?' she asked.

'*For God's sake, woman, I love her!*'

'Oh!' Rosa's mouth dropped open and her eyes widened. Well, what a turn of events! This prosperous-looking gentleman in love with little Lissie!

She said, 'Oh, you've missed her. She collected her things and left. In a hurry she was, to catch the evening carrier on the turnpike.'

'Dammit, no! Which way was she heading?' The horse was spooked by Blake's raised voice and he whinnied and pulled at the reins.

'Search me! She never said. But she's been living on a farm somewhere since . . . since her father died.'

'How many farms are there in the South Riding?' he groaned.

'Look here, sir,' Rosa suggested. 'There's no point in chasing after her now. That horse needs a rub down and you need to calm down a bit too. All I can tell you is that she sometimes goes to market in town. She told me she makes pies and has a stall there.'

Town? In town? He lived near the town now! The market square was just up the hill from Sir William's ironworks. He could find her. He *would* find her.

Martha saw Lissie struggling down the track with her travelling box. It was early morning and she had just unbolted the front door and stepped out on to the porch.

'Lissie! Oh, Lissie, what happened? You look tired out!'

'I came on the night carrier. And walked from the turnpike.'

'You walked? All that way on your own! Come inside, there's porridge on the hob. Here, let me take your cloak.'

After porridge with milk and honey in their warm farmhouse kitchen, Lissie felt better and was able to tell Martha everything that had happened to her.

'I should have been with you,' Martha commented.

'At least I know a little about my birth now. That was quite a shock and then the attack . . .' She shuddered. 'It was horrible and I did have a feverish reaction. It brought back all the memories of that first attack. But Mickey Jackson's dead now and he can't hurt me any more. What's done is done. I have had time to think on the long walk from the turnpike.'

'And?'

Lissie paused and took a deep breath. 'I have to move on. I shall go and see Edie as often as I can, and Eliza will always be my friend, but I have to look forward now and make something of my life.'

Martha's heart turned over. She did not want Lissie to leave. She nodded silently and waited for her to go on.

'The man who I believed had killed my dad was there and it was him, Martha, who rescued me and stayed with me until I was safe at Eliza's.' Lissie covered her face with her hands. 'I pushed him away, Martha. He only wanted to care for me, to be kind to me, and I pushed him away. He went off then. Said he had to get back to work. I didn't want him to leave me. I didn't.'

'You'd had a rough time of it. He'll understand, I am sure.'

'But I love him! I love him and I could not stand for

him to touch me. Twice, Martha, I turned away from him twice. He'll not come looking for me again.' Lissie gazed into the red glow of the fire and let out a long sigh. 'I don't know if I'll ever be able to let . . . let him touch me.'

Martha reached across the table to hold her hand. 'There are good, kind men in this world, Lissie, love. He sounds like one of them. You have to give yourself time. He will too.'

'But what if . . . what if . . . I mean, would I have to tell him about . . . about the rape?'

'Yes, my dear. You have to be honest with each other.'

'But he won't want me then, will he? What will he do when I tell him?'

'It will be hard for both of you. But if you are right for each other, you'll come through it together.'

'He is right for me, Martha. But I'm frightened that he has left me for good now.'

'He doesn't sound to me like a man who gives up easily. Are you sure you really love him?'

Lissie nodded silently.

'Then we shall have to see what we can do. Where is he now?'

She shrugged. 'In town, I suppose, or hauling coals on the canal. I was so . . . so numbed by events that I could barely speak to him.'

Martha tried to cheer her. 'Why don't you show me your mother's things?'

Lissie took the pouch out of her box.

'There's nothing about your real father?'

Lissie shook her head. 'These are all the things I have.

I expect Rosa was right and he didn't know – or didn't want to know about me.'

Martha examined the trinkets. 'You look a lot like your mother. Pity there's nothing about your father.'

'I don't think I shall ever know now, Martha. But Luther Dearne was a good dad to me and I loved him. He did his best for me and Edie, even though Edie was like she was. I know my real mother was a lady. But she's been dead and gone since I was born and her family hasn't come looking for me.' She looked directly into Martha's brown eyes. 'My real family is here, Martha.'

'Welcome home, Lissie,' the older woman replied tearfully.

They celebrated that evening when John came in from the fields. Martha killed a fowl which Lissie plucked and drew and stuffed with sage and onions to roast in the bake oven. John tapped a new barrel of ale in the cellar and they both complimented him on his brew.

'The sow has farrowed,' Martha commented as they finished up stewed pears and clotted cream. 'I thought we might keep more of the piglets this time, to fatten for your pie meat.'

'What a clever idea! I'll look after them. Can we give them more buttermilk and whey in their feed? It makes for very tasty pork.' Lissie sat back in her chair at the kitchen table. 'Oh, it is good to be home again.'

'I'll be taking the rest of the litter to market as soon as they're weaned. You know, now you're here to stay, we could go to market more often.' Martha cast her a knowing glance. 'You need to get to know the folk in town better now. Find a friend or two of your own age. When you're ready.'

'Oh, I am ready, Martha. Quite ready. When is the next market day? I should make a start on my pies.'

Market day was breezy and sunny. The smoke and grime had been blown over to the east and the air was clear. Gusts of wind ruffled Lissie's skirts about and she had to tie her bonnet on with an extra-broad ribbon. She looked for Rosa to give her some of the pie money for Edie, but there was no sign of her that day. Next time, Lissie resolved, for already she was planning a weekly stall for her pork pies.

The cobbled market square was thriving with pens of cattle, sheep and pigs. Live poultry squawked in baskets and farmers' wives displayed their garden produce for sale. Trade was good and there was talk of Sir William starting up new furnaces and more work for the townsfolk. John went off to watch the livestock auction while Martha and Lissie looked after the stall.

'This breeze is a bit parky today,' Lissie commented as it swirled round her head.

'Why don't you go into the Lion for some soup?' Martha suggested. 'It'll warm you up a bit. Don't go in the tap room though, it's rough there. The saloon will have ladies in today, it being market day.'

'Thanks, I shall.'

The Lion was busy and noisy. She took her bowl of soup and found a chair at a table in the window, opposite two women who were warming themselves with brandy.

'Good morning,' she said breathlessly. 'Can I sit with you?'

The women were squashed together in the window seat, their full skirts taking up all the space. They nodded and smiled at her. The older one had grey hair under her bonnet and a plain, lined face. But her dark dress was made of good woollen cloth and she had a matching small cape with a grey silk lining. Her companion was younger, her daughter maybe, Lissie thought. She had a lovely face and wore fashionable ribbons on her bonnet that were echoed by the trimmings on her maroon dress.

She returned their smile tentatively and drank her soup. After a few minutes she was aware that the older woman was staring at her intently. Eventually, the woman said, 'I hope you don't mind me asking, but do you come from round here?'

'Swinborough way,' Lissie answered politely. 'Just past Sir William's estates. On the way to Mexton.' After a pause, she added, 'I'm Lissie,' and offered her hand.

'Lissie, did you say?' the younger woman enquired slowly. 'Are you fr—'

'Grace,' the older woman interrupted quickly, taking Lissie's hand. 'And this is Clara, my niece.'

Sitting opposite her, Grace thought that Lissie was the image of her mother. Same glossy black hair, coiled and tamed under her bonnet. Same green eyes and delicate white skin. Thank goodness she didn't have her father's jaw to spoil it! She had inherited the beauty of her mother and the upright bearing of her grand-father. She looked reasonably well turned out too.

Grace recognised that the stuff of her gown was one of this year's woollens from the draper's shop on the high street.

'Have you come for the market?'

'I've brought my pork pies in to sell.'

'Clara,' Grace added briskly, 'why don't you get me another brandy? Would you like one, dear?'

'Oh, no thank you,' Lissie replied. 'This soup is enough for me.'

As Clara left, Lissie was jostled from behind and a male voice said, 'Excuse me.'

She turned to face Mr Kirby, well dressed in a tweed suit, fancy silk waistcoat and polished boots. He held a glass of whisky in his hand and it was clear to Lissie that he had already drunk several before that one.

'Well, well,' he sneered. 'The Lion is indeed honoured today. The ladies of the town, all gathered together to ply their trade.'

Grace leaned forward. 'Don't take any notice, dear. This man is drunk.' She turned to Mr Kirby and added, 'If you carry on like this, you'll get through your new money like you got through your father's.'

'Mind your own business,' he slurred.

'I'll do that all right,' Grace replied smartly.

'I heard you were selling up, anyway.'

'Now where did you hear that, Mr Kirby?'

'And it's not before time! We don't need your sort here,' he replied belligerently.

'No, well *you* don't. Not now you're a respected alderman. But I remember when you were very happy to visit . . .' She stopped, glanced across at Lissie, then finished lightly, 'You wouldn't like me to talk to your sister, would you, or that preacher friend of yours?'

He had been a regular afternoon visitor to Grace's, when he told his sister he was at the Institute. Grace wondered how he would continue to satisfy his appetites now that he no longer called.

He spluttered into his whisky. 'I'll have you run out of town, you—'

'No need, Mr Kirby. You will be pleased to hear that you are right and I am leaving.' Grace patted her throat. 'The smoke from the furnaces is not good for me. Clara and I are moving to Harrogate for my health. They have healing waters there.'

Mr Kirby made an impatient, grunting response and moved on.

'So sorry, my dear,' Grace apologised.

'Oh him! Don't be sorry about him. He's always laying down the law for other folk!'

'Do you know him?' asked Grace, surprised.

'I was a pupil at his sister's school and when their housekeeper died I was given her position.'

'Oh?' Luther had looked after her little Lissie well, she thought. 'What did you think of Mr Kirby?'

'I didn't like him. He was strict with everyone except himself.' Lissie shook her head. 'Strange fellow, if you ask me! I couldn't fathom him at all. Where has he got all his new money from anyway? Not the school, surely?'

Grace laughed. She knew that he had been responsible for the furnaces closing down and the buildings being rented out. Sir William had bought them up and taken on young Blake Svenson, who would run the new ironworks one day.

Grace also knew that, for all his self-righteous preaching, any money Mr Kirby had gained from the sale of his father's ironworks would soon be spent on drink and gambling and women.

She answered, 'No, not the school. He sold his father's bankrupt ironworks to Sir William. It's about time those furnaces got going again.'

Lissie finished her soup and got up to leave. Martha needed a break, also. She gave Grace a brief nod and said, 'I have to get back to my stall. Thank you for your company. I wish you well in Harrogate. Good day.'

Out in the square, with its animal smells and noise, Lissie thought how much she wanted to stay here. She liked it here. It had a future and so did she. What had happened to her in the past had been harrowing and, yes, it had wounded her. But wounds can heal and although the scars, whether they were visible or hidden, would always be there, they gave her protection from further damage and reminded her that she had healed. She could go on, she would go on and be part of this town, with its ironworks and forges, its people and its future. She had an extra strength now because she knew she could survive. No matter what happened in the future, she would be able to endure it.

Blake reined in his horse just before he reached the market square. He winced a little as he dismounted. But the aches in his muscles were nothing compared to the ache in his heart as he had searched for Lissie. The works' manager had lost patience with him and told him to take a day off to sort himself out.

He had asked around the town. A newcomer, he was looking for. A young woman, a beautiful young woman, you would remember her if you saw her, black hair and green eyes. The draper's assistant remembered because she had been there a while back, with widow Thorogood, for woollen cloth to make winter gowns. Yes, Mrs Thorogood lived on a farm on the edge of the Swinborough land. She was often here on a market day, had a stall with her son, big man he was, impossible to miss him . . .

Thorogood farm. It had to be where Lissie lived now! If she doesn't come to market today, I'll ride over there tonight.

The market crowds were thinning as Lissie threaded her way from the Lion through the pens and stalls. Farmers and butchers were herding off their newly purchased beasts. Martha and John were selling the last of their vegetables and preparing to pack the cart for their journey home. There was a man with them, holding a horse, a fine chestnut, and talking to Martha. Lissie recognised him at once and her heart rose in her breast.

She quickened her pace. Blake was here. In town. At the beast market. As she approached she heard Martha explaining about John and telling Blake how Lissie had taught him to read. Blake had his back towards her, bowing his head to John.

'Oh look,' Martha said. 'Here she is.'

Blake turned his head. He was smiling. How striking he looked when he smiled! She wanted to reach out and touch his face, trace her fingers around his eyes and nose and lips and kiss him, right there, in the market square.

'Lissie!' He had found her at last. He dropped the reins. His arms came forward to hold her and she did not flinch from him. Gently, he rested his hands lightly on her upper arms and gazed at her. She had a radiance about her that made his heart turn over. She was smiling! She was pleased to see him! It took all his will-power to stop himself scooping her up and carrying her away that minute.

'Blake! Oh Blake! You're here, you're here.' Her face was beaming. She could barely get the words out. She loved him so much that her heart was swelling in her breast and her throat was closing with emotion. How could she have ever rejected him? 'You have recovered from the beating?' she asked.

'Oh yes. Eliza told me what happened in the chapel last Sunday. How could the preacher be so cruel? It's that Kirby fellow! I could tell you a thing or two about him!'

John took the reins of Blake's horse, smoothing his hands over its nose and neck and flanks in a close examination of its form. Martha busied herself tidying the cart. Lissie sat on their makeshift stall as they talked. The noise and bustle of the beast market faded into oblivion. She loved listening to Blake. She loved everything about him. 'Have you settled in the Riding for good, now?' she asked.

'Sir William has taken me on in his new ironworks,' he said. 'I'll be manager one day and live in my own house.' How could he wait until then? He desperately wanted to have her to himself *now*, to hoist her up on his horse and ride away with her to the hills. But he knew she needed time, healing time, and he could wait. It would be hard for him but he had time. *They* had time. Time to be together, and to grow together.

He went on, 'Will you go back to Mexton?'

'Only to see Mam and Rosa. I live with Martha and John now.'

Martha glanced up at them and smiled.

'Mrs Thorogood,' Blake asked, 'may I come and visit you – all of you – out on the farm?'

'Of course you may,' Martha replied. 'It's no distance at all on horseback if you cut through Sir William's estate. I'm sure he'll not object.'

'Thanks.' He turned to Lissie. 'Promise me that you will never run off from Martha's like you did from Eliza's.'

'I promise,' Lissie agreed solemnly.

He put his arm round Lissie's shoulders and gently kissed her cheek. She did not recoil. She did not reject him and his heart soared.

Lissie leaned against him, soaking in the warmth of his body. This is where I belong, she thought. With him. With Blake.

Grace stumbled on the cobbles as she left the Lion.

'Here. Take my arm,' Clara said.

'It's this stiff hip of mine,' Grace complained.

'You'll be better when we get to Harrogate. Does wonders, apparently.'

'We'll see,' Grace responded sceptically.

Across the market square they saw Blake and Lissie talking together, his arm resting comfortably around her.

Clara said, 'Look, Grace, there's Blake. He's with that young woman we met in the Lion. Lissie, wasn't it? He talked of a girl he had met when he was working on the flyers. Do you think it is her?'

'Fine-looking woman,' Grace added. 'They make a handsome couple, don't they?'

'Mmmm, yes,' Clara responded. 'He is a gentleman, is Blake. I hope she is worthy of him.'

'Oh yes. She is,' Grace answered. 'She has good blood in her veins. And he will look after her all right. He'll go far, he will. He's already secured Sir William's patronage.'

They walked on to their waiting carriage.

'How do you know about her blood?' Clara ventured.

'It's a long story, Clara. I'll tell you when we get to Harrogate.'

But Clara was not put off. 'Is it her?' she pressed.

'Who?'

'That baby you talk of sometimes. Is Lissie that baby?'

'Might be.'

Clara was aghast. 'She isn't yours, is she?'

'No, my dear. Not mine.'

'Then whose? Come on, Grace! You can tell me.'

Grace gave a rare smile. 'Yes, you're right and I shall. One day. Her mother was a real lady, you know.'

'What about her father?' Clara urged.

'I've never told a soul about him and I don't think I should start now. She doesn't need him. She's in good hands with Blake.'

'She would want to know who her father was, surely?'

'Perhaps. But he would never own her. He did not know about her and he married and had other children. He is a gentleman though,' Grace replied.

'*Is* a gentleman?' Clara pursued. 'He is still alive, then?'

Very much so, Grace thought. Lissie's grandfather had been a successful iron master in the South Riding and his only son, Lissie's father, had gone on to build all kinds of new things with it. He was famous now, for his railways and his bridges. News-sheets reported his progress. He lived in London with his family and had travelled to the Americas twice.

But she would not risk his rejection of Lissie, as reject her he surely would if ever the truth came out. He had been a highly charged and active young man when he had been a visitor to the Admiral's home in London, a trait he had carried on into adulthood with his ideas and his work. Now, no doubt, he valued his exalted position in society too much to lose it.

Lissie's future was secure with Blake. She hoped fervently that they would have a long and happy life together, with children and grandchildren. They were young, strong and had each other. If any couple could survive in this danger-strewn world of the nineteenth century, they could.

Grace said, 'Did I say her father *is* a gentleman, Clara? Slip of the tongue. He *was* a gentleman. He's dead now.'

CLOTH GIRL

Marilyn Heward Mills

Matilda Quartey is fourteen years old when sophisti-cated black Gold Coast lawyer, Robert Bannerman, sets eyes on her and resolves to take her as his second wife. For Julie, his first wife, this is a colossal slap in the face. For Matilda it is an abrupt – and cruel – end to childhood.

Matilda must harden her heart to the world she has left behind. And yet as she struggles to understand this strange new life, she is also learning that it can offer exciting new possibilities . . .

'Warm, moving, delightful'
The Times

'This unusual tale of the colonial experience hits
the spot'
Guardian

'A debut novel of substance that movingly captures the
meaning of loss and the cost of gain'
Scotland on Sunday

978-0-7515-3815-1

THREE BITES OF THE CHERRY

Emma Blair

In the Glasgow of the 1920s, life is changing all around. And it's just changed again for Georgie Mair.

It is Georgie's close-knit family who help her get through the terrible time of her husband John's early death. And it is they who watch Charlie Gunn come into her life – and her heart – and offer her a second chance at happiness. To Georgie it seems that this second chance is simply too good to be true. It is.

But then it's not as if her family don't have problems, not to mention secrets, of their own: if Georgie's staid community are shocked by her decision to separate from Charlie, they should see what her sister Lena is now up to . . .

And so when she meets Bill Bailey, her world is thrown upside-down. Can she find, with Bill, the same sort of bliss she had known with John? Or will this third bite at the cherry be something completely different?

978-0-7515-3699-7

Other bestselling titles available by mail